The Choice

Susan Lewis is the bestselling author of *A Class Apart, Dance While You Can, Stolen Beginnings, Darkest Longings, Obsession, Vengeance, Summer Madness, Last Resort, Wildfire, Chasing Dreams, Taking Chances, Cruel Venus, Strange Allure, Silent Truths, Wicked Beauty, Intimate Strangers, The Hornbeam Tree, The Mill House, A French Affair, Missing, Out of the Shadows* and, most recently *Lost Innocence*. She is also the author of *Just One More Day*, a moving memoir of her childhood in Bristol. Her website address is www.susanlewis.com

Susan
LEWIS
The Choice

arrow books

Published by Arrow Books 2010

2 4 6 8 10 9 7 5 3 1

First published in Great Britain in 2010 by
Arrow Books
Random House, 20 Vauxhall Bridge Road,
London SW1V 2SA

www.rbooks.co.uk

Addresses for companies within The Random House Group Limited can be found at: www.randomhouse.co.uk/offices.htm

The Random House Group Limited Reg. No. 954009

ISBN 9780099525677

A CIP catalogue record for this book is available from the British Library

The Random House Group Limited supports The Forest Stewardship Council (FSC), the leading international forest certification organisation. All our titles that are printed on Greenpeace approved FSC certified paper carry the FSC logo. Our paper procurement policy can be found at: www.rbooks.co.uk/environment

Mixed Sources
Product group from well-managed
forests and other controlled sources
www.fsc.org   Cert no. TT-COC-2139
FSC   © 1996 Forest Stewardship Council

Typeset by SX Composing DTP, Rayleigh, Essex
Printed and bound in Great Britain by
CPI Mackays, Chatham, ME5 8TD

For John and Sandie Holton,
friends for many years past, and I hope for many more to come

Acknowledgements

First and foremost I would like to extend my warmest thanks to Loraine Stern MD for such invaluable support, guidance and insight into her specialised world of paediatrics. Dr Anirban Majumdar and Dr Andrew L. Lux were also extremely generous with their expertise in the same field. An enormous thank you to Carl Gadd who makes just about everything possible; to Sean Goodridge of the Avon & Somerset Child Abuse Investigation Team; Bob Somerset of the Avon & Somerset Ambulance Corps for his help with the paramedic scenes; and to Andy Hamilton in the Bristol Coroner's office.

A very special thank you to Susie Mulcock for such detailed and painstaking help in drawing the character of Mrs Adani; and to Jane Piscopo for teaching me everything I'd never known or experienced about child birth.

Also my thanks go to Simon Pearce and Adele Lovett for reminding me what it's like to be young and working in TV and film.

I am once again very deeply in Ian Kelcey's debt for so much invaluable legal help, and for putting me together with two ex-inmates of Eastwood Park who would prefer not to be named. They will know who they are and I thank them warmly for their willingness to share their 'inside' stories.

Last, but by no means least, much affection and an enormous thank you to my agent, Toby Eady, and to my wonderful editor Susan Sandon. This is also warmly extended to the fantastic team at Cornerstone, most particularly Georgina Hawtrey-Woore, Rob Waddington, Kate Elton, Louisa Gibbs and Louise Campbell.

Chapter One

'So, which do you want first, the good news, or the bad news?'

Nikki Grant's luminous blue eyes were sparkling with mischief as she regarded her parents. The anxiety behind her smile was well hidden, like an actor hovering in the wings ready to make its big entrance the instant it picked up its cue. For the moment, however, there was only silence, unnerving in itself, but Nikki managed to keep her merriment going, trying to make everything seem like a great big tease.

Neither her father nor her mother spoke.

They were in the drawing room of her parents' grand Georgian house in Bath where they'd lived for the past five years. Before that, all through Nikki's schooling, they'd resided in London, first in a smart Belgravia town house, then, when Nikki was around eight, they'd moved to a spectacular Italianate villa on the right side of Holland Park. As far as Nikki was aware the reason they'd relocated to Bath was because it was a city her mother adored and it was close enough to London for her father to be able to commute a few times a week, which was all that was necessary since his company and finances were so well established. So, aged sixteen, Nikki had said goodbye to her friends in London and with her irrepressible enthusiasm for life and new experiences, had thrown herself into sixth-form college in Bath. This was more or less when all the problems between her and her parents had begun.

Now, her parents were seated, a stately duo, side by side, on one of the elegant cream sofas that blended so perfectly with the carefully chosen antique furnishings and draperies around them. Nikki was perched on the edge of an overstuffed Queen Anne wing chair with neatly scrolled arms and a fine set of cabriole legs. It was bizarre, the way her parents entertained her to tea whenever she came these days, as if she were some kind of vicar or ageing aunt.

Actually, she wouldn't mind being one of those right now. Better still would be if her grandmother was around to lend some moral support, but she'd died last year and Nikki was still angry and sad that her parents had never allowed her to spend more time with Granny May. OK, Scotland wasn't exactly around the corner, but even when they did go to visit she was hardly ever left on her own with Granny May, who, in spite of being ancient and virtually wheelchair-bound, had always seemed so mischievous and carefree and was never in the least bit intimidated by her autocratic son.

'This is why you can't be trusted,' Jeremy Grant would inform his mother whenever she encouraged Nikki to do things of which he didn't approve, such as winking, or painting her nails, or doing handstands in the garden so anyone passing would be able to get a good look at next week's washing. Hardly deadly sins, and since Nikki had arrived for that particular visit wearing a pale pink nail varnish her own mother had applied, and her father himself had praised her before coming for how long she'd been able to stay on her hands (in their back garden), it had seemed grossly unfair of him to pick on poor Granny May the way he had.

'Och, don't you worry about me, lassie,' Granny May always told her. 'He doesn't scare me, and you mustn't let him scare you either.'

'I don't,' Nikki assured her hotly. 'He can be very bossy though, sometimes.'

'Just like his father, but the important thing to remember is that you're more precious to him than anything else in the world, and there's nothing he wouldn't do to make you happy.'

Though Nikki had never doubted how much her father adored her, over the last few years she'd come to learn just how determined and intransigent he could be. Once he'd set his mind on something he wouldn't even listen to what she might want, especially where her career choices were concerned, and it seemed she was just like him. In spite of her naturally sunny nature and laissez-faire ways, she could be every bit as theatrical in her temper, and even more stubborn when it came to deciding what she was going to do with her life.

Now, trying to cover her unease, Nikki widened her smile as she struggled for her next words, even though, by rights, it was her parents' turn to speak, since she'd asked them a question. They clearly weren't going to answer, though, in fact her father seemed to be checking an email on his iPhone. Apparently whatever news it might contain was more important than anything his daughter had to say, except that she knew he was doing it to unnerve her. It was one of the ploys he used in business, apparently with great success.

Out of nowhere a quick memory of how close they used to be flashed through her mind. He was forever swinging her up in his arms and teasing her that she put the eyes in mesmerise – or mesmer-eyes, as they'd spell it for a joke. He used to plant big kisses on her cheeks, and glow with pride at all her little accomplishments. He was loving and attentive, always ready to help with her homework, or take her to special exhibitions and shows. It saddened her a lot that he was nothing like that now. In some ways he could even be a different person, because once the serious business of her further education had kicked in she'd sometimes wondered if an alien had crept under his skin one night and taken him over. Suddenly all his lofty ambitions for her future were all that mattered. He had some finely honed plan that would take her to the very top of *his* chosen profession. Provided she studied all the right subjects, made all the right friends and went to the right university there was no reason why she shouldn't become as successful a financier as he was, and therefore as rich.

The only problem with this grand design of his was that it hadn't come even close to chiming with Nikki's ambitions. She didn't give a flying fig about high finance, investment brokerage or hedge funds. All she wanted to do was write.

Her parents had been so aghast when she'd announced her decision to read Creative Writing at Falmouth that she might have laughed, if her father hadn't looked as though he was on the verge of a heart attack. Needless to say he'd set his sights on his own alma mater, Cambridge, or, if she hadn't managed that, Edinburgh. He'd have found Bath acceptable too, since it was where her mother had read English before going on to study law at LSE. However, Nikki had especially not wanted to go to Bath, since her parents would almost certainly have expected her to live at home if she did, and by the time she was eighteen she was so ready to fly the nest she was practically flapping her arms as she went out the door.

Now she was twenty-one, and had graduated five months ago with a first class degree after spending three of the happiest years of her life at the university of her choice. She'd even managed to scoop a prize for one of her scripts – actually, it was the ITV West award for best short film, but since she'd written it at least part of the glory was legitimately hers, and Spencer, the producer-director, had insisted, during his acceptance speech, that he couldn't have done it without her. It was a pity her parents hadn't been around for the ceremony, but they'd had some major charity function to attend in London that night, so popping over to Bristol from Bath simply hadn't been possible. She hadn't minded too much though, since it wouldn't really have been their scene, cooped up in a non-de luxe cinema with a bunch of grungy bohos, forced to watch some mind-boggling arty animations or borderline obscene docudramas in a festival they'd never even heard of, until her and Spencer's film had been accepted for entry.

'Well, we're waiting,' her mother prompted.

Nikki was tempted to remind her that she hadn't chosen yet, good news or bad, but decided that would be a tad disingenuous, since it was highly probable that her parents weren't going to like anything she had to say. In fact, she wished she'd started this off differently now, because the way her mother's steely blue eyes were watching her, too closely and full of suspicion, made it clear that she was expecting Nikki to do no more than let them down again.

4

Nikki cleared her throat and braced herself. Although her small, beautifully shaped yet quirky mouth was continuing to smile, and her eyes continued to sparkle, her nerves were close to the surface now. She gave a casual flick to her shaggy dark hair which was swinging loosely around her collar today, not the way she usually wore it, because her father didn't approve of the unkempt ponytail that seemed to suggest to him that she hadn't washed it or picked up a comb for over a week. When she was at home, which was less and less these days, he implied that she should respect his rules and make herself as presentable as if he were about to stick her in front of the Queen. Well, maybe that was a bit of an exaggeration, but he was so starchy at times he might start to split at the seams if he made an unexpected move. Anyone would think he was a bloody duke the way he carried on, not some clever dick who had run mega invest-ments funds and raked in small fortunes for the already filthy rich and uselessly elite. She'd actually said that to him once, and had promptly earned herself one of his famous, holier-than-thou lectures on manners, language, respect, and the immense good fortune she'd enjoyed, growing up in a loving and stable home, with two parents who'd provided her with a first-class education, most of the privileges money could buy (not all, because he was a stickler for not spoiling her, even though he had, really) and the security of knowing that when the time came all the right doors would open to see her on her way to a dazzling career.

Back to the same old sticking point. Was he really never going to forgive her for not bending to his will? How much umbrage could one person have roiling away inside them? Was all of it really directed at her, or had something else happened to turn him into this cold and distant man who was so unlike the daddy of her early years? If she could get through to that man who used to tuck her in at night with a bedtime story, who'd built a tree house for her in the garden and who'd always welcomed her friends whoever they were, she was sure her news wouldn't prove too much of a bombshell. As it was . . .

'OK,' she said, pressing her hands together. 'The reason

I'm here . . .' She flicked them a glance. They weren't making this easy, either of them, sitting there staring at her like a couple of head teachers or policemen. She could just imagine her father arresting her if he didn't like what she had to say – handcuffs, frogmarch, throw away the key – it would be just his thing. Or her mother putting her in detention for a week and sending her outside the door with her hands on her head. She wasn't afraid of them, though, and never had been, though sometimes she thought they'd like her to be. She was grown-up now. She had a mind and a life of her own and didn't have to answer to them any more, whether they liked it or not. In fact, she was doing them a favour by coming here to tell them her news, when she could have done it by phone, or even email.

She was starting to wish now that she had.

Taking a deep breath and squeezing her hands even more tightly together, she suddenly blurted out the words, 'I'm going to have a baby.' After a moment's pause, her face lit up as though with relief that the words were finally out. Or maybe it was to lessen the impact of her news, turning it into some sort of joke that wasn't actually a joke, but it wasn't all that serious either.

It didn't work, because her father's face was already darkening with the threat of a terrible storm, while her mother's seemed to be draining of life. Ordinarily they were quite a good-looking couple in a Fortnum & Mason sort of way, all upper-middle-class perfection and only ever the best. Her father's black-rimmed spectacles made him look a bit owlish at times, however, and his beaky nose didn't help much, but when he laughed, which, it had to be said, didn't seem to happen often these days, his smile offered a glimpse of what he used to be like before he'd gone all Victorian and dictatorial on her. Her mother, who was fifty-two (the same age as her father), had aged quite well, actually, with hardly any lines round her aquamarine eyes and no visible grey in her short fair hair, mainly thanks to immaculately applied highlights that were turning her more blonde by the day. At five foot six she was an inch taller than Nikki, and still in great shape, but the way she dressed in white-collared dresses, or pleated skirts and twinsets, was seriously *old* and *weird* as far as Nikki was concerned. Still, each to their own, was Nikki's philosophy, and she was more than ready to admit that on a good day, both her parents could probably pass for mid-to-late forties.

This was no longer a good day.

'Go on,' her father said. The low Scottish burr of his voice was like a dreadful tide starting to roll in, warning her what dangerous waters they were now heading for.

She shrugged. 'That's it,' she said, trying to stay upbeat, while already feeling herself going under. She was also horribly aware of the way her mother was scowling in her father's direction, making it clear that whatever stand he took on this, she would back him. It wasn't that Nikki had expected any different, because her mother *never* took a stand against her father, but just this once, over something like this, it would have been nice if she could have drummed up a little female – even motherly – support.

It was asking too much.

'And the good news?' her father enquired. His square-set jaw was as implacable as she'd ever seen it, and his eyes were so piercing she was starting to feel like a kebab. 'Perhaps we should hear that before we go any further.'

Nikki flushed with anger. It was so typical of him to assume her pregnancy was bad news, and to act as though she thought so too. 'That was the good news,' she told him tartly, 'and actually, there's more good news, because Spence and I are getting married.'

Silence.

Then more silence.

Followed by some really deadly silence.

Finally, Jeremy Grant rose to his full six foot two inches and went to stand in front of the hearth. It was where he always planted himself when he meant business, spacing his feet about fifteen inches apart, and clasping his hands behind his back. 'Clearly,' he said, eyeing his daughter with enough chilly disdain to make her shiver, 'we have a very different understanding of good and bad news. So maybe, before we address the issues you've just raised, you'd like to enlighten us with your bad news.'

Nikki regarded him helplessly. She'd lost sight now of

what was supposed to be what, but she had to admit there really hadn't been anything he'd consider good anyway.

'Perhaps it would be the termination you're planning,' he suggested, 'for which you would presumably like me to pay.'

Nikki banged down her preposterous little teacup and leapt to her feet. 'I don't care what you say,' she informed him, 'this baby is mine, and I'm keeping it.'

Her father regarded her with steely eyes. 'You don't have the first idea what it means to be a mother,' he told her sharply. 'You're barely more than a child yourself, and if you think we're just going to stand by and watch you throw everything away on that poor excuse of a human being you've got yourself involved with . . .'

'You don't even know him,' Nikki broke in furiously, 'so before you start calling him names . . .'

'I'm not arguing with you over this,' her father shouted. 'You're not having that child, and nor are you going to marry an individual whose background is as lacking as his moral fibre . . .'

'You are such a snob,' Nikki cried. 'Just because he grew up in south London and his father isn't rich . . .'

'I thought you said he didn't have a father,' her own interrupted.

'He doesn't. He died when Spence was five. So did his mother. He had a really difficult start in life, so to have achieved what he has . . .'

'Spare me the sob story,' her father broke in. 'That boy grew up on a *sink* estate; he was arrested for trafficking drugs . . .'

'He had to in order to survive. You've got no idea what it's like for people . . .'

'I know a lot more than you think, young lady, none of which gets us away from the fact that he has neither the character nor the income to take on the responsibilities of a husband and father.'

'Since when did you become such an authority on his character, when you've never even met him?'

'The fact that he's not here, now, lending you his support at a time when you clearly need it, speaks for itself.'

'He's not here because you've always made it clear that you don't want to see him, and anyway, I didn't want him to come. I knew you'd go off on one, and if you two . . .'

'*Off on one,*' he interjected scathingly. 'Please don't come into this house with gutter vernacular, I don't appreciate it, and I don't want to hear it. If you mean you knew I'd be angry, then say so.'

Nikki growled in hopeless frustration. 'You are impossible to talk to,' she spat. 'Who cares about bloody vernacular and what you do or don't want to hear? I'm pregnant, I'm getting married and whether you like it or not, it's going to happen.'

His eyebrows rose in a way that was meant to cow her, and it did, a bit. 'I'm perfectly aware that you're old enough to make your own decisions,' he retorted smoothly, 'but before you start running with them you might like to consider *how* you're going to live, the three of you. As far as I'm aware this boy has no proper job, and your *writing* assignments are sporadic at best. So how are you going to feed and clothe yourselves, never mind a baby? Where are you going to live?'

Her cheeks were burning with anger and resentment. He was expecting her to ask for money, she knew it, but no way was she going to give him the satisfaction of turning her down. 'We'll manage,' she replied tartly. 'We've talked about it, and if Spence doesn't manage to get the backing for his next film by the time the baby comes, he'll find another kind of job.'

'Doing what?'

'I don't know! Anything that pays.'

'And this is the kind of uncertainty you want to bring a baby into? A father with no meaningful employment or prospects that I can see; a mother who's thrown her chances away to pursue some romantic whim . . .'

'It's not a whim!' she seethed. 'It's what I want to do, and for your information I'm quite good at it.'

'Quite is not good enough,' he informed her, 'but luckily you're still young enough to retrain and get some decent qualifications behind you.'

'I already have decent . . .'

'It's also high time you left that miserable squat you're wasting . . .'

'It's not a *squat*. It's a perfectly good house that we pay rent for.'

'And how many of you live there? Six, seven?'

'Five, actually. And it's where . . .'

'When are you going to get yourself some normal friends, that's what I want to know? All this hanging around with people from broken homes, ethnic minorities, council estates, homosexuals . . .'

'Just stop with your disgusting prejudice,' she shouted. 'I hate it when you say things like that, and I hate *you* for saying it.'

'It's not prejudice,' he told her, 'I'm simply pointing out that you are not mixing with people from your own background, which I presume is a way of getting at me . . .'

'It's not about you,' she cried. 'If you lived in a real world you'd know that everyone has issues, and there's nothing wrong with . . .'

'And your issues would be?' he said cuttingly.

She flushed angrily. She couldn't think of one, and he knew it. Then it came to her. 'Actually, being an only child is my issue,' she informed him, 'especially when you behave like this.'

'That's an absurd argument,' he told her, and turning to his wife he said, 'You'll arrange a termination for her . . .'

'Don't you dare!' Nikki shrieked.

'It's for your own good. You'll thank me for it one day.'

'I'm already twenty-seven weeks,' she shouted, 'so it's too late. They won't give one after twenty-six, and anyway, I'd have to be willing.'

Her father's eyes had turned to granite, but she could see the pain in their depths, glimmering flecks of confusion, frustration and defeat. He knew she'd deliberately outmanoeuvred him by waiting till now to break the news, so, no matter what arguments he put forward, he'd have no chance of persuading her to change her mind. At least, not about the baby – but he wasn't going to talk her out of marrying Spence either, because her mind was as totally made up about that as it was about having his child.

Jeremy Grant began shaking his head in dismay and disappointment. Then, turning to his wife again, he said, 'She's your daughter. Talk to her,' and walking to the door he let himself quietly out of the room.

Were she not so upset Nikki might have laughed at his exit line. She was always her mother's daughter when being unruly or rebellious. At all other times she was very definitely his. 'My daughter's planning to follow in her old man's footsteps,' he used to joke to his clients and colleagues. Or: 'Let me introduce you to my daughter, Nikki. She's going to get a First at Cambridge, aren't you, my darling?' Or: 'I know my daughter can be a handful on occasions, but I like to think of it as spirit and a challenging mind.' He'd trotted that one out to the dean of the sixth-form college after Nikki and her best friend, Joella, had fronted a picket line outside the gates following the abrupt and unexplained withdrawal of several long-standing privileges. He was always proud of her for having the courage to muscle up against authoritarian oppression, unless it was his, of course, when he didn't like it at all.

As his footsteps faded across the hall her mother rounded on her. 'You're a fool,' she said angrily. 'We've given you everything, and this is how you repay us?'

'I didn't ask you to give me anything,' Nikki cried. 'You did it because it was what *you* wanted.'

'And there's something wrong with wanting the best for your daughter?' Adele Grant's smooth oval face was quivering with frustration. 'Don't you realise how much you mean to us? Or how important your future is? If you mess it up now . . .'

'What's messing up about having a baby?' Nikki cried. 'You had one, and from where I'm standing you seem to have survived.'

'I wasn't twenty-one, and I . . . I had your . . . father.' As Adele's voice broke with emotion Nikki felt the annoying heat of guilt flaring up inside her. She really didn't want to hurt them, but she wasn't going to back down over this, no matter how small and ungrateful, or bad, they made her feel.

'This boy, Spencer,' her mother went on.

'He's not a boy, he's a man.'

11

'How can you be so sure he'll stand by you?'

'Because he's as thrilled as I am about the baby. And it was his idea to get married, not mine. I'd be just as happy if we went on living together.'

Her mother's eyes narrowed like a cat's. 'You don't have the first idea what you're doing,' she said bitterly. 'You haven't given a single, sensible thought to what really lies in store for a parent, especially one who's as young and unprepared as you . . .'

'You're making all these assumptions! Did it ever occur to you to *ask* me what I'm thinking? To try to discuss . . .'

'You haven't left us with anything *to* discuss,' her mother cut in furiously. 'If you're past the legal limit for a termination, it's already too late. Now you're going to find out what it's like to lose everything. Your opportunities, your friends, your aspirations, even your dreams, because that's what having this baby is going to cost you, Nicola. Mark my words. While you're sitting at home, tearing out your hair because it won't stop crying, and bouncing off the walls with sleep deprivation and mindless worry, your *boyfriend* is going to be out there living the kind of life you'd be having if you hadn't made such a stupid mistake. He'll hang on to his freedom, so will your friends, and eventually they'll all start moving on without you. No baby will hold them back. It'll be your responsibility and yours alone. And don't make the mistake of thinking I don't know what I'm talking about, because I do. I gave up my career for you, young lady, so you could have a safe and loving environment to grow up in, with a parent here every time you came home, not some foreign nanny, or airhead au pair. It was me, your mother, who was waiting at the school gates, who helped with your homework and made everything all right when your world was going wrong. I'm the one who's spent my life as a nobody in your father's world, the housewife and mother who can't possibly have anything interesting to say, who's had to watch people's eyes looking past her as soon as the requisite pleasantries are out of the way. My friends didn't take long to disappear. They all had careers to pursue, places to go, people to see. They didn't have time for someone like me, and those who did I never really fitted in

12

with, because we hadn't started out wanting the same things. They were happy being full-time mothers. Most of them didn't have the affliction of unfulfilled ambitions, because having children *was* their ambition. It's not yours, Nicola, any more than it was mine, so I'm damned if I'm going to stand back and watch you throw your life away as if you know everything it's possible to know at your age, when you absolutely *do not*.'

Nikki was staring at her mother with wide, unblinking eyes. She'd never heard her sound off like that before, much less go on about giving up a career and being unhappy with her lot. 'Are you saying Dad made you give up your job?' she asked, sliding her hands around the barely noticeable bump of her unborn child.

'No, I'm saying that I know what it's like . . .'

'So you had a choice?' Nikki interrupted.

'Yes, but . . .'

'So don't you think I should be allowed the same?'

'Of course, but when I see you making the wrong one, you can't expect me, or your father, to . . .'

'No one's expecting you to do anything,' Nikki cut in angrily. 'I'm sorry if your whole life's been a waste of time, thanks to me, but I doubt I'll see my child in the same light. In fact, I know I won't, because I'm going to make sure it feels loved and wanted . . .' Her voice almost faltered. 'I can see now that I was a real inconvenience for you,' she pressed on, using anger to block her emotions. 'Well, again I'm sorry. If I'd known you were going to feel like that I wouldn't have bothered being born.'

'Nicola, don't walk out,' her mother shouted, as Nikki grabbed her bag and started for the door. 'You misunderstood what I was saying . . .'

'No, I got the message, loud and clear. And now here's one for you. You don't get to tell me what to do any more. It's none of your business how I live my life, or who I live it with.'

'If you leave, your father and I will wash our hands of you,' her mother warned.

'Good. You keep telling me it's time I stood on my own two feet . . .'

'That means no more bailing you out when money gets tight. And just in case you think I don't mean that, spare a thought for what's going on in the wider world. People are losing everything in this global meltdown, and your father hasn't remained immune. We don't have anything like the funds we used to have, we're not even sure how much longer we can stay in this house. Yes, Nicola, there are other issues in our lives besides you, things that are causing your father sleepless nights and problems with his heart.'

'*Stop* with the emotional blackmail,' Nikki shouted, 'because it's not going to work. I've told you already that it's too late for a termination even if I wanted one, which I don't. This baby's kicking even as I speak, so, as a mother, you should know how bonded that makes you feel. But hey, I'm forgetting, you didn't want me, so . . .'

'I never said that. I always wanted you. I was just trying to point out how difficult it can be . . .'

'Well, thanks. Now, here's your *difficulty* signing out. I won't be troubling you for anything else. If you like, you can forget I exist.'

'Don't tempt me,' her mother raged. 'And don't even think about bringing the child to me when you can't cope any more . . .'

'After what you've just told me you'd be the last person I'd turn to, but don't worry, I'm going to manage just fine, because I already care about my child ten times more than you've ever cared about me.'

As she stormed into the hall she found her father standing at the open front door, ready to see her out. Though the coldness of his gesture cut her to the core, she was too angry and proud to let it show.

'One day you'll come to understand just how selfish and misguided you are,' he informed her as she passed.

Though she flinched, her voice was steady as she said, 'Don't ever expect to see me again, or your grandchild when it comes.'

As she ran down the steps and out through the black iron gate into the street he stood watching her, his dark eyes showing the frustration and love churning around inside him. His thoughts were hurtling back and forth over the years, swinging into focus and then out again. He could hear her squeals of laughter as a child, feel the clutch of her arms around his neck, smell the sweet scent of her as he laid her down to sleep. Then she was screaming in a fit of teenage rage, singing at the top of her voice when he'd asked her to stop, challenging him on topics she knew nothing about. She'd always been wilful and opinionated, but generous and forgiving too. She'd driven him to the very limits of endurance, swamped him with love and pride, and an overwhelming sense of protectiveness. No one had ever reached as deeply inside him as she had, and it was unlikely anyone ever could.

Hearing his wife come out into the hall, he closed the front door and turned round to face her.

In those moments Adele could see every one of his fifty-two years gathering on his face.

'I don't want to discuss it now,' he told her. 'I just want you to know that I'm not going to make it all right for her to have a child at her age, nor am I prepared to suffer that cowardly excuse of a man as a son-in-law.'

Nikki was walking fast towards Pulteney Bridge. It was a place she'd loved from the moment she'd first come to Bath, with its quaint little shops either side of the narrow road, like the Ponte Vecchio in Florence, and its encompassing air of romance that seemed to float up from the foaming river below.

Reaching the steps that led to a café and a small park below the bridge, she ran down and made towards the weir. There were a lot of people around, mainly tourists, plus elderly folk out strolling with their dogs, and a group of young mothers who might actually have been nannies, sitting on blankets on the grass with their charges, partly hemmed in by a wall of assorted toys and buggies. Nikki's smile as she passed them twisted with a sob, but no one noticed, because no one was watching her.

Reaching her favourite tree – a giant maple with branches that fanned out over the grass like a vast, leafy umbrella – she slumped down in front of it and began to rummage about in her bag for her notepad and pen. Finding them, she pulled them out, then let her head fall back against the scaly bark, as though she'd found oxygen at last, or some small treasure that she was afraid she might have lost.

For several seconds she kept her eyes closed, trying to empty her mind of everything beyond the sound of children playing, and the river splashing down over the weir. The rich tang of earth and freshly mown grass began to reach her, along with the warmth of the autumn sun, pushing its rays down through the colourful mass of maple leaves, as though trying to find her.

Eventually, as the storm inside her began to pass, she let her eyes flicker open. She was still angry and hurt, but most of all she was resolved not to allow the bitterness of the past hour to settle around her heart for fear of it pumping through her veins to the baby. It was important, vital, that his innocent little life not be contaminated in any way by the negative attitude of her parents, or the resentment she was feeling.

Opening her notebook, she took out the precious photograph of her first scan and felt her heart spilling over with love. She knew she was carrying a boy, but she hadn't told anyone yet, not even Spence. She'd meant to, as soon as she'd found out, but then something inside her had pulled the words back. For now, over this precious, short time, it was a secret she and the baby would share. There would probably be others, throughout his life, but this one was special because it was the first, and because it was happening at a time when they were still one.

She loved being pregnant. The feel of the baby inside her was so beautiful and tender, so enriching and humbling that she could only wonder at the miracle of it all. The whole world seemed different to her now. Everything was special, from the air she'd always taken for granted, to the strangers she passed in the street, to the music of the birds and the gathering of a storm. She felt strong and courageous in a way she never had before. She had no dread of becoming a mother, and hadn't had since she'd found out she was pregnant. It had been an accident of course, but from the moment she'd seen the blue line on the test she'd wanted the baby more than she'd ever wanted anything. Even more than Spence, though that came a very close second, and what made it all so much more wonderful was that he was as excited as she was about becoming a parent.

Going back to her notebook, she turned to a fresh page, and balancing the pad on her knees she began to write.

My darling Zac (this was the name she and Spence had agreed on if the baby was a boy),

At this moment I am sitting under a tree next to Pulteney Weir in Bath. It's a beautiful red maple, and as I write its leaves are changing colour and drifting to the ground like paper fruit. I think I can hear them whispering as they pass. I shall bring you here again after you are born to let you play on the grass and watch the leaves too. I am imagining your exuberance, and I want to laugh out loud as you chase the birds and shriek with joy.

One day, many, many years from now, after I've gone, you will be able to come here with this letter and know that we sat here together as I wrote it. You will be a grown man by then, probably with children of your own, and you'll be able to share this with them. I think that will be a very special thing to do.

The memory of what happened today, with my parents, will be long gone, and maybe even forgotten. My mother thinks I won't be able to cope, but she's wrong. She says I'm too young to know my own mind, but she's wrong about that too. Today I gave them a choice, they must either accept you or lose me. They have chosen, for now, to let me go. They're going to starve me of money – and their affection, it would seem – to try to make me bend to their will, but I won't. We don't need their support in order to survive, my darling. We'll have one another, you, me and Daddy, and whatever life throws our way, we'll find a way to get through it.

Breaking off as a dog came bounding over to greet her, she ruffled its ears and smiled up at the owner. Maybe Zac would like a dog, she was thinking. Not right away, because they couldn't afford it, but later, when she and Spence had their careers properly on track. This was one of the great joys of being a writer, she'd quickly come to realise, she could be at home with her baby and still work.

She wondered what career her mother had sacrificed for her. Obviously not the Aga-training sessions Adele was currently giving for the shop on Widcombe Parade. Or the flower arranging she'd studied for a whole year at Bath Spa just after they'd moved here. Whatever it was, she certainly seemed bitter about it now. When things had settled down, and they all felt ready to forgive one another, she'd ask, and try not to feel guilty that she had, in some way, ruined her mother's life. After all, the decisions hadn't been hers to take, so how could she be to blame? She felt hurt, though, and angry, that her mother seemed to resent her for being born, and bitterly stung by the way her father had opened the door for her to leave.

It would serve them right if she never went back.

She sighed shakily to herself. This was one of the worst parts of being an only child, the fact that she had to carry all her parents' expectations and dreams – and disappointments when she didn't conform to their ideals. How much easier it would have been if she had a brother or sister to share the burden, but she didn't, so there was no point thinking that way. The fact was she meant everything to them, and in spite of how acrimonious their showdown had been today – one of their worst, in fact – she doubted they'd be able to shut her out for long. They'd end up forgiving one another eventually, because they always did.

However, she was of a mind to let them sweat for a while, and was fairly sure they were going to do the same to her. It was going to be interesting to see which of them ended up backing down first.

Chapter Two

After catching the train back to Bristol, Nikki decided to save the bus fare to Bedminster and walk home. It should only take about forty-five minutes and the exercise would do her good.

As she started down the slip road from Temple Meads station where taxis were pulling up and away, and other travellers hurried to their cars, or bus stops, she wrapped her scarf around her mouth and nose to stop herself inhaling the traffic fumes and gusts of gritty wind that were sweeping up from the road. Since the battery had died on her mobile phone she couldn't call Spence to let him know she was on her way, but if the phone box on Coronation Road was working she'd ring from there, and maybe he'd come and meet her halfway.

She wondered who else would be at home when she turned up, beavering away on their laptops in the dining area of their shabby, but cosy, through sitting room. They were a close-knit bunch, Spence the producer-director, Nikki the writer, David the cameraman/editor, Kristin the actress and Danny the journalist who doubled as a production manager when they were shooting. They'd decided to base themselves in Bristol after winning the ITV West award for *Done with the Night*, since it might give them a head start in the city that they probably wouldn't get in the much more competitive arena of London. Also, David was from Bristol and as everyone adored his family, it hadn't been a hard choice to make.

More than anything the five of them wanted to work together again, but since that day might be some way off, they were taking the pragmatic approach of throwing themselves into whatever jobs they could get in the meantime, either behind bars, stacking shelves, or pulling shifts at one of the cinema complexes – always a favourite, since they got to see the films for free. Not that they didn't manage to work at their chosen careers: Nikki frequently submitted articles on spec to the local press, and even saw some of them published, while David, who everyone agreed was a gifted cinematographer, as well as probably the most handsome guy on the planet with his classic Indian features and devastating smile, had managed to get some freelance camera work with a couple of the independents in town, as well as with ITV's local news programme. It was through David, or a friend of a friend of his father's, that they'd first made contact with the Encounters Festival who'd accepted their film into the contest that had won them their award. It was also through David's father, who was a pharmacist in Totterdown, that they'd found their Victorian terraced house in an area of the city that everyone said was up and coming these days, with a landlord who wasn't out to fleece them.

Kristin Lyle, the only other female in the house, was David's stunning blonde girlfriend, who'd starred in Spence and Nikki's award-winning short. Like Nikki, she'd read English and Creative Writing while at uni, but since receiving some great reviews for her performance in *Done with the Night*, she'd decided to focus on acting from now on. So far, she hadn't managed to find an agent, or to become a member of the actors' union, Equity. However, another of David's family contacts had slipped her into a non-speaking part in *Casualty* a few weeks ago, which was shot in the city. And she'd recently read for the part of Maria in a 'radically cut, fast-paced version' of *Twelfth Night* for the Tobacco Factory Theatre, which, along with its vast café-bar, dance studio, live music events and Sunday market, was the hub of the local community. No news yet, but all fingers were crossed.

Danny Williams had been Nikki's best friend at sixth-form college, along with Joella, who'd ended up going off to Aberdeen to study marine biology when it had come time to leave. Nikki and Danny were rarely in touch with Jo now, but the two of them remained as close as ever, which presented no problem to Spence, since Danny's personal-relationship requirements didn't swing Nikki's way.

Thinking of Danny now as she crossed the yellow footbridge that curved like a giant banana over the cut, Nikki felt her usual sense of protectiveness closing in around the image of his cherubic face. Not that he needed her to look out for him these days, but he had when he'd first started college. She'd found him, one day, surrounded by a gang of fellow students all apparently getting some sort of kick out of belittling and threatening him. One glimpse of his face had told Nikki that he was terrified out of his life, and if there was one thing she couldn't stand it was bullying, so without stopping to think, she'd shoved her way through the crowd to rescue him. To her amazement, apart from a few unsavoury remarks, no one had challenged her, and as the crowd of morons started to disperse she put an arm round Danny, who was shaking so hard he could barely stand.

After that she and Joella had encouraged him to tag along with them, not only to take care of him, but because the more they got to know him the more attached they became to him. Like a lot of gays he had a wicked sense of humour, but he had a tender and loyal side too, and a way with him that was both comfortingly female and deliciously male. After a few weeks of knowing him Nikki had invited him home so they could do some revising together, not dreaming for a moment that her parents would behave so appallingly. She'd felt so embarrassed by the way they'd barely hidden how unsuitable they considered him as a friend for their daughter, that she hadn't spoken to them for an entire week, and then only grudgingly. She hadn't invited Danny home again after that, and though he never said so, she knew he was glad not to be put in the position of having to turn her down.

Not wanting to think about her parents now, Nikki hurried along past St Mary Redcliffe school and on to Coronation Road where Zion House preened like an old Greek temple in modern clothes over the passing traffic, and Asda squatted at the back of its car park like a giant spider pulling everything it could into its web. Finding the phone box out of order, she pressed on alongside the grimy river into a darkening overhang of trees, then past a row of dusty old shops before turning into Greenway Bush Lane to cut across Southville to North Street. Everyone said this part of Bristol was becoming desirable now, and there were definitely signs of it in places, with all the trendy cafés and health-food stores that were sprouting up. However, there was still some way to go before her parents would consider it even remotely suitable for their precious daughter, or, indeed, entirely safe.

Huddling deeper into her jacket she kept her head down as she passed gangs of young kids hanging about on street corners, always stepping out of the way when someone came towards her. She knew better than to start some stupid confrontation about who had pavement rights in this neck of the woods.

By the time she finally turned into their street which dipped steeply at first, then flattened out at the bottom where it T'd with Carrington Road, and where the terraced houses were packed as tightly as a deck of cards, it was past six o'clock and starting to get dark. She loved this time of day, when the sun was setting over Dundry Hill in the distance and front rooms began to light up like tiny private stages, allowing her to catch glimpses of the action inside. She'd become very fond of some of their neighbours, especially the old folk who'd lived and worked in the area since the days when the Tobacco Factory had been just that, churning out Woodbines and Embassy Gold. They'd seen a lot of changes in their time, including a world war, a cold war and even a couple of turf wars, and loved to tell Nikki about the old days whenever she had time to stop and chat.

There were lots of younger residents too, who, like Nikki and her friends, couldn't afford the grander environs of Clifton and Redland, but that was fine, they were happy enough here, meeting up regularly at the Factory, and helping the area to take on a new lease of life.

Spotting Mr Gladstone, the neighbourhood curmudgeon, about to pull his curtains, Nikki scowled and turned away before he could beat her to it. His house was on the opposite side of the street to theirs and because, when they'd first arrived, she'd noticed that no one ever seemed to visit him, she'd gone over to introduce herself and to ask if there was anything she could do. She'd had in mind a spot of shopping, or perhaps some company now and again. The answer she'd got wasn't one she'd been prepared for at all.

'Yeah, you can get those bloody Pakis out of our street,' he'd snarled, apparently referring to David and his parents, who'd helped with the move in. 'Send 'em back where they belong, or tell them to bugger off over to St Pauls, we don't want 'em round here.'

At the time Nikki was so shocked that she'd been unable to think of a thing to say before he'd slammed the door in her face. She'd ended up shouting through the letter box that the world would be better off without people like him, before storming back across the road to where Spence was waiting to find out how she'd got on. Now, as far as she was concerned, Mr Gladstone was beneath contempt, and if he starved in there with no one noticing it would be fine by her.

As she reached the green front gate to their house with its flaky paint and wonky bottom hinge she glanced in through the bay window. Her heart surged with happiness to see Spence's worried face light up as he caught sight of her.

'I was about to send out a search party,' he chided as he pulled open the door before she could find her key. 'Are you OK?'

'I'm cool,' she answered, as he wrapped her tightly in his arms. 'Glad to be home.'

Standing back to get a better look at her, his velvety brown eyes narrowed their focus as he searched for signs of tears, or joy, or anything else that might give him an early indication of how her news had gone down with the parents.

'I'm fine,' she assured him, smiling at the way his thick fair hair tumbled over his collar and curled in a random sort of burst around his ears and forehead. She could rarely resist touching it. His features, though ruggedly handsome, were oddly aligned, which lent a kind of rakishness to his intensity that she found as appealing as his lazy, but radiant, smile. At five foot nine he wasn't especially tall, but his physique was as well honed as an amateur athlete's, and as she was only five foot five – five six in her Doc Martens – it hardly mattered that he was shorter than David and Danny, since there wasn't a contest.

'Everyone's home already,' he told her, closing the door as she hung her coat on top of the pile bunched up on the stair rail. 'We're all waiting to hear how it went.'

Having caught the mouth-watering drift of exotic spices coming from the kitchen, Nikki felt a beat of pleasure as she looked at him in surprise. 'Is David's mum here?' she asked, already knowing the answer, since none of them could rustle up the kind of culinary magic Mrs Adani managed to produce with seemingly no effort at all.

'Apparently we're in for a Navratri treat this evening,' he informed her. 'I think I've got that right.'

Though David's parents were Anglo-Indian and practising Catholics, Mrs Adani wasn't one to let religion or culture stand in the way of fine cuisine. She loved to cook, and since there didn't seem to be a day in the Indian calendar not given over to one kind of festival or another, she always had an excuse, as well as five deeply appreciative mouths to feed.

'Do you know what Navratri is?' Nikki whispered as they headed towards the sitting room. They all knew not to interrupt Mrs Adani when she was at work in the kitchen; she'd let them know when she was ready to serve up.

'Not a clue,' he whispered back, and after treating her to a tender kiss on the mouth while smoothing his hands over the baby, he opened the door.

'Hey, here she is,' Kristin cried, bouncing up from the floor to give her a hug. 'We were starting to worry about you. How did it go?' Kristin's pretty, heart-shaped face was showing genuine concern in its frame of a damp blue towel.

'It was a blast,' Nikki said drily, taking the child-size carton of Ribena Danny was passing her, and giving him a quick hug too. Danny's shaggy auburn hair was standing out like broken bicycle spokes, the way it always did when he'd been working at the computer, since he was forever dashing his hands through it as though trying to rake out something that made sense. Apart from his hair colour he was a dead ringer for Leonardo DiCaprio, which got plenty of heads turning whenever they went out, but alas for him most were female. In truth, his big passion was for David, but though David had once, during a very drunken night at uni, let things get a bit out of hand with Danny, he was very definitely with Kristin now.

'How's Junior?' Danny asked as David plumped up a threadbare cushion ready for Nikki to sink down on the sofa.

'Lively,' Nikki replied, placing a hand on top of Spence's as his splayed over her bump. 'Thanks,' she smiled at David.

Though David was quite simply drop-dead gorgeous he was as thin as a noodle, and as modest about his looks as Kristin was proud of hers. Of them all, he was the biggest earner to date, but as far as he was concerned everything went into the kitty and they all lived on the same allowance. In his way, he was as generous and irresistible as his mother's food.

'So come on, spill,' Spence said, slipping an arm round her as Kristin hunkered down on the floor in front of David's armchair, and Danny sank cross-legged into a beanbag.

Nikki let go of the tiny straw of her Ribena and sighed. 'They weren't pleased,' she said flatly. 'In fact, they went mental, or my mother did. My father played his usual trick of treating me like I'm still five, then he more or less showed me the door.'

Danny's jaw dropped. 'You're not serious. You told them you were pregnant and they threw you out?'

'Actually, I was already walking in that direction, because there was no point in staying. They don't want me to have the baby . . .'

'You told them it's too late?' Spence jumped in.

Nikki nodded and squeezed his hand. 'They won't be coming to the wedding,' she told him, her smile showing only irony.

'Have you decided yet when it's going to be?' Kristin asked.

Nikki glanced at Spence. 'Definitely not till after the baby's born,' she said. 'For one thing we can't afford it yet, and for another, I'd like the baby to be there in person.'

Spence's eyes shone as he nodded in agreement – anything that made her happy was OK by him.

'Your parents are sure to come round once they see their grandchild,' Danny declared decisively.

Nikki's eyebrows arched. 'That depends if we let them see it,' she retorted testily.

'So how have you left it with them?' Kristin wanted to know.

'Well, let's put it this way, I'm not going to be the one to call them, and they made it pretty clear that there won't be any more bail-outs.'

'Jesus Christ,' Spence murmured. 'How are we going to manage without . . .'

'We will,' Nikki said forcefully. 'We'll have to.'

Cupping her face in his hands, he turned her to him. 'Of course we will,' he said, starting to grin, 'which gives me the perfect segue into *my* news.'

'You are so going to love this,' Kristin told her, excitedly.

Everyone was smiling now, apparently already in on the secret, while Nikki was trying not to feel let down by how abruptly the scene with her parents was being dismissed. On the other hand, if the news was good, she could certainly do with some cheering up, so let them bring it on.

'Drake Murray's office has been in touch,' Spence announced, practically glowing with pride, 'and I've only been offered second unit on the feature he's currently shooting.'

Nikki's mouth fell open. 'No way,' she murmured. 'You mean *the* Drake Murray?'

Spence was grinning from ear to ear. Everyone was. 'I got a call about an hour ago,' he told her. 'Apparently he looked at the show reel I sent, but he knew about me anyway because Philippa Sawyer, the agent we met at the Encounters Festival?' Nikki nodded. 'Well, she'd already told him about me.'

'Oh my God, this is amazing,' Nikki cried. 'If you can get in with him . . .'

'It's only a week's shoot,' Spence went on, 'but if it goes well this could be the gateway to the big time.'

'It definitely is,' Nikki insisted warmly. 'Once he sees how good you are . . . Are you getting paid?'

'I don't know, I didn't ask.'

Everyone laughed, because they all understood that this job wasn't about money, it was all about prestige – and the dream chance of being invited to join Drake Murray's team of protégés, legendary in the industry for the number of careers which had been launched from there.

'When's it happening?' Nikki asked.

'The week after next, in London. I'm going to take your new script with me to show to him. You never know, he might have some backers who are just waiting to throw their money at something new.'

'Has anyone got any money these days?' Danny wanted to know.

'Good question,' David said soberly. 'This is a helluva time we're going through, everyone losing their jobs and pensions . . .'

'The markets have gone up again today,' Spence informed them.

'Yeah, by half a per cent,' Danny added.

'Apparently my dad's been hit,' Nikki told them. 'Or so my mother claims. She was probably just trying to make me feel guilty, though – and anyway, he's got so much that he probably won't even notice if he loses some.'

'A lot of people are suffering,' Danny said darkly. 'They're having their homes repossessed and . . .'

'Hey, come on, you guys,' Spence cried, throwing out his hands. 'I'm giving you some fantastic news here, and you're going all market slumps and negative equity on me. Not everyone's lost everything. There's still plenty of cash out there, and if I can pull this off, there's a chance some of it might be coming our way.'

'You haven't told her about David yet,' Kristin reminded him.

'I was just getting to it,' Spence assured her. To Nikki he said, 'We're being hired as a team. David and me. Apparently Drake was so impressed with the camerawork on

Done with the Night that he wants us both for the second unit.'

Nikki's eyes sparkled with joy as she turned to David.

'Chris Doyle, stand aside,' David warned, referring to one of the world's leading cinematographers, 'Adani's a-coming on through.'

'You can joke,' Kristin said, 'but you're just as brilliant as Doyle.'

'Yeah, right,' David laughed. 'Says my girlfriend. No bias there then.'

'Says everyone,' she told him. 'And don't forget the rest of us, either of you, when your names are up there in lights, cos we'll be wanting some of the action.'

'Hey, baby,' Spence drawled in his best movie-director drawl, 'wherever I go, you go, got it? You're my leading lady.'

'Ahem,' Nikki coughed.

'On-screen,' he hastily added, making them all laugh. Then, burying his face in her neck, he cupped a large hand around her abdomen and whispered, 'I'm going to make our baby so proud of us he's going to pop out with Oscars in each hand and a great big fat cheque doubling as a diaper.'

Smiling, she said, 'What makes you think it's a boy?'

'A gut feeling, but hey, if it's a girl, and she's like you . . . Well, how much happiness can one guy take?'

As Kristin and Danny began playing air violins and David started to croon a silly love song, the kitchen door burst open and Mrs Adani appeared in the dining area, all bright smiles and turmeric-smeared cheeks. Though she was in her late forties she was still an exceptionally lovely woman with exquisite sloe eyes, a deliciously full mouth and the bearing of a Manipur dancer. However, the floury apron, tumbling hair and wayward twinkle in her eye grounded her firmly in the real world.

'My God, it's Madhur Jaffrey,' Spence teased.

'Pff! An amateur,' Mrs Adani scoffed. 'Ah, Nikki, you're back, dear. Excellent. Are you hungry? We are having magnificent dishes tonight to celebrate the festival of Navratri, which means nine nights and marks the start of autumn. David, my boy, I asked you to clear the table, but still all your computers are filling it up.'

'I'm on it,' he cried, leaping to his feet, even though his own computer and state-of-the-art equipment was in a niche of its own next to the fireplace, taking up no table room at all.

Passing her son as she came further into the sitting room, Mrs Adani took Nikki's hands and held them warmly between her own. 'How did it go with your parents?' she asked kindly.

Nikki pulled a face. 'I think I've been cut off,' she told her.

Mrs Adani's gracefully plump features creased with regret. 'This is very sad,' she stated, 'but I am sure it will all be repaired when the baby comes. They have a way of sorting out priorities and perspective, you know?'

Nikki smiled. Since David's mother was a health visitor who'd seen more babies come into the world and family disputes erupt and resolve than most, she was very probably right. It pleased Nikki to think so, in spite of being in no mood to forgive her parents yet.

'What time is it?' Nikki grumbled, rolling on to her back as Spence sat up in bed and flooded the room with light.

'Quarter to seven,' he whispered. 'Go back to sleep.'

'Why are you up so early?' she mumbled, keeping her eyes closed.

'I'm catching the eight o'clock train,' he told her, getting out of bed and dragging on a pair of boxers.

She screwed up her nose. She couldn't remember him saying he was going anywhere today.

'I told you last night,' he said, coming to sit on the side of the bed. 'I'm meeting the agent, Philippa Sawyer. She's taking me out to the set so I can spend some time with Drake, going over the script and stuff, before I start prepping next weekend.'

'Oh,' she murmured, wondering where her mind had been when he'd told her that. 'Is David going with you?'

'No, not this trip.'

'Mm,' she mumbled. 'What time will you be back?'

'Late. Drake's giving a talk at BAFTA tonight, and Philippa's got me a ticket to go.'

Peering through half-open eyes, she said, 'Great. You never know who you might meet.'

He smiled, clearly pleased she understood. 'And I got a hundred quid off the full price, which is brilliant,' he added.

She blinked. 'So how much was it?' she asked.

'Three hundred, but I only have to pay one. Course, it means my credit card is maxed out again, but hey, when isn't it?'

Having no answer to that, she ran a hand up into his hair and gazed lovingly into his eyes.

'How's the boss this morning?' he asked, pulling back the covers to kiss the flesh that was exposed between the top and bottom of her pyjamas.

'Still asleep,' she smiled, and shivering, she pulled the duvet back. 'Call me when you get to London,' she said, snuggling down again, 'let me know how it's going?'

'Sure,' he promised, and after ruffling her hair he tugged the light cord hanging over the bed, and left her in darkness while he went to take a shower.

When she finally woke up again it was gone nine o'clock, and realising she had no recollection of him coming back into the room, or leaving, she smiled to herself to think of him tiptoeing around as he dressed, trying not to wake her.

'Ah, at last,' Danny declared, putting his head round the door. 'I was beginning to think you'd never wake up. How are you?'

'OK,' Nikki answered, actually feeling a bit light-headed as she struggled to sit up. 'I was awake half the night, though.'

Danny grimaced. 'The baby, or your parents?' he asked, coming to sit on the bed.

Nikki sighed. 'Both, I suppose. I mean, the baby wasn't kicking, or anything, it's just that I love lying in the darkness imagining how it's going to feel when I can actually hold him – or her.' She yawned and stretched. 'Are you working today?' she asked.

'Yep. I'm doing a shift at ITV, but I don't have to be there

30

till one, so I was thinking I might come for a swim with you this morning, if you're going.'

Nikki's spirits rose. 'Great,' she said, stifling another yawn. 'Where's everyone else?'

'David's gone to shoot some vox pops for his blog, and Kristin caught the train with Spence.'

Nikki frowned. 'She's gone to London too?' she said, not remembering that being mentioned either.

'Apparently Spence is introducing her to Philippa Sawyer because someone at her agency looks after actors too. They went off all full of how there might be a small part in the movie for Kristin.' He shrugged. 'You never know, I guess there might.'

Nikki's expression wasn't warm. 'It would be good if there was,' she said, and feeling Danny's eyes on her she flicked him a glance, knowing he could see straight through her. It wasn't that she disliked Kristin, exactly, but there were certainly times when she regretted David bringing her into their group. On the other hand, she felt sorry for Kristin too, or she had when they were at uni, for the way other students – usually female – often ostracised her, not for her beauty, but for how self-centred and full of herself she could be. Once Nikki had got to know Kristin she'd discovered that she really could be a pain in the butt, but she had her good points too, and since Spence, who Nikki had already been involved with for a year, was committed to creating a partnership with David, there was nothing more to do than to try to get along with Kristin.

'With any luck,' Danny muttered, 'they'll cast her in *EastEnders* and she'll have to move up to London. Or better still, *Hollyoaks*.'

Nikki choked on a laugh. 'Yeah, but that means David might go too,' she reminded him, 'and I don't think we want that.'

Danny shuddered. 'Definitely not,' he agreed. 'Except they don't seem quite so close any more, or at least not to me. What do you think?'

Squeezing his hand, Nikki said, 'If things are cooling down between them, then all I can say is I hope she doesn't start coming on to Spence again. That really got to me when she tried it before. I don't know what's wrong with her, the way she has to go after other people's partners all the time. It's why no one wanted to know her at uni.'

'It's called narcissism,' Danny reminded her, 'she has to be the centre of attention and admired by all, no matter who they are, or who they're involved with.'

Nikki was pouting thoughtfully. 'It's because her dad abandoned them when she was little,' she said. 'Then her stepdad goes and walks out on her mum, who goes and gets breast cancer . . . It's no wonder she's so insecure really.'

Much less prepared to cut Kristin any slack, Danny rolled his eyes. 'Anyway, you don't need to worry,' he said. 'Spence is totally mad about you, and he's so not interested in her. He knows exactly what she's like, and it bugs him too, the way she's always going on about how fantastic everyone thinks she is, and how she's going to blow everyone's mind with her auditions and stuff, when the only part she's ever actually been cast in is Thea in *Done with the Night*.'

'Which was when she tried to seduce Spence,' Nikki murmured.

'And didn't succeed.'

Nikki threw him a glance. 'She's still got no idea he ever told me about that, you know.'

'I always said you should have brought it up with her.'

'Yeah, but the timing was really bad. We were about to start shooting, and it was too late to find anyone else for the part. Actually, I didn't want anyone else, because she was perfect for Thea, and putting everything else aside, you have to admit she's got talent.'

Danny grimaced. 'If I must,' he retorted grudgingly. With a playful grin he flipped back the duvet, saying, 'So how's Buster this morning?'

'Hungry,' Nikki replied, batting him away, and pulling the duvet back. Then, smothering another yawn, 'God, I really need a swim to wake me up. And please someone tell me how I can be starving when I ate so much last night. What a feast! Wasn't it amazing?'

Danny groaned in ecstasy. 'Tell me about it,' he drooled. 'That sabudana puri was to die for. There's loads of leftovers, by the way, so we can have it for dinner tonight. So, now, what's on your agenda today, after the swim?'

Nikki frowned as she gathered her thoughts. 'Actually, I might get the bus to Stroud. There's some kind of wedding fair going on, according to the ITV news diary – thanks again for letting me see it – so I thought I'd do a piece on the romance versus hard cash of it all, and try to sell it to *Gloucestershire Life* or maybe the weekend *Evening Post* or something. Oh, I've just remembered, Spence and I are supposed to be going for our second antenatal class tonight.' She rolled her eyes. 'He obviously forgot too, not that he'd have cancelled today . . . I don't suppose you fancy coming in his place, by any chance?'

Dan pulled a sorry face. 'I'm seeing Gus later,' he confessed. 'We're going to the opening of some new wine bar on Whiteladies Road. You can come with us, if you like?'

'I know you don't mean that,' she laughed, 'and anyway, I'd rather not miss the class. So, how are things going with the new man on the block?'

Danny shrugged and blushed. 'Still early days,' he said, 'but so far, so good.'

Nikki gave him a playful nudge. 'Trust you to find someone with a proper job, a car and his own flat,' she teased. 'My parents would be proud of you.'

Danny laughed. 'Especially with him being an accountant,' he added. 'Even my own parents approve, but there again, they'd go for anyone with the potential of making sure their youngest's not left on the shelf. I think they'd rather Gus was a girl, though. Can you believe it, twenty-one, and my mother's already on my case about grandchildren, even though she knows I'm gay?'

Smiling in sympathy, while wishing her own mother was of the same mind, Nikki flipped back the duvet and swung her legs to the floor. 'I've decided that nothing we do will ever be right for our parents,' she said, 'so we might as well give up trying. God, I could kill for a cup of coffee.'

'Sorry, not allowed,' Dan reminded her.

Nikki's eyes softened as she cradled the bump beneath her pyjamas. 'No binge drinking, no spliffs, no caffeine, no aerobics, no sugar . . . The things I've had to give up for this little blob.'

'But it's worth it?'

'You bet.'

Danny smiled. 'You know, it suits you, being pregnant,' he decided. 'It's like you've got this inner-calm thing going on that's totally awesome and like, *Zen*.'

Nikki laughed. 'You wouldn't say that if you'd seen me at my parents' yesterday. You know my mother practically accused me of ruining her life, the cow! Amazing how she always manages to make everything my fault, just because she gave up some stupid career that I never even knew anything about until she suddenly decided to bring it up. She wouldn't dare to blame my father, of course, even though I'll bet anything he made her chuck it in, because we all know what a control freak he is. But hey, don't let's go there. It only winds me up thinking about them, and no way do I want all those negative vibes going through to the babe. They're not controlling my life any more, and if they ever decide they want to play a part in their grandchild's future, I can tell you this much, they'll have to change their attitudes big-time.'

Knowing only too well what a volatile relationship Nikki had with her parents, Danny merely shrugged, and led the way downstairs to the kitchen. Last night's dishes were still soaking in the sink, and piled high on the draining board, waiting to be washed.

'Bloody hell,' Nikki groaned. 'Why's it always me who gets left with the chores these days?'

'Because you're the one who's always here,' Dan reminded her, 'but come on, I'll wash, you wipe, then we'll have a great big breakfast after our swim.'

Much later in the day, after Danny had cycled off to the studios, Nikki decided to abandon the idea of going to Stroud and took a bus to Broadmead instead, intending to have a no-spend browse round the baby shops. They were going to have to be seriously careful with money now that her parents weren't providing any fallback, but that was fine, they'd manage, especially if Spence got paid for this job with Drake Murray. But even if he didn't, David and Danny, the two real earners in the house, were still insisting on covering the rent, should the need arise.

'We're family,' David had said firmly over dinner last night. 'And that baby is going to have nothing but the best when he or she comes along, because I'm not having any godchild of mine going without.'

'Me neither,' Dan had echoed.

'And you know I'm up for babysitting, or bathing, or anything but nappy changing,' Kristin assured them. 'And if I get a job, same goes here, what's mine is yours.'

Spence had been so moved by their loyalty that he hadn't really known what to say as he'd taken Nikki's hand. 'I promise you all,' he'd finally managed, 'that as soon as I'm a mega Hollywood director, and Nikki's picking up Oscars for her screenplays, we won't forget this.'

'We're going to the top together, all of us,' Nikki reminded him.

'Definitely,' he confirmed.

No one ever mentioned the fact that Danny's ambitions lay in a different direction, least of all Dan, since there was a tacit understanding that whatever they did he'd be involved somehow, either getting all the exclusives when it came to interviews, or managing their publicity, or whatever other role he felt might suit him.

On arriving at Broadmead, the town's main shopping area, Nikki decided to have a stroll around Waterstones first, since bookshops were always a magnet to her. She'd been known to spend entire days in them in the past, and to come out at the end of it with nothing more than a newly translated novel, or some obscure reference book for writers to add to her growing collection. The baby manuals were now piling high next to the bookcase in their bedroom, along with reams of parenting tips that Spence had downloaded from the Internet, so deciding to give that section a miss today, she meandered off to the poetry shelves. Emily Dickinson had long been a favourite of hers, along with the metaphysical poets such as Donne and Marvell, and since Mrs Adani had given her a small volume of Indian verse for Christmas last year, she'd developed a taste for this, too.

Indian poets weren't very well represented in this particular shop, but finding a book of Upanishads, she took it down from the shelf and started to flick through. Moments later she was smiling dreamily to herself as she read the words.

> *From Delight we came into existence*
> *In Delight we grow,*
> *At the end of our journey's close,*
> *Into Delight we retire.*

Simple, yet unutterably lovely, she was thinking as she copied the lines into her notebook. She'd speak them aloud to the baby later, then add them to the next letter she wrote him.

Though she'd have dearly liked to buy the book, she restrained herself, remembering that they still had so much else to buy, like a crib, a buggy, clothes, petal-soft blankets and a whole wonderland of toys that she'd already started to collect and was keeping stored in a large wicker drawer under the bed. The cost of Spence's ticket for Drake Murray's talk at BAFTA tonight flicked through her mind, but that was a necessary investment, because the place would be full of industry people and it was vital he made the right contacts.

After leafing through a few more pages of the book she tucked it back in its place and strolled outside on to Union Street, where the traffic was pouring downhill towards the cinema and the sky overhead was turning a leaden grey. If she was with her mother now, she knew they'd almost certainly walk round to Cabot Circus to browse Harvey Nichols and the House of Fraser, and if she was being completely honest with herself, in a very deep and secret part of her heart she wished they were together, shopping for the baby and enjoying the same closeness that she'd noticed several other pregnant girls sharing with their mothers. However, there was nothing to be gained from feeling sorry for herself; she was here, her mother was in Bath and a serious apology and change of attitude had to happen before that distance closed. Besides, all those high-end shops were way, way over her budget, so turning in the opposite direction she covered her nose and mouth with her scarf to block out the fumes and began traipsing across to the Centre to catch the bus home again.

As she went, she was talking to Zac in her mind, giving him a guided tour of what they were passing, from the old area of Castle Street that had been bombed out during the Second World War, *no sign of any damage now*, she assured him, to the fabulously smart limestone building of the Corn Exchange where, back in the nineteenth century, Bristol's merchants used the flat-topped pillars outside, called nails, for the exchange of money. *And that*, she told Zac, with her pocketed hands cupping his little bulk, *is how we got the term 'to pay on the nail'*.

Her scant knowledge of the city's history had come from Mr and Mrs Adani, who'd given them all a guided tour not long after they'd moved here. She felt warmed by the memory of the Adanis' reverence as they'd talked them through Isambard Kingdom Brunel's mind-blowing accomplishments, from the world-famous Clifton suspension bridge, to the world's oldest railway station at Temple Meads, to the legendary SS *Great Britain*. Their bubbling sense of pride in the old steamship, the fastest of her day apparently, had practically set them afloat on the vessel, which had been launched from Bristol in 1843, and was now at rest in the very dock she'd been built in, gloriously restored. The Adanis were clearly as in awe of Brunel as they were attached to the city they'd called home for the past thirty years.

Nikki tried to imagine her parents taking the time to show them around Bath the same way, but couldn't.

On reaching the Centre, she spotted her bus coming and ran to the stop, arriving just ahead of it. Twenty minutes later she was alighting in North Street, and because a cup of herbal tea at Pete's café was half the price she'd have had to pay at the Factory she decided to pop in there instead of going to find out if any of the regular crowd were around.

As she waited at the counter, behind a deaf old couple, she turned her back on the temptations of the cake trays in their shiny glass cabinets, and spotting a little girl standing in front of her pushchair, staring at her, she gave her a smile. She was probably no more than two, she thought, and looked dead cute in her pink hair slides and matching coat.

The little girl's expression didn't change, but she blinked a couple of times, then made two fists that she punched in the air.

Nikki laughed, then all of a sudden someone was shouting.

'What the bloody 'ell do you think you're staring at?' the woman was yelling.

To her horror Nikki realised the woman was talking to her.

'Never seen a kid in a pink coat before?' the woman growled savagely.

Nikki flushed red. 'No, I was just . . .'

'Yeah? Just what? Gawping, that's what you was doing. Well, fuck off and gawp somewhere else, why don't you? Get on my bloody nerves, you posh gits coming round here, staring at us all like we was in the bloody zoo or something. Go on, get lost . . .'

'Kay, settle down,' the woman with her sighed, tugging at Kay's sleeve. 'I don't expect she meant any harm.'

'How do you know?' Kay snarled, and pulling the little girl on to her lap she started shouting at her for looking at strangers.

Shaken, and not sure what to do, Nikki decided it might be best if she left. However, as she started forward, the woman suddenly stuffed the child in her pushchair, picked up her coat and marched out of the caff.

Nikki looked at the other woman as she dropped some coins on the table and started to follow.

'Had a good eyeful?' the woman asked nastily.

Nikki flinched.

'Take no notice,' Pete said, coming round the counter as the door banged shut behind the woman. 'They come in here, mouthing off at everyone who dares to even look at that poor kid. It's people like them who give this area a bad name. Wish they'd go somewhere else for their tea, scaring off my customers all the bloody time.'

'So you know them?' Nikki asked.

'They lives down on St John's Lane. I heard that the mother, the one called Kay, hasn't been right since the kid was born.'

Nikki was confused. 'Why?'

Pete looked surprised. 'You didn't notice? She's got the Down's syndrome.'

Feeling a swell of pity Nikki said, 'Oh, I see. What a shame. It didn't show.'

'It do if you looks closely enough,' he told her. Then to the old couple who were still doddering about the counter, 'That's all right Mr Audley, I'll bring your cake over. You and the missus go and sit yourselves down now, before your tea gets cold.'

A few minutes later Nikki was sitting at a window table with her herbal brew staring out at the passing traffic, while still thinking about the woman, Kay, and her dear little girl. She wished there was a way she could stop the mother shouting at her child like that ever again. It might not be any of her business, but it wasn't the girl's fault she had Down's, she probably didn't even understand she was different, much less why her mother got into such a state when people spoke to her. However, when all was said and done, no matter how angry, defensive or confused the woman was, she must surely love the child, or why would she feel so protective?

Sipping her tea, Nikki looked up as Pete slid a saucer of biscuits towards her with a wink. He was chatting to someone on his mobile phone, so she smiled her thanks and started to nibble one of the digestives. She was wondering now how it might affect her if there was something wrong with Zac. The mere thought turned her cold to the core, but she'd had the necessary blood test at fifteen weeks and the results had come back way below the danger line of 295, so she knew already that there was absolutely no risk of Down's.

However, that didn't stop her worrying, the way all expectant mothers did, especially with their first. She'd seen enough stories on the news and in the papers to know what some people had to go through, and she could only wonder if she had it in her to be as brave as some should it ever happen to her.

Except it wasn't going to, so she must stop tormenting herself with the fear of it, or she'd end up transmitting those negative feelings to Zac, and she'd promised herself from the start that she'd be careful not to do that. She wanted him to come into the world full of courage and confidence, a real little fighter, with way too much charm and kindness, like his father, and with total belief in himself. So, drinking up her tea, she helped herself to another biscuit and went back to the counter to pay.

Her parents didn't have the first idea about the way real people lived, she was thinking to herself as she walked back to the house. All shut up in their fancy Georgian house with more money than most ordinary folk could ever dream of, and a daughter who'd never been ill in her life, apart from the usual colds and tummy bugs. Sure, she'd been wilful and hotheaded, and perhaps not always as grateful as she should have been, but since that was all they had to complain about maybe they ought to start considering themselves lucky they had her, instead of opening the door to show her out for the great crime of making up her own mind about what she wanted to do with her life.

It would serve them right, she decided, if her father did lose all his money in this global credit crunch. They might start seeing life a bit differently then, and valuing things that really mattered, like, for instance, their perfectly healthy, intelligent, law-abiding, socially aware, award-winning writer of a daughter, not to mention their own grandson when he came. However, given her father's famously astute gift for handling financial matters, she wouldn't be holding her breath for long for disaster to strike them.

Chapter Three

'Hey, I was wondering where you were,' David said, glancing up from his computer as Nikki came in the door. 'Been anywhere nice?'

'Just into town,' she answered, unwinding her scarf. 'Any news from Kristin, or Spence?'

'Yeah, I had a text from Kris around lunchtime saying she was blown away by Drake Murray.'

Nikki nodded as she glanced through the mail. Nothing for her, so putting it aside she hung up her coat and went to look over his shoulder. 'Oh my God, who's that?' she laughed, as a seriously weird individual wearing half a rabbit suit and braces hopped across the screen.

David grinned. 'He was in Clifton, doing his shopping, he said, and he didn't mind me filming him, so there he is.'

For a while now David had been running a weekly blog of people going about their business in the city, and having been blessed with an unerring eye for an event about to happen, he'd already managed to capture some pretty outlandish stuff. One of the best, everyone agreed, was the bride whose wedding car had broken down, since he'd managed to grab images of her father punching the driver, then the bride promptly smacking her father, and when they'd realised they were being filmed they'd tried to set upon David. In the end David had flagged down a passing driver, who'd happily agreed to transport them all to the church, and David was there at the end waiting to shoot more footage of the bride emerging, all smiles, with her slightly baffled, and not entirely sober, new husband. The edited package had made the local news – with the couple's permission – and ever since David had been getting thousands of hits on his site, mainly from people searching for themselves in case he'd caught them without them knowing, or for someone they knew, or simply to have a good laugh at the idiots who often put themselves up for the taking.

'There sure are some strange people out there,' Nikki commented, as she went to open up her own laptop.

'Bring 'em on,' David chuckled, going back to his editing. After a quick blitz on the keyboard he said, 'I was thinking I might go to that gay club with Danny and his new bloke again one night. I got some pretty good stuff the last time I was there. Fancy coming, if I do?'

'I might, depends when it is,' Nikki answered, opening up her email. Nothing from her parents, which irked more than it should, no offers of work, but some interest in an article she'd submitted to the *Western Daily Press*. After replying to say she'd be happy to come in and discuss it further, she clicked off again and said to David, 'So is Kristin going to this talk tonight?'

David was intent on his editing again. 'What talk?' he murmured. 'Oh yeah, the BAFTA thing. Not sure, but I guess so, because she's coming back on the same train as Spence.'

Deciding not to read any more into that than the fact that Kristin was going to the talk too, Nikki said, deadpan, 'If you're at a loose end later, you can always come to the antenatal class with me.'

His fingers slowed on the keyboard, then quickly set off again. 'Actually, I was going to catch a film with a couple of the guys,' he replied, referring to the crowd they generally hung out with at the Factory.

She laughed and he peered at her guiltily.

'Sorry,' he groaned. 'It's just not really my thing, you know, all those pregnant women playing with dolls and stuff.'

'It's all right,' she said, 'I was only joking. What are you going to see?'

'Haven't checked what's on yet, but there's a copy of *Venue* over there, if you feel like coming with . . . *Shit* I've just lost . . . Ah, there it is.'

Getting to her feet, Nikki was about to go and fetch the

local entertainment mag when her mobile bleeped with a text.

Aymazing day. U shd b hr. DM raving abt Done with the Night. *Rckn he's gonna luv yr nu scrpt.*

She was in the middle of sending a message back when another came through. *How's my boy/girl and his/her mother? Lv u all x*

Feeling a surge of love that made her eyes shine, Nikki hit the reply key and wrote, *Both msng u. Will try to w8 up. Hope talk is intrstng and hlpful. Dying 2 hear abt it. Lv u2 xx*

'Spence?' David asked as she put the mobile down.

She nodded. 'Sounds as though they're having a great time up there, so don't see why we shouldn't too, even if it is only the local . . .'She gasped and laughed as Zac gave her one of his mightiest kicks yet. 'You rascal,' she told him, putting a hand over her belly.

David's boyishly handsome face split in a grin as he realised what was happening. 'Can I?' he asked, holding out a hand.

'Of course, but I think he or she's settling down again . . . Or no, there he goes,' and taking his hand she pressed it to her bump, holding it in place with her own.

'That is so awesome,' David murmured as Zac started to wriggle about, causing butterfly ripples across their palms. It wasn't the first time David had felt the baby move, but he was still as blown away by it as the rest of them, and rarely missed a chance to connect with his unborn godchild.

'So,' he said, as Nikki plopped back down in her chair with the copy of *Venue*, 'Spence says you're OK about us shooting the birth.'

Nikki's head came up.

'With a camera, in the delivery room,' David explained.

'I know what you mean,' she said. 'When did he tell you that?'

He shrugged. 'Yesterday? The day before. He was dead chuffed about it. Something to keep to show the baby when it's older, he said, and great material if we ever need it for a birth scene.'

Nikki blinked once or twice.

David grimaced awkwardly. 'You're looking at me

strangely,' he told her. 'Please don't say I've put my foot in it. He said you were cool with it.'

She smiled. 'No, it's fine,' she said brightly. 'I mean, he happens to have forgotten to mention it to me, but you know Spence, when he runs with an idea he thinks he's told everyone, and half the time it's still in his head.'

David chuckled. 'That's him,' he confirmed, clearly relieved that he hadn't messed up. 'So, are you going to pick us a movie?' he suggested, going back to his editing. 'No chick flicks, because we're all guys, and if *Mamma Mia!* is still on, none of us want to see it again *ever*.'

Nikki laughed, since she, Danny and Kristin had been to see it twice, they'd loved it so much, and had dragged David and Spence along both times, reminding them that it was as important to keep up with the big commercial successes as it was with the more serious art-house stuff they generally went for.

In the end, she decided not to go to the cinema after all. Instead she went to her antenatal class, as planned, where she wasn't the only one without a partner, nor, by a long shot, the youngest expectant mum there. One girl, who was due around the same time as her, was only fifteen, and another, whose mother waited outside, chain-smoking and arguing with someone on her mobile phone, was just sixteen, and this was her second! In fact, of the entire class, which consisted of ten women tonight, only two looked older than Nikki, though even they couldn't have been much more than mid-twenties. Part of Nikki would have taken great pleasure in informing her parents of this; however, knowing they'd be decidedly unimpressed, not to mention deeply critical of the kind of people she was mixing with, she felt almost thankful that they weren't in touch.

On returning home she settled down in front of the TV with a very generous helping of last night's leftovers and a glass of Ribena. She was feeling quite tired by now, but managed to stay awake for an episode of *Desperate Housewives*, then switching off she picked up her notebook.

Dear Zac, she wrote, feeling a swell of pleasure at the connection this small, simple exercise seemed to effect, *we played hooky today, you and me, and went into town. I copied out a little poem for you from the Upanishads, which is above, and I think you enjoyed your mini guided tour on our way back to the bus stop. I met a lovely little girl in a café, where the owner gave me some biscuits to cheer me up after the little girl's mother shouted at me.*

Should she tell him why the mother shouted, she wondered, and decided not to.

Daddy's in London this evening. We're all very excited, because he's had the most fantastic offer to direct the second unit of a Drake Murray film. David's going to shoot it, and they're hoping to get Kristin a part.

She put the tip of her pen in her mouth as she wondered how she might feel if Kristin did land a part. Then her heart twisted as her mother's words suddenly echoed past her thoughts. '. . . your *boyfriend* is going to be out there living the kind of life you'd be having if you hadn't made such a stupid mistake. He'll hang on to his freedom, so will your friends, and eventually they'll all start moving on without you. No baby will hold them back. It'll be your responsibility and yours alone.'

Though she felt shaken, Nikki's expression quickly hardened. It wasn't going to be like that, she told herself firmly. Her mother didn't know Spence, or her friends, so how could she speak for them when she didn't have the first idea of how close and supportive they all were to one another? Anyway, it seemed pretty unlikely that Kristin *would* get a part in the movie, since it must surely already be cast. However, if there did happen to be a small role she could play, Nikki would be nothing more than really pleased for her, and would even hope that it might lead on to something much bigger.

Going back to her letter she wrote, *I wonder, when you come to read this, what will have happened. Are we really on the brink of something big for us all? I hope so.*

Breakfast the following morning was a rowdy affair as they all got caught up in the excitement Spence had transported back from London with him. He'd also brought an enormous teddy for the baby and a bright purple scarf for Nikki – purple being the in colour this season. Though she'd been asleep when he'd come in, just after midnight, he'd woken her up crashing over her boots in the dark, and she'd laughed herself silly when she'd turned on the light to find him wrestling about on the floor with a giant fluffy bear.

They'd made love then, not in the frantic, no-holds-barred way they used to, because he was afraid of hurting the baby, but in a gentler, more tender way with him tucked in behind her as though she was sitting on his lap, the faint smell of beer on his breath and autumn cold still in his hair.

Now, as he sat with his arm around her on the sofa, crunching toast and infusing them all with his infectious energy, Nikki felt so full of love for him that she wanted to grab his face in her hands and kiss him senseless. This was Spence at his best, when he was telling them how brilliant life was going to be; what he, as a director, was going to do for them all, and how the seriously big time was right around the corner.

'He actually reckons we should get ourselves over to Hollywood,' he was saying, meaning Drake Murray. 'He's got loads of contacts, agents, producers, you name it, that he can put us in touch with, plus his own set-up over there.'

'He rated *Done with the Night* that highly?' David cried, incredulous, but thrilled.

'Absolutely. He said it was dead professional, slick, moody, that we all showed real talent . . .'

'Except me,' Danny pointed out.

'Yeah, but you're going to be our manager, or publicist, or co-producer,' Spence reminded him. 'We can't do anything without you.'

'You should have heard what he said about my performance,' Kristin piped up, flicking back her hair.

'He reckons she's sexier than Bardot in *And God Created Woman*,' Spence said for her. 'In fact, the whole thing, my directing, David's lighting, put him in mind of that film, he said.'

'Have you ever seen it?' Nikki asked.

'No, so we have to get it.'

David was already at the computer, going online to find a copy.

'He thinks we should take a closer look at some of Buñuel's stuff too,' Spence told them.

'God, I love Buñuel,' Nikki swooned. '*Los Olvidados* is, for me, one of the best movies ever.'

'No, no,' Kristin retorted, shaking her head, 'it has to be *Belle de Jour*. Everyone knows that's his absolute masterpiece.'

Nikki didn't argue, there was no point.

'The other director he mentioned,' Spence went on, 'was Fernando Meirelles . . .'

'*City of God*,' Nikki cried. 'That was so brilliant. We've got it here somewhere. And *The Constant Gardener*. I wasn't so keen on that, actually.'

'Me neither,' Spence agreed. 'Anyway, what matters is that David and I do a fantastic job for him with the second unit. We are so lucky to get this, you know. It's only because the other guy dropped out that it came up . . .'

'Hey, I haven't told you my brilliant news yet,' Kristin cut in, focusing on Nikki. 'I had a call yesterday from the producer of *Twelfth Night*. I've only got the part of *Olivia*.'

As Nikki's face lit up Danny said, 'I thought you were up for Maria?'

'I was, but apparently they think I'll be better in the lead.' She waggled her eyebrows playfully, showing how pleased she was with herself. 'We start rehearsing on the 28th of this month, which means I'll be free to go up to London with you guys the week after next while you're shooting the second-unit stuff.'

'Does that mean you didn't get a part yesterday?' Danny prompted.

Kristin shook her head. 'They're already fully cast, which is what I expected actually, but it was definitely worth going, because Philippa's put me in touch with another agent in her office who deals with actors. I'm seeing him next Tuesday.'

'Great,' Nikki cheered, actually meaning it. After all, it wasn't as though she wanted to see Kristin fail, it was simply that she wished she had some good news to impart too.

'It'll be really cool to have you around,' David said,

sinking down in the armchair and pulling Kristin off the arm on to his lap. 'Are you going to come too, Nikki?'

'Sure she is,' Spence answered for her. 'We go as a team, all of us. You too, Dan. We can stay with Sam Preddy in Vauxhall.'

'Who?' Kristin said.

'You remember him from uni. He's going out with Kayla McClane, or he was back then. Anyway, his place is so big, he won't have a problem fitting us all in.'

'I can't get the time off,' Danny informed him. 'I've just been offered four more shifts on the news.'

'And I've got my twenty-eight-week check next Wednesday,' Nikki grimaced, 'plus I'm seeing someone at the *Western Daily Press* on Tuesday. Anyway, we can't all go. They only want you and David. If the rest of us are hanging around like spare whatsits at a wedding, it's going to look really dumb, like we're your groupies, or something.'

Spence laughed and treated her to a resounding kiss on the cheek. 'I guess I want to show off to the baby,' he confessed, 'you know, so we can tell him he was there when I shot the first movie I was paid for.'

Nikki turned to him with widening eyes.

He whispered in her ear and her mouth fell open. 'Are you serious?' she murmured.

He nodded. Then, grinning at the others, 'Three grand a day, for five days,' he told them, his eyes on fire with pride. 'And David's getting two.'

David looked about to faint.

'We're going to be rolling in it,' Nikki declared. 'Fifteen grand from you and ten from David! Oh my God, we can get everything we need for the baby.'

'And the rent's sorted for at least the next nine months,' David piped up.

'If we're not in Hollywood by then,' Kristin pointed out. 'I really reckon we should take Drake's advice and up sticks and go. I mean, what have we got to lose? We're young, none of us has any commitments, or a serious job . . .'

'Ahem,' Danny interrupted.

'Apart from you,' she conceded, 'but you're only freelance, and you can be a journo anywhere.'

'Oh yeah, just like that,' Danny said sarcastically. 'Anyway, aren't you forgetting something?'

Kristin looked puzzled. 'Oh you mean the movie, and my play. Well, I don't mean we should go before they're over, but with all the money the guys are going to make next week, and the little bit I'll get from the play, we can easily buy tickets to LA, *and* afford somewhere to rent when we get there.'

Spence and David definitely appeared up for the idea.

'I think Danny meant the baby?' Nikki suggested.

Danny nodded and Kristin had the grace to blush. 'Sorry, yeah, of course,' she said, 'but hey, what's the difference between here or Hollywood? It can be born anywhere, right? And we'll all be there for you, the same as if you were here. Plus, think how fantastic it'll be for him, or her, to grow up in the movie capital of the world with a famous director as a dad.'

'And an even more famous writer for a mum,' Spence added, hugging Nikki to him.

'Well, I'm sorry to burst everyone's bubble,' Danny said, sounding annoyed, 'but there's a small matter of healthcare that none of you seems to have considered, and where are we going to get the money for that? Nikki can't just go into a hospital over there and deliver it, like you can here. You have to pay, and we definitely won't be able to afford that *and* rent *and* food when we're trying to get established.'

As they all fell silent, Nikki felt herself flooding with guilt. She was spoiling the dream already and it had only just got going.

'I know, it's easy,' Spence declared. 'We just wait till the baby's born, *then* we go. How long's that? Another four months, five tops, by the time it's home and everything.'

'That works,' David agreed. 'We can always start making plans now, but we won't actually leave until Nikki's ready.'

'*Or*,' Kristin came in deliberately, 'we could go on ahead and Nikki and the baby could follow when the time's right for them.'

Danny looked as though he wanted to smack her. 'Are you . . .?'

'Why don't we take one step at a time,' Nikki said, cutting

Danny off before a row flared up. 'Let's get next week over first and you never know, something else might come up here in England as a result of it, and we wouldn't want to miss out on that, would we? It might even give us a bit more money to get started in LA.'

'Good point,' Spence agreed, 'because there's always a chance Drake's going to go overboard about your script, and if he does, it has to be shot here.'

'Yeah, but if he doesn't,' Kristin said, 'I still think we should start making plans . . .'

'Yeah, we know what you think,' Danny butted in, 'but let's not get too carried away, eh? A lot of that fifteen grand's got to go on stuff for the baby, don't forget . . .'

'Sure, but David's going to have ten, so what's to stop us two going on ahead?'

'No, we go together, or not at all,' David told her. 'Anyway, we want to be here when the baby comes.'

Kristin's face darkened. 'Speak for yourself,' she muttered, and getting to her feet she stalked out of the room.

Danny's eyes were murderous. 'I could swing for her sometimes,' he seethed, not bothering to keep his voice down. 'Just because she's not getting her own way. I don't know how you stand it, David.'

'She has other qualities,' David said tactfully, even though he didn't look especially impressed either.

'Anyway,' Spence said, running on as though nothing had happened, 'I need to start working out how I'm going to shoot these scenes we've been given, and you, David, should take a look at the script.'

'Do you have a copy I can read?' Nikki asked, allowing him to haul her up from the sofa.

'I sure do,' he replied, gathering her into his arms, as the others started preparing to leave, 'but I'd kind of like the house . . .'

'. . . to yourself for the next couple of hours,' she finished for him. 'No problem. We need some things at the supermarket, so I'll make myself scarce just as soon as someone coughs for the groceries. Kitty's empty, I'm afraid. So five quid each?'

'Here's a tenner,' Danny said, digging one out of his

pocket and handing it over. 'I have to get going now, or I'll be late. And leave the heavy stuff for me to pick up on my way home,' he said bossily. 'Just text me what we need and I can put it in the basket on my bike.'

'Or I can go to the supermarket with you,' Kristin offered, coming back into the room all pouty lips and guilty eyes. 'I'm sorry about just now,' she apologised, going to put her arms round Nikki. 'I got a bit carried away with everything . . .'

'It's OK,' Nikki responded, raising her eyebrows at Danny, who was scowling at Kristin's back.

'Kris, do you know where I put my wallet when I came in last night?' David asked, searching his pockets.

'I wasn't here last night,' she reminded him.

'Course not. It must be upstairs in my other jacket. OK, here's another fiver to be going on with,' he said, slapping a screwed-up note in Nikki's hand. 'Got to run now. I'm doing a day's edit at Available Light. I'll take the script with me,' he told Spence. 'Any chance you can meet me in Clifton around six?'

'I'll be there,' Spence told him, and after kissing Nikki on the forehead, he disappeared up to the bedroom where his small desk in the bay window overlooked the street below. Not quite the view he'd have in Hollywood, but it was suiting him just fine for now.

Nikki and Kristin looked at one another and shrugged.

'I'm ready if you are,' Nikki said.

'I'll get the shopping bags,' Kristin offered. 'Do you have the list?'

'It's still stuck to the fridge. Feel free to do the washing up while we're gone,' she shouted up the stairs to Spence. 'It might help focus your mind,' and deciding to put his fiver in herself rather than interrupt the onset of his creative flow, she went to put on her coat.

An hour and a half later Nikki and Kristin were slumped cosily in the deep red leather sofas at the Factory, a clutch of Aldi carrier bags at their feet as they drank rose and camomile tea and tucked into the Clark's pies they'd picked up from the pie shop opposite. The place was enormous, with exposed steel ducts trafficking around the ceiling like some elevated endurance game, a long zinc bar with chalked menu boards on the walls behind, high sash windows overlooking the busy street outside, and a lively collection of Aubrey Beardsley-style paintings hanging around the red brick walls.

None of the usual crowd was in right now – they generally weren't during the day. However, a group of young mums Nikki was coming to know were filling up the sofas and pouffes on the other side of the room, and several old folk she recognised from shopping on the high street were spread out around various other tables. She'd spoken or waved to most on arriving, making a fuss of the babies and stopping to ask one of her neighbours if he'd received the letter that had come through their door by mistake, while Kristin had gone to order their tea.

'At least you've got an excuse, eating for two,' Kristin was grumbling through a mouthful of tasty minced beef and gravy pie. She picked up her cup. 'I'm just disgustingly weak-willed, but this is definitely it now, because the last thing I want is to waddle on to the stage like some disgustingly pregnant duck next month . . .' Her eyes rounded as she realised what she'd said, then a spray of pastry flakes shot from her mouth as they both started to laugh. 'Sorry,' she said, dabbing her lips with a serviette, 'you know what I mean.'

'I don't think one Clark's pie's going to do much damage,' Nikki said comfortingly. 'If you were scoffing them all the time, maybe . . . God, they're so delicious. I wouldn't mind another. Anyway, tell me more about yesterday and what . . .' She broke off as Kristin's mobile started to ring.

'My mum,' Kristin said, checking the screen. 'Hey, how are you?' She grimaced an apology to Nikki as she listened to the reply. 'Oh, right. What time do you have to be there?'

As she chatted on Nikki finished the rest of her pie and was just taking a sip of tea when she spotted a girl from her antenatal class waving through the window. It was the one with the chain-smoking mother.

Waving back, Nikki mouthed, 'How's everything?'

The girl patted her eight-month bump and gave her the thumbs up.

'Sorry about that,' Kristin said, glancing over her shoulder as she rang off. 'Who were you waving at?'

'I don't know her name,' Nikki answered. 'She goes to my antenatal class.'

Kristin instantly lost interest. 'My mum's got her six-monthly check-up today,' she sighed glumly. 'She gets a bit stressed before she goes and my sister's not around, so she has to go on her own. Maybe I should have stayed in London last night and gone with her today.'

Knowing how much Kristin worried about her mum, Nikki said, 'Is it too late to get there now?'

Kristin nodded. 'Her appointment's at twelve. What an idiot,' she muttered angrily. 'I should have thought of it yesterday. Anyway, it's too late now, and actually, she'll be fine.' She gave a toss of her head and forced a smile.

Nikki reached out to squeeze her hand. 'Of course she will,' she said warmly. 'It's just a check-up.'

Kristin smiled gratefully, then making an effort to dismiss it, she said, 'So where were we? Oh yes, I was about to . . .'

'Sorry,' Nikki grimaced as her own phone started to ring, and checking who it was she broke into a smile. 'David's mum,' she said and clicked on.

'Give her my love,' Kristin mouthed.

Nikki nodded. 'Hi Mrs A,' she said. 'How's tricks?'

'Hello my dear,' Mrs Adani chirruped cheerfully down the line. 'I hope I am not interrupting, but I have something to tell you. Is this a good time?'

'It's fine,' Nikki assured her, intrigued. 'And by the way, the Navratri dinner was amazing the other night. You should have stayed and had some with us.'

'Oh no, you do not want me to be hanging around,' Mrs A protested, 'and I have many things to do at home with Mr Adani away.'

'Any news on when he's coming back yet?'

'I am afraid not. His mother is still very ill, and they think she will not recover, so he will stay with her to the end.'

'I'm sorry to hear that,' Nikki murmured, thinking of how close the Adanis were, and how much they were probably missing one another.

'That is very kind of you,' Mrs Adani told her. 'This will

not be an easy time for my husband, because, as you know, we have not seen our families in India for many years. Now he is feeling very guilty that he did not visit sooner. They had an argument, you know, he and his mother, before we left, and it was a very long time before they spoke again, and then it was only on the telephone. This is not a good thing between a mother and her child, not good at all. However, God in his mercy has brought about their reunion, and they will be at peace with one another before she goes.'

'That's good,' Nikki mumbled, suspecting this was Mrs A's way of telling her to mend the fences with her own parents before it was too late. However, as far as Nikki was concerned, it was her parents who should be doing the mending, not her.

'So, now the reason for my call,' Mrs A chattered on. 'I know how important it is when having a first baby that everything is new, so this is why I would like to buy for you a very nice buggy from John Lewis, which is where I am now. If it is not . . .'

'Mrs A, you can't do that,' Nikki protested.

'Now, don't you be telling me what I can and can't do. I have already talked it over on the telephone with Mr Adani last night, and he agreed that this is the gift we would like to make for the godchild of our son. We would be very happy if you would be baptising the baby a Catholic, but of course we will not be insisting. Everyone has the right to their own religion, even though there is only one true faith.'

With a smile, and a heart brimming with affection, Nikki said, 'Honestly, you really shouldn't . . .'

'If it is not to your taste,' Mrs A interrupted, 'then we can be changing it, but I think it is the one you said you liked when we were looking through the catalogue last week. I will be bringing it over in the car on Friday evening on my way home from work. Now, please say hello to my son, if he is with you, and to everyone else. I must go because I have more shopping to do before I pick up the buggy down at the collection point,' and before Nikki could send Kristin's love she was gone.

'Sorry,' Nikki apologised, 'she didn't give me a chance . . .'

Kristin waved a dismissive hand. 'So what can't she do?' she asked.

Nikki coloured slightly as she said, 'She only wants to buy a buggy for the baby.'

Kristin's eyes widened. 'Why? It's not as if it's *her* grandchild you're carrying.'

Feeling more awkward than ever, Nikki said, 'She says it's because David's going to be the godfather, so maybe, in her world, that kind of makes the baby family.'

Kristin was still looking miffed. 'You know, she's always preferred you to me,' she said snippily. 'It's like I'm not good enough for her son, or something.'

'That's not true!' Nikki protested. 'She's really sweet to you. Remember the lovely Ganesh she gave you on your birthday . . .'

'Excuse me, what am I supposed to do with an elephant god? Do I look Indian? Even she's not Hindu.'

'That's not the point. It was a lovely gesture, and it's something you can keep for your daughter, if you ever have one.'

Kristin shuddered. 'No way am I having any children,' she retorted. 'Not yet, anyway. I've got things to do, and places to go . . .'Her eyes flicked uneasily to Nikki. 'Sorry, I don't mean to be rude,' she said, 'but honestly, the last thing I need is some kid holding me back at this stage of my life.'

Nikki's smile faded as her eyes fell to her tea. 'It doesn't have to,' she heard herself saying, even though she was becoming increasingly unsure of that. 'The way Spence and I see it is that the baby will come with us, wherever we go . . .'

'Yeah? And what about when it's at school, or sick, or whatever? Look, I know it's too late to do anything about it now, and I'm not suggesting you should, but honestly, Nikki, if you'd seen Spence on that set yesterday, chatting to the actors and everyone like he already knew them, he was seriously into it, and they loved him. You know what he's like, an instant hit everywhere he goes. And you heard what Drake Murray said to him. He's got amazing talent, and it needs to be exploited, now, while he's young, before fatherdom and domesticity start weighing him down.'

'I'm not weighing him down,' Nikki objected. 'Whatever he wants to do is fine by me. He knows I'll support him.'

'Really?'

'Yeah, really.'

'You mean, like this morning, when we were all for making plans to go to Hollywood, until he realised you couldn't have the baby there. In my book, that's weighing someone down.'

Annoyed, Nikki said, 'It's *you* who wants to go right away, not Spence. He was perfectly cool about waiting and if something else comes up over here, it's where he'll want to be. And you never know, it might.'

'Yeah, and it might not, so what's the harm in thinking about going where the action is?'

'None. I'm only saying that there's no rush. He hasn't even shot the second-unit stuff yet, and what about your play? You might get offered more work after that . . .'

'I don't want to do theatre. It's OK for now, to put on my CV, but movies and TV are where it's at.'

'So? Movie and TV people go to the theatre too. Anyone could be in the audience . . .'

'Here? At the Tobacco Factory?' Kristin scoffed. 'Give me a break.'

'It's the only decent theatre in town since the Old Vic closed,' Nikki pointed out, 'so it's where the talent spotters go.'

'Mm,' Kristin grunted grudgingly. 'Anyway, I'm just saying, everyone seems to think Spence's got a great future ahead of him . . .'

'And I agree with them,' Nikki broke in. 'Look, OK, this baby was a mistake when it happened, but deciding to go through with it was something we discussed at length, and if anything, Spence was more for it than me.'

'Oh come on, you know him better than anyone. He's all for anything if it makes someone happy. Look, I wasn't going to tell you this, but do you know what he said on the train coming back last night? He said, "I'm totally responsible for Nikki and the baby now that her parents are acting up." I know to you that might sound all cool, and honourable and everything, but think what a pressure that's putting on him, when he hasn't even really got started.'

Nikki's face was growing pale. 'We're responsible for one another,' she argued. 'We're both perfectly capable of . . .'

'He also said,' Kristin cut in, 'that he actually wished you were a bit more like me.'

Nikki stared at her, dumbfounded.

Kristin's cheeks flamed crimson. 'I'm sorry, but it's what he said,' she murmured awkwardly, 'and I knew what he meant. I'm much more ambitious than you are. I'm prepared to take chances, and do all the networking and stuff you have to do in this business.'

'And you think I'm not?' Nikki challenged.

Kristin shrugged. 'There's no point arguing about this,' she replied, 'I'm just telling you what he said. Anyway,' she went on, looking at her watch, 'I'm supposed to be meeting David at twelve, so I have to go.'

Nikki watched her pick up her bag and get to her feet.

'I'll see you later,' she said, looking down at Nikki.

'Yeah, right,' Nikki murmured, and it wasn't until Kristin had gone and she'd finally managed to think up a couple of withering put-downs that she realised she now had to carry all the shopping home alone.

'Did you seriously say that?' Nikki demanded, glaring at Spence across the bedroom where rogue rays of sunlight were streaking through the venetian blinds, creating a bizarre zebra effect over the unmade bed. 'Do you really wish I was more like *her*, because . . .'

'No way,' he cried, starting to laugh.

'So why did she say you did?'

'I've got no idea. I mean, I guess I said something she took the wrong way. You know what she's like. She always makes everything about her . . . Oh come on,' he said, leaving his desk and walking over to give her a hug. 'You're letting her get under your skin and you know better.'

Gazing into the gentle depths of his eyes, she said, 'She really seems to think I'm holding you back, or weighing you down, as she puts it. Is that what you think too?'

Dropping his forehead on to hers, he said, 'Look, I'm not getting into this. You know I'm crazy about you. I can't wait for the baby to come and no way do I wish you were more like Kristin Lyle. So please don't go dyeing your hair blonde, or deciding to take up acting, or getting everyone's back up, because then we really will have a problem. I want you just the way you are.' He frowned. 'Isn't that a line from an old song?'

She shrugged. 'Who cares, I just want to be sure you're being honest with me.'

He tilted her face so he could look directly into her eyes. 'When am I ever not?' he asked seriously.

Knowing that he always was, she managed a smile. 'I'm sorry. You're right, I shouldn't let her get to me, but I have to be honest, sometimes I have a problem remembering what her good points are. In fact, if it weren't for David . . .'

With a laugh, he pressed a kiss to her mouth and said, 'I really need to get on with this script, OK? There's a copy for you to read downstairs, next to your computer. I've marked the scenes I'll be shooting, so let's have a chat about it before I go to meet David later, yeah?'

Feeling annoyed with herself for wanting even more reassurance, she forced herself to let him go, and watched him return to his desk. Almost immediately she sensed him detaching from his surroundings, as though he was stepping out of this world into another that only he could see. It happened so fast, she almost felt the draught.

When she reached the door she turned back, not really wanting to say what was on the tip of her tongue, but unable to stop herself. 'If you're feeling pressurised by this split with my parents . . .'

'Nikki, please,' he groaned. 'I really need to focus.'

'Sorry,' she mumbled, and closing the door behind her she wandered back downstairs, feeling more bothered than ever as she went to find the script.

A while later, realising she wasn't really paying attention to what she was reading, she put the script aside and returned to her computer. Whether she liked it or not, Kristin was right about her not being proactive enough. She needed to start making more contacts herself, instead of always relying on Spence to carry them to fame and fortune. True, they knew mostly the same people, but that was beginning to change now that he and David were spending more time mixing with other directors and cameramen, here in Bristol as well as in London. They were also becoming quite skilled at promoting themselves to local production companies who had network commissions, and various businesses that might benefit from a promotional or training video. For Spence, just about everyone he met was a potential backer, or client, or connection to someone who might be the next big step in his budding career, and the way he overflowed with charm and talent and infectious energy, most were willing to go out of their way to help him.

Whereas she was . . . what?

The writer of an award-winning short film, and another full-length feature yet to be produced. Both positives, she had to admit, but the latter didn't actually mean anything unless someone decided to back it. Naturally, Spence was already on the case, and had given it to Drake Murray to read, but maybe she should be doing more to get it out there too.

Opening up Google, she typed in *Agents for screenplays.*

After searching a few of the results she felt more despondent than ever. There was absolutely no submitting a script on spec. None of them wanted it, and most were right upfront about saying so, as if unsolicited material was the next best thing to anthrax. First, she'd have to write a letter, send a sample of her work and then wait up to three months for a reply, which she might only get if she supplied a stamped addressed envelope. Presumably, if they decided her work was of high enough quality, they wouldn't worry too much about springing for a stamp, or even a phone call, so it seemed a bit mean to be asking writers to pay the postage for their own rejection letters.

Going back to Google she typed in *Finding finance for films.*

Twenty minutes later she wished she hadn't bothered. There was absolutely nothing straightforward about it, and no decent books she could find on the subject that Spence didn't already have. Moreover, she knew what he'd say if she told him what she was doing – that she should just focus on coming up with great scripts and let him take care of everything else.

So maybe that was what she'd do, and Kristin bloody

Lyle, Queen of the Networkers, star taker of chances, who hadn't actually come up with a single useful contact herself now Nikki came to think of it, *or* taken any risks that Nikki could remember, could just go screw herself.

Happy with that decision, she opened up a fresh page in her screenwriter programme and sat looking at it for a while. Unlike a lot of writers she loved blank pages. To her they were an invitation to a party full of people she hadn't actually met yet, but already knew a great deal about, and the instant she opened the first scene, so the party began. The interdependency between writer and character, the journey they made together and the tussles and triumphs along the way, were as exciting – no, exhilarating – for her as appearing in front of a camera, or on a stage, would be for Kristin. And just because Kristin had an audience when she strutted her stuff didn't make what she did any more skilful or valuable than what Nikki did. In fact, without someone like Nikki, Kristin wouldn't actually have any stuff to strut.

Pleased with that timely reminder, she began filling the page with various ideas she had for new scripts, and as words, characters, scenarios, even snatches of dialogue flowed from her fingertips, time passed in a blur. She finally saved what she'd written, and opened up her emails. She wasn't in the right head space to start an actual script today. She needed to work up to it, spending time with the characters in her mind first, then she'd discuss her ideas with the others, going over everything from background to motive, plotline to structure, and mood to denouement before she began committing to dialogue and action. Getting their input was as vital a part of the process for her as sitting down at the computer to compose the right words. She loved it. They all did. It was, more than at any other time, perhaps apart from shooting, when they really came together as a group, sparking off one another like a bunch of comedians, running with each other's suggestions, trying to outdo one another and generally testing each other's imaginations and intellect to the full. Which, she decided, kind of made her the glue that held them all together. So let Kristin stick that in her ambition pipe and smoke it.

Feeling the baby move, and picturing him in there, floating about like a little astronaut, she spread her hands over him, saying in her mind,

'I hope you weren't listening when Kristin was going on with all her crap earlier. She talks such a load of BS. sometimes, and she can be a real b.i.t.c.h. too when she wants. Actually, I should have told her she was right, Mrs A doesn't really like her much, that would have shut her up, because she can't stand anyone not liking her. To be honest, though, Mrs A's never mentioned what she feels about her, but I definitely get the impression she's not too keen. Kristin wouldn't even be a part of our set if it weren't for David. Until then, we were a foursome, me, Daddy, Danny and David. Daddy and I have often wondered if David might be using Kristin to convince everyone he's a full-blooded hetero. Not that he doesn't like her or anything, because I'm sure he does, but Daddy and I reckon he's a bit more the other way than he wants to admit. In fact, we're sure he is, but with his parents being Catholic he's probably too afraid to come out. Whatever. It's not something he's ever talked about, so we're only surmising. He and Danny are going to make fantastic godparents for you, just you wait and see. I've had to ask Kristin if she'd like to be one too, sorry about that, because she's way too up herself to be any good at it, but it just seemed a bit mean to leave her out. Actually, I probably would have, but Daddy's such a softie when it comes to people's feelings that he said we couldn't possibly hurt hers, so we had to include her.'

'Nikki? *Nikki*?'

Starting, she looked up.

Spencer laughed. 'You were miles away,' he told her. 'I've been calling you for ages.'

Heaving a tremulous sigh, she said, 'I was having a little head-to-head with Bonzo.'

He looked amused. 'Really? What about?'

She shrugged. 'Just keeping him/her up to speed with what's going on around him. She's dead chuffed about your second-unit gig, by the way,' her gaze sharpened slightly, 'but she's not too sure about making his film debut through his mother's legs.'

Spence's eyes narrowed.

'Did we discuss it, and I've blanked on it?' she asked.

He pulled a face. 'I don't think so,' he confessed. 'I know I meant to mention it . . . It's a great idea though, isn't it?'

She reached for his hand and held it between her own. 'I can see why you might think so,' she said, 'but I doubt he's ever going to want to watch it. I mean, would you, if it was your mother giving birth to you?'

As he thought about it she started to regret the question, since the few memories he had of his mother were of her either enraged by drink, slumped in a near coma because of it, or bringing strange men into the house, presumably to earn cash for more. Were it not for the aunt who'd taken him in after his mother had broken her neck falling down the stairs of their high-rise, heaven only knew what might have happened to him. The aunt lived on the same estate, and wasn't really much better than her sister, but at least she'd fed him and made sure he went to school most days. It was largely thanks to one of his teachers that his love of film had been eased past all the aggression and fear he had stored up inside. It was the same teacher who'd got him through his GCSEs by coaching him after school, and another caring tutor had taken him on for his A's. Without them he might never have escaped the vicious down-ward spiral he'd been born into. Thank God he had, because he was so special and talented and had so much to give to the world, as well as to their relationship and their baby, that she couldn't even imagine her life without him in it now.

With his nose screwed up he said, 'I take your point. In fact, thinking about it some more, we want the whole birth thing to be a private time for us two, three come the end.'

She laughed and hugged him. 'Sounds about right,' she told him.

'Anyway,' he continued, his mind doing a quick flit back to where they'd left off, 'the reason I was calling you was to find out if you've reached Scene 88 yet, because I can't seem to get my head round it, and it's one of the scenes I'm supposed to be shooting.'

Using his hands to pull herself up, she said, 'I have to

admit I got a bit sidetracked, but I'll make a start on it now, and come up as soon as I've got that far.'

'Brilliant,' he declared, already starting back to the door. 'I mean, I think I know what's going on, but then . . . Well, you'll see. Oh yeah, any chance of a coffee when you come up?'

'Every, if you make it.'

'Nik,' he groaned. 'Come on.'

'OK, just as long as you don't start treating me like the tea lady just because I'm a girl.'

'Never going to happen,' he assured her, taking the stairs two at a time. 'Oh, by the way,' he said, turning back as he reached the top. 'David just texted to say Stevie Munster's having a party on Friday night at Bar Humbug. Reckon it's time we all went out and got smashed, don't you?'

He'd gone before she could remind him that getting smashed was no longer an option for her, but she wouldn't have anyway. He'd remember soon enough, and then feel really bad about all she was having to give up for the baby, but maybe she could have one glass of wine, he'd say. She'd refuse and he'd agree it was the right decision, then he'd offer to stay at home with her if she didn't want to sit around sober while everyone else was getting off their face. She didn't, but she'd go anyway, because she was finding that she didn't actually have to be smashed to have a good time.

Picking up the script, she flipped open to the first page and curled into a corner of the sofa to start reading. Now Spence wanted her opinion, she'd probably find it easier to focus.

However, she was on Scene 33 before she realised she'd barely registered a word. Instead, she was aware of feeling agitated and uneasy about something, which wasn't going to be good for the baby at all. She needed to be chilled and calm, but something wasn't feeling right, and it was really starting to get to her.

Did pregnant women get premonitions about things?

She'd never heard that they did.

Was there some gloomy little hormone that went round the system like a video nasty, scaring all the others?

Or was it just a pain in the neck called Kristin Lyle who was making her wish she wasn't pregnant at all, when actually it was the best thing in the entire world, and she didn't regret it one bit.

Chapter Four

Ten days later Spence and David took off for London to start prepping their shoot, while Kristin's rehearsals for the wacky version of *Twelfth Night* started early, preventing her from tagging along, and Danny got a job offer from E! Online.

'You didn't even tell me you'd applied,' Nikki accused, after congratulating him. 'What's it all about? When's it going to happen?'

Grinning all over his face, Danny said, 'I'm going to be part of the news team, you know, interviewing celebs and getting all the goss, which is brilliant, because of all the contacts I could make for you and Spence.'

'It's brilliant for you too,' she told him. 'It's *so* you, getting it on with the rich and famous, prancing down red carpets, slapping on the sequins for all those glitterati parties. I can see you now. It's fantastic. When do you start?'

He grimaced. 'The beginning of December – and, wait for this . . .'He was looking as though he might duck. 'I have to be based in London.'

Nikki's heart gave a jolt. *'My friends didn't take long to disappear,'* she heard her mother shouting. However, she managed to keep her euphoria going as she said, 'Perfect. It's absolutely where you should be.'

'Yeah, but you and David and Spence are all here, and I really want to be around when the baby comes. Actually, I will be,' he declared decisively. 'I'll just take the time off.'

'And if you can't, you'll see him or her soon enough after,' Nikki assured him. 'And before you know it, we'll all be moving in with you, because London's definitely where it's at. I mean, we might love it here, but all the big chances are there.'

'You're right,' he agreed, 'but until you can make it, I'll be visiting as often as I can, so you're not getting rid of me that easily.'

'As if I'd want to,' she laughed. 'Now, what about Gus? Have you told him yet?'

'No, but really, we're not that serious. I don't think it'll be a big deal for him. Leaving you's going to be much worse, like having my teeth removed without anaesthetic.'

Managing a laugh while fighting back a silly rush of emotion, she said, 'We have to celebrate. I might even have a glass of champagne. Or half, anyway.'

Danny winced. 'Oh no, I'm not being responsible for screwing up your resolutions,' he told her. 'You promised yourself no alcohol while pregnant, and I'm always up for a glass of Ribena. We can use sparkling water and pretend it's a Kir royale.'

Squeezing him hard just for being him, she said, 'I can't tell you how pleased I am for you.'

'And I can't tell you how crap I feel that I might not be there when my first godchild comes into the world.'

'Don't worry, you'll be first on the list for Spence to call,' she promised. An image of her parents flashed into her mind, causing an uneasy twist in her conscience. She'd have to tell them too, she supposed – on the other hand, did she really want to give them the chance to ignore her?

She'd decide when the time came.

'OK,' she said, leading Danny into the kitchen to mix their cocktails-lite, 'do you want to hear how I got on with the *Western Daily Press* today?'

Danny's face became a picture of guilt. 'Oh my God. I forgot you were going,' he cried. 'That is so typical, always thinking about myself first . . .'

'That's so not you,' she interrupted, 'and let's face it, your news was pretty big, whereas mine is . . . Actually, it's OK. They want me to produce a series of articles on people who live and work in this area, you know, tradesmen, restaurateurs, teachers, doctors, kids at school, the unemployed, anything I can come up with that says something about who we are around here. I'm feeling quite jazzed about it, actually, and the pay's not bad, considering the measly sums they've shelled out in the past. Two profiles a week for the next three weeks, to include domestic hardship, unusual love stories, coping with bereavement and family feuds if I can get them.'

Danny was clapping his hands with pride. 'This is absolutely right for you,' he told her. 'You are *so* good with people that I can't see you having any problem at all getting them to open up. If anything, you'll probably have them beating at the door begging to be on your A list once word gets out. They'll bring their digital cameras and their families . . .'

Nikki gave a choke of laughter. 'Yeah, that would be me,' she said drily. 'Princess Di and Brad Pitt stand aside, Nikki Grant is about to top the list of people you'd most like to meet.'

As it turned out, Danny wasn't entirely wrong about Nikki proving popular with her interviewees, since she really did have a gift for getting people to talk about themselves, even when life wasn't serving up a whole lot of good luck for them. Of course, there were always the awkward types who tried to make her look foolish, or told her to get lost, and one bruiser of a female car mechanic who actually threatened to whack her if she didn't eff off p.d.q. She didn't venture into Hartcliffe again after that. Or Knowle West. There were too many women like the mechanic, and Kay, the mother of the little girl with Down's, who'd think nothing of giving her a mouthful of abuse, or worse, if the mood took them that way.

So on the whole she stayed in the safer areas of Southville, Ashton and Victoria Park, and the interviews she delivered were impressive enough to earn her a few more commissions from the paper, and the offer of some part-time work with the *Bristol Magazine*.

By then David was back home and working with a local independent, and Kristin's play was about to open. Spence was still in London working on a rough edit of the scenes he and David had shot, and the great news for Nikki was that Drake Murray was making some positive noises about her script. He wanted to talk to her about it when the movie he was still shooting was finished, but as there was no actual date for that at the moment, she wasn't going to get too excited yet.

When the curtain went up on *Twelfth Night* Kristin delivered such an amazing performance in the quirky production that it was no surprise to anyone that she earned herself glowing reviews in the local press. Seizing the exclusive, Nikki interviewed her for David's blog, which ended up being aired on both local TV stations and on other websites too, including E! Online, thanks to Danny's submission.

A week later Kristin received a call from her new London agent telling her she had an audition for a part in *The Bill*. Her character was an ex-catwalk model hooked on cocaine, whose rock-star boyfriend had been arrested for the rape of a fifteen-year-old girl.

Kristin was ecstatic, and in spite of a tinge of envy Nikki couldn't help being pleased for her.

Though Spence had returned to Bristol for the opening of Kristin's play – 'have to show support,' he'd declared – he was back in London by the time she knew about her audition. On hearing about it he immediately told Nikki to get Kristin to come up the day before, so he could give her some coaching before she had to turn it on for the casting.

'She's right here if you want to talk to her,' Nikki told him. 'I'll pass you over.'

Leaving them to sort out the details, Nikki returned to the article she was polishing before submitting, only half listening to Kristin's gushes of gratitude and excitement as Spence made his offer.

'Fantastic, I'll text you when I get to Paddington,' Kristin was saying as she walked back towards Nikki. 'What's the nearest Tube . . . OK . . . If you can meet me there . . . That's great. I'll see you tomorrow, then, outside Vauxhall station at . . . Cool. Do you want to speak to Nikki again? Sure, bye,' and barely pausing to pass the phone back, she scooped up her own phone and dashed up the stairs to start texting everyone she knew with the great news.

'Hey,' Nikki said to Spence. 'That seems to have worked.'

'Sure,' he said, sounding distracted. 'Hang on, just a minute, I've got a text from . . . Great, I know where I have to be tomorrow now. So, how's everything with you?' he asked, focusing again. 'Did you go for your check-up today?'

'Yep, and everything's great. Baby's heart's beating like a little drum. The midwife let me have a listen again, it's so cool.'

In a voice husky with pride he said, 'How's your blood pressure this time?'

'Still perfect. Apparently we're a textbook pregnancy.'

'That's what we want to hear. I'll make sure I'm there the next time you go. When is it?'

'In four weeks, which makes it ten days before Christmas. After that I'll be seeing her every two weeks until . . . our lives change for ever.' As soon as the words were out she regretted them, and the silence that followed didn't help one bit. Evidently, deep down, he was as daunted and nervous about it all as she was.

'It's coming around so fast now,' he murmured. Then, 'I can hardly wait to see him, or her, can you?'

Forcing a smile, Nikki said, 'I keep imagining you holding him, or her, and it makes me want to cry.'

He laughed. 'I won't be that bad,' he joked. 'I've got myself a doll now, so I'm practising every day.'

Loving the image, in spite of knowing it wasn't true, she looked up and gave Danny a wave as he came in the door.

'Someone's nicked my bloody bike,' Danny growled furiously. 'I had to walk all the way from Clif . . .'Noticing Nikki was on the phone, he came to a stop and turned back into the hall to start peeling off his coat and scarf.

'Danny's bike's been stolen,' Nikki told Spence.

'Oh God, that sucks,' he said sympathetically. 'He's not having a lot of luck lately, is he, what with breaking up with Gus too. How is he about that now?'

'OK, I think. It was his decision, remember, but that didn't stop him feeling bad. Gus has rung a couple of times, actually, but I don't think Dan's going to change his mind.'

'If you ask me he's still holding out for David,' Spence commented.

'Mm, I rather think you're right,' Nikki murmured, 'but let's not get into it now. Will you be back for his going-away party?'

'Absolutely. When is it?'

'Next Saturday. We're going to start off with everyone at the Factory, then he wants to take us five to the Clifton Sausage for a meal. I keep saying we'll pay, but he's . . .'

'Hang on, someone's calling on the mobile,' he interrupted. After checking who it was he said, 'It's OK, they can call back. Tell Danny we're paying and that's an end to it. How's he getting to London with all his stuff?'

'His dad's taking him on the Sunday.'

There was a moment before Spence said, 'It's going to seem strange without him.'

'Tell me about it, but he had to take the job. It's too good an opportunity to miss.'

'Of course. Actually, I've been meaning to bring this up . . . I reckon we should all move to London, after the baby comes. I've been thinking about it for a while. I know it's not Hollywood, but that's just Kristin and her big ideas. There's a lot going on here too, and with all the contacts I've been making . . . Well, let's talk about it when I come back next weekend.'

'I'm happy to do whatever you want,' she told him, meaning it. 'If London's your choice, then we can just as easily live there as here, and you're right, I think we should be there. I mean, it'll be more expensive, obviously, but if we're finding more work . . . David and Kristin are bound to be up for it, unless she's still got her sights on Hollywood.'

'We all have,' he reminded her, 'but that's for later. London's for now, until we've got ourselves established. Drake reckons one more movie as good as *Done with the Night* and we'll have the kind of calling cards that'll open all the doors.'

'You mean another short?'

'Possibly. Or your feature, but that's a much bigger project, so maybe a short's the way to go for now. Drake's happy to work with us on getting the script into shape, once we have one, and I'm hoping he'll offer to produce it, because we won't have any problems raising the finance if his name's attached.'

'That would be amazing,' Nikki murmured, sharing his excitement. 'Do you think he will?'

'I reckon there's a chance, yes. He's a really great guy, no bullshit, no ego, no side to him at all. You're going to love him when you meet him. Everyone does.'

Looking forward to the day, Nikki said, 'So I guess I should start work right away. I've had a few ideas, actually. We could brainstorm them next weekend, if you like.'

'Fantastic.' Then after a beat, 'God, I miss you. This is the most we've been apart since we met, do you realise that?'

Smiling, she said, 'Yeah, I had kind of noticed, but you have to do this. Mentors like Drake Murray don't come along every day, and as long as you're here when the baby comes . . .'

'You can count on it. Anyway, I guess I should be going now. Sam and the others left a while ago, they'll be wondering what's happened to me.'

'Where are you going?'

'Just for a Chinese.'

'OK, well send them all my love. Where's Kristin going to sleep when she gets there?'

'Kayla's away at the moment, so Kristin can have her room. It's dead lucky I got that fifteen grand now I'm paying rent here and there, not that Sam's asking for much, but he's not exactly rolling in it so every little helps. Which reminds me, are you OK for money? I can always transfer some if you need it.'

'Actually, I'm quite flush at the moment,' she answered. 'The *Western Daily Press* have just coughed for my series of articles on South Bristol and I've had a couple more cheques come in from *Venue* and the easyJet in-flight mag, would you believe?'

'Brilliant,' he laughed. 'Now, before I go, can I speak to my son or daughter please?'

Feeling her heart melt, she put the phone to her swollen belly and listened to him telling the baby that he'd be back soon, and that he was sorry he hadn't been there for the thirty-two-week check today, but he wouldn't miss the next one, just before Christmas. 'And I'm going to take you to Bristol City the minute you're born,' he informed him, 'because Mummy tells me you're already seriously into the game.'

'I think you're going to be disappointed if it turns out to be a girl,' Nikki chided, putting the phone back to her ear.

'Don't you believe it,' he replied. 'Now, I really have to go. Be good. I'll call again tomorrow.'

As she rang off Nikki was still smiling, though inside she was tensing against the anxiety that had started to sweep over her at times now, leaving her shaky and disoriented and not at all sure what to do. She put most of it down to missing Spence, and the continuing rift with her parents, and weirdy old hormones, of course, but in her worst moments she was no longer coping very well with the thought of how drastically the baby was going to change their lives. Her mother's words kept echoing through her mind, making her want to run and hide, as though that single mindless act would somehow make the awful sense of dread disappear. No matter what she and Spence told themselves, or how brave a face they put on for each other and the rest of the world, maybe they really weren't ready for this.

A couple of times lately she'd become so torn and confused, and so afraid of the nightmares she'd started having where she was doing terrible things to her baby, that she'd mentioned it to Mrs A when she'd called in the other day. In her usual unflappable way Mrs A had only chuckled, and promised Nikki that she really wasn't the first expectant mum to get cold feet, or feel spooked, during the last couple of months of pregnancy.

Though Nikki had felt reassured at the time, the unease and slight twinges of paranoia kept coming back, and if she were being totally truthful with herself she might have to admit that she didn't actually want the baby any more. Denial clamped down on that thought like a vice. Of course she wanted him. Definitely, she did. It was just that she was starting to worry about the way everyone else was racing up and down to London, being mentored, or auditioned, or getting fantastic jobs, while she was stuck here in this little house most days, getting fatter and fatter and more and more scared of what was going to happen when the baby finally came.

I'm really sorry, Zac, she wrote in her notebook that night, *I'm not doing so well at the moment, but I don't want you to think this is going to last. It's just a phase I'm going through, feeling a bit nervous about giving birth and being a good enough mum to you.*

She had to write something like that, because she'd never want him, or anyone else, to know her darkest thoughts. She was too young for this. She was throwing away her chances of a glittering career. She might want to tell herself that it was all going to work out perfectly once she and the baby got used to one another, but what if it didn't? What if it all proved too much for her, or for Spence, and he decided to leave?

'Are you crazy?' David laughed after she blurted this fear out to him in the early hours of one morning. 'No way in the world would Spence ever abandon you, or the baby. You're working yourself up into a state over nothing.'

They were standing in the kitchen, huddled in their dressing gowns and shivering with cold as they waited for the kettle to boil. In David's right hand was the cricket bat he'd brought down with him to use on the burglar he'd half expected to find when noises downstairs had woken him.

'I know, I know,' she said, pressing her hands to her cheeks. 'It's just that I keep getting these feelings . . . The midwife says they're not unusual, so I should listen to her and calm down. In fact, actually I'm fine now. I just couldn't sleep and . . . No, I'm fine.' She took a deep breath, and then another. Her eyes went to his and seeing his tender, trustworthy face so full of concern, she felt the last dregs of her panic starting to slide away. 'I promise, I'm fine,' she assured him, pulling her dressing gown more tightly around her.

'I'll make the hot chocolate,' he said decisively, and propping the bat against the flip-top bin he opened the fridge to take out some milk. 'Why don't you go back to bed to keep warm,' he suggested. 'I'll bring it up to you.'

By the time he came up, carrying two steaming mugs of cocoa, she was snuggled cosily under the duvet with the baby's giant teddy lying next to her.

'Does Spence know about this other guy you're sleeping with?' David quipped, putting her cocoa down beside her.

Nikki giggled as she sat up, keeping the duvet tucked under her chin for warmth. 'Thanks,' she whispered, cupping her hands round the mug. 'I'm sorry for waking you.'

'I'm good,' he assured her, perching on the edge of the bed as he sipped his drink. 'Now I know you're not some pondlife trying to steal my camera and doby premier pro.'

She smiled again, then flinched as the hot cocoa burnt her lips.

'Sorry,' he apologised.

'It's OK. Not your fault.' Then, after taking a more careful sip, she let her eyes drift about the room, taking in all the photographs and posters that were barely visible in the shadows, and the brand spanking new cot, still unassembled, leaning against Spence's desk.

Looking around too, David said, 'Do you remember how we used to sit up all night chatting and smoking dope and drinking cheap wine when we were at uni? Seems a long time ago now, doesn't it?'

She smiled. Then on a whim, she said, 'Fancy having a chat now? Or no, I expect you're tired . . .'

'I'm good,' he said again, and turning himself round to lean against the headboard next to her, he wrapped his feet in the dressing gown she'd left at the end of the bed and dragged the teddy over him to help keep him warm.

'No dope or booze, I'm afraid,' she told him.

'Really?' he said, sounding surprised and disappointed. 'In that case, I'm gone.'

He stayed where he was and after taking another mouthful of cocoa, he said, 'So what do you want to chat about? I'm up for historical and contemporary cinema in the genres of documentary and short film; soccer 1952–88; or babies and how they get their pregnant mothers belted round the head with cricket bats.'

She spluttered a laugh. 'Would you really have used it, if it had been a burglar?' she asked.

'Dead right I would,' he assured her in his best macho bluster. 'Then I'd probably have dropped it and scarpered back upstairs to hide behind this teddy, and the burglar would probably have come up with the bat and bludgeoned us all to death and do you think you're going to sleep well now, after this cosy little chat?'

Losing a yawn to a laugh, she said, 'It doesn't seem as though I woke up the others, thank goodness.'

'Takes a lot to wake Kris, once she goes off,' he commented wryly.

'She'll probably have trouble sleeping tomorrow night though, before her audition.'

'I'm sure you're right. It's really good of Spence to go over the part with her. He got such a great performance out of her for *Done with the Night*, so he knows how to get her to play to her strengths.'

'Mm,' she murmured, the pride and affection in his voice as he spoke about Kristin deciding her not to mention Danny and whether there might actually be any hope for him. 'How long have you and Kris been together now?' she asked. 'It must be almost two years.'

'Almost,' he agreed.

'So it's pretty serious?'

He seemed surprised by the question. 'I think twenty months is long enough to qualify, don't you?' he said.

She nodded.

He smiled as he gazed into the semi-darkness. 'I think she gets a bit fed up with me at times,' he confessed, 'but hey, she hasn't chucked me yet, so I must be good for something.'

Nikki glanced at him, and felt her heart flood with feeling. 'If you ask me, she's lucky to have you,' she told him earnestly.

He laughed. 'Now you're making me blush.'

'I mean it.'

He took another sip of his drink.

'So you really are keen on her?' she ventured.

His eyebrows arched playfully.

'Sorry, I'm being nosy. I'll mind my own business now, just tell me, are you going to be spending Christmas with her and her family?'

He gave a laugh of surprise. 'Are you kidding? Can you imagine how my mother would take that, especially with Dad being away? Unless she decides to join him in India, of course, which is on the cards. My sisters are definitely going with their husbands and all three kids.'

'Wouldn't you like to go too?'

He shrugged. 'Not really. I'm not as keen as they are to explore my roots.'

'I'm amazed,' she commented. 'I'd give anything to have a heritage as fascinating as yours. India always strikes me as such a magical place. I know there's loads of poverty and everything, but all that history . . . and the wildlife. Imagine doing a safari there. That would be so cool, wouldn't it?'

'Maybe you and Spence should go for your honeymoon?'

She smiled at that. 'It would be a bit difficult with Junior,' she reminded him, while thinking that this was something else they'd be missing out on, a real honeymoon adventure, 'but it's a lovely thought. Anyway, back to Christmas. Danny's promised to come and spend it with us, so it would be great if you were here too.'

'Isn't he going to his parents?'

'No, apparently they're off to Australia for a month at the beginning of December to stay with some friends who emigrated last year.'

'Honestly, parents! No sooner do you fly the nest than they get lives of their own! What do they think they're doing? No news from yours, I suppose?'

Nikki's heart tightened. 'Not a word,' she answered, 'and frankly I hope it stays that way.'

He turned to look at her. 'You don't really mean that.'

She sighed. 'No, I don't,' she admitted. 'Or maybe I do. The longer it goes on the easier it gets, not having to watch their eyes roll whenever I say something that irritates them, which is most of the time, or be treated like some kind of delinquent whenever I exhibit signs of having a mind of my own.'

'Most parents are like that.'

'Then please shoot me if you ever see me treating my child that way. Freedom of expression needs to rule in our house, alongside freedom to decide what he or she wants to do with their lives.'

'They're only like it because they care,' he said softly.

She looked at him askance. 'You're starting to sound like your mother now,' she warned.

He laughed.

After that they sank into a cosy silence for a while, each with their own thoughts, until the way to memory lane seemed to open up and as they began recalling experiences they'd shared over the past three years, Nikki could feel their bond tightening. He was the brother she'd never had and had always longed for, kind, funny, always looking out for her, and seeming able to understand things about her that she barely understood herself. It was curious, she was thinking, as she listened to the gentle timbre of his voice, how she'd never fancied him, in spite of how heart-stoppingly attractive he was. She loved him, though, she was in no doubt about that, and she adored his mother too. A spark of guilt flared in her heart as she thought of her parents, and wondered if she was letting too much pride stand in the way of being in touch with them. Sometimes she felt sure she was, but then at other times she found herself becoming angry and resentful that they hadn't swallowed their pride and contacted her. It was a ridiculous stand-off that they probably weren't enjoying any more than she was, but considering the way they felt about Spence she had to wonder if it wasn't better this way.

It was almost five o'clock when Kristin tiptoed into the bedroom to find David snoring softly next to Nikki, whose head had lolled on to his shoulder, and whose hand was touching his on top of the teddy bear. Though Kristin's eyes narrowed, instead of waking them up and throwing a fit, which was her initial instinct, she found herself backing out quietly, and closing the door so softly that no one but her could have heard the click.

'I am so going to miss you guys,' Danny was lamenting with tears shining in his eyes as he gazed at their familiar, beloved faces. 'You're like my family. No, this is worse, because I couldn't wait to leave home, whereas I really, really don't want to leave you.'

They were in the Clifton Sausage now, already fairly tanked up from his going-away bash at the Factory, where he'd got emotional too.

'You'll be back in less than four weeks,' Spence reminded him, having to shout to make himself heard above the buzz, 'and we'll be coming to London as soon as Nikki and the baby are ready.'

'Don't forget, you have to find us a place near you,' Nikki told him. 'I don't know Shepherd's Bush, except it's fairly central, so it's bound to work for us too.'

'Absolutely,' Spence agreed, nodding a thanks to the waiter who'd just delivered their third bottle of wine.

'Don't forget us,' Kristin piped up.

'I know,' David cried, 'why don't we try to get a house for us all, the same as we have here, but bigger?'

Spence shrugged, and glanced at Nikki, seeming to like the idea.

'Nikki and Spence will want to be on their own with the baby,' Kristin reminded David. 'Actually,' she said, putting a hand over Spence's, 'I could see you living somewhere like Hampstead, or Kensington . . . Or no, in one of those fantastic riverside apartments in Battersea. You know, the ones close to the bridge, where we went the other night.' To Nikki she said, 'You should have seen this place. It was out of this world. It belongs to this distributor guy that Drake wanted Spence to meet. Everything was white, or chrome, and the view of the river was ay-mazing. Yeah, definitely,' she said to Spence, 'that's exactly the kind of place I can see you in.'

Danny was eyeing her nastily.

'With a baby?' Nikki said, wishing Spence would remove his hand from under Kristin's, even though he had an arm draped protectively around the back of Nikki's chair. She never used to mind about how tactile he was with other girls, but it was bugging her tonight, especially with the way Kristin didn't seem able to keep her hands to herself. She was also sitting at the head of the table with Spence and David either side of her, which was where Danny should have been, considering it was his night.

'Great, who's for dessert?' David said, as a waiter began handing out the menus. 'I've *got* to have the cheesecake.'

'Think of your figure, darling,' Danny chided.

'He doesn't have to worry,' Kristin retorted, 'but I'm definitely on a diet now I've got this part. I'm supposed to be a catwalk model, for God's sake. I think it's amazing that they chose me. I mean, I've never had any modelling experience, and I'm only five seven, but the casting director said it was my legs that did it. And my acting, obviously. Did I tell you, they said I did a fantastic audition? Apparently they didn't bother to see anyone else after I went in, and it's all thanks to you,' she informed Spence, squeezing his hand again. 'If you hadn't given me that coaching the night before, I'd have been all over the place.'

'You're looking a bit spread out now,' Danny muttered, loud enough for her to hear.

As Nikki smothered a laugh, Kristin cast him a look, then hiccuped and giggled. 'Sorry, I know I've had too much,' she admitted, 'but I'm on such a high right now. Everything's going so brilliantly. Did I tell you, I've got another audition next week, for a part . . .'

'Yes, you told us,' Nikki informed her, the only one amongst them who was stone-cold sober, and wishing she wasn't. 'David, have you heard anything yet about the Paris job?' she asked, determined to cut Kristin off.

'They're getting back to me on Monday,' he replied.

'How long will you have to be there?' Danny asked.

'First couple of weeks of January, apparently.'

'Is there a part for me, do you think?' Kristin wanted to know.

'Not unless you've taken up cooking,' he laughed.

'Oh yeah, sorry, I forgot, it's a foodie show, for some cookery channel. *Boring*.'

Nikki's eyes widened as David flushed.

'It's paying twice the rate I get for the news jobs,' David reminded Kristin.

'Just as well, or it would be a waste of time,' she retorted. 'No, I'm sorry,' she said, as Nikki and Danny glared at her, 'he's a really talented cameraman, so he should be doing features or at least TV drama. Look at me, I'm not messing about . . .'

'Kris, I think you've had enough,' David told her.

'I'm just saying . . .'

'Yeah, we know what you're saying, but let's make this about Danny now, shall we?'

Kristin's nostrils flared and Danny glowed. It wasn't

often David made a stand, but it was pretty exciting when he did.

'Excuse me for breathing,' Kristin muttered sarcastically.

Ignoring her, David said, 'So come on, Dan, talk us through what's going to happen over the next few days.'

With a theatrical fan of his hands, Danny said, 'Sweetie, you know most of it. My dad's coming tomorrow . . .'

'When are they going to Oz?' Spence asked.

'The end of next week, and you'll never guess what they're giving their precious boy for Christmas?'

Everyone waited.

His eyes rounded and his lips circled as he put a finger to his cheek. 'A brand-new bike,' he announced, in a baby voice, 'and it doesn't have stabilisers.'

As they laughed and toasted the new bicycle, a must for getting around London, a waiter came to take their orders, and Spence refilled their glasses.

'More orange juice?' he whispered to Nikki.

'If I do, I'll start changing colour,' she groaned.

'Are you feeling OK?'

'A bit of indigestion, I think, but I'm fine.' She wanted to tell him to move his hand so Kristin couldn't touch it again, but it would sound petty and jealous and that wasn't her. Or it never used to be, anyway.

David was about to encourage Danny to go on, when Danny said, 'Darlings, we all know I could talk about me all night, but I thought we were supposed to be brainstorming Nikki's ideas for a short, and it might be the last time I get to do it for a while. So come, Nikalula, get us started. What new genius is fluttering about in that gorgeous head of yours?'

Laughing, and leaning in closer to Spence, Nikki said, 'Well, actually, I've been thinking about doing some kind of new take on . . .'

'Oh God, I'm sorry, sweetheart.' Spence winced as his mobile started to ring. 'It'll be the call I'm waiting for. I'll have to take it outside.'

As he left, weaving through the crowded restaurant with the phone pressed to his ear, Kristin said to Nikki, 'Who's it from?'

'Drake, I imagine,' Nikki replied.

'What's it about? Any idea?'

Nikki shrugged and shook her head. Even if she knew, she wasn't sure she'd have told Kristin.

'He probably won't be long, so let's crack on with the brainstorm,' David said. 'You were thinking of doing a new take on . . .?'

'Ah, yes. *The Merchant of Venice*,' Nikki finished. 'It came to me when we were watching Kris in *Twelfth Night*, actually. Not that it's anything like *that* production . . .'

'Why? What was wrong with it?' Kristin demanded frostily.

'Nothing,' Nikki assured her. 'It was great. What I meant was, I'm not envisaging the same kind of comedy approach, but it did get me thinking about Shakespearean adaptations and with the way things are at the moment, you know with the recession, and everything being about money, I thought this might lend itself really well to a modern-day pastiche of the Shylock story.'

David and Danny were looking impressed. Actually, so was Kristin.

'Go on,' David encouraged. 'No, hang on, what kind of duration are we talking about first?'

'No more than forty minutes,' Nikki answered. 'I thought we could keep the character names, but I don't see Shylock as Jewish per se, he'll be the head of a merchant bank, you know, like Lehman Brothers . . .'

'Hello! Who would have been Jewish,' Kristin cut in.

'You're missing the point,' Danny told her. 'What she's saying is that religion's got nothing to do with it. It's about our culture of greed.'

'Exactly,' Nikki confirmed. 'Just about everyone's being affected by the fallout from this sub-prime fiasco, so if we can draw the right parallels I think it could be really effective.'

'So do I,' David agreed warmly.

'You know, I think you're amazing,' Kristin told her seriously. 'I could never have come up with anything like that. Spence is going to love it, you just wait and see.'

Though Nikki didn't much appreciate Kristin speaking

for Spence, she was flattered by the praise and felt a little warmer towards her again.

When Spence returned, all apologies and cold-reddened cheeks, he threw himself straight into the idea, and as they came up with all kinds of angles and analogies and a whole slew of possibilities that stimulated as many hilarious as serious suggestions from everyone else, even more wine was consumed.

'I think we should all go clubbing now,' Danny announced when the bill came. 'Are you up for it, Nik?'

'Definitely, count me in,' she replied, in spite of being half asleep on Spence's shoulder by now.

'You know, I've always wanted to play Portia,' Kristin announced as they went out into the cold night to find a taxi. 'Who are you thinking of casting as Bassanio?' she asked Spence.

'God knows,' he replied, 'but there's someone on the cast of Drake's movie who'd make a great Shylock, if I could talk him into it. Before we start getting into that, though, we should have a script to show him, so it's over to you, Mrs Shakespeare.'

Nikki laughed, then winced as a sharp pain cut through her side.

'Are you OK?' Spence demanded, immediately worried.

'Yes, I think so,' she said faintly.

'It'll be wind,' Kristin informed her. 'My cousin used to get it really badly when she was pregnant.'

'Has it gone now?' Danny asked, looking as worried as Spence.

Nikki nodded. 'Just about.' She blew out a large mouthful of air.

'Has it happened before?' David wanted to know.

'Not like that, but a bit, yes. I think it's my muscles expanding. Actually, I'm a bit tired too, so why don't you all go on to the Queen's Shilling, and I'll get a cab home.'

'I'll take you,' Spence said, pulling her against him.

'Actually, let's all go,' Danny said. 'I've got a busy day tomorrow, so an early night's not a bad idea, and it's never any fun without you, sweetie.'

Nikki laughed. 'If I believed that, I'd believe anything,'

she retorted, as she leaned into Spence and hooked Danny's arm.

In less than an hour they were at home, but while the others were all for watching a DVD and smoking some pot, Nikki and Spence were ready for bed.

'Are you sure you're OK?' Spence asked, as they gazed at one another across the pillows. 'You've seemed a bit down lately, and if you're worried, you know, about the baby, or anything, I want you to tell me.'

Smiling as she cupped a hand round his face, she said, 'I promise I will if it gets out of hand, but really I'm just happy to have you home for the weekend, and excited about us moving to London.'

'It'll be great,' he murmured.

'Everything will,' she assured him, because in her heart she knew it would.

His eyes were dancing as he said, 'This is quite some roller coaster the little monster's got us on, isn't it?'

Since the pregnancy had been perfectly smooth so far, she knew he was alluding to the inner concerns they shared, but didn't really discuss. It was as though if they did, they'd breathe some life into them, and there was nothing at all to be gained from doing that.

'Would you like me to rub your back?' he offered.

'Mm, yes please,' she murmured, and turning on to her other side she closed her eyes as he started one of his wonderfully gentle massages.

'By the way,' she said sleepily, 'I take it that was Drake on the phone earlier?'

'Mm?' he said, sounding sleepy too. 'Oh, yes. It was.'

'What was he calling about?'

'Oh, um, nothing really . . . Just a change in the schedule next week. It was good of him to let me know.'

Several minutes ticked by before his hand came to rest on the baby as he drifted off to sleep. She'd been very close to getting there too, until the feeling that he'd just lied to her had stung her awake.

Chapter Five

After Danny left the following day it was as though all the energy had been sucked out of the house, leaving it feeling sad and empty and a place Nikki didn't really want to be any more. She was going to miss him so much, especially with Spence being away all the time, but at least Spence was coming back, eventually, whereas Danny wouldn't be.

'He'll be here for Christmas,' Spence reminded her, as she heaved a tremulous sigh after waving off Danny and his father until they'd turned the corner at the end of the street.

'I know,' she said, leaning into him as he put an arm around her, 'but that seems a long time away right now, and it's starting to feel as though our little family is breaking up, and I want it to stay the same.'

Hugging her close, he pressed a kiss to her forehead and started to walk her inside. 'It will,' he promised. 'This is just the beginning of the transition to London, that's all, then we'll either be sharing a house again, or living as close to one another as we can.'

'Mm,' she murmured, wanting to believe him, but not sure she could. However, it wasn't in her nature to stay pessimistic for long, and since there was a good chance he was right, they would all be together again in a few months, she forced a smile and turned her mouth for a kiss. 'What time are you leaving?' she asked as he held her.

He glanced at his watch. 'In about an hour.' Then, sliding his fingers into her hair, 'Why don't you come with me?' he suggested.

Feeling a lovely warmth spreading inside her, she considered it for a moment, but then shook her head. 'I can't,' she said. 'I've got a lot to do here, and anyway, you'll be out all day, so I'd hardly see you.'

'True, but at least we'd be together in the evenings.'

'Not with how late you're working these days,' she reminded him. 'No, I'll be fine. David's still around, and I've promised to do some vox pops with him on Tuesday, plus I want to make a start on the new script.'

Since he was keen for that to happen too, he didn't argue any further, only kissed her forehead again, then went to use her laptop to check his emails.

'Hey you two,' Kristin said, coming down from her bedroom as Nikki slumped into the armchair with a Sunday paper. 'Anyone seen my mobile? I had it just now, but I must have put it down somewhere.'

'It's over there, on the floor,' Nikki answered, pointing towards where it was lying in front of the TV. 'Any idea what time David's coming back from his mum's?'

'He said around three, so any minute now, I guess. *Great!* There's a text from the costume designer.' She gave a little squeal of excitement. 'We're going shopping tomorrow, isn't that fab? So I'll definitely get the same train as you today, Spence.'

'Cool,' he replied, distractedly. Then, 'Actually, Sam's just sent an email saying Kayla's back so I'll sleep on the sofa and you can have the spare room.'

Kristin's eyes were mischievous as she looked up from her mobile. 'We could always share,' she joked, giving Nikki a wink.

Though Spence's eyebrows waggled playfully, showing he'd heard, he appeared much more focused on the email he was reading.

'So how long are you going to be in London?' Nikki asked, trying not to sound snippy, or as if she particularly cared.

Kristin shrugged. 'Not sure yet. Depends what they might need me for, I suppose. We don't actually start shooting until two weeks before Christmas, but who knows, something else might come up while I'm there. Ah, here he is,' she said, spotting David coming in through the gate, and rushing off to the front door she tugged it open and immediately started jabbering away about going to London earlier than she'd expected, and could he come upstairs to help her sort out what to take.

'Poor guy's obviously in for some kind of fashion show,' Nikki remarked, throwing aside the paper and heaving herself out of the chair. 'Anything interesting?' she asked, going to stand over Spence.

He shook his head and clicked off the inbox. 'Just the usual stuff,' he replied, 'apart from something Philippa's working on that might earn us a few quid, if she can pull it off.'

'Go on,' Nikki prompted, intrigued.

He grinned. 'Would you believe, it's on *The Bill*? Apparently they're really open to trying out new directors, and she's having lunch with one of the producers tomorrow, who's a great mate. I know it's telly and we'd rather do film, but it's all good experience and with this little rascal on the way,' he added, his voice softening with tenderness as he spread his hands over her swelling belly, 'we need to keep the cash coming in.'

She laughed as the baby kicked. 'I think that was a vote of approval,' she told him. 'So, that means you'll be working with Kristin?'

'Oh God no,' he replied. 'She'll be finished long before I'd start – *if* I start,' and stooping to blow a raspberry on her navel, he said, 'Hello, Buster, don't think I'm not aware of how expensive you're going to be, especially if you're a girl, so I'm doing my best. You know,' he said to Nikki, 'if something does come of this thing with *The Bill* . . . Well, they must need as many scriptwriters as directors, so maybe we could put your name forward?'

She almost laughed. 'You know me, I'm up for anything, but I don't know the first thing about police procedure.'

'There'll be a writer's handbook, I'm sure, and loads of real police officers they can put you in touch with. Anyway, it's a thought. The main thing is trying to get your own scripts off the ground.'

'Or written even, but I'll definitely make a start on the Shylock one this week.'

As it turned out, she became so busy with more articles

for the *Western Daily Press*, and helping David with a workshop at the Watershed arts centre, that she didn't manage to get down to her new script until the following week. However, she'd only just begun when David asked if she'd do some more interviews for his blog, which turned out to be so hilarious and addictive that they were at it for four whole days, and ended up shooting so much material that it took them another five to view and edit it all.

'It's absolutely manic,' she told Danny on the phone, three weeks after he'd left. 'The only downside is that you and Spence aren't here to join in.'

'Sounds wild,' he laughed. 'Better than here, where they've got me working like a slave. *Crack that whip, move your butt boy!* I love it, though. Now, tell me, how's the little imp, and what would he or she like for Christmas? Before you answer, remember I'm still not earning megabucks, so the designer stuff will have to wait a while yet.'

Laughing, she said, 'Don't worry about gifts, Dan, just make sure you come, that's all that matters to us. Mrs A is definitely going to India, by the way, so David will be here.'

'Oh, heaven,' he swooned. 'You could really make my day now if you tell me Kristin won't be.'

'Then consider it made, because she's going to her mother's. David's been invited too, of course, but he told her he'd rather be here, with us, which wasn't very clever of him, because, as you can imagine, it seriously pissed her off.'

'Oh, shame,' he said, with mock pity, 'but I'm sure she'll get over it. Has she started *The Bill* yet?'

'Next week. Did Spence tell you that he's spending a lot of time trailing the programme's directors to get a hang of the style and schedule? They haven't said whether they're going to give him an episode yet, but he's really jazzed about it.'

'Oh, you know Spence, he has a way of making things happen, which is why we all love him.'

'Or one of the reasons . . . Oh hang on, someone's trying to get through,' and lowering the phone to check who it was, she felt her heart give a violent jolt. 'Dan, I'll ring you back,' she told him, and quickly switching to the other call she said, 'Hello,' in a voice that was as neutral as she could make it, considering how thrown she was.

'Nicola, it's Mum.'

'Yes,' Nikki said, not sure yet whether she could allow herself to feel as relieved as she actually was. 'How are you?' she asked cautiously.

'I'm . . . We're . . . fine, thank you. How are you?' Her mother's tone wasn't brimming with warmth, but that wasn't unusual, and she was probably anxious, too, about how her call was going to be received.

'I'm OK,' Nikki replied. 'It's nice to hear from you,' she added, going a step further.

Sounding marginally less strained now, her mother said, 'I'm glad you feel that way. We've been worried about you.'

Then why didn't you call sooner, Nikki wanted to say.

'Your father and I would like to see you.'

Nikki wanted to see them too, more than anything, but she was worried about how they might respond to the increasing evidence of her pregnancy.

'There are some things we need to discuss with you,' her mother continued. 'We're happy to come there, but it might be better if you came here. Would that be possible?'

Nikki swallowed. 'I guess so,' she said. 'What's it about?'

'It's not something we should talk about over the phone. Dad's saying he'll pick you up from the station if you let us know the time of your train. Would tomorrow suit? Why don't you come for lunch?'

'Um, OK, thanks, but there's no need to pick me up. I don't mind walking, if it's not raining.'

'Fine. Shall we say around midday?'

'Mum,' Nikki said, before her mother could ring off, 'I'm still pregnant, and it shows, so . . .'

'We weren't expecting anything else,' her mother assured her. 'It's why your father offered to pick you up. He still will if you change your mind. Just let us know.'

For several minutes after the call had ended Nikki sat staring into space, wondering what it had really been about. She'd have loved to think that they'd changed their minds about the baby, and wanted to be involved, the way most grandparents would. With Christmas just around the corner, she guessed it was possible; however, her instincts weren't providing much of a response to the hope.

She didn't mention it to Spence when they spoke on the phone that night, mainly because she got so caught up in the details of his day that she actually forgot until after she'd rung off. For a while she considered calling him back, but in the end she decided not to. She wanted to find out what it was all about first, because if everything fell apart the way it had the last time she'd seen her parents, she didn't want him worrying about her and how upset she might be.

So, the following day, after spending a long time trying to decide what to wear, and rehearsing an endless number of possible scenarios in an effort to prepare herself for the big 'discussion', she caught the eleven o'clock train to Bath, and by ten to twelve she was heading down Great Pulteney Street towards her parents' house. Though it wasn't raining, there was a fine drizzle in the air, so the hood of her duffle coat was up, and the purple scarf Spence had given her was covering half her face to help protect it from the icy edge of the wind.

As she turned in through the gate she was just debating whether or not to use her key when the door opened and her mother, seeming reassuringly glad to see her, ushered her in out of the cold.

'You should have called from the station,' Adele told her. 'It wouldn't have been any trouble to come and collect you.'

'It's fine, and I'm here now,' Nikki said, starting to unbutton her coat, and feeling a lovely sense of belonging coming over her as she inhaled the familiar smell of her home.

After taking Nikki's coat, Adele seemed hesitant, even awkward, but then she cupped a hand round Nikki's cheek and leaned forward to press a kiss to her forehead. It was a rare but not unheard-of show of affection, that had the effect of triggering Nikki's unease while fuelling her need for a more enthusiastic embrace. Was there going to be an apology for the harsh words they'd exchanged the last time she was here, she wondered, hoped? Certainly she was ready to offer hers, and to forgive and forget, provided they accepted the baby, of course. She'd even stopped at the baker's on the bridge to bring some apple turnovers as a kind of peace offering, knowing they were her father's favourite.

'Dad's in the drawing room,' her mother told her. 'We thought we'd have lunch after our chat. He's going to make us some smoked salmon and cream cheese crêpes.'

Since that had long been Nikki's filling of choice she smiled at their similar efforts to please one another, and decided not to remind her mother at this point of the risk to pregnant women from soft cheeses.

'Go on through,' Adele said, hanging up the duffle coat and scarf. 'He's looking forward to seeing you.'

Realising how keen she was to see him too, Nikki went into the drawing room to find her father on his knees stacking fresh logs on the fire.

'Hi,' she said.

'Ah, you're here,' he said, and brushing the dust off his hands he started to get up.

It startled and unsettled Nikki to see how stiff he seemed, as though he'd injured his back, or had some sort of pain in his legs. Then he turned round, and her heart skipped a beat. He looked drawn and pale, and he'd definitely lost weight. A fear suddenly came over her that they might be about to tell her that he had cancer, or something equally as terrible, and her blood turned to ice. *Please, please God don't let him be ill*, she silently begged as she went to give him a hug. 'Are you OK?' she asked.

'Yes, yes, I'm fine,' he replied, hugging her back, not in the hearty way he used to when she was little, but with enough warmth to remind her of how much she loved him, in spite of their issues – and just in case his news was going to be as bad as she feared, she tightened her embrace. 'I've missed you,' she told him, wondering how he might feel about having his unborn grandson pressed up against him.

'I've missed you too,' he said gruffly. 'We shouldn't have let things get out of hand the way we did the last time you were here.'

'Would you like something to drink?' Adele offered, coming into the room.

When Nikki turned round her concern started to grow, because now she could see her mother more clearly she

90

didn't seem her usual self, either. Her face was strained, and her eyes seemed glassy and ringed with shadows. 'Uh, no, thank you,' Nikki said awkwardly. 'I'll wait . . . till we eat.'

'Sit down, close to the fire,' her father said, waving her towards the armchair opposite the one that he was sinking into. 'There are some crisps there, if you're feeling peckish.'

Vaguely aware that something was seeming different about the room, too, Nikki pulled her long jumper further down over her bump as she perched on the edge of the chair. Between them was the coffee table, which was more cluttered than she was used to seeing it, since both her parents were tidiness freaks.

'So, are you still going to Barbados for Christmas?' she asked, trying to sound chatty.

'No, we've cancelled,' her father replied.

Nikki's heart tightened. That wasn't the answer she was hoping for.

'We'll be here,' her mother said. 'In fact, we were hoping you might think about joining us.'

Afraid that it might be her father's last, but guessing the invitation wouldn't include Spence, Nikki hedged, saying, 'Um, well, I guess that depends . . . I mean, obviously I have to be with Spence.'

Her father nodded and clasped his hands together. 'We have something to tell you,' he began, glancing at Adele as she settled on the sofa next to his chair.

Please God don't let him be dying, Nikki was inwardly panicking.

'It won't be easy for you to hear this,' he continued, and her heart virtually stopped, 'but I think it's important for you to know what we've discovered, especially with the baby on its way.'

Thrown by the mention of the baby, Nikki could only blink as she looked at him.

'After you were last here,' he went on, 'I felt so concerned about the decisions you were making and where they might lead you that I took the liberty of employing someone to carry out a background check on your boyfriend, and it would appear . . .'

Outrage hit Nikki so hard that she could barely get her

words out fast enough. 'You did *what*?' she cried furiously. 'Are you seriously telling me . . .? How dare you? You have no right . . .'

'Nicola, please, listen to your father,' her mother cut in. 'It's very important for you to know what we've found out.'

Nikki was on her feet. 'Whatever it is, it won't change anything,' she informed them. 'Spence is the baby's father, and if you think . . .'

'Nicola, your boyfriend is the son of a convicted child molester,' her father told her bluntly.

Nikki reeled with shock.

'His victims were mostly under the age of five,' her father said quietly. 'So I have to ask you, is that the kind of risk you want to put . . .'

'His father's dead,' Nikki shouted.

'Indeed, but that doesn't change who or what he was. And the question we have to ask ourselves is, how like his father is your boyfriend? Has he inherited . . .?'

'Don't you dare even say it,' she warned, her voice deepening with menace.

'What has Spencer ever told you about his father?' her mother asked calmly.

Nikki turned on her furiously. 'Not *that*,' she spat, 'because it's not true, and even if it is, it doesn't mean Spence is like it too.' She pressed her hands to her head. 'I can't believe I'm standing here letting you get away with this,' she raged. 'How dare you go snooping into things that are none of your business, and now, without ever even having met Spence, you practically accuse him of being a paedophile, when he'd never hurt *anyone*, least of all his own child . . . You disgust me for even thinking it,' she sobbed. 'I wish I'd never come here. I should have known you were going to try and turn me against him, or do something vile to . . .'

'Please, calm down,' her father interrupted. 'I understand how upset you are, but we did it for your own good . . .'

'*No!* You did it for *you!*' Nikki yelled. 'You can't stand it that I'm going my own way, so this is how you try to bring me back under your control. Well, it's backfired, because the only person it's turning me against is you . . .'

'I'm merely the messenger,' he reminded her.

'Spy,' she corrected. 'And how do you know the person you found was his real father? I told you what his mother was like . . .'

'It's the name on his birth certificate.'

'Which doesn't mean a thing. She could have made it up for all we know, so to start accusing Spence . . .' She choked on a sob. 'He's done everything he can to break free of his past, so for you to bring it up like this . . . I feel so . . . *ashamed* of you. Don't you have any compassion or forgiveness in your souls? No, don't bother to answer that, because I already know.'

As she headed for the door her mother came swiftly after her.

'Darling, please try to see reason,' Adele implored. 'Leaving like this isn't going to help you or the baby . . .'

'It's not doing either of us any good being here,' Nikki shot back. 'God, I can't believe you went that far. And to be telling yourselves that someone you've never even met, so don't have the first idea about, has to be some kind of monster just because his father – who might not actually be his father – is . . .'

'We have the investigator's report,' her father told her, 'so why don't you take a look at it yourself?'

Nikki spun round, her eyes still blazing with fury. 'I don't need to see it to know with all my heart that whatever it says, Spence is nothing like you're trying to make . . .' Her voice fractured with frustration. 'I'm not listening to any more,' she shouted. 'I don't want any lunch. In fact, after what you've done . . . Your vile efforts to try and control everything I do and everyone I mix with . . . I'm through here. I don't want any more to do with you.'

'Nicola, there are other things we need to discuss,' her mother cried, as Nikki wrenched open the door.

'I don't care. I'm not interested in anything you have to say,' and storming out into the hall she grabbed her bag, coat and scarf and slammed with all her might out of the front door.

It wasn't until she was almost back at the bridge that she stopped to put on her scarf and coat, keeping her head down so that no one passing could see she was crying. Though she was still boiling with anger, she felt utterly devastated for Spence, and so protective towards him that she longed to go to him right now and throw her arms around him, as though it might stop anyone else from trying to malign or hurt him. Thank God she hadn't told him what she was doing today, because she never, ever wanted him to know what her parents had done. It was disgusting, reprehensible, and utterly unforgivable. The fact that he'd never mentioned his father's conviction to her told her quite plainly that he was so ashamed of it that he couldn't bring himself to speak of it. On the other hand, there was a very good chance he might not even know, and if he didn't there was no way in the world he was going to learn about it from her, or her parents, she was absolutely sure about that. So no matter how much it might hurt her, or them, as far as she was concerned they really had seen the last of her now, because she wasn't going to allow them and their nasty little minds anywhere near Spence.

During the journey home Nikki did everything she could to push her parents out of her mind, but it wasn't easy, until she received a very timely call from Spence. Though he detected a flatness in her voice at first, she assured him she was simply a bit tired, and in next to no time he had her laughing and sharing his excitement as he passed on his news.

'Two episodes of *The Bill*,' she cried. 'That is so major.'

'I know, fantastic huh? Good old Philippa, she really pulled it off.'

'So when do you start?'

'Ah, now there's the hitch. The first week of Feb.'

Nikki's heart sank. It was dangerously close to her due date.

'Which is why,' he continued, 'I've turned it down.'

Nikki was stunned. 'But Spence, you can't,' she protested. 'It is such a . . .'

'Don't worry,' he interrupted, 'I explained why I couldn't do it then and they were very understanding and said they'd keep my name on file for later in the year.'

'But . . .'

'No buts, it's done, and I'm cool with it.'

Wishing her parents could hear this conversation, so they'd understand just how wonderful he was, Nikki smiled as she said softly, 'Thanks, because I really do want you to be with me when it all happens.'

'It's where I'll be,' he assured her. 'But there's more. I told Drake about your *Merchant of Venice* idea and he's interested to know more.'

'No way! What did he say?'

'He thought it had some real merit, so as soon as you've got something to show him, he'll be happy to read it.'

'Oh my God! I better get started.'

'Too right you had. And now, wait for this, because this is the big one. I've only got a commercial to shoot in January courtesy of Drake.'

Feeling her head starting to spin with euphoria, Nikki could only wish they were together so they could wrap each other in their arms and dance around for joy. Everything was going so well for him, which was absolutely what he deserved, and she truly couldn't be happier, because she loved him so much that whatever happened to him felt as though it was happening to her.

She was still smiling when half an hour later she let herself into the house, where the lights were on, telling her that David was in. 'Hi, I'm back,' she shouted, closing the door and taking off her coat.

There was no reply, so assuming he was in the shower, or on the phone, she went into the sitting room to check if he'd put any mail on the table, and found, to her surprise, that he was sitting at his computer, but staring out through the back window, clearly miles away.

'Hey,' she said gently. 'I'm home.'

Starting, he turned round, and though he immediately gave her a welcoming smile, she could see the troubled look in his eyes.

'Is everything OK?' she asked, immediately concerned.

'Yeah, everything's cool,' he assured her. 'Where have you been?'

'Oh, just out doing a few things. You seem a bit . . . I don't know, worried?'

He laughed and shrugged. 'I'm good,' he insisted. 'Just having a think about stuff, and trying work a couple of things out in my head. So, what's new with you?'

Realising that he didn't want to discuss whatever was on his mind, Nikki let it go, and, beaming with pride, told him Spence's news.

'That's amazing!' David cried. 'And he seriously turned *The Bill* down? That's a major gig. What's the commercial for?'

'Some chocolate bar, he couldn't remember the name because he'd never heard it before, and the budget's not huge, but it's a great opportunity.'

'Are you kidding? Do you know how many top Hollywood directors have made it through commercials?'

She was laughing. 'Ridley Scott, Alan Parker . . . Oh, and did you know that David Lynch was only twenty-one when his daughter, Jennifer, was born? I just read that, yesterday.'

'And she's a director now too,' David added.

Nikki's hands splayed over Zac. 'See what you've got in store, you lucky thing,' she told him. Then, in a burst of euphoria, 'Oh God, David, everything's so brilliant, isn't it? I can hardly wait for Spence to come home so we can start celebrating Christmas with him too.'

'On which note,' he said, 'my mother's coming over later to dump all her fairy lights and stuff on us so we can decorate the house, seeing as she won't be needing it. So, if you're up for it, I thought we could go out and buy a tree before she gets here.'

'Fantastic. Shall we go now? I'll get my coat.'

'Right with you,' he laughed. 'I just need to finish this email to Kris.'

'Send her my love. How's she getting on? I haven't heard from her since she started shooting.'

'She's loving every minute, apparently, apart from one of the regulars is giving her a bit of a hard time.'

'Male or female?'

His expression was dry. 'What do you think?'

Grinning, she left him to send his message and went upstairs to change into her fake Ugg boots. She was so large now that the only way to drag them on was to lie on the bed and put her legs in the air. Spence had found this hilarious when he'd caught her in the act at the weekend, and it seemed the baby was quite keen on it too, the way he kept jumping about in what felt like glee.

'It's all right for you, all snuggled up and cosy in there,' she scolded playfully. 'It's freezing out there, so I need these things.'

She wasn't sure if he really hiccuped, but it was what it felt like, so she rubbed her tummy gently, as if somehow she could wind him. 'I'm going to write you a lovely letter later,' she told him, 'all about Daddy's news today, and our trip to the market with David to buy your very first Christmas tree. We'll take photos, which I'll put in the book I've started for you, so you'll see yourself as a great big bump with me and Daddy on your first Christmas Day, surrounded by all the lovely things Santa's going to bring you.'

She wouldn't mention what had happened with her parents in her letter, because it was so horrible that she'd do almost anything to make sure Zac never knew about it. In fact, she'd already decided that she was going to delete any emails they sent, or erase texts unread and ignore their calls, because what really mattered to her, more than anything, was protecting Spence from their utterly *loathsome* assumptions.

It was late on Christmas Day, with a sluggish fire sighing and shifting in the hearth, and the room still littered with gifts and wrapping, when Nikki's mobile bleeped with a text.

'Who's that?' she said irritably, not wanting to stir from the comfortable position she'd finally snuggled into on the sofa with Spence.

'Ignore it,' he mumbled drowsily.

Opening her eyes a fraction, she looked at the others. David was sprawled out on the floor, fast asleep, his head pillowed on a bright orange fluffy ostrich, and Dan was curled up in the armchair, his paper party hat tilted at a rakish angle and fluttering in the draught of his gentle snores. They'd eaten so much, all of them, that Nikki was starting to regret their rash decision to throw a party tonight. Luckily they'd told everyone to come at ten, so by then they might have recovered from the morning's euphoria of present-opening, cooking and phone calls to family and friends – and the afternoon's great indulgence of roast turkey, cheesy parsnips, sautéed sprouts and carrots, and enormous helpings of Fortnum's Christmas pud.

As her mobile bleeped again and *102 Dalmatians* cavorted about the TV screen ignored by all, she decided she really didn't have the energy to force herself up and over to the table. Anyway, if she did, she might feel compelled to start clearing it, and it was David and Spence's job to wash up, after the amazing feast she and Danny had miraculously concocted.

Since the phone would only bleep once more before giving up, she snuggled back in against Spence and closed her eyes. It would probably only be another Happy Christmas message to add to the dozens of others they'd received from old university friends and the crowd here in Bemmie today, or someone asking if they could bring someone else to the party tonight, so no urgency attached.

She murmured sleepily and inhaled the wonderfully masculine scent of Spence's skin. It was so lovely and cosy lying here like this with the four people she loved most in the world, if she included Zac, which she had to, particularly considering how lively he'd been today. He seemed to have settled down now, though, no doubt dazed by the amount of food and sip of wine that had come cascading his way. It must have seemed like an avalanche, she smiled to herself, and rubbed a hand gently over her tummy as though to soothe him.

Mrs Adani had given her another book of Indian poetry for Christmas, which she was looking forward to settling down with tomorrow while the others nursed hangovers from the party, or braved brisk walks on the Downs. Later they were planning to meet up with everyone at the Factory, if it was open. If not, they'd just come home again and hang out here, which was more or less what they intended to do until after the New Year, when Spence and Danny returned to London and David took off to Paris for a week for his foodie show. She wondered what Kristin would do, since her episode of *The Bill* was now in the can. Was she thinking of coming back to Bristol, or had she decided to inflict herself on Sam and Kayla in Vauxhall again?

As the phone bleeped for a third time Nikki kept her eyes closed, as though to lock in the lazy sense of happiness and contentment that was infusing the air with as much warmth as the fire. All that could be more wonderful than lazing here like this would be to have little Zac snoozing contentedly on his father's chest, or kicking about in the cute Moses basket Danny had bought, trying to make sense of the mountain of toys Santa had stacked up around the tree. In all her life Nikki had never seen so many gifts for just one tiny person, and actually, not many were from her and Spence. Mostly they were from friends and neighbours who'd been dropping in all week to deliver cards and gaily wrapped parcels that had turned out to be everything from Babygros, to musical mobiles, to a little chair to hang on the door for him to bounce up and down in, to teething rings and animal rattles. The generosity had been amazing and had touched her so much that she had ended up in tears.

'There go the hormones again,' Spence had teased.

She'd laughed and hugged him, and refused to admit to a sadness, or anger, that the only people who hadn't made the effort to make the baby feel welcome this Christmas were her parents, because this would cast a shadow on an otherwise perfect day.

Thinking of them now, she began wondering how they might have spent the day themselves. Most likely they'd invited friends over for lunch, since her mother loved to cook, or maybe they'd gone to someone else's home where there were staff and lots of rosy-cheeked extended family and a Christmas tree that reached the ceiling. She wondered what they were saying to anyone who asked about her. Were they telling them in that long-suffering way, typical of most parents, that she was making a stand for independence so hadn't come home this year? Or maybe they'd lie and say she'd gone skiing or backpacking across Asia or somewhere equally distant. No way could she imagine them telling anyone she was pregnant and at home in Bristol with the baby's father, who'd grown up on a south London housing estate and whose father, albeit dead, was one of society's worst kind of criminals. She wondered how much they'd thought about her today. At least last year, which she'd also spent with Spence while they were in Barbados, they'd called to wish her happy Christmas and thank her for the presents she'd sent. This year there had been no crossing in the mail of cards, or gifts, and no exchange of phone calls or texts either. Not that she wanted anything, but it hurt, nonetheless, to know that they hadn't even attempted to get in touch.

Then a spark of suspicion, or was it hope, began to flicker in a small corner of her heart. But no, she wasn't going to start telling herself the text might be from them, only to end up disappointed if it turned out not to be. (Not that she'd read it, but she'd like to have the chance to erase it, at least.) If only she didn't care. Should anyone ask she'd swear she didn't, but the truth was, in spite of still being furious with them for snooping on Spence's life the way they had, whenever she thought about them apart from that, a kind of emptiness opened up inside her, or a yearning, or a sadness that things had to be like this. In her heart of hearts she'd really believed they'd get in touch today, but as so many hours of silence had passed, she guessed she had to accept they weren't going to.

Unless . . .

Unable to doze now that the hope, or suspicion, that the text might be from them had taken root, she rolled off the sofa on to her hands and knees and tried not to laugh at what an unladylike spectacle she made of getting to her feet.

Finding her mobile under a gold paper hat that had a blob of Christmas pudding stuck to the side, she felt a wave of nerves go through her as she clicked to open her messages.

After reading the text she simply stood staring at it, too bemused by the content for the moment to feel irked or upset that it wasn't from her parents.

Have just sent you an email by mistake. Pls do NOT open. Just delete. Kristin x

She jumped as her mobile suddenly started to ring. Seeing it was Kristin, she clicked on.

'Hi, did you get my text?' Kristin demanded, sounding flustered, or rushed, or even slightly panicked.

'Yes, just. What . . .'

'You didn't open the email, did you? Please tell me you didn't open it.'

'I haven't even turned on my computer,' Nikki told her.

'Great. When you do, just delete the message from me. OK? It was one of those stupid things . . . You know how it happens, I was thinking about you, wondering how you were today, and everything, and I ended up putting your name in the address box instead of the person I was writing to. I only noticed after I sent it. So don't read it, OK? It's nothing, but it would be, you know, better if . . . Well, you know what I'm saying.'

Half suspecting that she did, Nikki said, 'OK, I'll delete it.' She was careful not to add *without reading it*, which Kristin didn't seem to notice.

'Great,' Kristin said. 'I'm sorry to make a fuss. I mean, like I said, it's nothing. It's just that I'd end up feeling really embarrassed if anyone else got to read it, because, well, you know . . .'

'So who was it supposed to go to?' Nikki asked.

'No one. It doesn't matter. Anyway, sorry, I have to go. My gran's just arrived. Say hi to everyone and tell David I'll call him later.'

After ringing off, Nikki went on standing where she was, staring at her laptop which was tucked in next to David's computer in the niche where all his equipment was stored. She knew very well that she'd just been spun a load of rubbish, but did she really want to go online now to find out what was in the email and why she wasn't supposed to read it?

The answer was no.

It was early on Boxing Day morning and everyone, apart from Nikki, was still fast asleep, some having only recently passed out after partying most of the night. There were bodies sprawled all over the place, on floors, sofas, chairs – she'd even found someone wrapped in a duvet in the bath whom she'd had to turf out so she could go to the loo. When she'd returned to the bedroom he was curled up next to Spence in the bed.

So far she hadn't even attempted to do anything about the bomb site the place had turned into, so there were still beer, wine and spirit bottles cluttering up just about every surface, along with overflowing ashtrays, empty plates, Santa hats and baby toys. However, she'd cleared one small space on the table for her laptop, because curiosity had got the better of her just after she'd woken up.

Now she was staring in cold disbelief at the email she wasn't supposed to have read. Though it didn't mention any names, it was clear from the content who it had been meant for.

I can't stop thinking about you. Today has been really miserable without you. I keep wondering if you've told her anything yet. You'll have to sometime, but I guess it would be a bit mean to do it at Christmas. You need to tell her about the writer you're working with though. She'll find out sooner or later, so better that you do it now. She can't expect you to work exclusively on the stuff she writes, that would just be egotistical and she's not really like that, so it should be fine.

Please email or text me to let me know how you are. I hope you liked the card I left for you at Sam's. I can't wait till we're back there in January.

All my love K

Nikki's heart was thudding so hard that she put her hands on the baby as though to protect him. Her mind was reeling, her whole body was starting to shake. When she tried to stand up, her legs were like jelly and she sank back down again.

She surely had to be misunderstanding something, because Spence wouldn't do this. It just wasn't in him to be dishonest or duplicitous, and nothing about him even remotely suggested he'd been pretending they were happy when what he really wanted was to be with someone else.

Putting a hand to her mouth to stop herself crying, or shouting, or maybe choking, she made herself read the message again. As she took the words in, she could feel a surge of fury and denial beginning to push its way through the barrier of shock. Whatever had happened, it would be Kristin's fault, she felt certain of that, because whatever Kristin wanted she had to have, regardless of whom it might hurt. But Spence couldn't be blameless. She had to confront him over this. He needed to explain why Kristin was sending him this sort of message, but even as she got to her feet she wasn't sure she could bear to hear it.

'Oh my God, she is such a bitch,' Danny hissed, after Nikki had dragged him out of bed and downstairs to her laptop. He read the message again. 'You know what I think?' he said.

Nikki's eyes were heavy with dread as she waited.

'I think she did this deliberately to make trouble,' he stated, with so much conviction that Nikki clung to it like a lifeline. 'I think she knew exactly what she was doing when she sent this email,' he continued, 'and all that BS about making a mistake and begging you not to read it . . . Of course you're going to read it. Anyone would, and she knows it.'

Nikki looked at the email again and tried to decide what to do.

'You have to show Spence this,' Danny insisted. 'Let him speak for himself.'

'But what if they are seeing one another? They've been staying together at Sam's all this time, and there's only one spare room. I even heard her offer to share it . . .'

'Because she wanted you to hear. She's so jealous of you, darling, she's practically got green oozing out of her pores. She always has been, because everyone adores you and no one can stand her.'

Though the words were comforting in their way, they didn't actually prove anything, either. 'This is going to ruin the rest of Christmas, if there is something going on,' she said.

'It'll ruin a lot more than Christmas,' he pointed out, without thinking, and seeing Nikki's face he quickly added, 'but I promise you, there's *nothing* going on. You know Spence better than anyone. He couldn't hide something like this if his life depended on it.'

Nikki nodded and swallowed. 'You're right,' she said. 'Except he's obviously keeping something from me, if he's developing someone else's script. And I have to admit, there have been a couple of times lately when I've thought he might be . . . Well, maybe not lying exactly, but it's like he might not be telling the whole truth.'

'You have to talk to him,' Danny said firmly. 'No hanging around, letting this fester, because we've already agreed no negative vibes for Junior . . .'

'There'll be a lot more than negative vibes if . . .'

'Stop! Take the laptop upstairs now and show him the email.'

'Jasper's in bed with him.'

Danny blinked. 'I won't even go there,' he decided. 'I'll sling him out, then keep the coast clear while you get to the bottom of this crap.'

Ten minutes later Spence was staring, bleary-eyed, at the screen, trying to take in what was written there. 'Are you sure this is for me?' he said, stifling a yawn. 'I can't see my name anywhere.'

'Who else would it be for?' Nikki challenged.

She was sitting next to him on the bed, her legs tucked in under her, while her heart seemed to stop and start like a faulty machine.

He read the email again, then suddenly his eyes closed as he gave a protracted groan of dismay. 'I know what this is about,' he said. 'Jesus Christ . . . Listen,' he said, taking Nikki's hand firmly in his, 'I swear on the baby's life it didn't mean anything, but there was one night, when we were all out clubbing . . . I danced with her and then . . .'

Nikki's face was turning white. 'Then what?' she prompted.

'Then I kind of kissed her. I didn't mean to . . . I was off my head . . . We'd all had a lot to drink, and she'd been coming on to me for days, you know, flirting and stuff, the way she does. Anyway, that's all that happened. One kiss that lasted about three seconds tops.'

Nikki was staring at him hard, wanting to believe him. She was almost certain he was telling the truth, but she wasn't sure if it was all right or not. 'What about this other writer she mentions?' she asked.

He took a deep breath and blew it out slowly. 'Yeah, well, that is something I've been meaning to talk to you about. She's one of Drake's protégés. She's written a script for a short that Drake quite likes, so I thought . . . Look, you haven't had time to get one together yourself, and with the baby coming, I thought it would ease the pressure on you a bit if I . . .'

'Why didn't you tell me?' she cut in.

'Because I didn't want you to think I was trying to move on without you. You've been a bit skittish lately about us all being in London, so I decided to make sure I knew the project was going somewhere before I told you. If it doesn't there was no need for you to know.'

'But that's having secrets from one another, Spence, and if we start doing that now, where's it going to end?' His father flashed through her mind, to be quickly dismissed, because that was entirely different.

'Look, I'm sorry,' he said, wiping his hands over his stubbly face. 'It was a bad judgement call, and this . . . *email* is Kristin in some kind of world of her own. Jesus, think how David would feel if he saw it.'

Nikki looked away. 'Actually, I'm not sure he'd care that much,' she replied. 'Did you see him with Yasmin last night?'

Spence nodded. 'I did, but did you see him with Danny, later?'

Nikki's eyes widened. She'd gone to bed before everyone else, so no, she hadn't.

'Well, they were kidding about, you know the way Danny is sometimes with David, but David was definitely egging him on.'

Nikki wasn't sure what to say.

Spence shrugged. 'It's their business,' he said, 'but I bet David's got a sore head this morning.'

Nikki looked at the email again. 'Do you think we should show him this?' she asked doubtfully.

Spence embarked on another yawn and shook his head. 'Probably not,' he replied. 'If I were you I'd just delete it and make out like it never happened.'

Nikki regarded his sleepy face, and told herself that he could never be this relaxed if he was lying. 'Are you going to say anything to Kristin?' she asked.

He opened his eyes, seeming surprised.

'Well, she must have sent the email to you too by now, so how are you going to answer it?'

He appeared baffled by that. 'You know what,' he said in the end, 'I'll just ignore it.'

'And when you get back to Sam's, what's going to happen then?'

Clearly confounded again, he shook his head. 'Nothing's going to *happen*,' he said, 'or not the way you're thinking.'

'She'll be there, though, and if she's going to keep coming on to you . . .'

'Tell you what,' he broke in, 'how about I shack up with Danny till you're ready to make the move to London? I know he's only got one bedroom, but I don't mind the sofa, as long as he's cool about sharing. That way I won't be under the same roof as Kristin.'

As the last of Nikki's doubts evaporated in a rush of love, she launched herself forward to throw her arms around him. 'That's a fantastic idea,' she laughed as he winced. 'I know Dan'll go for it, and while you're there you could look for somewhere for us all to share, because it's a great area.'

Grinning as the baby began kicking about between them, Spence rolled her on to her side and spooned in behind her so he could splay his hands all over the mound of their child. 'I wish you were coming back with me in January,' he murmured into her hair. 'I miss you when we're not together, and I love it when we can lie like this, pretending we're the only people in the world, or that you're already a famous writer, and I'm directing your movies.'

She smiled. 'Shall we make our base in Hollywood or London?' she mused, loving the feel of his hands stroking her naked skin.

'Why not both?' he replied. 'We'll be so rich that we can fly back and forth between the two.'

'First class.'

'Of course.'

'And the baby will always come with us?'

'Definitely. We can get a nanny to help, and personal assistants and publicists to deal with the pap.'

She laughed and moved in closer to him.

After a while, as the sounds of people coming awake

started to crump and groan around the house, he said, 'Are you upset about your parents not calling?'

Feeling a stain of darkness merge into her happiness, she said, 'No, not really. All that matters is us.'

His arms tightened around her. 'We can go to see them if you like. I'll come with you.'

Her heart jarring at the mere thought of how awful that would be, she said, 'If they can't be bothered about me, which they clearly can't, I don't see why we should bother about them.'

Chapter Six

They saw the new year in with a raucous fancy dress party at the Factory, digging out costumes from various charity shops and old prop stores around the city, and resorting to cobbling together what frills and fancies they couldn't find. Nikki went as a pretty convincing Humpty Dumpty, Spence as a dashing Captain Jack Sparrow, David as a magnificently swashbuckling Zorro, and Danny as the highly imperious grand old Duchess of York. Kristin came back for the celebrations, decking herself out in a very sexy catwoman suit, and making Nikki feel about as attractive as a lump of dough standing next to her.

'Just keep your claws out of Spence,' Nikki muttered to her, when the party was in full swing and Kristin was getting carried away, slinking around every man in sight.

Startled, Kristin turned to look at her.

'I know the email was meant for him,' Nikki told her, 'but I don't want to argue about it. Just back off, OK, and feel lucky I didn't show it to David.'

Beneath her cat mask Kristin's mouth had paled. 'So you read it,' she said. 'I thought you said . . .'

'We're at a party,' Nikki reminded her with a smile, 'so drink up.'

'Are you sure you didn't show him?' Kristin demanded, as Nikki turned away.

'I just told you . . .'

'Only he's being really distant with me. You don't think . . .'

'Not now,' Nikki said, 'it's nearly midnight,' and moving off she began searching for Spence. They found one another with seconds to spare and quickly dragged Danny and his candyfloss wig into their New Year embrace. At the stroke of twelve the place erupted as everyone cheered and fired off poppers while balloons cascaded from the ceiling, and champagne corks started to fly.

Twenty minutes later Nikki and Spence sneaked out quietly to carry on the celebrations at home. The upcoming year was going to be a big one for them, and now they'd seen it in with their friends they wanted to be on their own, with no interruptions and nothing more to think about than each other.

By the time everyone left for London on the third of January Nikki was as convinced as she'd ever been that nothing was going on between Kristin and Spence. For one thing, Kristin barely paid him any attention, and didn't even seem particularly surprised, or put out, when he announced that he was going to be moving in with Dan. She might not even have heard, because she was so totally focused on David now he wasn't seeming quite so interested any more, that she didn't appear able to concentrate on anything else.

It wasn't until a couple of weeks into the new year that Nikki, alone in the house since David had gone off to Paris, learned from Danny that Spence was intending to cast Kristin in the lead of the short film, *Celeste*, he was due to start directing as soon as the final tranche of financing was in place. She'd known it was starting to move ahead, and had even read the script by now, which she'd found both inspiring and dispiriting, since it was better than anything she could have written; however, Spence hadn't mentioned anything about casting Kristin. Nor had it entered Nikki's head to wonder if he might, when the principal female character was Asian, overweight and in her early forties.

'Actually, there have been some changes since you read it,' Spence confessed when Nikki challenged him over it.

Nikki blinked. 'Are you saying you had it rewritten so Kristin could be in it?' she cried, praying it wasn't true.

'Not me,' he protested. 'She did it herself. She went to Drake, who thought it would be a really good experience for Val – the writer – to rewrite her material to suit an actor, because it happens all the time in the real world. So now Celeste is younger and Italian instead of middle-aged and Indian.'

'So how does that work? I thought the whole point of the story was Celeste's struggle with integration. A piece of Continental totty isn't going to have much trouble in that department.'

'You'll have to read it,' he told her. 'It works, and actually, in some ways it's better.'

'So you're going to be with Kristin every day while you're shooting?'

'Nikki, don't do this,' he groaned. 'She's right for the part as it's written now, and she's a good actress. Anyway, it's not due to happen for ages yet.'

'Is she going to move into Danny's with you?' Nikki snapped.

Spence sighed. 'No, of course not. Look, I'll be back at the weekend. I'll bring a copy of the script with me, then you'll see for yourself why I'm not having a problem with the change.'

Still not satisfied, Nikki said, 'Do you know what's really getting to me? It's the fact that I had to find out from Danny. If you'd told me yourself, I might not be so worried, but hiding it from me . . . How the hell did you think that was going to work? I was bound to find out sooner or later . . .'

'I was going to tell you at the weekend, after you'd read the script,' he cut in. 'I thought, once you'd seen it, that you'd probably suggest Kristin yourself.'

'God, you are so naive at times,' Nikki seethed. 'All this pretence she's putting on about David . . . She's definitely after you, and you can't even see it – or you're making out you can't. Or maybe you're pretending to me that nothing's going on when it is. So what's the plan? Wait till the baby's born, then goodbye Nikki, we're off to Hollywood?'

'Don't be ridiculous. No way in the world am I letting anyone, or anything, come between us, so just keep that in mind next time your hormones start beating you up like this.'

'It's not hormones,' she raged furiously, 'it's frustration and paranoia and loneliness and fear. I know you love me, really, but I'm so huge now that I wouldn't blame you if you fancied someone else. We don't even have sex any more . . .'

'That's because I'm having a problem getting my head round the fact that I'm not going to hurt the baby if we do.'

'But you spoke to Mrs A yourself, you heard . . .'

'I know, I know, I just can't get there, but it'll be all right once the baby comes. Everything will. Wait and see. You'll move up here to London – which reminds me, I'm going to look at a house in the next street tomorrow. I haven't told Dan about it yet, but hopefully he'll come with me. It's got three huge bedrooms, apparently, and two bathrooms, so it would be plenty big enough for all of us, especially after our little gaff down there, and the rent's more or less affordable, provided we all keep working.'

Nikki's expression turned mutinous. 'I don't know if I want us all to live together if it's going to include Kristin,' she said stubbornly.

'Nik, it was your idea in the first place,' he reminded her. 'But hey, if you want to change it, I'm cool. Whatever makes you happy.'

Realising how hurt David would be if she suggested getting a place that was only big enough for Danny to join her and Spence, she said, 'Why don't I catch a train tomorrow and come to look at the house with you? I don't have anything on, or nothing that can't wait a day.'

Not sounding too keen on that, he said, 'Nik, the baby's that close now . . .'

'There's another month to go!'

'Even so, I don't like the idea of you travelling alone, especially on a train. No. If David could come with you, it might be different. When's he back?'

'On Sunday. So we could come next week, if he's free, and if you think the place might be suitable. I'd like to see it myself before we make a decision.'

'I don't have a problem with that. Actually, why don't you get David to bring you towards the end of next week, then you can stay over with me at Danny's until I can catch the train back with you at the weekend?'

With a tremulous sigh she said, 'I guess that should work, just promise me you won't let Kristin see it before me.'

'You have my word. I'll take Dan, though.'

'Definitely.' Then, sighing again, 'I'm getting really fed up with being pregnant now. Being this big is seriously cramping my style.'

'I know,' he said sympathetically, 'but it's not for much longer, and think how wonderful it's going to be when we have him, or her, with us.'

'Mm,' she responded, feeling both doubtful and daunted, but now wasn't the time to start voicing any of that.

She saved it till later when Mrs A came round, overflowing with gifts from India, and so pleased to be back that, reading between the lines, Nikki guessed her mother-in-law hadn't been too thrilled at having to share her son with his wife for a couple of weeks.

'I do miss Rajan so much,' Mrs A confessed, referring to her husband, 'and it was very lovely to see him, but our life together is here, in England. Over there, with his family and mine, things are different between us.'

'When do you think he'll be back?' Nikki asked.

A roguish light sparked in Mrs A's eyes. 'Not until the old dear croaks,' she said mischievously, 'and now she has her prodigal boy with her, well, heaven only knows when that will be. As soon as he starts saying he is going to leave, she becomes unwell again. But now, enough about that, how are you, my dear? You're looking like a rose in full bloom.'

'You mean because I've doubled in size, and my cheeks are constantly red?'

Mrs A laughed. 'Do I sense you are a little out of sorts?' she asked kindly.

Nikki nodded. 'It's all the books I've been reading,' she complained. 'They keep going on about how a baby changes things, and now I can't stop wondering if Spence and I have been a bit naive, you know, thinking we can carry on the way we always have without the baby making a difference.'

With her wonderfully jocular warmth Mrs A said, 'All new parents are naive. How can you be anything else, when you've never had a child before? But life will go on the way it did, you'll just have different priorities and a whole lot more joy than you ever imagined before he arrived.'

'But what if he turns out to be one of those babies that never stops crying?'

'Then we shall find out what is upsetting him, and do something to make him happy.'

Nikki wanted to hug her. It was amazing how the minute Mrs A was around everything felt OK again. 'I wish you could move to London with us, when we go,' she said. 'We'll really miss you.'

'And I shall miss you, but I will be coming to visit often, given that I have two daughters already living there. And perhaps you will come back from time to time too. Now tell me, what is everyone doing? And where is my son?'

'He didn't let you know he was going to Paris? That is so typical. He's due back on Sunday, but you can probably get him on his mobile, if you need to speak to him.'

'I shall try later. Is his relationship with Kristin still ongoing?'

Nikki eyed her carefully as she nodded. 'They definitely don't seem as close as they used to be, though,' she said.

'Mm, well that doesn't surprise me. I don't think they are each other's types, if the truth be told, but it's best to let them find this out for themselves. And what about Danny? How is he?'

'As gorgeous and outrageous as ever. Loving London, of course . . . Spence is going to look at a house tomorrow for us all to share.'

'Oh? Where?'

'Close to where Danny is now, in Shepherd's Bush. I wanted to go with them, but Spence isn't happy about me travelling alone – and to be honest, I don't think I am either.'

'Then why don't I drive you?'

Nikki's eyes widened in astonishment.

Mrs A threw out her hands. 'I am not due to start back to work till next Monday, and as I am very well qualified to deal with you, should the baby decide to put in an early appearance, I think this is an excellent idea.'

Not holding back on hugging her this time, Nikki said, 'But you've only just got off a long-haul flight.'

'That was yesterday, and I am made of very strong stuff, you know. So, if you would like to go to London tomorrow, I will take you.'

Nikki didn't want to admit that part of her was trying to catch Spence out, but in her heart she knew that was why she hadn't told him when they'd spoken on the phone last night that she and Mrs A were coming today. She'd simply asked, in a chatty sort of way, what time he was going to view the house, and if Danny was going with him. Apparently Danny wasn't, because he had a big interview scheduled that he couldn't change, so Spence had arranged to meet the agent alone.

'The trouble is,' he'd said, 'these places go so fast that if it does turn out to be suitable I think I'll have to give an answer straight away, or we'll lose it.'

Nikki's suspicions immediately kicked in. 'Is that you trying to make up an excuse to take Kristin with you?' she asked bluntly.

'*What?*' His laugh was incredulous. 'Honest to God, the way your mind works . . . It hadn't even entered my head. I'm just saying that nothing decent ever stays on the market for long, so if it is any good I'll be snapping it up and the rest of you better just like it.'

Unable to argue with that, she'd let her defences down then and the rest of the conversation had been much easier, in so far as Spence did most of the talking about what had been happening in his world during the day. She'd merely listened, making all the right noises, until eventually he had to go because he was meeting Sam and the others in the West End.

As she'd put the phone down Nikki was close to hating her mother for her prophecies of doom, as though simply by pronouncing them she was making them happen. Then there was the really perverse part of it, which was how much she longed to talk to her mother, the way she used to as a child, when her parents could make everything all right. Those days were long gone, though, and it saddened her more than she wanted to admit that she couldn't foresee a way of allowing them to be close again.

Now, as Mrs A sped past the Bath turn-off, Nikki shifted in her seat to make herself more comfortable. It wasn't possible to avoid thinking about her parents when passing the city they lived in, but she made a supreme effort to push her thoughts aside. She didn't want to become embroiled in the conflicting emotions they always triggered, especially while experiencing a contraction.

Sensing Mrs A's glance in her direction, she said, 'I'm fine,' before Mrs A could ask.

Mrs A chuckled. 'Braxton Hicks or fisticuffs?' she said.

'The former,' Nikki replied, clasping her hands around the balloon of her belly. 'I think the car's sending the baby off to sleep.'

Mrs A glanced at her again. 'You're looking a little tired yourself,' she commented. 'Is he keeping you awake at night?'

Nikki's eyes went down as she shook her head. 'Not really,' she answered. Then, after a pause, 'It's more the way I keep worrying about things. I know it's normal, and everyone does . . . I suppose I just don't like being on my own in the house too much.'

'What kind of things are you worrying about?' Mrs A asked gently.

Nikki shrugged. 'You know, the usual stuff, will he have all his fingers and toes? Will Spence and I be good parents? Is it the right thing to move up to London?'

Mrs A seemed surprised. 'I thought you were quite decided about that,' she said.

'I am, but if Spence takes this house today, I'll have to go sooner rather than later, because it would be madness to pay two rents, and I'm not sure I'll feel ready to go . . . No, that's not true, I think I'll be OK about going, as long as I'm breastfeeding properly and everything's fine with the baby, but I'm feeling a bit daunted by the thought of trying to get work in London, where I don't know anyone.'

'But Spence has already made some good contacts, hasn't he?'

'Yeah, that's true, and actually, I'm sure it'll all work out just fine.'

Reaching out to give her hand a reassuring squeeze, Mrs

A said, 'I have no doubt of it. All you're experiencing now is a little touch of pre-baby blues. All perfectly normal.'

Nikki felt a lump rise in her throat. She didn't want to admit how much she was dreading leaving Mrs A, because if she did she might have to admit how safe Mrs A made her feel, and if she admitted that it would be like saying she was afraid she and Spence couldn't cope. Actually, not Spence, because he'd be great, she just knew it, except her mother's warning was flashing through her mind again, ripping like knives at her confidence . . . *While you're sitting at home, tearing out your hair because it won't stop crying, and bouncing off the walls with sleep deprivation and mindless worry, your boyfriend is going to be out there living the kind of life you'd be having if you hadn't made such a stupid mistake. He'll hang on to his freedom, so will your friends, and eventually they'll all start moving on without you. No baby will hold them back. It'll be your responsibility and yours alone.*

Her eyes closed as she leaned back against the headrest. She already loved this baby more than she could put into words, but now the time was drawing close she couldn't deny how anxious she was becoming.

Out of the blue, Mrs A suddenly said, 'Did you hear from your parents at Christmas?'

Nikki swallowed. 'No,' she answered shortly.

For a while Mrs A said nothing, simply drove on at a steady seventy, careful to check her mirror every time she overtook, then steering safely back into the slow lane to allow others to pass. It was typical of her to be so considerate. Second nature. Nikki's mother always hogged the middle lane, while her father usually charged along at somewhere around ninety, flashing his headlights for anyone in the way to move aside.

'I take it you haven't attempted to contact them,' Mrs A said in the end.

Nikki swallowed hard as she prepared to lie. 'No,' she replied, except it wasn't a lie really, because they were the ones who'd contacted her. In many ways she'd have liked to confide in Mrs A, and tell her what her parents had found out about Spence's dad, but it would be disloyal to Spence to discuss something so personal, and awful, with someone else when she hadn't even mentioned it to him. 'I think it's best if we go our separate ways,' she mumbled.

Mrs A let that lie for a moment. 'Are you going to tell them when the baby comes?' she asked.

Nikki started to answer, then stopped as Zac gave her a sudden kick. Was he dreaming, she wondered, or listening and trying to tell her something? Then, moving past her fanciful thoughts, she returned to Mrs A's question, trying to decide how to answer it.

'I think,' Mrs A said, 'that when the baby comes many things will change, on both sides, so perhaps you should leave the decision till then.'

Though Nikki took comfort from the words, her insides started to churn. There was that word 'change' again, making her feel edgy and fretful and as though she wanted to run away and hide. What made it worse was that until now, apart from the odd hormonal blip, she'd felt truly excited about becoming a mother. Most of the time she'd wanted to dance and sing in the joy of it, but these last couple of weeks hadn't been like that at all. 'I expect,' she said, because she felt she needed to say something, 'that I'll be too busy to worry about them very much then.'

Mrs A nodded. 'This is possibly true,' she conceded kindly, though her tone suggested that she wasn't entirely convinced.

It was just before two when Mrs A's satnav announced that they'd reached their destination. Coming fully awake and trying to straighten up, Nikki looked around at the tall red-brick houses rising up either side of them, some scarred with age and neglect, others shining with new paint and chic modern blinds. Danny's bijou apartment was on the top floor of number forty-two, four flights up, which Nikki wasn't much looking forward to climbing, but far, far worse was the returning dread of blundering into a little Spencer/Kristin love tryst.

She was out of her mind, coming here like this. Everyone knew that those who went looking for trouble always found it. She was asking to be hurt, deceived, devastated, a month before the baby was due. Why would she do that? What was wrong with her that she wanted to disrupt, or even destroy, her whole life, when all that really mattered was Zac and how safe and secure he needed to feel? She didn't understand herself. She wasn't thinking straight. She was falling victim to some bizarre paranoia that she had to get under control.

But how could she tell Mrs A, now they'd come this far, that she'd changed her mind, she didn't want to see the house, or even let Spence know she was here? Mrs A would smile in her kind, knowing way, understanding on a level that was deeper than Nikki could even imagine that everything was perfectly normal, and there was no need to worry.

Suddenly words were blurting out of her. 'I think Spence and Kristin might be . . .' She stopped abruptly, as though she'd hit a brick wall.

Mrs A was ahead of her, at the front door, and after pressing the bell she turned around saying, 'Sorry, dear, what was that?'

Nikki only looked at her. She felt suddenly dizzy and faint, as though words and feelings were blending with the sky and the cold, and nothing could be touched, so nothing was real. Then the front door was opening and Spence was there, blinking with shock.

'Hello dear,' Mrs A said.

'Hey,' he cried, clearly delighted to see them. 'What are you doing here?'

'We thought we'd surprise you,' Mrs A replied.

Nikki almost jumped. She'd told Mrs A that Spence was expecting them, so why had she said that? Was she really so intuitive that she could actually read minds, or at least sense when she wasn't being told the entire truth?

As Spence's arms went round her Nikki promptly started to cry. 'Hormones,' she sobbed as she laughed.

'Oh, so that's how you got here,' he grinned. 'Probably more reliable than First Great Western. How much longer is this going to go on?' he asked Mrs A. 'She's a mess.' Then, holding Nikki back to look at her, 'It's great that you came,' he told her softly. 'I want everything to be right for the baby, and you'll be better at deciding that than me.'

As guilt dragged its evidence over her cheeks, she quickly glanced at her watch. 'How far is it?' she asked. 'We don't want to be late.'

'I told you, it's the next road, so we can walk. The agent's just rung to let me know that he's already there.'

Overcome with gratitude and relief that she'd been wrong, and love that she was so right in choosing him, Nikki grabbed his arm and held on tight until they rounded a leafy corner at the end of the street and came to a stop in front of a bright end-of-terrace house, with a very important-looking black front door and tall sash windows with bamboo blinds that were lowered partway, like sleepy eyelids.

'No way can it be this one,' Nikki gasped in awe.

Spence was grinning. 'Cool, huh? Dan and I came round last night to have a look at the outside. We were totally blown away.'

'Can we really afford something like this? I mean, we have to. Whatever the rent is, we're going to find it.'

'Maybe we should take a look at the inside before making a decision,' Mrs A suggested as the front door opened and a man in a grey wool coat and slick dark pinstripe suit came out.

'Mr Curran?' Spence said, going forward to shake his hand. 'I'm Spencer James.'

Curran's expression managed to appear both amicable and distant. 'Good to meet you,' he said politely. 'The landlord's not joining us, I'm afraid, something came up, but he's instructed me to go ahead without him. Would you like to come in?'

As they stepped into a spacious front hall with pale laminate flooring and matching staircase, Nikki felt a wonderful sense of happiness come over her. She almost didn't need to go any further, because the vibes in the house were already enough to persuade her. 'Hi, I'm Nikki Grant,' she said to the agent, holding out a hand to shake. 'And this is Mrs Adani.'

The agent's smile was warm enough as he shook hands, but he was glancing at his watch as he turned away. 'I have a lot of viewings lined up for this afternoon,' he told them, 'so if you'd like to come this way . . . The kitchen's recently been fitted, the cooker hood's due to arrive tomorrow, so it'll be in before the place is rented, and those IKEA boxes against the wall are the table and chairs. I'm guessing they'll be put together before anyone moves in.'

'I hope so,' Spence smiled, 'because none of us lot has mastered the science of IKEA.'

Nikki was gazing around in rapture. Though it clearly wasn't the most expensive kitchen in the world with its plain white cabinets and grey Formica worktops, to her it was like a dream. There was even a TV on the wall, and a stable door leading out to a tiny patio garden.

'The space where the table's going means we'd all be able to eat in here,' she said, still drinking it all in.

Mrs A was opening drawers and cupboards, finding the fridge, an assortment of cooking pans, enough crockery and cutlery for six and plenty of empty space for their own odds and ends, plus a pull-out pantry for food. 'And a dishwasher,' she declared, tugging it open.

Nikki almost swooned, and as Spence's arm went round her she could feel his excitement merging with her own.

Next came a large sitting-cum-dining room, much like the set-up they had in Bristol, but bigger and much posher thanks to the smooth wooden floors, mock leather sofas and smart black marble fireplace. There were also built-in shelves and cupboards, a long table that could easily double as a desk for them all, and all the requisite wiring to set up a plasma TV, broadband, Wi Fi, and whatever else they needed to install.

'This is amazing,' Nikki murmured, walking over to the large bay window and gazing out into the street. It was much like any other in the area with its stoic Victorian terraces and winter-bare trees, but to her it was as magical as Hollywood.

'There's no niche for David's stuff,' Spence pointed out. 'But I guess we need to see the bedrooms. He might be able to work upstairs.'

When they got there, there was no doubt that David could, because after the master suite, which had its own bay window, a king-size bed, still in its cellophane, and its

own shower and loo – sink yet to be fitted and tiling
finished – the next room was almost as big, so plenty of
space for both David and Kristin to set up their computers.
The third bedroom, which would be Danny's, was smaller,
but large enough to house a spanking new double-size
bed, also still in its cellophane, built-in cupboards and a
window overlooking the patchwork of tiny back gardens
that joined the parallel terraces together. The bathroom
was on a small half-landing partway up the stairs, and was
all blue and white tiles with a deep claw-foot Victorian
bath, a separate shower, a double-basin unit running the
entire width of one wall and plenty of space to set up a
table for the baby bath, until he was old enough to go in the
big one.

It was all so perfect that Nikki's euphoria was starting to
shred with doubt. It seemed too good to be true. 'Are you
sure we can afford all this?' she muttered to Spence as they
followed the agent back downstairs and Mrs A stayed
behind to test the plumbing. 'How much is the rent?'

As he told her, Spence was flipping open his mobile to
answer a call. 'Hey, Jen,' he said. 'Can I call you back in ten?
Great. Speak then,' and repocketing his phone he said to the
agent, 'Can you give us a minute to have a chat?'

The agent, in the process of answering his own phone,
waved them into the kitchen, then disappeared outside.

'We have to take it now,' Spence stated. 'You heard him
say he's got lots of viewings lined up.'

'So we offer the full rent? No negotiating?'

'I think so, don't you?'

She nodded. 'Yeah, we don't want to lose it by faffing
about, but sixteen hundred a month's a lot more than we're
paying now. Are the others OK with it?'

'I haven't had a chance to talk to David yet, but Danny's
cool for three hundred, he says. That means the rest of us
have to find six hundred and fifty a couple. Or, three
twenty-five each. David won't have any trouble affording
that, given the amount he's working now, and he's got this
short coming up, with me, plus more second-unit stuff for
Drake. Kristin's still flush from her stint on *The Bill*, and I've
got the commercial next week . . .'

'But what about me? I'm not going to be earning for a while, so . . .'

'You've got the most important thing of all to think about, and it's my place to make sure you don't have to worry.'

Smiling into his eyes and seeing how excited and happy he was, she felt all her misgivings melt away. They could afford it, and it wouldn't be long before she was chipping in with the finances too.

'So,' Mrs A said, joining them in the kitchen, 'have you come to a decision?'

Nikki laughed. 'It's a bit of a no-brainer, wouldn't you say?'

Mrs A smiled. 'But possibly not in those words. Have you asked about the deposit, and when it'll be ready for you to move in?'

'Not yet,' Spence answered, 'but whatever, I think we have to take it.'

Mrs A nodded. 'I'm happy to give you David's share of the deposit if you need it before he gets back.'

'So you think he'll go for it too,' Nikki said, already knowing the answer.

'If he doesn't,' she replied, 'I'll move in myself.'

As they laughed the agent came along the hall saying, 'Sorry, but my next appointment's arrived, so do you want to give me a call at the end of the day?'

'No, we want to take it,' Spence told him. 'We can get the deposit to you by five o'clock, we just need to know how much it is, and when we can move in.'

The agent blinked at the speed. 'The deposit's three thousand,' he told them, 'and it's renting from March 1st. I can't make you any promises right now, though. I'll need to speak to the landlord first, and get some references.'

'I'll give Mr Farrell a call,' Nikki said, taking out her phone. 'He's our landlord in Bristol,' she explained to the agent. 'Do you have an email or fax number he can reach you on?'

After handing over his card, the agent began steering them towards the door. 'I'll be in touch as soon as a decision's been made,' he told them. 'Thanks very much for coming.'

Back out in the cold, where a couple in their early thirties were waiting to go in, Nikki suppressed the urge to scowl at them and quickly told Mr Farrell's secretary what needed to be done and how soon. 'We have to get it,' she said urgently to Spence as she rang off. 'We just have to.'

'We will,' he said confidently. 'Hey, Jen,' he said into his phone. 'What's up?'

As he walked on down the road, Nikki followed on with Mrs A, linking her arm as they negotiated the slithery leaves and cracked pavement. 'By the first of March the baby should be a few weeks old,' she said.

'You'll have the hang of it all by then,' Mrs A assured her. 'And I'll pop up at the weekends to make sure you're all settling in. And eating.'

Nikki smiled and felt a flood of love fill her heart as Spence came back towards them. 'That was one of the production managers at Drake's office,' he said. 'I've got a meeting in an hour with the clients for this commercial. Apparently they want to discuss the location again, so I'm going to have to get myself back over to Soho p.d.q. Fancy coming?'

Nikki's eyes widened with surprise.

'Come on, it'll be a great opportunity for you to meet some of Drake's team. And the writer of *Celeste* is there today, so you could have a chat with her. She knows all about you, and she said some really cool things about *Done with the Night*.'

Nikki looked at Mrs A, who surely wouldn't want to come too, and was probably even quite eager to get back on the motorway before the rush hour started.

'Actually, if you could go off with Spence for a couple of hours,' she said, 'it would give me a chance to pop over to Great Ormond Street to see one of my babies.'

Nikki blinked, and feeling instantly concerned for the mother without even knowing her, she said, 'What's he in for?'

'It's a she,' Mrs A corrected, glancing at Spence as he whipped out his mobile to take another call. 'She's having surgery on her hips today. Her mother rang this morning, needing to talk, so I told her I'd drop in before returning to Bristol if I could.'

'Oh yes, you definitely must,' Nikki urged. 'She'll be needing all the moral support she can get.'

Mrs A smiled and patted her hand. 'Let's keep in touch by phone,' she said, 'and arrange a time to meet up later.'

'That is so cool,' Spence declared, ending his call. 'Drake's just rung in to say he's on his way to the office, so you'll get to meet him too.'

Nikki immediately experienced a bolt of nerves. 'Are you sure he won't mind you dragging your pregnant girlfriend . . .'

Spence's hand went up as he took another call. 'Hey, Mark. Yes, I'm on my way now. I heard. We can sort it. Is Drake going to . . .? Yes, she's with me now. Great. Fantastic. OK. See ya,' and ringing off he wrapped Nikki in an exultant, though slightly awkward embrace as he said, 'Drake's looking forward to meeting you. He wants to talk about your take on the Shylock story.'

'Today!' Nikki cried. 'But I'm not ready.'

'You will be by the time we get there,' he promised, and folding her arm in his he began marching her towards the Tube, laughing delightedly as the baby jiggled about under the hand he'd slipped inside her coat.

Chapter Seven

At first glance Drake Murray reminded Nikki so much of her father that the warmth of her smile started to seep away. With his iron-grey hair, intense, hawkish features and imposing stature he was definitely the man she'd seen on umpteen TV shows, but there was a severity about him that didn't come across at all on-screen. Then he looked up and saw her, and as his face lit with pleasure it threw her into an uncanny sense of having met him many times before. She hadn't, but the relief of finding him to be every bit as friendly as Spence had claimed put the heat back into her smile, as he scooped one of her small hands between both of his and held it warmly.

'Nikki, at last,' he said, gazing directly into her eyes. 'I hope Spencer's told you what a great fan I am. The nuances and undercurrent of menace in *Done with the Night* were masterly, especially coming from someone of your tender years. Excellent. A very well-deserved award for Spencer, but in my opinion you should have received a trophy too.'

Nikki was beaming and blushing. 'Thank you,' she said, glancing at Spence, who was smiling all over his face. 'It really was a team effort, though,' she added.

They were in the penthouse suite of Drake's Soho-based offices which occupied all four storeys of the complex, just off Beak Street. It was where many of his protégés had begun their careers, and several were still working there, some in the ground-floor editing rooms, others, such as fledgling producers, writers and directors, in the productions offices on the second level. A handful of experienced technicians staffed a third-floor studio where they ran various training programmes when the space wasn't being hired out to other companies, or used for an in-house production.

Drake's eyes were twinkling merrily. 'I don't doubt it,' he responded, 'but it was you who provided the material for the others to work with. Without it, there would have been nothing to direct, light, shoot, act or edit, and what you gave them turned out to be a superb showcase for their individual talents.'

Nikki glanced at Spence again. 'I'm starting to feel embarrassed now,' she confessed, aware of Drake's two personal assistants, Mark and Diana, who were at their desks but apparently enjoying the moment.

He chuckled kindly. 'Don't be,' he said. 'I'm simply giving praise where it's due. You'll get used to it if we're to work together, and I'm sure we shall if things go to plan. Now, come on through, and we'll have a little chat about your new ideas. I know one of them is particularly interesting, so I'd like to hear more. Will you have a drink of something? How about a hot chocolate to warm us up a bit?'

Nikki's eyes were shining as her mouth started to water. 'Hot chocolate sounds great,' she told him.

He gave her a playful wink. 'Cakes too, I think,' he whispered, and after signalling for someone to do the honours, he strode on into his office, unravelling a bright red scarf as he went.

'I'll have to leave you to it,' Spence said, coming to help Nikki off with her coat. 'My meeting's about to start downstairs.'

Resisting the urge to drag him after her, Nikki said, in a voice she felt proud of, 'OK. Will I see you before I leave?'

'Maybe. If not, I'll call as soon as I come free. Good luck with the old bear, I know the two of you will get along great,' and after draping her coat over an empty desk he made off towards the lift.

'Give me a shout if you need me,' Drake called after him, 'but I'm sure you won't.'

Spence raised a hand without turning round, impressing the heck out of Nikki with how self-assured he was in this major big-time environment.

'That's it, come in, come in,' Drake encouraged, as she

stepped gingerly through his open door. 'We'll sit on the sofas, I think. You'll be able to put your feet up more easily. So when's the little monster due? Any time now, by the look of you.'

Surprised and heartened by how casual he seemed about her pregnancy, she said, 'Just over three weeks, unless it's late. Or early.'

He made a soft growling sort of noise. 'You can count on it being one or the other,' he told her confidently, while picking up a cushion to slide behind her back. 'I've had six of the little perishers, and not one of them had the good sense, or manners, to turn up on time. And believe me, they haven't changed. They might all be in their teens or twenties now, but the earlies still invariably turn up ahead of time, just when you're not ready for them; and the lates keep you waiting for hours, as if you've got all the time in the world and it's theirs to spend.'

Loving the fondness of his tone, and doing a quiet effervesce inside at how amazing this was, she settled as comfortably as she could on the sofa, and even allowed him to lift each of her booted feet, one at a time, on to the table. The whole thing was blowing her mind. Here she was, in Drake Murray's office, being waited on hand and foot and told she was a good writer. Did it get any better than that? 'You know,' she said, in a sudden rush of jubilance, 'not even in my wildest dreams did I see myself going to my first-ever meeting with a big-time movie director, eight and a bit months pregnant, still aged twenty-one, dressed in all my preggie gear, and have him offer me hot chocolate, a pillow to prop me up and a table for my fake Uggs. This was definitely not a scenario I'd have written.'

He gave a shout of laughter as he sank into the sofa opposite. 'That is exactly what I love about people your age,' he told her. 'You're not afraid to say what you're thinking.'

She blinked in amazement. Had she overstepped some invisible mark, or said something she hadn't quite registered?

'It's how my daughters speak to me,' he confided. 'Without restraint. I like it. They go a bit far sometimes, it's true, but I'm their dad, it happens, and I can get over it.'

She suddenly liked him so much that she had to bite her lips to stop herself gushing it out. He was making her feel so at ease, as if she could say anything and he'd try to understand before he even thought about getting into judging. Not like her father at all.

'You know, I was afraid you'd think I might hold Spence back,' she told him, in a rush of confidence, 'what with the baby and everything.'

His eyes narrowed slightly and gazed into hers, not in a bad way, but in a way that seemed to see things about her that she might not even know herself. Mrs A could do that, she was thinking. She had a way of seeing, or under-standing, or sensing that went beyond anything Nikki could put into words. How weird that Drake should remind her of her dad *and* Mrs A. She wondered if it was bad in the former and good in the latter, or both good, and ended up being not quite sure.

'The way I see it,' he said, 'is that how you cope with the baby, and your family and career, is down to you. I think you, Nikki, have already decided that you can have it all – and believe me, if you choose to, you can. It's easier for you than for some, because being a writer means you can work from home. But it'll be frustrating at times, and you might want to bring someone in to help take care of the blighter when you're fighting a deadline, but whatever you're working on, and whoever you're doing it for, nothing's ever going to mean more to you than him, or her – take that from someone who knows.' He waved a hand, gesturing around the walls that were covered in posters from all the movies and commercials he'd made, along with the many awards he'd won. 'All this you can see, these trappings of success,' he said, 'none of it means more to me than my kids. And it never will – just don't tell them that!'

She laughed and felt the bubble of joy inside her growing so big she might float.

'Being a mother will give you a perspective on life that you can't even begin to imagine right now,' he went on, clearly warming to his theme. 'The world, the people around you, who you are, who Spencer is, your friends, your ambitions, your dreams . . . This baby will change everything as far as you're concerned, which I expect sounds a bit scary, but believe me, being a parent will complete you as a person in ways that just aren't possible to understand until you're there. You can write as many scripts as you like, Spencer can make as many movies, but that child is the most important thing either of you will ever produce. I know that, and I think you do too, but my guess is you're nervous of it right now. You're young. You've hardly got started, so it's not surprising you're worried, but take it from me, it won't stand in your way unless you let it. But you won't. You'll cope. I can see it in you.'

Nikki was glowing. She felt so exhilarated she wanted to throw out her arms in joy, or sit down and start drafting a script for him right now.

He hadn't finished. 'You're made for success,' he told her, 'so is Spence. And David and Kristin are right there with you. Personally, I don't think it's any accident you all happened upon each other down there in Falmouth, I think destiny's hand was at work when it brought you together.' He grinned so widely that it almost made her blink. 'Do you believe in all that guff?' he asked. Then, waving a hand, 'It doesn't matter whether we do or don't believe, the fact is you're a gifted bunch of beginners, and I don't have any trouble seeing you go all the way to the top, provided you put in the work – and the right breaks come your way, of course. They're always a vital part of the process, but happily I'm here to help with that. So now, lecture over, let's get down to this modern take on *The Merchant of Venice*. I like it in principle, so I want you to talk me through how it could work as a short film.'

Nikki's head was spinning, but she was so high on his enthusiasm by now that after the timely pause offered by the arrival of their hot chocolate and cakes she was ready to launch into her idea. It helped enormously that she'd gone over it with Spence during the Tube journey here, but Drake's belief in her, coupled with how possible he was making everything seem, had given her imagination wings.

'What kind of duration are you thinking?' she asked. 'And should I be keeping a budget in mind?'

He started to laugh. 'Spoken like a true professional,' he

told her. 'OK. Let's go for thirty minutes, forty tops, and a budget of say, ten thousand?'

Her eyes almost popped. *Done with the Night* had been shot on a shoestring of less than two grand, most of which had been raised on their credit cards. Then, reminding herself that he hadn't actually offered that sum, and was in fact only posing it as a hypothetical to get her started, she decided to run with the freedom of cash and set her opening scene in New York.

Twenty minutes later, as they wrestled with how the pound of flesh could best be represented, there was a knock on the door and Diana put her head round.

'Sorry to interrupt,' she said, giving Nikki a quick smile, 'but Alan Gleeson's on the line. He says it's urgent.'

'OK, switch him through,' Drake said, and heaving himself up from the sofa, he walked over to his desk and picked up a receiver. 'Al, what's up?'

Nikki was just wondering if she should leave the room, or stay put, when her own phone started to ring. Seeing it was Mrs A she quickly clicked on.

'Hey, how's it going?' she asked quietly.

'I'm still at the hospital,' Mrs A replied, 'but the operation was a success, so mother and baby are fine. I'll be leaving in about half an hour, so I was wondering where to pick you up.'

Nikki pulled a face. 'I'm in Soho at the moment,' she said, still keeping her voice down. 'I'm having the most amazing meeting. We're discussing my script and he really seems to like it.'

'Then take your time, dear. I can always pop in to see Nanette and the boys. Just give me a call when you're ready.'

'Mrs A, you're the most wonderful person in the world,' Nikki told her. 'It probably won't be much longer now. Oh, please give my love to Nanette,' she added, even though she'd only met David's oldest sister twice, but hey, why not? She was in such a great mood today, she had plenty to spare.

As she rang off she heard Drake saying, 'OK, I guess it's best if I come over there. Tell her I'm on my way, and if she walks again she won't get a second chance.' After putting the phone down he turned back to Nikki, looking distracted and not very pleased. 'I'm afraid something's come up,' he told her, 'so I'll have to curtail our meeting, but I want you to keep thinking, and as soon as you've roughed out a draft email it to me and we'll either meet again or discuss it on the phone.'

'I can hardly wait to get started now,' she told him, as she struggled to get up. 'I'm really buzzing.'

Coming to give her a hand, he tugged her to her feet and put his hands on her shoulders. 'Don't go too fast,' he advised. 'There's a big event coming up . . .'

'Yes, but not for three weeks or more, and in that time I could probably complete a first draft.'

He smiled. 'Then I'll look forward to reading it. Now, I must go. Are you waiting for Spence, or can I drop you somewhere?'

'Oh, don't worry about me,' she told him, appalled by the idea of putting him out. 'I'm meeting a friend who's driving me back to Bristol.'

'OK, then go safely,' and after treating her to an avuncular peck on the cheek he left.

Not quite sure what to do now, Nikki stuffed her notebook back in her bag and followed him out of the door. Both Diana and Mark were on the phone. She didn't want to leave without saying a proper goodbye, so she went to pick up her coat, put it on slowly, then bought some more time by calling Mrs A to arrange when and where to meet.

Moments after Nikki rang off Diana came free and turned to her with a friendly smile. 'Everything OK?' she asked.

'Yes, thank you,' Nikki replied. 'It was a great meeting. He's really nice, isn't he?'

Diana laughed. 'Oh, he's definitely that,' she confirmed. 'Those of us who work for him know how lucky we are.'

'He has an office in Hollywood too, doesn't he?'

'On the corner of Sunset and Sweetzer. Do you know LA?'

Nikki shook her head. 'But I'd love to.'

'I'm sure you will from what we've been hearing about Spence. Drake's really taken to him. The commercial Spence is shooting next week? Drake hardly ever gives anything as

131

big as that to someone with no experience in shooting commercials. That's how much confidence he has in him. And how much the client trusts Drake. They're prepared to go with his recommendation, just because it's his.'

Nikki felt so thrilled for Spence that she wanted to hug him and Diana and Drake and everyone else in this wonderful, magical tower. 'When he comes out of the meeting will you tell him . . .?' She broke off as the lift doors opened and with impeccable timing Spence walked out.

'Hey, you're still here,' he said. 'Drake just popped his head round to say you were leaving. How did it go?'

'Fantastic. Amazing,' she told him. 'I'm going to make a start as soon as I get home. No word from the agent about the house yet, I suppose?'

'I don't know, my phone's been switched off,' and taking it out of his pocket he fired it up to find several voicemails and texts, but nothing from the agent.

'We have to get it, we just have to,' Nikki said desperately.

Laughing, he put an arm round her shoulders and walked her to the lift. 'We will,' he said confidently. 'We were first in, and we offered the asking price, and we're OK about waiting till March. Everyone else will probably be looking for somewhere straight away.'

Taking comfort from that, she called a goodbye to Diana and Mark and as the lift door closed she put her arms round Spencer's neck. 'I really, really love you,' she told him. 'You're so brilliant, and everyone here is amazing. Can we really be this lucky? Is it all going to come true?'

He grinned. 'I don't see any reason why not. The clients for this commercial are giving me some grief, but hey, I can deal with it. Then David and I are due to start shooting *Celeste* right when we could be moving to Shepherd's Bush, but no problem, we'll make it work. By the way, did you get to meet Val Fleming?'

'You mean who wrote *Celeste*? No, I didn't.'

Quickly hitting a button, he stopped the lift at the first floor and led her out into an open-plan office where a dozen or more people were on phones, at computers or in front of video screens. 'It'll have to be a swift hello,' he said, weaving a path through the desks, 'because I have to get back. Hey, Val,' he said to a woman who was sitting gazing out of the window.

Apparently starting out of a reverie, the woman turned round and Nikki felt her heart falter. With her glossy mane of sleek black hair, exquisite sloe eyes and honey complexion she was stunningly beautiful and clearly Chinese, but when she spoke there wasn't even the trace of an accent. 'Spencer, hi,' she said, getting to her feet and towering over him. 'I heard you were in. And you must be Nikki,' she said, turning her enchanting smile on Nikki. 'I wonder how I guessed.'

The twinkle in her eyes, as well as the words, made Nikki laugh. 'I loved your script,' she told her earnestly. 'I haven't read the revised version yet, but Spence's bringing one home . . .'

'I have a copy here, if you're interested,' Val broke in, taking one from the top of a pile. 'It's a pretty drastic rewrite, but everyone seems to think it works. I'd love to know what you make of it, once you've had a chance to read it.'

Nikki felt almost overwhelmed as she took the script.

'I'm enjoying working with Spence,' Val continued, throwing a quick smile his way. 'He has some very – how shall I put it? – *challenging* ideas, such as changing the central character from a middle-aged Indian frump to a thirty-year-old Italian bombshell. Definitely not how I saw her, but it's interesting, and I agree it's good practice for dealing with drastic rewrites.'

Nikki's blood was turning cold. She glanced at Spence, expecting him to look awkward or guilty, since he'd told her the change was Kristin's idea.

'It was,' he laughed, when she challenged him back in the lift. 'It happened exactly the way I told you – she went to Drake, they called me in, told me what they were thinking, and I was OK with it. Then we went to Val, so she's obviously assumed it was my idea. Don't worry, I'll put her straight, and be prepared, because Drake's likely to put you through the same thing when your script's being developed.'

Feeling a thrill at the mere thought of that, Nikki let go of her ire and gave a small gasp as a contraction tightened inside her.

'You're getting a lot of those lately,' Spence said, looking worried as they walked into the lobby.

'I'm supposed to,' she assured him. 'Anyway, you'd better get back to your meeting. Call me the minute you hear about the house, OK?'

'You got it, and keep reminding that little rascal in there that he's not due for another three weeks.'

'Don't worry, he's staying put, because I want the time for myself now to get going on the script.'

'Famous last words,' Mrs A laughed, when Nikki repeated them as they drove back down the motorway. 'He's bound to come early now.'

Nikki was laughing too. 'I don't really mind if he does,' she admitted. 'I'm fed up of being this huge, and the longer he stays in there the bigger I'm going to get. I can always write while he's sleeping.'

Mrs A cast her a look, but all she said was, 'I spoke to David just before I picked you up. He's very excited about the house.'

Nikki's heart lurched. 'Me too. It's got to happen, Mrs A. It just has to, because everything's so perfect, the house, the rent, the location, the timing, absolutely everything. It's meant for us, I just know it.'

Two hours later, as they were driving past Temple Meads station on their way to Bedminster, Spence rang.

'Nik,' he cried excitedly. 'Wait for this! Provided the references are OK, and we can pay the deposit by the end of next week – and the cheque doesn't bounce – the house is ours from the beginning of March.'

'Oh my God!' Nikki squealed. 'Mrs A, we've got it. I told you, didn't I? It's meant for us. Oh, Spence, you're brilliant.'

'I didn't do anything,' he laughed.

'You did, you found it. And now we're going to have the most perfect home for the baby, and for the rest of us, while we work for Drake and make movies and turn ourselves into amazing, fantastic, fabulous megastars.'

The Merchant of Venice
Act One
Scene 1

Nikki looked at the screen, took a moment to ponder the '1', then changed it to '*One*'.

Deciding she liked the first version best, she swapped it back again, hit the return key a couple of times and typed: *Ext. Wall St. Day.*

It was early on Tuesday evening, and this was the first opportunity she'd had to make a start on the script since returning from London last Wednesday. However, she'd discussed it some more with Spence over the weekend, and with Kristin, because she'd come back too, full of how fabulous the new house was, and how amazing it had been of Spence to find it. She was upstairs now with David, who was running lines with her for a small part she'd managed to land in a low-budget feature shooting next week. It was only a day's work, but the way she'd been carrying on anyone would think she was playing the lead in some major Spielberg production. Heaven only knew what she was going to be like when she started rehearsals for *Celeste*. Or when her episode of *The Bill* was transmitted.

Leaning her elbows on the desk, Nikki regarded her reflection in the darkening window for a while, then focused on the screen again and tried to remember how they'd decided the film should begin. Spence had described his ideas for various openings, and she'd particularly liked one of them, but for some reason she couldn't bring it to mind. Maybe she should ring him. She'd like to speak to him anyway, not for anything special, just to hear him really, because she seemed to be missing him more than usual this week. And she was feeling a bit low – or not low, exactly, just big and tired, and kind of lonely in a way.

She reached for her mobile, then decided she couldn't call, because he'd be up to his eyes preparing for his first day's shoot on the commercial. She could always ask Kristin and David what they'd decided, because they'd been part of the discussion, but they'd been up there for a while now, so there was a good chance they'd moved on to other things.

Though certain she hadn't written the opening she needed

135

into her notebook, she picked it up anyway, and began flicking through. Seeing so many letters to Zac, penned in a neater hand between scribbled notes for everything else, she felt a flutter of happiness coast over her heart. She'd written to him even more than she'd realised, keeping him up to date with everything that was happening to him and her, and everyone else, especially his dad. She'd made sure to pack a fresh notepad in her hospital bag along with the new dressing gown and slippers Spence had bought her for Christmas, two nursing bras, some toiletries and a pack of sanitary pads. It felt important to record how he came into the world. She hoped, when the time came, that it wasn't going to hurt too much, but even if it did, she wouldn't tell him. She didn't want him to feel bad for causing her pain, and besides, being a boy he probably wouldn't appreciate the gory details of his birth. It was likely he'd want to know other things, though, such as how she got to the hospital, who was with her, the things his daddy said or did during the labour, and how loud he cried when he came out.

Of course, she wasn't naive enough to think that she'd be writing all the way through the birth, but as soon as she was able she'd note it all down, ready to put into gentler, or at least more readable words when she had time.

Groaning as an ache began carving a path through her back, she tried as best she could to rub a hand up and down it.

'Can I help?' Kristin offered, coming into the room.

Starting, Nikki turned round. 'I didn't hear you . . .' She stopped abruptly as her eyes widened with shock.

Kristin's face turned pale. 'What is it?' she asked urgently. 'Why are you looking like that?'

Nikki swallowed hard. 'I think . . . Oh my God, I think my waters just broke,' she said, in a voice that seemed to trail at the end of a thread.

'Oh shit!' Kristin gulped. '*David! Get down here!* What shall I do?' she urged Nikki. 'Just tell me . . .'

'We have to call the hospital,' Nikki cut in, trying to stand up.

'No. You sit there,' Kristin insisted. 'We'll do everything. David!'

'I'm here,' he said, bundling in behind her. 'What is it?'

'Nikki's in labour. Call a taxi. Or an ambulance. What do we do?' she asked Nikki.

'Ring the hospital,' Nikki said again. 'The number's here,' she flipped to the inside cover of her notebook. 'Actually, I'll do it. You call a taxi.'

'I'm going to ring Mum,' David declared, taking out his mobile as Kristin dashed upstairs for hers.

A few minutes later Nikki had confirmation from the hospital that she was to come straight in. 'I need to get my bag,' she said, starting from the room.

'Is it upstairs?' Kristin demanded. 'I'll get it. Taxi's on its way.'

'So's Mum,' David announced, clicking off his mobile. 'Have you called Spence yet?'

Nikki gave a choke of laughter. 'Oh my God, I almost forgot,' she confessed. 'Don't ever tell him, will you?'

David grinned. 'Sealed lips,' he promised. 'Do you want me to do it?'

'No, I will.' Her heart was already flooding with the joy of uttering the words *the baby's on its way*. Or, *it's time*. Or whatever she might say, she wasn't sure yet. She only knew that she'd never wanted to see Spence more in her life, and had never felt so close to him, in spite of the miles between them.

However, when she connected to his number she was diverted through to voicemail. Trying hard to swallow her disappointment, she looked at David. 'Shall I leave a message?' she said. Then, 'No. I'll try again in a minute.'

'What do we do now?' David asked.

'I need to go and change,' she answered.

Seeming not to have heard, he said, 'Shall I rub your back?'

She wanted to laugh. 'I think it's OK,' she replied, then suddenly gasped as the first contraction started to make itself felt.

David's eyes rounded. 'Are you all right?' he demanded, and putting an arm around her he sat her back in her chair.

'Here's your bag,' Kristin said, wrestling it down into the hall. 'What's happened?' she asked, noticing David's worried face.

Nikki smiled. 'I had a contraction,' she answered proudly.

Kristin looked at her in a bewildered sort of way. 'Cool,' she muttered.

'I can stand up now,' Nikki told David.

'But I don't think you should,' he argued. 'Let's wait till Mum gets here. Or the taxi.'

'I need to change. Actually, I'm going to try Spence again.'

Kristin immediately baulked. 'But you can't,' she protested.

Nikki blinked with shock. 'Why not?'

Flushing red, Kristin threw out her hands and looked to David as though seeking support.

'Why not?' he echoed.

'Well, what can he do?' she demanded. 'He's miles away and he starts shooting first thing in the morning.'

Nikki looked lost as she turned to David.

'She has to call him,' he told Kristin. 'He's the baby's dad.'

'Duh, like I don't know that,' she retorted. 'But this commercial's a really big deal for him. He can't just take off. It'll mean leaving everyone in the lurch and no way will he want to do that, especially not when Drake's gone right out on a limb to give him this job.'

'But we can't not tell him!' David protested.

'I repeat myself,' Kristin snapped. 'What can he do? Nikki's the one giving birth, not him.'

'That's not the point.'

'It's exactly the point. Look, I know it's a harsh truth for a man, but I'm sorry, you're surplus to requirements at a time like this. As long as the midwife's there, and the doctor if she needs him . . .'

Nikki started to interrupt, but a dart of pain shot down her side, stealing her words.

'Anyway, we'll be there,' Kristin went on insistently, not noticing, 'so it's not as if she'll be on her own. We can keep her company and do whatever . . .' She broke off at the ring of the doorbell. 'That'll be your mum, or the taxi,' she declared, and went to find out.

The moment Mrs A stepped into the room, her hair glistening with raindrops and her lovely face as calming as one of her poems, Nikki felt so much relief that she was sure she could go through anything now.

'OK, let's have a little feel of where the rascal is,' Mrs A said, putting her bag down. And easing Nikki to her feet she began a gentle massage of the baby, using her expert fingertips to tell her what was happening in his world. 'Lovely,' she smiled, and cupping a hand round Nikki's face she said, 'I expect you'd like to go upstairs and change before we leave.'

'Do I have time?' Nikki asked.

'Of course,' Mrs A chuckled. 'I'll take you in my car. We'll be there long before anything serious starts to happen.'

As Nikki disappeared upstairs, Mrs A looked from David to Kristin and laughed. 'Well, anyone would think this was *your* first baby,' she teased.

'It is,' Kristin answered with feeling.

'That'll be the taxi,' David said as the doorbell rang again. 'I didn't know who'd get here first,' he explained to his mother. 'I thought it was urgent.'

'You did the right thing,' she told him. 'So now the taxi's here, why don't you and Kristin use it to follow me? My back seat's crammed full of things I need to take to the clinic tomorrow. Now, I'll give the hospital a call and find out who's on duty tonight to let them know I'm coming.'

After going to ask the driver to wait, David returned to the room and stood waiting with Kristin until his mother had finished her call. They were like two spare parts that hadn't quite discovered where they fitted in yet, but remained hopeful that they would somehow.

'That's good,' Mrs A announced as she rang off. 'Mattie Jarvis is the duty midwife tonight. She'll take excellent care of our girl. Has anyone called Spence yet?'

Kristin glanced at David. 'Actually, we were just discussing that when you arrived,' she answered. 'I don't think we should, because everyone's booked to do this commercial tomorrow. Crew, actors, location . . . It's quite a big budget, and it all hangs on Spence, so there's no way he can get down here tonight.'

Mrs A's eyes went to David as he said, 'He's always said he wants to be there when the baby's born. It's why he turned down *The Bill* and organised everything so he'd have a couple of weeks off either side of the due date. So I think we should tell him.'

Mrs A looked up as Nikki came down the stairs. 'What do you want to do?' she asked, guessing that Nikki must have heard. 'It's your baby, so it has to be your decision.'

Nikki looked at her helplessly. 'I don't know,' she answered. 'I mean, I really, really want him here, but Kristin's right, he can't just leave everyone without a director, and it's too late to get anyone to step in.'

Apparently deciding not to express her own opinion for the moment, Mrs A said, 'OK. Let's get you out to the car. David, go back upstairs to make sure Nikki hasn't forgotten anything.'

'Like what?' he cried in alarm.

'I'll do it,' Kristin said with a roll of her eyes. 'You go and check the back door's locked and I'll meet you outside.'

Ten minutes later Mrs A was driving along the cut towards St Mary Redcliffe, wipers surging back and forth in a near-futile effort to clear the screen, while Nikki sat nursing her mobile in one hand, and the hardening mound of her belly in the other.

'Am I being selfish if I tell him?' she wondered out loud. 'It'll put him off what he's doing, and Kristin's right . . .'

'Kristin is entitled to her opinion,' Mrs A cut in, 'but in mine, I think you should let Spence decide for himself whether or not he wants to come.'

'I know he does. It's just . . .'

When she didn't say any more Mrs A glanced at her, then had to hit the brakes hard as the lights ahead turned to red. 'There will be other commercials,' she said reasonably. 'There will only ever be one first child.'

Nikki looked down at her phone. 'Put like that,' she whispered, but it was still several minutes before she pressed in Spence's number and tried again.

'Hey,' he said cheerily down the line. 'I was about to call you. How's things?'

She swallowed hard, wanting to suppress her misery. She'd so been looking forward to this moment and now it was all going wrong. 'I'm on my way to hospital,' she told him, while gazing out through the steamy windows and seeing her reflection travelling over the offices and restaurants of Welsh Back. 'The baby's coming.'

'What!' he exploded. 'You're kidding me. It can't.'

'I know, but it is. I'm sorry . . .'

'Nik, this is terrible timing.'

'It's not my fault,' she cried. 'I didn't tell it to come now.'

'But you know what's happening tomorrow. I can't get down there tonight . . .'

'It's OK,' she said tartly. 'You don't have to. I'm just letting you know that your baby's on its way, and that the next time we speak you'll probably be a dad.'

'Oh, Nik, don't do this to me,' he groaned. 'I can tell you're pissed off, but you've got to know if there was any way I could . . .'

'I just told you, you don't have to come,' she snapped. 'Mrs A's with me, so I'll be absolutely fine.'

'I know you will, but that's not the point. Oh God, Nik, you're not going to hold this against me, are you?'

'No. I understand you have to stay there. I just thought you'd want to know . . .'

'Of course I want to know. I want to be there, for God's sake. It's just I can't let Drake down now. There's a quarter-million budget riding on this . . .'

'I have to go,' she broke in, and ringing off she put her head back, squeezing her eyes tightly as the gnawing ache of another contraction began working to a peak.

'Don't forget to breathe,' Mrs A said mildly. 'Did you remember to bring your birth plan?'

Nikki nodded. 'It's in my bag,' she gulped.

'What have you decided about pain relief?'

Nikki let her breath go in a laugh. 'Whatever it was, it's not going to be enough,' she declared. She looked at her phone as it rang. 'It's him,' she said, and clicking on, she listened as Spence said, 'Nikki, please try to understand. You know how important Drake is to our future . . .'

'It's all right,' she told him. 'I don't want you to let him down, either. Just promise me you'll leave your phone on and I'll call as soon as there's some news.'

'Of course. Stay on the line all night, if you like. If it's the only way I can be with you, it'll have to do.'

After ringing off, she sat quietly watching the rain whipping around the city centre, misting the inky darkness

141

and turning the slick wet roads into pools of shimmery light. People were hunched under umbrellas, scuttling to bus stops or in and out of doorways, wet, stressed and eager to get home. She wasn't really registering them, because she was thinking of Spence and trying desperately not to mind that he wasn't coming. It was hard, though, because she almost couldn't bear the thought of someone else, like David, or Kristin, or even Mrs A holding little Zac before his daddy had the chance to do so. He should be with them now, and yet she understood why he couldn't.

'I expect he's feeling really bad now,' she said to Mrs A.

Mrs A reached over to give her hand a squeeze. 'He's a big boy, he'll deal with it,' she said. 'You just concentrate on the baby, because I'm getting the impression he's in a little bit more of a hurry to join us than I thought.'

Chapter Eight

It was three o'clock in the morning. Nikki was so tired and frustrated she barely knew what to do with herself. Every instinct she possessed longed to start pushing but the midwife kept telling her she mustn't, or she'd tear her cervix, and maybe even damage the baby.

During the lulls, when the fierceness of the urge subsided, she found herself drifting towards sleep, only to be woken by the kind of pain she never wanted to experience again in her life. It was as though her entire lower body was being ripped apart with bare hands. She gasped hard on the gas and air, drawing it in like a drowning woman taking her last breaths, squeezing David's hand so tightly she feared his knuckles might break.

'It's all right,' he whispered raggedly, trying to stop his face contorting with the pain. 'You're doing great.'

Right now Kristin was dozing in a comfy chair next to the monitor, a magazine half sliding from her lap, while Mrs A dabbed Nikki's face and whispered softly, reciting lines from a poem Nikki had never heard before, but sensed, on a level that ebbed and flowed like a tide, that she might one day come to love.

> From the private ease of Mother's womb
> I fall into the lighted room.
> Why don't they simply put me back
> Where it is warm and wet and black?
>
> They tuck me in a rustling bed
> I lie there, raging, small, and red.
> I may sleep soon . . .

She opened her eyes as the midwife, a cheery, round-faced woman in her early forties, came back to check how far she'd dilated. To Nikki's unutterable dismay she shook her head, saying, 'Not there yet, but shouldn't be long now.'

Nikki turned to Mrs A in despair. It was exactly what the midwife had said the last time she'd popped in. Meanwhile, two babies had been born in neighbouring rooms, their tiny cries rising up like little fountains of music from the laughs and cheers of happiness around them.

She began speaking to Zac in her mind again, urging him on, reminding him how much he was loved and telling him not to be afraid. *I'll be here for you*, she whispered silently. *And Daddy will be soon. Everyone's longing to see you and hold you and give you a very special life.*

A few hours had passed since she'd last spoken to Spence. He needed his sleep, and when there was nothing to tell it would serve no purpose to keep him awake just because she wanted to feel he was there, even if it was at the end of a phone.

Her eyes started to droop. Zac seemed to be sleeping too. 'He's being really stubborn,' she murmured. 'I'm going to have something to say to him when . . . ' She suddenly cried out as her cervix flexed like a disc blade scything through her insides.

Kristin started awake; Mrs A quickly passed the inhaler; David bravely offered his other hand.

Nikki sucked in hard as tears streamed down her cheeks and sweat beaded on her skin. She didn't want this to go on any longer. She couldn't stand it. *She couldn't stand it.* She should have had an epidural, or a Caesarean, a lobotomy, anything that would have saved her from this indescribable pain. She wanted Spence. He should be here. She couldn't do it without him. Somehow he would make it all right. Her tears were turning to sobs. She disguised them with short, heavy pants. This was all wrong. It wasn't how it should be. She wanted to phone him again, but he had a six o'clock call so she had to let him sleep.

She cried out again – and again. Nothing, but nothing had prepared her for this. How bad was it going to get? She was starting to feel afraid. Very afraid.

The midwife came back, looking busy and approving. 'Ah ha,' she announced with a satisfied smile, 'I think we're getting there at last.'

In a sudden incoherent flash, Nikki wanted to go home and come back when the baby was supposed to be born. Spence would be with her then. It would all be happening properly. It might not even hurt so much.

Everyone was watching her, except the midwife, who was strapping two wide belts around her belly to begin monitoring the baby's heart. Above the clear shell of the oxygen mask Nikki's eyes followed her every move, then heady surges of joy began to chime with the rapid bleep, bleep, bleep of the little life inside her. Her eyes drifted to the ceiling as though some divine presence might be there for her to thank. Then the lights suddenly began blooming like giant flowers, and seemed blinding, as the walls started to float and the bed rocked back and forth like a swing. She heard music, tinkling and sweet, bleep, bleep, bleep. Someone, a long way away, began speaking in a voice that was coming from the bottom of the sea.

The nurse was saying something to Mrs A, who gently lifted the mask from Nikki's face.

'OK, let's get pushing,' the midwife said.

Nikki clutched the sides of the bed. Her knees were already raised and as she strained with all her might her lower body felt as though it was igniting, ready to explode. *Spence*, she cried inside. *Spence, Spence, Spence.* She wouldn't shout it out loud, because someone might tell him and she didn't want him to feel bad for not being there. But then she was screaming and hardly knew what she was saying as white-hot pain sliced through her like molten glass.

It seemed an eternity before the midwife finally said, 'Good girl. I can see the head.'

Nikki grabbed the mask from Mrs A, took several giant gulps and began pushing again.

Kristin was standing next to the midwife, transfixed, and horrified.

Nikki wanted her to go. She shouldn't be here. No one should. She clenched her teeth and her fists, tensed her whole body, then seethed and pushed with all her might and wanted to die, the pain was so bad.

'Not long now,' the midwife murmured. 'Almost there.'

Nikki gave a sob of laughter. Any minute now she'd be holding Zac in her arms. It was the only thought that kept her going. He was all right. His heart was beating, she could hear the blips, steady and strong. She tried to see the monitor, but David was in the way.

Mrs A was still dabbing her face and neck.

With an almighty growl she pushed and strained with every ounce of energy she possessed. She could feel the mass of the baby moving down and down, splitting her open and seeming to drag her with him.

'One more and he should be with us,' the midwife chirped encouragingly.

Nikki braced herself, sucked in more gas and air, then more. She sensed rather than saw David leaving. Kristin's hands were clasped to her mouth, her face as white as the gown she'd been given to wear. Nikki pushed and seethed and yelled, as though the noise might snag the pain and carry it off into a place of senselessness and silence.

'Here he is,' the midwife laughed. 'The head's coming through.'

'Oh my God!' Kristin gasped.

Nikki clasped the mask again, took a mammoth inhalation and was starting to push when Spence burst through the door, harried, dripping wet and panting for breath.

Nikki laughed and sobbed and growled furiously as a new energy heaved itself behind the final push, and a moment later Zac came boldly into the world where his daddy was waiting to catch him.

Nikki wasn't sure where the others had gone now. All that mattered was the tiny bundle Spence was holding, his hands seeming so large around the tender little limbs.

After delivering him on to Nikki's chest, the midwife had allowed several minutes of contact before gently lifting Zac up for Spence to hold while she cut the cord and dabbed him clean. He was still red and mottled and seemed to have too much skin for his tiny sparrow bones, but he was whole and healthy and his hair was an inky-black fuzz, while his eyes, blinking and squinting against the bright lights, were a deep night blue.

He was as perfect as perfect could get.

As the midwife tucked a soft white blanket around him, Spence looked on in awe, still hardly able to grasp the fact that he'd made it in time. He was wearing one of the hospital gowns now, and his damp hair was tousled and spiked from the quick rub Mrs A had given it with a towel. His eyes were wet with tears.

'He's amazing,' he murmured, unable to stop looking at the baby. 'Hello,' he whispered, over and over. 'You're Zac and I'm your daddy.'

Nikki's heart was expanding with so much love that she couldn't get any words past it.

With a happy chuckle, the midwife started to boss them around again, reminding them that the placenta still needed to be delivered, so could Spence please stand aside with his son while she brought things to a close.

Nikki almost wept for joy as she saw Spence beam with pride. *His son.*

Twenty minutes later the midwife had gone, saying she'd be back in a while to check the baby was feeding, and Nikki and Spence were laughing with delight as Zac's little mouth opened like a fish trying to take the bait. After a couple of failed attempts they gave a soft cheer of astonishment and triumph when he finally clamped on.

As he began to suckle, the sensation was like nothing Nikki had ever experienced before, as was the happiness and feeling of being so much more than the person she'd been less than an hour ago. She wasn't just Nikki any more. She was a mother, and if she'd thought she loved Zac before he was born, it was nothing to the emotions that were overcoming her now.

'I can't believe he's here at last,' she whispered, gazing at him rapturously.

'Me neither,' Spence said shakily.

Their heads were touching as they watched him feed, their eyes absorbing his every slurp as hungrily as he was taking the colostrum.

'I'm so glad you made it,' Nikki whispered. 'Talk about great timing.'

'Don't,' he said, his eyes closing as he shuddered at the thought of how close it had been, 'another five minutes and I'd have missed it, and even if you'd forgiven me, which I doubt, I know I'd never have forgiven myself.'

She smiled and brushed her fingers over his unshaven cheek. 'So what's happening about the commercial?' she asked. It was almost five in the morning, he'd never get back to London in time to start shooting now.

His eyes were still fixed on the baby. 'Drake's taking it over,' he said, touching a large knuckle to Zac's spotty little face.

'No way! So what happened?'

He gave a smile of disbelief as he shook his head, clearly still blown away by it all. 'It was after your last call,' he said, 'the one around midnight? That's when I did what I should have done right at the start. I rang Drake to tell him you were in labour and he didn't even give me a chance to ask. He just laughed and said something about having warned you things wouldn't go to plan, then he told me to bring my notes and everything to his place, and to get myself down here. It's just lucky that his movie's not shooting again till next week, but he said even if he hadn't been able to do it, he'd have found someone who could.'

Though Nikki's eyes were shining, exhaustion was starting to creep through her bones in a way she couldn't fight off. She could feel twinges in her lower body, but they were like feathers in comparison to the claws she'd suffered for the past nine hours. She looked down at Zac as he let go of the nipple, and breathed a gentle sigh as he snuffled and seemed to settle into sleep.

'So how did you get here?' she mumbled, not realising tiredness was slurring her words.

Brushing a hand over her hair, he said, 'I was too late for the last train, so I hitched and got a lift in a Tesco truck.'

Hearing the words from the end of a long tunnel, she said, 'We'll do all our shopping there from now on. Did Danny come with you?'

'He's in Manchester, but I called to let him know you'd

gone into labour. He's coming straight here in the morning. Well, in a couple of hours, I guess.'

'Mm,' she murmured, no longer able to keep her eyes open.

Putting an arm under hers to help support the baby, he gently eased the little bundle free, then swinging his legs up on to the bed, he rested Nikki's head on his shoulder and held them both as they slept.

When the midwife returned a few minutes later, mother, father and baby were deep in dreamland, and since David had managed to go home to fetch the camera he'd forgotten earlier in the rush, she allowed him to tiptoe in to capture the touching little scene of a brand-new family in their first precious hour of existence.

By the middle of the afternoon Nikki and Zac had been moved on to a ward where half a dozen other new mothers were either sleeping or feeding or limping cautiously to the loo, usually helped by a nurse or a husband or an excited relative.

The space around Nikki's bed was already filling up with cards and presents, including a large wicker hamper from Drake Murray and his wife filled with everything from booties, to bottles, to fluffy toys and Babygros, to a magnum of Moët & Chandon. The guys from the Factory had had a whip-round to send an enormous bouquet of flowers, which Kristin and David had taken home with them.

Danny had swept in just after ten this morning, gushing with happiness and congratulations and demanding a blow-by-blow account of the birth. Once he'd finished fanning himself down and making Nikki laugh so hard that the rest of the ward started joining in without knowing why, he'd minced and swaggered about the bed, using up his entire memory card taking shots of little Zac blinking, sleeping, feeding, screwing up his face, and punching his tiny hands in the air. When it was time for the nappy change, however, he'd threatened to faint and passed the camera to Spence.

Though she was still tired and sore, Nikki managed to stay awake through the ebb and flow of visitors that came and went all day, as their mates from the Factory dropped in to welcome Zac into the world, and seemed to adore him on sight. He fed and burped, threw up and pooed and even, to her and Spence's great delight, managed a little fart after his tea.

She'd managed to take a shower earlier, while Spence stayed with Zac, who'd slept the entire time, snuggled into his dad's shoulder as though, Spence claimed, he already knew who he was.

'I feel so proud,' he told Nikki, when they were alone before the early evening brought more visitors. 'I can't believe we made him, can you?'

'It's amazing,' she murmured, gazing at him in Spence's arms, all downy black hair and wrinkled little face. 'I always knew he'd be perfect, but I have to admit, I started to get scared towards the end.'

Keeping his eyes down, Spence said, 'Do you think we should call your parents to let them know?'

As Nikki's heart turned over, she closed her eyes to hide her feelings. Though part of her wanted more than anything to tell them, she couldn't run the risk of them spoiling this magical time for Spence. So all she said was, 'Let's leave it for now.'

Seeming happy to let the subject drop, Spence continued gazing down at Zac. 'We're so lucky,' he murmured, 'but even if he'd had something wrong with him, we'd have loved him just the same.'

'Of course we would,' she said, leaning forward to kiss Zac's velvety soft cheek. 'The paediatrician hasn't seen him yet, but the midwife says we can probably take him home tomorrow.'

When Spence's eyes came up to hers they were so full of love that tears welled in her own.

'How long can you stay?' she asked, already dreading the answer. *Please don't let him have to go back to London right away.*

'I haven't spoken to Drake yet,' he replied, 'but I'm hoping he'll cover the entire three days. If he does, I won't have to go back till the weekend.'

'To do the edit?'

He nodded. 'He's already said he wants me to do it, because he has to get ready for his own shoot next week. So there's a good chance I'll have to spend Sunday with him, at least, to look at rushes and talk about how he sees the package going together.'

It felt wrong to Nikki to be discussing other commitments when Zac was all that mattered, but she had to force herself to be practical – and brave. After all, it wasn't as if she was afraid of coping on her own, she'd just rather Spence was there. Or her mother. But she always had Mrs A, who'd be popping in and out all the time, lending as much moral and expert support as Nikki could possibly need. The community midwife would be coming as well, and David would be around all week, possibly Kristin too, and they had so many friends in the area that she was going to have all the backup she could wish for, if she needed it, which she probably wouldn't.

'Are you still going to take two weeks off at the beginning of Feb?' she asked Spence.

'Of course,' he replied with feeling. 'No way am I changing that. Actually, we'll have to start packing for the move by then, so it's a good thing I'll be around.' He looked down at Zac again, gazing at him as though he might never get enough of him. 'It's going to be so amazing once we're all in the London house,' he murmured. 'Just don't you keep us all awake at night crying,' he chided gently.

'Shall I take him now?' Nikki offered, feeling an overpowering need to fill up her arms with her son.

Spence gave her a pained look. 'Two more minutes?' he asked plaintively.

Loving that he felt so possessive too, she repressed her own urges and glanced up as some visitors approached one of the opposite beds, all coos and aaahs and arms loaded with gifts.

'What are you going to do this evening?' she asked, as Spence pressed yet another kiss to Zac's forehead.

He grinned. 'Provided I don't have to go back to London, we'll be wetting the baby's head,' he reminded her.

She laughed and rolled her eyes. 'Is Danny staying?'

'Yep. He'll be back to see you with Kris and David around

six, he said, then we're meeting everyone at the Factory around eight.'

Her eyes were never far from Zac. Did she wish she could join in the celebration tonight? Be amongst her friends, throwing back the booze and kicking up her heels? No, not a bit. She was too tired, for one thing, breastfeeding for another, and all she really wanted was to go on getting to know her son.

Her son.

She was a mother.

I'm a mother!

It was so hard to take in: the most exhilarating and yet sobering feeling she'd ever had in her life.

'He's awake,' Spence announced as Zac's eyes started to open. 'I think he's looking at me. Hello, my boy. How are you?' he murmured. 'Did you have a nice sleep?'

Zac's tiny mouth pursed and smacked. Then his eyes screwed up tightly and he let out a wail.

Spence looked worried. 'Do you think he's hungry?' he asked.

'He could be,' Nikki replied. 'Shall we find out?'

Spence handed him over, so gingerly he might have been made of glass.

As Nikki put him to her breast a nurse came over and gave a nod of approval at the way Zac latched on to the nipple straight away.

'He's a clever boy,' she told them. 'Not everyone can do that as young as you,' she informed Zac. Then, after checking Nikki's chart, 'Seven pounds eleven ounces. A good weight. And a nice meconium nappy – sticky greenish-black,' she explained in real language. 'He's doing very well. You understand he'll probably lose a few ounces before he starts gaining again?'

Nikki nodded. 'A good friend of ours is a health visitor. She's explained most things.'

'Excellent. Are you going home tomorrow?'

'I hope so. The paediatrician's seeing him around ten, and if everything's OK we should be able to leave just after.'

The nurse smiled brightly. 'I'll leave you to it then,' she said. 'Call if you need anything.'

As she walked away, Spence said, 'I have to be here to take you home. I can't go back to London yet.'

'You might not have to,' Nikki reminded him.

'I'll rent a car,' he decided.

'We can get a taxi.'

'Yeah, that's probably best.'

'Or Mrs A might . . . What?' she said as he started shaking his head.

'Everyone can be at the house when we get there, if they like, but I think it should be just the three of us when we leave here.'

Smiling, she tilted her mouth up for a kiss. 'How are we going to get all the presents home?' she asked after he'd touched his mouth lovingly to hers.

He looked stymied, then the question was forgotten as Zac lost the nipple and started to fret.

Moving him over to the other breast, Nikki murmured to him softly while Spence looked on, so entranced by the amazing vision of his girlfriend and son engaged in something that was so natural, and yet so magical, that his eyes filled with tears again.

'You're such a softie,' Nikki teased when she noticed.

'It chokes me up just to look at you both,' he confessed. 'I never guessed it was going to make me feel like this. I mean, I always wanted him, but now he's here . . . Seeing you together . . . It's the most beautiful thing in the world.'

Swallowing a lump in her own throat, Nikki looked down at Zac again, watching him suckle and running a finger over his fluffy dark hair. 'I think he's going to be like you,' she said, wanting to bring Spence closer into the moment.

Sitting beside her and putting a hand over hers on Zac's head, his voice turned husky with emotion as he said, 'You've given me something I've never had before, Nik, something I was always afraid to want because it meant too much and if it didn't happen . . .' He swallowed hard. 'I always used to dream about being part of a family, to have someone to love and who'd love me back.' He lost it for a moment, then said, 'We're going to give this little fella everything I never had. There won't be any gangs, or drugs, in his life, no mum and dad going AWOL, or aunts who only just care then up and die anyway. We're going to make him feel safe in a way I never did when I was growing up . . . He's going to know we're always there for him, no matter what. We won't let him down, *ever*.' His voice was a soft growl at the end, fraying with feeling. 'I swear, Nik, I'm going to do everything I can to be the best dad in the world. I'll never let anyone hurt him or you, because you mean more to me than anything else ever has or ever will.'

He lifted his head to gaze into her soft blue eyes.

'Thank you for my son,' he whispered. 'And thank you for loving me. I'm always going to love you too, and I know this already, that nothing, not even an Oscar, could ever make me happier than I am now.'

Later that evening, after helping Nikki give Zac his first bath and being peed on for his efforts, Spence left them to sleep while he took off to the Factory, where their mates were already half-cut with the celebration. As soon as he walked in everyone began cheering and singing 'For He's a Jolly Good Fellow' and then a couple of bawdy ditties, not at all suitable for the occasion, while four-pint jugs of beer were passed over the counter to keep the glasses full. David had spent the entire afternoon downloading and printing over a hundred photographs, including a still image from the footage he'd shot of Spence, Nikki and Zac fast asleep in the delivery room.

Having spoken to Drake a couple of hours ago Spence was in a position to really let rip now, since he didn't have to go back to London till Sunday. However, no way was he going to allow himself to be cracking apart with a hangover when he went to collect his son tomorrow, so he was determined to keep a lid on his intake by staying off the vodka chasers and going easy on the beer.

In no time at all the place was throbbing with music and celebration. Even people he didn't know were coming up to congratulate him, and stealing a look at David's photos to tell Spence what a gorgeous son and girlfriend he had.

'I know, I know,' he shouted back merrily. 'They're the beauties, I'm the beast and you know what happened to him in the end.'

'What was that?' Kristin cried in his ear.

He turned to her in confusion. 'What was what?' he asked.

'What happened to the beast?'

Astonished, he said, 'You've got to have seen the film.'

'Sure. So the beast turns into a really fit guy and marries his princess, but that can't happen.'

'Why?'

She grinned. 'Because you're already a really fit guy, and Nikki's no princess.'

Wanting to move away, he said, 'You're taking it too literally. It was just a joke.'

'I know. Anyway,' she went on, grabbing his arm, 'I wanted to say I'm sorry for nearly screwing it up for you and Nikki over Christmas. It was just, I thought, you know . . .'

'It's cool,' he told her, not knowing, or caring, what she thought. They'd had one kiss, for God's sake. If she'd read any more into it, he was sorry, but she'd have to get over it. 'Where's David?' he said, searching the crowd. 'Is he shooting any of this?'

Going up on tiptoe to shout in his ear, she said, 'I think you're trying to run away from me.'

He looked down at her. 'Yep, that's right,' he agreed, and turning round he began looking for David again, until spotting Danny coming back in from outside he shouted, 'Dan! *Danny!* Over here.' He pushed towards him, while thanking everyone for their offers of drinks and good wishes, and finally grabbed Danny's arm to steer him into the 'quiet area' at the back of the room, where an old couple were tucking into a delicious-looking Turkish stew.

'I've been thinking,' Spence said, keeping his voice down, 'I reckon I ought to tell Nikki's parents the baby's arrived. What do you say?'

Danny's eyebrows shot up in surprise.

'I know she doesn't want to give them the chance to ignore her,' Spence went on, 'but I thought, if I ring and they don't want to know, I don't have to tell her about it, so she won't be any the wiser.'

Danny regarded him dubiously. 'What happens if they do want to know?' he asked.

Spence shrugged. 'Zac's their grandson. If they want to see him no one's going to stop them. Anyway, it would be good for him to have grandparents. You know, like a proper family.'

Danny gave it some more thought, apparently not convinced it was a good idea, but in the end he said, 'All right, why not? I mean, the worst they can do is hang up, and if they do, well it's their loss.'

Spence was already taking out his phone. 'Precisely,' he said. 'I'll do it now, before I go back in there, but I need their number. Do you have it?'

Danny fished out his own phone. 'I used to,' he replied, starting to scroll through. 'Yep, here it is . . .'

Moments later the connection was made, but as Spence heard the electronic voice at the other end he rang off. 'Let me check that number,' he said, glancing at Danny's mobile.

Danny read it out.

Spence shrugged, and tried again.

'What?' Danny prompted, as Spence started to frown.

'You try,' Spence said.

Clearly perplexed, Danny clicked on the number and put the phone to his ear. A beat later an automated voice came down the line telling him that the number he'd dialled was no longer in service. 'They must have changed it,' he said.

'Mm,' Spence replied. 'If they have I don't know how else we can get hold of them, do you?'

Danny shook his head. 'Unless we send a card. Or we could check Nikki's mobile to see if she has a different number.'

Spence looked at him. 'Let's sleep on it,' he said, 'because I don't know about you, but I'm suddenly not having a great feeling about this.'

Chapter Nine

Over the next few days, in spite of still being sore and almost constantly tired, Nikki remained in a bubble of happiness like she'd never known before. Bringing Zac home was yet another magical moment amongst so many, with everyone there, waiting to greet them, big welcome banners strung across the front of the house, cameras to record it all, and the heating turned up high inside so the newcomer wouldn't catch cold. Mrs A had prepared a special banquet with all mild flavours so as not to upset Zac's tummy, and Danny had helped David to assemble various toys, a playpen that wouldn't be required for at least four months so had to be taken down again, and the beautiful wooden crib that Spence and Nikki had chosen together, which Kristin had draped with copious frills of blue and white lace.

The first weekend was exhilarating in every way, but exhausting too, mainly thanks to the unpredictable surges of emotion that kept creeping up on her like mischief at its worst. However, with everyone around to support her, her bouts of anxiety and helplessness didn't last long, nor did the tears, or feelings of being completely overwhelmed. In her rational moments she understood, because all she'd read on the subject had told her, that the sudden changes in her hormones following the birth were causing the problems, and that eventually they would subside. Besides, in her heart of hearts, she knew she could do this. She wasn't afraid. She was going to make every possible effort to be a great mother, because nothing mattered more than Zac, and she was so happy being with him that apart from the diaries she was creating for him, she didn't feel remotely inclined to do any other writing.

'Don't rush it,' Drake told her when he called to congratulate her. 'The madness of our economic situation isn't going away any time soon, so the modern *Merchant* can wait, and I can't believe we're even having this conversation when the little chap's barely a week old.'

Nikki laughed. She'd only mentioned her script because she thought Drake would expect her to, and being let off the hook so easily was another boost to her joy.

'I wish we'd thought of keeping diaries for our kids when they were young,' Drake continued. 'Or that my parents had done it for me. Now they're dead there's no one to ask what I was like when I was Zac's age, or how they felt about having me. Why aren't we interested in these things until it's too late?'

Rising to the question, Nikki said, 'You know, that's exactly what I thought when my gran died. We didn't see her that often, but I always loved it when we did. There's so much I wish I'd asked her. I never had the courage when my parents were around, because they were always telling me to stop bothering her, but I always felt she knew a mountain of things that she was dying to tell me. She even said as much to me once.'

'Really?' Drake prompted, sounding amused. 'Lots of skeletons and black sheep, do you think?'

Nikki laughed. 'I don't know, but I'd love there to be, because they have to be more interesting than the sterile anecdotes my parents conjure up on request.'

Chuckling, Drake said, 'Then I hope for your sake that your family is rife with scandalous secrets, and even if it isn't, pretend that it is, because we none of us wish to be dull, or lacking in history. And besides, there's only so much breastfeeding and nappy-changing a chap can take when reading back on his life.'

In spite of recalling Spence's skeleton, Nikki bubbled with laughter, and felt Drake's enthusiasm continuing to buoy her right through to when the dreaded time came for everyone, apart from David, to return to London. She'd been putting off thinking about it, certain that the place was going to seem horribly empty without them, but amazingly it didn't. In fact, it astonished her to discover just how much one tiny little person could fill up a house, not to mention time and thought and capacity to love. The wonderful baby scent of him was everywhere, drifting like a charm through every room, lightening its ambience and making their home a really special place to be. When she took him out people she'd never met before all wanted to take a peek at him, and thrilled her no end when they said how lovely he was. He soon became so popular around the neighbourhood that virtually all the tradesmen and their regulars knew his name; he even acquired his own parking space next to the big red sofas in the Factory, where she took him most afternoons for a cup of tea and to mingle with his new friends, young and old.

Though his mop of inky-black hair didn't last, a fair, downy fluff began to emerge over his scalp, and because he was feeding so well he was starting to fill out his wrinkly skin like a fat little sausage. She often longed for her parents to see him, and felt devastated for them that they were missing out on their only grandchild's first precious weeks. But then she'd remind herself of how set against her having the baby they'd been, and even if they'd changed their minds, well, she was sorry, but they only had themselves to blame that they weren't being included now. They should never have gone digging around in Spence's past the way they had. If they hadn't, she wouldn't have trashed the only email she'd received from them since the day she last saw them, and she'd have let Spence call them when he'd suggested it.

However, she couldn't allow herself to dwell on this, when all that really mattered was Zac, who hadn't taken long to develop a fine pair of lungs that made sure he was heard from one end of North Street to the other. The odd thing was, no one ever seemed to mind about the noise he made, or if they did, they never let on. He wasn't much of a crier, though, and on the whole he slept quite well, though there was the odd night when he wouldn't settle, and the days that followed were testing, due to tiredness and worry that she was doing something wrong.

'All that's going on here is a spot of colic,' Mrs A assured her, during one of her regular visits, 'so try to watch your diet, and avoid the foods that seem to upset him. Now, let's see how his weight's coming along, shall we?' and taking out her baby scales she began to set them up on the floor. 'Do you have your Health Record so we can fill in his chart?'

'Of course,' Nikki replied. 'I never go anywhere without it,' and delving into the nappy bag she produced the flimsy red booklet that documented every single aspect of his progress from head circumference, to length, to every tiny gram he might lose or gain.

After popping a naked and vaguely curious-seeming Zac in the weighing tray, Mrs A broke into a smile. 'Marvellous,' she stated, lifting him up, then she gave a cry of laughter as a fountain of pee curved up as if shot from a water pistol, and almost caught her in the face. 'You rascal,' she told him as Nikki quickly dabbed him down. 'Something tells me you're developing a very wicked sense of humour.'

'Don't worry, we've all been in the firing line,' Nikki laughed. 'It's turning into a bit of a party trick.'

Chuckling at the very idea, Mrs A continued her check-up, until declaring his development to be very satisfactory indeed, she held him up and gave him a playful little jiggle. 'You're a star,' she told him, 'and such a handsome fellow too.'

With his hands bunched in front of his face Zac kicked his legs and gave a funny little yelp.

Glowing, Nikki said, 'I did as you said, and bathed his eyes in cooled boiled water, and the stickiness seems to have gone.'

Mrs A nodded, and after testing the soft spot on the top of his head, and making sure his mouth was clean and pink and moist, she handed him back to Nikki to dress. 'And how are you?' she asked.

Nikki laid Zac down on his changing mat to start rubbing olive oil into his dry skin. 'Actually, I'm great as long as I don't read too many of the books they give you,' she replied. 'There's so much that can go wrong with a baby, it terrifies the life out of me.'

'Like what?' Mrs A probed.

'Well, you know, everything from whether his poo's the right colour, to why he's throwing up, to not using baby oil because of the perfume, right through to possible signs of meningitis or whether or not I'm lying him down properly, in case he suffers a cot death. Honest to God, I keep waking up in the night thinking he's not breathing . . .'

Mrs A put a hand on hers. 'This will pass,' she told her gently. 'The more you get to know him, the more confident you will feel. Having said that, you're doing marvellously already. In fact, I'm very proud of you.'

Nikki's frown was lost in a beam.

'Babies aren't as fragile as you think,' Mrs A continued, 'they simply need you to be vigilant and,' she added with a wink, 'to eat the right foods.'

Nikki pulled a face. 'So no more of your curries for a while?'

Mrs A laughed. 'I'm afraid not, but there are plenty of other dishes you'll both enjoy, so I'll bring some over at the weekend. Now, I must be on my way. Love you as I do, Zac James, there are other babies that require my attention, and not all of them are as robust as you.'

After she'd gone Nikki gazed down at Zac on his changing mat and started to laugh at the way he looked up at her. 'I'm your mummy,' she whispered, still getting used to the words and the thrill they gave her. Lowering her head she pressed a kiss to his fat little cheek, then winced as he grabbed her hair. She'd learned fairly quickly that though babies could grip, they didn't know how to let go, so the next couple of minutes were spent extricating herself as painlessly as possible before pulling the plucked strands out of his fists.

Then, after Velcroing him up in a Huggy, a weeny white vest and a Desert Storm Babygro, she buttoned him into the cutest little cardigan and combat boots, tugged a dark green bobble hat over his head, enveloped his hands in furry mittens, then settled him down in the Maclaren buggy while she ran upstairs to tug on her own boots. This was a much easier exercise now she wasn't carrying him any longer, however her weight remained an issue, which Kristin, 'as one of her closest friends', had very kindly pointed out last weekend.

'I'm only mentioning it,' Kristin had said, 'because everyone knows how important it is for a woman to get back in shape after she's had a baby, or she'll be in danger of losing her man.'

It was with those words ringing in her ears that, on Monday, Nikki had started avoiding the Clark's pie shop, even crossing the road rather than pass it, since the smell was irresistible, and had also signed up for yoga and stretch at the local church hall. Today was her second class, her first having been a bit of a disaster thanks to her leggings ripping virtually the entire length of the crotch when she tried to assume some impossible position. She'd sewn them up now, double stitch, and was wearing a pair of black tights underneath as extra protection for her modesty.

She and Zac arrived in plenty of time, and Mrs Gillam, who ran the crèche, which was in a roped-off corner of the hall, seemed delighted to see her youngest charge again. Since he was fast asleep by now, Nikki parked his buggy just outside the pen in order to give the older children plenty of room to play, then went off to bag herself one of the well-used exercise mats a local health club had donated to a jumble sale, which Maggie, who ran the class, had quickly scooped up.

By the three o'clock start-time half a dozen women had shown up, all with toddlers who were banging noisily about the crèche, while Maggie collected the £2 entry fees before putting on some soothing music to start the limber-up.

With no embarrassing rips to bring things to an hilarious halt this time, the next hour passed in a dreamy kind of blur as Maggie took them through the routine she'd devised to improve posture, circulation, muscle control and relaxation. When it was over, Nikki was feeling rather pleased with herself for how well she'd done. Then she turned towards the crèche, and after a beat of confusion, her insides turned to ice. A stranger was standing next to Zac's buggy, cradling him in her arms and kissing his cheek.

Trying not to make herself look foolish by panicking, Nikki all but ran across the hall. As she approached the woman her expression must have conveyed her horror, because the woman immediately handed Zac over, and after mumbling an apology she fled.

Nikki's heart was thudding so hard as she held Zac to her

that she was barely aware of Martina, a dark, curly-haired girl who lived over the ironmongers on North Street, coming up beside her.

'You know who that was,' Martina said, while hoisting her two-year-old on to one hip. 'It was Terri Walker.'

Nikki's face was flushed as she turned to look at her.

'Mrs Gillam shouldn't leave the kids on their own,' Martina remarked, 'even if we are in the same room.'

'Who's Terri Walker?' Nikki wanted to know.

Martina's chubby features couldn't disguise her love of gossip. 'She lives on Luckwell Road,' she replied. 'Poor thing's desperate to have a baby, but she was just about to start her fertility treatment when her husband upped and left. And do you know why? Because he'd knocked up some eighteen-year-old tart from Hartcliffe, the bastard.'

Nikki's heart twisted, though whether with pity or unease, she couldn't be quite sure. Maybe it was both. 'Has she done it before?' she asked. 'I mean, come in here and picked up a baby?'

Martina shrugged. 'Not that I know of, but this is only my fourth time. Everyone says she's really cut up by what's happened, though. She told one of my friends that if she could afford it, she'd have a kid on her own, but apparently she's having to put her house on the market to pay off that cheating scum she's married to. Life just isn't fair for some people, is it?'

'No,' Nikki murmured, 'no, it isn't.'

After tucking a grizzling Zac back into his buggy, she unhooked her coat and scarf, wrapped up tightly to brave the biting wind outside, and hurried home.

By the time she spoke to Spence that evening she'd more or less recovered from the shock of finding Terri Walker holding Zac, but she still couldn't stop thinking about her. 'It must be so hard for her,' she said when she told him what had happened, 'seeing other women producing babies with seemingly no effort at all, while her chances of having one walked out of the door with her husband.'

'Tragic,' he agreed, 'but it still doesn't mean that she can go round plucking babies out of prams to give them a cuddle without asking permission.'

'I know, but when I think about her now . . . She seemed so lonely, as well as sad. Maybe she doesn't have many friends . . .'

'Nik, I can sense where you're going with this,' he interrupted, 'but you can't solve her problems. Apart from anything else, you're not going to be there much longer, so think how hard it would be on her if you got to know her, then left. She could end up feeling even more bereft than she does already.'

In spite of knowing he was right, after ringing off Nikki still couldn't stop thinking about Terri Walker, and even began to feel guilty for how blessed her own life seemed in comparison. She had a perfect baby, a partner who adored them both, friends who were as supportive as other people's parents, and a future that was looking as bright as Terri's seemed bleak. It just didn't seem fair that she should have so much, while others were made to suffer through no fault of their own.

It was funny, she reflected a couple of days after the incident, how she'd never noticed Terri around the neighbourhood before, but now virtually every time she went up to North Street she spotted the royal blue coat and tight blonde ponytail either coming out of Wherlocks, the butchers, or browsing in the window of The Real Olive Co, or drawing cash from HSBC on the corner of Luckwell Road. She didn't show up at the church hall again on Wednesday, but Nikki spotted her the next day waiting for a bus outside the chemist. Though she smiled as she passed, Terri Walker seemed to look straight through her, apparently miles away. Had she responded, Nikki might have asked her if she'd like to have coffee sometime, but Terri was clearly in a world of her own, trapped, no doubt, in a place that was full of the kind of sadness and loneliness Nikki had never experienced.

'Nik, listen to me, you've got to stop trying to save the world,' Spence told her when he came home that weekend and Nikki brought the subject up again. 'I know it's horrible that she doesn't seem to have any friends, and life's dealt her a really bad hand, but there's nothing *you* can do to change that. Like I said before, if anything it'll make it worse for her if you let her get to know Zac, then take him away. She needs a child of her own, not one that belongs to someone else.'

Before Nikki could respond, Kristin said, 'Personally, I wouldn't trust her an inch. You let her in this house, or into your life, and the next thing you know she'll be running off with him, and we might never see him again and we definitely don't want that, do we?' she said to Zac, whom she was holding up so he could do some air-running on her knees. 'Oh no, we don't, because you're the best boy in the whole wide world and we'll never let anything bad happen to you, oh no we won't.'

Since Kristin was actually voicing Nikki's worst fear, Nikki didn't try to defend herself, or Terri, she simply turned to Danny as he said, 'For what it's worth, I'm with Kristin. It really sucks what's happened to this woman, but you don't know her, Nik, so you've got no idea how damaged, or you know, wacko, she might be.'

'It's OK, I hear you all,' Nikki told them, 'and I'm not arguing. I just feel really sorry for her, that's all. Anyway, it's time for his lordship's lunch, so if you're all going up to the Factory for yours, we'll join you when he's finished.'

'I'll stay with you,' Spence said, collecting the baby from Kristin and laughing as a trail of drool followed in his wake.

Doubting she'd ever get tired of seeing Zac in his daddy's arms, Nikki took him and giggled delightedly as Spence propped her feet up on the pouffe he'd bought specially for when she was feeding. Zac was looking really cute today in a navy blue Babygro with red teddy-bear buttons, yet another of the many gifts Spence had come home with these past two weekends – and now he was here for a whole two weeks!

As she settled Zac down and the others began pulling on scarves and coats to face the bitter wind, Spence said, 'I just want to have a quick word with Dan before he goes. Will you be OK?'

Raising her eyebrows, she said, 'I think so. You can bring me some baby wipes from the bathroom when you come back, though. There's a new packet on top of the cabinet.'

Saluting obedience, he went out to the hall, and grabbing

Danny's arm before he could leave, he said to the others, 'I need to pay my rent or he won't be able to buy the drinks,' and ignoring Danny's startled expression he steered him into the kitchen and closed the door behind them.

'No calls or messages before you left this morning?' Spence asked.

Understanding immediately, Danny said, 'No, nothing.'

Spence looked baffled. 'So the number at her parents' house is out of service, and the mobile number I got from Nikki's phone isn't working either. Or it is, and her father's just ignoring my message.'

'I take it the email didn't work either?' Danny asked.

Spence shook his head. 'And the girl who answered the phone at his office said she couldn't tell me when he'd be back.'

'Mm, curiouser and curiouser,' Danny muttered. 'I've heard of missing children before, but never missing parents. Did you find a mobile number for her mother?'

Spence shook his head. 'I might try to get over to Bath during the next couple of weeks, now I've got some time off. Do you have the address?'

'Sure, and it's dead easy to find. Great Pulteney Street's an extension of the bridge, if you know where that is. It's in one of those fantastic Georgian terraces that you see all over Bath. I'll check the number and text it to you so you'll have it in your phone. Obviously they haven't been in touch with Nikki?'

'If they had she'd have said something, so the answer has to be no. The problem is, how to get over there without telling her where I'm going. Still, I'll work that out when the time comes.'

'Tell you what, why don't I go on my way back to London tomorrow?' Danny offered. 'I can always jump off the train at Bath, pay them a quick visit, and get back on the next one. They run every half-hour.'

'That would be great,' Spence declared, slapping him on the shoulder. 'Just don't let Nikki know yet, because if they have taken off without telling her . . .' He shook his head, at a loss as to why they would have done that. 'Let's find out first if that is what's happened,' he said. 'If it is, well, I guess we take it from there.'

The following afternoon, true to his word, Danny jumped off the train at Bath Spa to make the fifteen-minute walk to Nikki's parents' house. Were it anyone but Nikki, then no way would he be doing this, because it was absolutely chucking it down, but he agreed with Spence, this mystery with her parents ought to be cleared up asap. Weird to think that they might have done a bunk, it definitely didn't fit with what he knew of them, but who could say how far they might go to try and punish her for not being a dutiful daughter.

As he hurried along Manvers Street, past the police station, he drew his hood string more tightly round his face in an effort to keep out the sleeting rain. Lucky he only had one small rucksack to carry, because he definitely wouldn't have fancied trying to lug anything unwieldy or heavy through this downpour. Nor would he have much welcomed the indignity of fighting with an umbrella, like one poor woman he passed who could have been mistaken for a budding Mary Poppins with a particularly lively form of transport.

Swerving against the wall to avoid being drowned by a Bright Orange Bus, he gave the driver the evil eye and found it particularly ironic to notice that the vehicle might have transported him to his own parents' house, up by the university, had it been in service. Actually, if he had had more time, he might have popped in for a quick cup of tea, but he didn't so he wouldn't. It was best not even to call to let them know he was in town, or they'd undoubtedly have tried to press him into coming over, particularly as he hadn't seen them since they came back from Oz. His dad would probably even have got the car out to come and fetch him, bless. This detour wasn't about them, though, or him, it was about Nikki, who meant more to him than his own sister and he didn't mind admitting it.

As he approached the bridge where the weir was gushing like Victoria Falls down below, he was reflecting on how different Nikki was to her parents. By some miracle she'd managed to detach herself from their chilliness and prejudices and turn herself into one of the warmest and most open-minded people he knew. In fact, if it weren't for her he probably wouldn't have had any friends at college, goodness knows he'd never had any at school, and he wasn't entirely sure uni would have been much different. As it was, she'd spotted his loneliness and the way others picked on him, and had drawn him into her magic circle, making him feel wanted and special in a way no one else ever had. This was apart from his parents, of course, but even they were still in semi-denial over him being gay.

'Don't worry,' his mother had said, patting his hand when he'd plucked up the courage to tell them, 'I'm sure it's something you'll grow out of. Now, what would you like for tea? Cheesy crumpets or some of Dad's home-baked scones?'

And the subject had never been mentioned again.

It was Nikki's fondness for underdogs, or outcasts, or life's victims that was uppermost in Danny's mind now, as he started past the quaint little Dickensian-style shops that lined the city's world-famous bridge. He wasn't the only one she'd taken under her wing since he'd known her, there had been plenty, including Spence, it had to be said, with his difficult upbringing and dodgy police record. True, Spence had all the charm in the world and was one of the nicest and most genuine guys Danny had ever met, but he was definitely not from the drawer Mr and Mrs G would have chosen for their precious girl. In their world, there was only one drawer which was acceptable: the top one. Then there was David, 'the coloured boy' as Nikki's father had apparently once witheringly described him. Nikki had introduced David into their group as one of the dishiest and most talented cameramen around, and she wasn't wrong about that, or certainly not in Danny's view. And the instant dynamic that had struck up between David and Spence was going to take them a long way, in Danny's opinion, and it seemed others were already agreeing. Kristin could be described as a bit of a rescue too, even though David had brought her in, probably, or possibly, to convince himself that he was completely hetero. (Danny still wasn't convinced by it, but he was hardly objective, considering the way he felt about David himself, he just knew that things definitely weren't going well between David and Kristin now.) Anyway, once again Nikki had welcomed Kristin in a way no one else had bothered to, seeing through all the superiority and me, me, me to the anxious, insecure little girl inside. Danny was still having a bit of a problem finding that person himself, but he guessed she was there somewhere, if Nikki said so.

In Danny's book, no one was more sensitive and special than Nikki, but her penchant for strays did worry him at times. Take this Terri Walker, for instance. Knowing Nikki as well as he did, he was afraid she wouldn't be able to resist reaching out to the woman, and considering the nature of the woman's problems . . . Well, the thought of it definitely wasn't giving Danny a good vibe. Not that he wished Terri Walker any harm, he just couldn't see anything good coming out of getting to know her. So it was a bloody good thing, Danny decided as he huddled deeper into his coat, that Spence was going to be around for the next couple of weeks to make sure Nikki's Mother Teresa tendencies didn't get the better of her. Or maybe he'd check this Terri Walker out before he allowed Nikki to wade in where your regular mortal feared to tread.

It was as he skipped across the grand Georgian circus of Laura Place to start along the equally grand Great Pulteney Street that Danny realised, with no little dismay, that Terri Walker's tragedy was turning her into some kind of monster in his eyes, or at least someone to be wary of. It was odd how bad luck could do that to a person, he thought, as though they were in some way responsible for the malicious fate that had chosen them as its victim. Still, he guessed he couldn't help the way his mind worked, and he was definitely thinking about this far too much anyway, because, as he'd already decided, Spence was there to take care of things, and provided all went to plan it would only be two weeks after Spence returned to London to start setting up his new film, that Nikki and Zac would follow.

So, pushing aside his concerns about someone he'd never even met, he brisked up his pace as he passed along the shiny black railings and gates that fronted the towering Bath stone houses whose extreme elegance was as captivating as their romantic past. At the far end of the street the magnificent Palladian facade of the Holburne Museum of Art seemed forlorn today, and almost embarrassed by its lack of exhibition banners and city flags, like a grand dame without her baubles and wig. It had closed for refurbishment over a year ago and wasn't due to open again until 2010, which Mr and Mrs Grant were no doubt more than happy about, since it would mean fewer backpacking tourists and open-topped buses streaming up and down their exclusive boulevard.

He was passing the Carfax Hotel now, all part of the endless flat-fronted terrace, which meant he was already closer to the Grants' residence than he felt comfortable with. However, he definitely hadn't come this far to start backtracking now. He might be feeling a bit less anxious, though, if he'd worked out what the heck he was going to say when they opened the door. Actually, he probably didn't need to worry too much, because as soon as they saw him they might well just close it again. Still, at least he'd know they were there, which was what he'd come to find out. However, it wouldn't clear up the mystery of why their phone was out of service and Mr G wasn't answering his mobile or emails.

In the event, the puzzle grew even stranger, because on reaching the house he could tell right away that he wasn't going to find anyone at home. The interior shutters were closed on all floors, preventing anyone from seeing in or out, and a jaunty rap of the polished brass door knocker travelled along the hallway in a lonely echo.

Taking out his mobile, he connected to Spence. 'Can you talk?' he asked when Spence answered.

'Sure. Where are you?'

'Outside the house in the peeing rain. No one's here.'

'Are you sure?'

'As I can be. Everything's closed up and no one's answering the door.'

'Can you see in through the letter box?'

Stooping to open it, Danny wiped the rain from his eyes to peer through. 'Oh my God,' he murmured, taking in the empty hall, 'no furniture, no anything.'

'So they've moved?'

Danny stood up. 'Would they really do that without telling Nikki?' he said.

'Try next door,' Spence suggested, 'see if anyone there knows where they are.'

Obediently Danny trotted along to the next house and gave the doorbell a jaunty little press. A few minutes passed, and he pressed again. 'Doesn't look as though anyone's here either,' he told Spence.

'What about the other side?'

Turning round, Danny trotted back up the street to try the other neighbour. This time an elderly man cracked open the door to the width of a security chain. 'Who is it?' he asked.

'I'm looking for Mr and Mrs Grant who live next door,' Danny explained. 'Do you have any idea . . .? Have you seen them lately?'

'No,' the old man replied, 'I've only just returned from my daughter's, so I haven't been here for the past couple of months.'

'Oh, I see.' Danny smiled. 'Well, thanks anyway,' and turning on his heel, he took the few steps back on to the street. 'I don't know what else to do,' he said to Spence.

Spence's silence suggested he was at a loss too. 'OK,' he said in the end, 'at least we tried. I just don't think either of us should mention it to Nikki, at least not until we've had a chance to work out what's going on.'

'Agreed,' Danny responded, wondering how on earth they were going to do that.

'Actually, I know this might sound weird,' Spence said, 'but before you leave, try calling his mobile again, will you?'

Danny baulked. 'Spence, you're starting to spook me,' he warned. 'You don't seriously think he's in there, hiding, do you?'

'I don't know what I think. Just try it.'

'What am I going to do if it rings?'

'We'll work that out if it does. Hang on, I'll try the number myself, from Nikki's phone, so stay on the line.' A few minutes later Spence said, 'Can you hear anything?'

Not enjoying this one bit, Danny put his ear to the letter box. 'Nothing,' he said, profoundly relieved.

'OK. I'd better erase this from her phone in case she notices. Thanks for going. I'll talk to you later.'

After ringing off Danny took one last look up at the house, then stuffing his hands in his pockets he set off back to the station, not sure how worried he was, or even should be. One thing was for certain, he was definitely glad to be walking in this direction now.

Chapter Ten

'Yay!' Spence cheered, clicking off his mobile. 'That was the agent in London. Everything's cleared, we can move in at the beginning of March, so . . . let's start packing.'

Laughing as he swept her up in his arms, Nikki wrapped her legs around him and held him tight. It was wonderful spending all this time with him, and now to know that they wouldn't be separated again after the beginning of March was the best news ever. 'We're registering the birth today,' she reminded him. 'And we'll have to give our notice here.'

'Everything's possible and nothing's standing in our way,' he grinned. Then, gazing lovingly into her eyes, 'God, I love you. You and Zac are the best things that ever happened to me. Did I already tell you that?'

'Once or twice,' she teased, 'and it's funny, because you and Zac are the best things that have ever happened to me.'

As his mouth came to hers she felt a rush of desire burn through her.

'Do we have time?' he murmured huskily.

'Who cares,' she responded, and moments later they were writhing on the bed, so lost in the passion that was joining them that it took several loud wails from Zac to bring them back to reality.

'You are a right spoilsport,' Spence told him as he reached into the cot to lift him out. 'We have to get a schedule worked out here, my son, so your mealtimes don't keep clashing with my sex life, or we're going to start falling out.'

Zac's wailing stopped as he settled in his father's arms and began blinking up at the familiar face staring down at him.

'I don't think he's hungry,' Nikki said, as Spence brought him to the bed, 'he probably just wants a cuddle.'

'Then he shall have one,' Spence declared, lying down with him and standing him on his chest.

Zac's tiny hands waved ecstatically as Spence held him up so his rubbery little feet could kick as though he was trying to run.

'He's going to be an athlete,' Spence laughed.

'A gold-medallist,' Nikki grinned, giving Zac a finger to squeeze.

Taking it, Zac held on tight. A moment later his face began turning red, signalling an upcoming nappy change.

'I'll do it,' Spence said, aeroplaning him down for a kiss. 'I think I'm getting quite good at it now.'

Not arguing, because he was, Nikki rolled off the bed and quickly reached for her robe.

'Hey, don't do that,' Spence protested.

'What?' she asked, tying the belt.

'Try to hide yourself from me. OK, so you're still carrying some weight, but do you think that matters to me?'

Coming to kiss him, she said, 'The point is, it does to me, but I'm working on it. It'll be easier when I'm not breastfeeding any more, I'll be able to start some serious aerobics.'

'Whatever,' he murmured, sitting up and lying Zac between his knees. 'Are you going to your class today?'

'Depends what time we get back from town, but I'd like to.'

'Do you hear that?' Spence said to Zac, 'Mummy's planning to abandon us again so we can party like animals while she's gone.'

Laughing, Nikki left them to it and went off to the bathroom to make herself ready for their trip to the registry office. Another little milestone in Zac's life that her parents were going to miss, but she couldn't help that. Later, she'd write it all down in her journal, including the lunch they were due to have afterwards with David and a few other friends at Carluccio's, to celebrate the important day. Kristin should have been coming with them, but her agent had called last night to tell her she had an audition in Soho today for a part in a commercial.

'I'm doing really well, aren't I?' she'd announced, after

ringing off. Then, with a twirl of euphoria, 'Look out world, Kristin Lyle will be coming to a theatre near you soon.'

They'd all laughed, and told her to break a leg when she'd left to catch the train at seven that morning, but Nikki knew, because in a private moment last night Kristin had told her, how troubled Kristin really was inside.

'I know I'm away a lot at the moment,' she'd said tearfully, 'but I have to think of my career, don't I?'

'Of course,' Nikki soothed, 'and David understands that.'

Though it was a reasonable assurance, Kristin hadn't looked convinced. 'He's going really distant on me now,' she said. 'He doesn't even cuddle me when we go to bed.'

'I'm sure it'll be different once we're all in London,' Nikki said comfortingly, even though she wasn't at all sure it would be. However, it wasn't her place to tell Kristin what she suspected was really happening with David, because if he was struggling to come to terms with his sexuality, it wouldn't be helped by her throwing out speculations that might actually be wrong.

'I absolutely love that house, don't you?' Kristin had gushed. 'It would be the worst thing in the world if David and I broke up, because I wouldn't be able to go there then . . . Oh God, I don't even want to think about it. I mean, we're a team, all of us . . .'

'Whatever happens, we'll all still be that,' Nikki assured her gently.

'Oh my God, that sounds as though you know something I don't,' Kristin wailed. 'Has he said something to you?'

'No, not at all. I promise.'

As she recalled the conversation now, Nikki could only feel relieved that David hadn't confided in her, because she was becoming increasingly convinced that, in spite of his inner battles, he was getting ready to break off the relationship with Kristin anyway. If he did, there wasn't much doubt that Kristin would take it hard, not only because of her abandonment issues, but because of how it might impact on her future with Spence and Drake. And Nikki could hardly blame her for being worried about that; Spence's star was clearly on the rise, so anyone with any sense would want to keep their career yoked to his, if they could.

Anyway, she wasn't going to obsess over it now, because until David decided what he was going to do it wasn't actually an issue, and if he did end the relationship, well, Nikki guessed she'd do her best to make sure that Kristin wasn't entirely shut out in the cold.

'Danny just rang,' Spence said as she walked back into the bedroom to find him still lying on the bed with Zac, who was now as naked as his dad. 'He wanted to wish us luck at the registry office and to offer his name if we were stuck for a middle.'

Nikki laughed and grimaced as she picked up the dirty nappy, which was only partially stuffed in a plastic sack. After dropping it out on the landing she said, 'Actually, I've been thinking about a middle name, have you?'

Spence shook his head, while walking his fingers, spiderlike, up and down Zac's tummy. 'Can't say I have,' he replied, 'but I'm happy to go for one provided it's not Cuthbert or Keith – never did like Keith, probably because it was my old man's name, and we definitely don't want you turning out like him, do we tiger?'

Though she laughed at the happy little squawk Zac gave in reply, Nikki was watching Spence closely, wondering what was really behind the words: a knowledge of the whole truth, or simply the impoverished drunk he'd told her about? 'How well do you remember your dad?' she asked, making it sound casual, as she started to dress.

Spence glanced up in surprise. 'Not very,' he replied. 'It's hard to remember anyone who was hardly ever there. Anyway, I've never been a hundred per cent sure he was my real dad, because my aunt told me once that he was banged up about a year before I was born, and he didn't come out until after my mum had had me.' He shrugged. 'She might have got it wrong, of course, but hey, who cares? They're history, and my boy here is the future, and we're going to make it the best one a special lad like him ever had, aren't we, my son?'

Nikki went to put her arms round them both and treated them each to a kiss. He was right, what did it matter who his father was when the man he'd vaguely known had been dead for sixteen years, and even if he was the despicable individual her parents had found out about, it was plain to anyone who knew Spence that he was nothing at all like him. 'You know, I was thinking,' she said, 'if we do go for a middle name, maybe we could use my dad's, if you didn't mind. I know we're not in touch with them now, but that could change one day, and if he realises his grandson has his name . . . Well, I think he'd like it a lot and it could help to improve relations between us all.'

Spence was lying very still.

'You don't like the idea,' she said, looking worried.

Rolling over to face her and bringing Zac with him, he said, 'It's not that I don't like it, in fact I think it would be good for you to try to sort things out between you, it's just that I'm surprised you want to do something so lovely for him when he's been the way he has with you. They didn't even get in touch over Christmas, remember?'

Nikki coloured slightly. 'Actually, I had an email about a week before,' she confessed.

He frowned. 'You never mentioned it,' he said. 'What did it say?'

'I don't know, I deleted it before I read it.' She shrugged. 'I know I probably shouldn't have, but I'm still angry with them, and until I know they can accept you and Zac, I don't want to hear from them.'

'But if you didn't read the email . . .'

'I didn't need to.' She hadn't even opened it, in fact, but realising she couldn't leave it at that, or he'd find it very odd that she hadn't given them the benefit of the doubt, she said, 'I mean, I saw a couple of things it said and they were still going on about you not being right for me, and me not knowing my own mind . . . It got me all worked up again, so it's not that I'm suggesting we go to see them or anything, we can just drop them a card to let them know they're grandparents now and that the baby's middle name is Jeremy.'

Spence looked at her askance. Then, cradling Zac in one arm, he leaned over to kiss her. 'If you want Jeremy, then Jeremy it'll be,' he said. 'Personally, I think it's a poncy name, but hey, what do I know? I'm telling you this, though, if he says one word to hurt either you or my boy . . .' He stopped as Nikki put a finger over his lips.

'Don't let's get into an argument about it,' she said softly. 'We can just as easily call him Zac Daniel, which sounds a bit like a whisky, come to think of it, but if it makes you and Danny happy, I don't have a problem with that,' and taking Zac from him she started to wrap him in a lovely fresh Huggy.

Thanks to a series of phone calls, all about *Celeste,* that kept Spence on his mobile from before they left the house, through the bus journey into town and all the way to the registry office, the subject didn't come up again until they were actually in front of the registrar.

'OK, so baby's name?' the registrar asked.

Nikki looked at Spence, her expression making it clear that it was his call.

Spence winced as he hesitated. Then in a rush he said, 'Zac Jeremy,' and feeling Nikki's eyes on his as he spelled it out, he reached for her hand.

'Are you sure you're OK with that?' she asked as they walked out of the Old Council House on to Broad Street, almost colliding with two robed barristers who were hurrying past.

He grimaced. 'Well, it's a bit late now if we aren't,' he pointed out. 'I just hope your old man appreciates it when we get round to telling him, but don't let's do it today, huh?'

'So what are you going to do if she suggests going over there?' Danny asked, when Spence stole a moment later to call him. He was outside Carluccio's in Cabot Circus, freezing his whatsits off as the shopping world whizzed and swirled around him, and the others tucked into starters of hot soup and crunchy French bread inside.

'I don't think that's her plan,' Spence answered. 'She mentioned sending a card, so with any luck she'll leave it at that until we can find out where they are.'

'I keep asking myself, what are we protecting her from?' Danny responded. 'Why don't we just tell her they've upped and disappeared?'

'I'm asking myself the same thing, but I've got this feeling something's not good about this. If they are trying to detach themselves from her – well, presumably they are or they'd

178

have let her know they were taking off to wherever the hell they've gone – then I don't think she needs to be dealing with that right now. She's got enough going on with Zac and the move.'

'Precisely. She's happy, so why spoil it? Crap always comes to find you in the end anyway, so don't go looking for it. Do you think you'll be able to get over there to see if they really have done a Bobby Ewing?'

'A what?'

'I heard one of the producers say it this morning. Apparently it's something to do with some programme back in the eighties where this bloke was supposed to be dead, then turned up in the shower one morning, like the whole thing had been a dream.'

Spence looked at the phone sideways. 'I don't think they're dead,' he protested. Then, after a beat, 'Do you?'

'No. Well . . . No, of course not. I just think the whole thing's weird. So, are you going over there?'

'I can't. We're together all the time, and if I take off for an afternoon I'll have to tell her where I'm going.'

'Have you told David about it? What does he say?'

'I haven't mentioned it yet, but I was thinking of having a chat with Mrs A if I can ever get her on her own. Being a woman she might be able to suggest how we should handle telling Nikki, if we have to.'

'Good idea. Now I'm afraid I have to go. I'm in the middle of editing a piece for tonight's programme, but we'll speak later, OK? I have to ring Nik anyway to give her the window measurements she asked for – this is provided I can get access to the house, but the agent said it should be fine.'

Going back into the restaurant, Spence found Nikki discreetly feeding the baby while David and the others who'd come from the Factory enjoyed huge bowls of pasta and loudly debated the reviews of the various films showing at the cinemas around the corner. It was where they were all planning to spend the afternoon, doing a back-to-back of two movies, yet to be decided.

'Do you want to go too?' Nikki asked, as Spence slid in next to her. 'I can always take Zac to the stretch class with me.'

'No, I'll come home with you,' he answered. 'It's easier for me to lift the buggy on and off the bus, and I kind of like our guys-hanging-out-together time when you're not around.'

Nikki rolled her eyes. 'I believe you,' she said, 'but I also know you're still worried about Terri Walker.'

'Who?' he asked, feigning ignorance.

She poked him. 'Don't play games with me,' she laughed, 'I can read you like a book. I promise, nothing's going to happen to him. Mrs Gillam had only popped to the loo, and she's sworn she'll never leave the children alone again, even if she's breaking her neck.'

'That won't be all that gets broken if some stranger lays hands on my son again,' he said darkly, 'but anyway, it's not about that. I'd rather come home. I can always use the time catching up on emails if Buster here lets me – otherwise, I'm happy to be with him.'

Leaving it at that, Nikki wound some spaghetti round her fork and took a mouthful before joining in the review debate, which was about as close as she was managing to get to a new release these days.

Later, as they wheeled Zac from the bus stop, calling into Parsons for some home-baked bread on the way, Nikki spotted Terri Walker through the window of The Dinkie Sweetshop. As usual, it was the royal blue coat that caught her eye, which, not for the first time, made her think of the little girl in the red coat from *Schindler's List*. The blue wasn't especially bright, but even so, it seemed to stand out the way the little Jewish girl's coat had in the film. It was as though it was supposed to attract her attention, making her aware of Terri Walker and the misfortune she carried inside.

Today, to Nikki's surprise, Terri seemed to be with another woman who was older, stouter and more scruffily dressed. At least, they were chatting to one another, so Nikki presumed they were together. Maybe they were just customers in the same shop, discussing the children they were buying sweets for. Whatever, it made Nikki feel better to see Terri talking to someone. She didn't seem quite so lonely or insular, the way she was pointing and nodding her head and relating to someone.

Though she saw Terri most days now, either on North

Street, or somewhere close by, she still hadn't spoken to her, but they'd made eye contact once or twice and a couple of days ago, as she was passing the florist and spotted her inside, Nikki was sure Terri had given her the ghost of a smile. There was no point trying to befriend her while Spence was around, though, and she still wasn't convinced she should, but the way she kept seeing her seemed, to her, like a sign, a kind of guiding hand trying to bring them together.

She was sure, if they weren't on the verge of moving to London, she'd have gone out of her way to invite her for a coffee by now, but what was the point when they'd all be gone in a couple of weeks?

Towards the end of Spence's second week at home he and Nikki began filling boxes with the many toys Zac had been given for Christmas and at birth, which he wouldn't be able to play with for months yet. They also packed up all their summer clothes, since they definitely wouldn't be needed this side of March, and all the knick-knacks Nikki had bought to help make their new house a home.

Since it was a great time for a clear-out, Spence rented an old van with David as an additional driver, to start ferrying accumulated junk to the tip, and taped-up boxes to Mrs A's front room for storage until they were ready to leave. When the time came they would hire a much bigger van, which, hopefully, would hold everything including Spence, David and Danny, while Mrs A drove Nikki and the baby in the comfort of her car to their new abode. Kristin hadn't made up her mind who to travel with yet, but seemed to be leaning towards the car, since David wasn't being very forthcoming about inviting her to join him in the van.

'I still can't get him to talk,' she confided to Nikki one evening as Nikki bathed Zac in a large bowl on the draining board. 'He keeps saying there's nothing to talk about. It's driving me nuts, like I'm supposed not to notice that he never kisses me now, or wants to have sex. Do you think he's met someone else?' Her face was such a tragic picture of insecurity that Nikki was as gentle as she could be as she said, 'If he has, he hasn't mentioned it to me, but I have to admit, I have noticed how . . . different he's been with you lately.'

Kristin's face turned paler than ever. 'He's going to ask me not to move into the house, isn't he?' she said shakily.

Nikki hiked Zac out of the warm soapy water and cuddled him snugly into a towel. (She was getting quite good at this now, even if she did say so herself.) 'You've already put down your share of the deposit and first month's rent,' she reminded her, 'so he can't.'

'But if he doesn't want to share a room with me . . . Oh Nik, what am I going to do? Can you talk to him for me? Find out what's going on in his head.'

Nikki pulled a face. 'Kris, it's not my place . . .'

'But he'll open up to you, I know he will.'

'He's very private, and he never has before.'

'Yeah, but over something like this, I think he will.'

With a sigh Nikki said, 'OK, if the opportunity comes up I'll see what I can do. Just don't blame me if you don't get the answer you're hoping for, OK?'

Kristin crossed her heart. 'I swear I won't. I just need to know where I stand, because if we're not . . . If he doesn't want to be with me any more . . .' Her eyes flooded with tears. 'I really love him, Nik,' she choked. 'Please don't let him chuck me. *Please.*'

'I'll do my best,' Nikki promised, not knowing what else to say. 'Are you going . . . Oh! Sssh, I think that's them coming back,' she whispered as a key slid into the front door.

'You'll talk to him, won't you,' Kristin urged, as Spence and David let themselves into the hall.

'I said I'll try. What time are you leaving tomorrow?'

'My call-back for the commercial's at eleven, so I'll probably get the eight o'clock train. Do you think you can do it before that?'

Nikki blinked with alarm. 'Like when?' she protested.

There was no time to answer, because Spence was coming into the kitchen.

'Hey, look at my boy, all squeaky clean and wide awake,' he grinned, holding out his arms to take him.

'His pyjamas are warming on the radiator in our

bedroom,' Nikki told him, handing Zac and his towel over. 'And there's a fresh nappy on the chair. I'll be up as soon as I've cleared things away here. God, will I be glad to move into our new kitchen. All that space. Heaven.'

'And we know who's going to fill it, don't we?' David teased as he came to stand in the doorway. 'How are you, little man?' he cooed, taking Zac's hand and giving him a finger to squeeze. 'You're looking pretty good to me.'

Zac's head jerked back against Spence's arm as he registered his godfather. His fat little cheeks were flushed red with warmth, and his deep navy eyes were opened as wide as he could make them.

'I know,' Kristin suddenly piped up, 'why don't David and I babysit tonight? It'll give you two some time to yourselves.'

Before either Spence or Nikki could respond, David said, 'Great idea, but I'm doing a late edit at Available Light, not due to finish till midnight.' He checked his watch. 'Actually, I should be making a move.'

'Why don't I come with you?' Kristin suggested.

David glanced at her awkwardly. 'I don't think the director would like it,' he answered. 'Maybe another time.'

Kristin's injured eyes moved to Nikki, but Nikki was careful not to meet them. 'You need to get him dressed before he catches cold,' she told Spence.

'Sure,' he replied, and hoisting Zac on to his shoulder he followed David down the hall, before turning to go upstairs.

'See what I mean?' Kristin whispered brokenly as the front door closed behind David. 'He didn't even say hello to me when he came in.'

'I don't think it was deliberate,' Nikki told her.

Kristin didn't look convinced. 'Do you reckon it's a lie about Available Light? He could be going to meet someone.'

Realising how much she was tormenting herself, Nikki dried her hands and gave her a hug. 'He might be terrible at confronting issues,' she said, 'but he's not in the habit of lying.'

'I know.' Kristin's eyes came to Nikki's. 'I just wish I knew what I'd done,' she wailed.

Not really wanting to get into that, Nikki said, 'Look, I

promise I'll find some time to have a chat with him. Obviously it won't be tonight, but I'll try to do it before you come back at the weekend.'

Kristin pulled a face. 'Actually, I might not be coming back till we move,' she confessed. 'My mum's a bit down again, so I said I'd stay with her for a while, and then I think they're going to offer me this commercial. My agent said they thought I was brilliant, so if it does work out I'll have to be in London next week for costume fittings and stuff.'

'OK, then I'll give you a call as soon as I have any news.'

It was in the early hours of the morning that Spence shouted, 'Nik! *Nik!* Wake up, for God's sake. Something's wrong.'

Nikki shot from the depths of sleep straight to her feet. 'What is it?' she cried, dashing to the cot.

Spence was holding Zac. 'He can't breathe,' he panicked. 'Listen.'

Hearing the tiny rasping breaths over the pounding of her heart, Nikki grabbed Zac and started to blow into his mouth. 'He's turning blue,' she exclaimed, looking at his face.

'We have to get him to hospital,' Spence cried, and snatching up his clothes he scrambled into them while Nikki continued blowing desperately into Zac's mouth.

'What's going on?' David demanded, bursting into the room.

'It's Zac. He's not breathing right,' Spence told him, hauling on his jeans. 'Call your mother, we're taking him to the hospital.'

David dashed back to his room.

'I've got him,' Spence said, taking the baby from Nikki. 'Put something on. We have to go.'

Minutes later they were thundering down the stairs, David hot on their heels.

'Mum says we're doing the right thing,' he told them. 'She'll meet us there. I'll drive,' and snatching the van keys from the hall table he followed them out into a howling gale.

Chapter Eleven

By four in the morning Zac was still not breathing normally, so the emergency paediatrician decided to admit him to the ward.

'He has what we call bronchiolitis,' the doctor explained to Nikki and Spence, who were still so traumatised that both looked on the verge of shattering to pieces. 'It's a very common virus that affects the small airways,' he continued, 'but don't worry, he's in no danger. The IV you see contains an antibiotic, and this gizmo here,' he was pointing to the one attached to Zac's right foot, 'is a pulse oximeter. At the moment it's showing an oxygen saturation of eighty per cent, which is slightly low, so we're going to keep him in for a few days to monitor his progress. I'm sure everything will be fine,' he added, with a smile that allowed the minutest trace of warmth to trickle back into Nikki's veins.

'Do . . . Do you know what caused it?' she managed to ask.

He shook his head. 'I'm afraid not,' he answered, 'but luckily you got him here in plenty of time.'

'Is there . . . ?' Spence cleared his throat. 'Is there anything we can do to stop it happening again?'

'Not really, apart from making sure that he doesn't sleep on his front, and that there's nothing blocking his airways, like a blanket, or toy.'

'Can we stay with him?' Nikki asked. 'I'm still breastfeeding . . .' Her eyes widened with alarm. 'Oh my God, you don't think . . . Is it my fault . . . ?' She stopped as the doctor put a hand on hers.

'No,' he told her gently. 'And yes, of course you can stay with him.'

'Me too?' Spence asked.

The doctor smiled. 'Naturally, you too. A consultant will be along to see him in the morning.' He glanced at the clock. 'In a few hours,' he corrected. 'One of the nurses will bring masks and gowns for you to put on, and you'll need to adhere to all the hygiene rules.'

'Yes, yes, of course,' Nikki responded, and turning back to the cot she clasped her hands around the rails as she gazed down at Zac's tiny little face, flushed and peaceful now, with no tinges of blue at all.

Spence stepped forward and slipped an arm around her. 'Hello my boy,' he murmured. His voice was thin and shaky, hardly like him at all. 'You gave us a bit of a scare,' he told Zac, 'but the doctor says you're going to be fine.'

Nikki swallowed hard and forced herself to speak clearly and firmly as she said, 'We're going to be here for a couple of days, sweetheart, while you get well, then we'll take you home.'

David and Mrs A had left the emergency waiting room after Zac had been transferred upstairs to a ward, and were now in the hospital's main lobby where only a security guard was on duty, and an early morning bin lorry was rattling along in the darkness outside. Neither of them was ready to leave the building until they'd spoken to Nikki or Spence to find out exactly how Zac was, and if there might be any more they could do.

Not for the first time, David's velvety eyes moved over the giant Kit Williams dolphin clock that dominated a wall next to the reception desk, then drifted on towards the stairs where a colourful tapestry called *The Heartfelt Tree* was brightening up the climb. He'd filmed here once, so he knew that the felt hearts had been made by children. He also knew a little about the other artwork that was on each floor of the hospital decorating the corridors, and wards, and even the Prayer Room on level four. He wasn't as religious as his mother, but a part of him wanted to go up there now to ask a higher authority to intervene and make sure there was a happy outcome to this terrible scare.

He was still buzzing subconsciously from the surge of adrenalin that had fuelled the crazy drive here, but a deadening exhaustion was starting to creep through his veins now. He wouldn't allow himself to sleep, though. Until he knew what was going on with Zac he'd be awake and here, ready to help in any way he could.

Feeling the vibration of his mobile he quickly snatched it from his pocket in case it was Spence. His heart sank when he saw who it was, and putting the phone away again he let the call go through to messages.

'Kristin?' his mother asked.

He nodded.

'Where is she?'

'At home. I can't believe she slept through it.'

Mrs A turned to look at him. 'Aren't you going to tell her what's happening?'

After a while he said, 'I guess I should.'

Taking his phone outside where it was still dark and starting to drizzle, he listened to Kristin's messages first, all asking where everyone was. She sounded panicky and afraid, which made him feel bad for not considering how frightening it must have been to wake up and find the place empty.

'David,' she cried, when he got through to her. 'What's going on? Where are you?'

'At the children's hospital,' he replied. 'Zac couldn't breathe.'

'Oh my God. Is he all right now?'

'I think so. He's out of emergency, but I'm waiting to hear from Spence.'

'On my God, oh my God, what shall I do? I have to get the train at seven, but if you think I should come over there . . .'

'It's up to you,' he said.

'I want to come,' she told him, 'obviously I do, but I can't miss this call back. I'm in with a really good chance.'

His tone was neutral as he said, 'Then you should go for it.'

'Do you think Nik and Spence will understand?'

He wanted to say no, but didn't.

There were tears in her voice as she said, 'I can tell you think I'm being selfish, but there's nothing I can do even if I do come.'

He didn't bother to point out how important moral support could be. If she didn't get it now, then she never would.

'David,' she whispered. 'I wish you'd tell me what's wrong. I keep trying . . .'

'Kristin, this isn't about you and me,' he interrupted. 'It's about Zac. Now I'm sorry, I have to go,' and cutting off the call he went back inside to rejoin his mother.

Moments after he sat down again the lift doors opened and Spence came out looking haggard and tired, and even vaguely surprised to see them.

Their faces remained sombre as he explained what he and Nikki had been told, until eventually Mrs A started to smile.

'Thank goodness,' she sighed. 'I thought it was probably something like that. They'll take very good care of him, and I have to tell you that I have had more babies rushed to A & E for this sort of thing than I've had hot dinners.'

Though Spence's eyes were grateful, he still seemed dazed. 'What if I hadn't woken up?' he said jaggedly. 'What if we hadn't got here in time?'

Mrs A shook her head admonishingly. 'There's absolutely no point in scaring yourself with what ifs,' she told him firmly. 'They didn't happen, so I want to hear no more of them. Zac is fine. They're just keeping him under observation for a couple of days, which is perfectly normal.'

Spence looked at David, who appeared as helpless and shaken up as Spence himself was feeling.

'I'm here for you, mate,' David said, clapping him on the shoulder.

Spence nodded, and dragged a hand over his unshaven chin. 'I'd better go back up,' he said. 'Nik was feeding him when I left.'

'Ah, a very good sign,' Mrs A beamed. And after giving him a hug, 'I will be going home now, but if you need me I shall be at the end of the phone.'

'Thanks,' Spence said. Then he told David, 'You did good getting us here. I could never have driven myself.'

David hugged him too. 'I'll call Dan,' he said. 'He'll want to know what's going on.'

Much later in the day, after managing to sleep for a couple of hours, Spence and Nikki followed a nurse's orders and took themselves up to the cafeteria, where the smell of food made both their stomachs rumble, though neither of them were sure if they could eat. 'You heard Mr Pearce,' the nurse had reminded them. 'Zac's doing just fine, and there's absolutely no reason for that to change, so off you go.'

Mr Pearce was the consultant. He hadn't stayed long with Zac, because there were other, much sicker children for him to see, whose parents were waiting anxiously next to their beds. Nikki had liked him right away, because in spite of their case being less urgent, he hadn't appeared rushed or distracted, and when he'd spoken to them he'd looked directly into their eyes.

'Not all doctors do that,' she said to Spence as he pushed a sausage around his plate.

'Unless it's bad news,' he responded. 'Maybe they find it hard to look at you then.'

'In which case, we really don't have to be worried,' she pointed out. She forked up some beans and put them in her mouth. 'He was a nice man, wasn't he?' she ventured.

Spence's eyes came up to hers. 'I just hope we never have to meet him again,' he said.

She tried to smile. 'We won't,' she assured him.

A few minutes later her mobile bleeped with a text. *Will be there about 7. Thinking of you. Love you all. Dx*

'Danny's on his way,' she said, clicking off.

Spence nodded.

Putting her fork down, she leaned forward and squeezed his hand. 'I think you should go to London on Sunday, as planned,' she said. 'You don't want to let Drake down . . .'

'He'll understand.'

'I'm sure, but he was so good over the birth, and the emergency's past now. No, listen,' she interrupted, when he started to protest. 'The doctor said he'll probably be able to go home on Monday, so we won't be here for long without you, and David'll be around . . .'

'David's coming with me,' he reminded her. 'He needs to start prepping for the film too, and Drake's got other things he wants him to do.'

'OK, well Mrs A is close by, and I can manage. Honestly.'

His eyes were dark with uncertainty as he regarded her.

'Spence, we mustn't start getting this out of proportion,' she said gently. 'Yeah, it gave us a scare, but you heard what everyone's saying, he's going to be fine. They wouldn't let him go home if they didn't think so.'

In the end Spence heaved a sigh and put his cutlery down. 'You're right,' he said, pushing a hand through his already dishevelled hair. 'Now the worst is over . . . I just thought . . . If anything had . . .'

'Don't go there,' she advised softly.

'No,' he agreed. His eyes came to hers. 'Don't you keep thinking . . .'

'Of course I do, but I have to stop myself. Think about all the other babies on the ward. He's nowhere near as sick as them, so we should be celebrating now, or at least thanking God that Zac's not in the same position.'

He nodded and reached for his coffee.

'Have you contacted Drake yet to tell him what happened?' she asked, picking up her juice.

'No. I haven't been in touch with anyone.'

'Then all the more reason to carry on as normal. Go to London, start setting up the film and by the time you come home next weekend Zac and I will be there, and this will already be fading into history.'

At last he managed the shadow of a smile. 'That sounds good,' he told her.

She smiled too. 'And in two weeks,' she continued, 'we'll be coming back to London with you and moving into our wonderful new house.'

His eyes connected with hers. 'Sounds even better,' he said, and taking her hand he pressed it hard to his mouth.

When it came time for Spence to leave on Sunday, Nikki found it much harder to let him go than she'd expected. Not that she let it show, she didn't want him worrying about her, but she'd got so used to him being around these past two weeks that she was feeling really strange about being on her own again, especially after what had happened to Zac. Also, the time they'd spent here, in the hospital, had brought them even closer together, so saying goodbye took every ounce of mettle she could muster.

'I love you so much,' he murmured into her hair, before leaving.

'I love you too,' she whispered, and pulled back to gaze into his eyes.

They were on the ward, next to Zac's cot, where he was kicking and punching the air like a little boxer in the making. Danny and David were standing over him, providing a mock commentary that was making the three-year-old in the next bed laugh with delight.

'You've been amazing through all this,' Spence told her softly.

'So have you,' she said. 'I'd have gone to pieces without you.'

Not seeming too sure about that, he said, 'He has the best mother in the entire world.'

'Then he's a lucky chap, because he has the best daddy too.'

With a smile he cupped a hand round her cheek, and the way he looked so deeply into her eyes turned her heart inside out.

'Call when you get to London,' she told him.

'Of course. Are you sure you don't mind me go . . .' She put a finger over his lips.

'I'm sure,' she said. 'We need to get back to normal, and this is the first step.'

He glanced down at Zac and broke into a laugh. 'Look at you,' he said, scooping him up, 'all that fuss and you've already forgotten all about it.'

Zac burped, loudly, and waved his fists.

As everyone laughed Nikki put her arms round Spence's waist and rested her head on his chest. Was there any lovelier feeling in the world than when the three of them were together like this?

Danny was looking at his watch. 'We'll have to make a move if we don't want to miss the train,' he said with a grimace.

Spence tightened an arm round Nikki, while pressing a kiss to Zac's forehead. Then, lying the baby back in his cot, he pulled her into an enveloping embrace.

'Don't mind us,' Danny said after a minute or two.

Nikki bubbled with laughter.

'Are you two still here?' Spence joked.

David came to pull Nikki into a hug. 'Mum will be here about eleven tomorrow to drive you home,' he reminded her. 'She said not to worry about food, she's got it sorted.'

With a laugh Nikki said, 'What would we do without her?'

'Only starve,' Danny replied, coming to get a hug of his own. 'Now I'm sorry, but we have to drag him away or we really will miss that train, and yours truly is working tonight, so I can't afford to.'

After one last lingering kiss, Nikki let Spence go, then lifted Zac up so he could watch his father and uncles walk down the ward. At the door Spence turned back to give them a wave, and as she waved Zac's hand for him she had to swallow hard on the lump in her throat.

A moment later the door closed behind them, and hugging Zac to her as he coughed she sat down on her own narrow bed, and began wishing away the time till they could all be together again.

Dear Zac, she wrote the next morning, while they were waiting for the consultant, *We're going home today, just as soon as the doctor's given you a final check, which is a great relief to me, I can tell you. You're so much better now – just a little cough which is happening less and less and is, the nurse keeps telling me, nothing to worry about. I won't go on any more about the fright you gave us, because I know it's all in the previous pages.*

You're asleep as I'm writing this, so you can't hear the children around you, but some of them are making lots of noise, and Todd, who's in the next bed, came over just now to ask if he could play with you. One of the nurses is doing some drawing with him now, so he's not on his own. It's sad that his mummy has to leave him, but he doesn't have a daddy, so she has to go to work. She'll be back later though, and I think his gran is coming for the afternoon.

She paused as she thought about her own mother, and how acutely she'd felt the need for her this past weekend. If she'd known her grandson was ill Nikki was sure she'd have come, her father too, but she hadn't wanted to run the risk of turning to them while Spence was there, in case they said something to make this stressful time even worse for him. She realised there was nothing to stop her calling them now, but though a part of her wanted to, what was the point? The crisis was over, and actually she'd got through it pretty well without them.

Turning back to her journal, she wrote,

Once again I realise how lucky I am that you, Daddy and I have one another. Our little family means the world to me, but I know it goes even deeper for him. Sometimes I can sense how afraid he is of losing us. This is because of the way his parents neglected him when he was little, and how lonely he was while growing up. I was too, as an only child, but it was nothing like what Daddy went through. I still had my parents and they loved me, probably too much, which is why we're having problems now.

Ah, looks like you're waking up, so I'm going to stop now and kiss you all over your squidgy little face. (I know you're going to hate that when you grow up, but hopefully we'll laugh about it together.)

By the time Mr Pearce, the consultant, swept into the ward, surrounded by a bunch of medical students, Mrs A had arrived too, and was holding a stark naked Zac on one shoulder, trying to wind him, while Nikki sorted out what he was going to wear for the day. Spence had gone home to fetch some navy dungarees and a pale blue hoodie yesterday, and the cutest little fur-lined dino boots which were still too big, but Nikki couldn't wait to put them on him.

As Mr Pearce talked the students through the bronchiolitis that had affected Zac, Mrs A laid him down in the cot, and was just turning away when everyone started to laugh. Zac was treating them to his favourite party trick.

'No, thank you, young man, we don't need any urine samples today,' Mr Pearce chuckled, as Nikki grabbed a nappy. Then to a pretty, dark-haired girl who was standing next to him, 'Trudie, why don't you do the honours?'

The student looked startled. 'You mean clean him up?' she asked.

Pearce's eyebrows rose. 'I'm sure his mother would be

delighted,' he replied drolly, 'but I was meaning, would you like to conduct a neurological examination?'

The student immediately seemed nervous and unsure where to start.

Nikki looked at Mr Pearce, who gave her a reassuring wink. 'You could begin by assessing his grip,' he prompted.

Trudie stepped forward, and after some initial hesitancy she seemed to gain confidence as she started pulling Zac up by the hands to test his head control.

'A bit of lag is normal at this age,' Mr Pearce informed the others, 'but as you can see, now he's upright, he's managing to keep his head fairly steady. OK, Trudie, pick him up.'

Putting her hands around Zac's middle, she raised him into her arms.

'If an infant is hypotonic,' Mr Pearce continued, 'he should kind of slip through the hands when you lift him, but as you can see little Zac here is bright-eyed and alert and easy to hold. OK, Trudie, on you go.'

For the next few minutes the student assessed Zac's muscle tone by gently shaking his arms and legs, then she stroked the outside of the bottom of his feet to check that his toes curled up and spread.

'In older children and adults the toes curl down when you do this,' Mr Pearce informed them, 'but with infants, until they walk, they turn up.' He looked at Nikki and smiled at the way she was glowing with pride. 'Right, Trudie,' he said, 'time to put the ophthalmoscope to work. Richard, what are we looking for here?' he asked another student as Trudie began shining a light in Zac's eyes.

'Uh,' he began anxiously, 'um, a red reflex, which is a reflection of the light from the retina.'

Mr Pearce nodded approvingly. 'Go on,' he encouraged. 'Why are we looking for this?'

'Because it will tell us that there is no cataract or tumour in the eye?' he replied.

'Precisely. So, Trudie, you're taking your time over that. How's it looking?'

'OK, sir,' she answered. 'I mean, the red reflex is definitely there, but it's . . . I don't know . . .' She looked up at him. 'I think there's a brighter spot that seems to come and go as he moves his eyes.'

Mr Pearce appeared interested, and using his own ophthalmoscope he stooped to examine Zac himself.

Nikki had become very still. No one was behaving as though there was a problem, but it seemed something wasn't right.

Standing up again, Mr Pearce called out to one of the nurses. 'Page Pete Laurence, find out if he's over at the eye hospital today,' he said. Then to Nikki, in a mock admonishing tone, 'Don't look so worried. I'm just going to get an ophthalmologist to have a look at him, because Trudie's right, there is something a little brighter going on in there.'

Chapter Twelve

It was gone four o'clock by the time Mrs A finally drove them through Bedminster, where a wash of late afternoon sun was turning the puddles and shop windows into mirrors of golden reflections.

As they travelled along North Street Nikki gazed out at the familiar surroundings and felt as though a very long time had passed since she'd last been here. It was like stepping back into a previous life and finding nothing had changed, when perhaps it should have. It was odd, and vaguely unsettling, to think of the place carrying on as normal while she'd been in the hospital with Zac, shops opening and closing, buses coming and going, people hurrying about their business, though she couldn't imagine what else she might have expected.

Behind her, in his car seat, Zac gave a little cough in his sleep. Nikki turned to check on him and felt her heart churn with love. He looked so sweet in his Tigger bobble hat and trendy dino boots, so scrumptious she could eat him.

'I expect he's exhausted after all that attention,' Mrs A remarked as they pulled up outside the house.

'Just thank God it's over,' Nikki murmured, and getting out of the car she opened the back door to begin unstrapping Zac. 'He'll need feeding again soon,' she commented as Mrs A went to unload the bags from the boot.

'I wouldn't wake him,' Mrs A advised. 'He's very good at letting you know when he's hungry, so you don't need to worry about that.'

Smiling as she held Zac against her, Nikki was about to carry him inside when her mobile started to ring. Fishing it out of her coat pocket she saw it was Spence and clicked on.

'Everything OK?' he asked as soon as she answered.

'Yes, we've just got home. I'll take him inside and call you back. Oh God, the keys,' she said as she rang off.

'Not to worry, David gave me his before he left,' Mrs A said, brandishing a set, and after filling Zac's car seat with bags she hefted the whole lot to the front door and led the way inside.

'Oh, it's lovely and warm in here,' Nikki cried, as she took Zac into the sitting room. Everything looked and smelled the same as when she'd left, except it seemed a lot tidier.

'I'll take this lot upstairs,' Mrs A called out from the hall. 'Are you hungry?'

Nikki thought about it. 'Starving,' she called back. Then to Zac, 'OK, sleepyhead, I'm going to lie you down here on the sofa and put some cushions around you to keep you safe. If you want me, yell.'

After making him comfortable and waiting a few moments in case he woke up, she went to take off her coat, before carrying the bags Mrs A had left at the foot of the stairs into the kitchen. To her surprise the place was spotless. Not even a single dish was waiting to be washed up. Finding a note from Kristin, she turned on the light and read it. *Sorry I didn't make it to the hospital, but have tried to leave place nice and clean for when you come back. If there's any mess it'll be down to the others, but I'll call and tell them to leave it as they found it. Thinking of you. Please call when you can. Love Kx*

'There is plenty to eat in the fridge,' Mrs A announced, as she came back down the stairs. 'I was thinking of making us a nice spaghetti bolognese. How does that sound?'

'Delicious. Are you staying?'

'If you would like me to.'

'I'd love you to,' Nikki told her with feeling. 'I should call Spence back, then I'll come and set the table and make us something to drink.'

A few minutes later she was sitting cross-legged on the bed, the phone in one hand, a fluffy dog with a musical collar in the other. 'The eye doctor said he didn't think it was anything to worry about,' she was telling Spence. 'He checked him over, then they took some blood, just to be on the safe side, and after that they let me bring him home.'

'So how is he now?'

'Fast asleep, and perfectly OK. He didn't like the needle much when they took the blood, you should have heard him.'

'I don't blame him,' Spence retorted, 'can't stand the things myself. Is Mrs A still with you?'

'Yes, she's staying to have something to eat, then I'll see what his lordship wants to do after he's been fed. With any luck I might be able to get an early night. I feel totally wiped out.'

'It's been a tough few days,' he reminded her softly, 'and you could have done without that extra business today. Still, as long as they don't think it's anything to worry about . . . When are they expecting the results of the tests?'

Nikki yawned. 'By the end of the week, I think. His cough's practically gone now.'

'Great. He's a champion.' Then in a lower voice, 'I wish I was there. I'm really missing you.'

'Same here, but it's not long till the weekend, and the week after that we'll all be in London. Oh, by the way, I had a text from our landlord, asking if someone can come to look at this house on Wednesday.'

'Is that convenient?'

'I don't see why not. I'll try to make it for when I'm at my stretch class, then they can have the place to themselves. So how's it going your end? Much to do?'

'Masses, but the production manager's got things under control. The schedule's more or less worked out already, and the casting session's all set up for this Friday. There aren't many people to see, because there aren't many parts, so I should be home by eight, nine at the latest. David's coming with me. We thought we'd rent a better van and bring some things back here on Sunday. We just have to check it's OK to store them in the house, because with all three of us staying at Dan's place, there's already no room to move.'

Even though she'd never been inside Dan's bachelor pad, it amused Nikki to think of them all squashed in there, Dan in the bedroom, Spence on the sofa and David . . .? She guessed on the floor, but who could say? 'Have you seen Kristin since you got back?' she asked.

'Yeah, she came into the office today, looking for David, but he was out on a shoot.'

Nikki blinked. 'He's working already?'

'No, just observing. He's got a pretty full schedule though, because Drake's put some editing his way, and he's shooting a corporate next week, because the guy who's supposed to be doing it has broken his wrist. Then, at long last, he'll be on board with me.'

'Yay!' she cheered. 'Bet you can't wait.'

'It'll be cool,' he agreed. 'Except it means you'll be settling into the house on your own, because the rest of us will be working.'

'But you'll be home in the evenings,' she reminded him, 'and it'll be good for me to get a routine going with Zac without too many distractions. I just wish we could take Mrs A with us. I don't fancy getting to know another health visitor. It won't be the same.'

'I know what you mean, but she'll always be at the end of the phone if you need her, and I'm sure the new one will be fine once you get used to her.'

'I guess so. Anyway, did Kristin get the commercial?'

'Yep. I'm sure she'll tell you all about it when you speak to her.'

'I'm sure,' she agreed. 'Has David said anything about their relationship to you?'

'No, but I'm definitely with you on thinking he wants out. Quite what's going on with him and Dan I wouldn't like to say at this point, but I reckon it's going somewhere. I don't say anything, though. It's their business, so if they want to discuss it with me they should choose the time. What it could mean, though, is that we'll find ourselves with one less sharer in the house. Or put another way, one less person to pay the rent.'

'Mm,' she responded, thinking more of Kristin's heart than their pockets for the moment. However, Spence had a point. 'That could be why David won't finish it,' she said, 'because he knows what a difficult position he'll put the rest of us in, financially.'

'Well, he can't stay with her because of that. I just hope he doesn't do it before we start shooting, because that could make things extremely awkward.'

'That's probably another reason he's holding back. Plus, he won't want to hurt her, because he can't bear hurting anyone.'

'Whatever. He's in a difficult situation, that's for sure, but so will we all be if we end up not being able to pay the rent.'

'I'll have to find work as soon as I get there,' she stated. 'I'll start putting out feelers this week to see if I can set up some meetings. And I'll create a kind of portfolio of my articles to email to editors. Ah, sounds as though our son and heir has woken up, so I'd better go and see to him. I'll call again later, before I go to bed.'

'OK. Love you.'

'Love you too.'

After ringing off she ran down the stairs calling out that she was coming, though Zac was yelling so loudly she doubted he could hear. When she reached the sitting room she found him all red in the face, and clearly too hot in his buttoned-up duffle coat, which Mrs A was already removing.

'There, there,' Nikki soothed, as Mrs A handed him over. 'Everything's all right now. Pff, he needs changing,' she grimaced as she caught the smell.

Mrs A chuckled, and tilted her head adoringly as Zac gazed up at Nikki, his eyes wet with tears and as blue as an indigo night.

'Hello,' Nikki smiled. 'We're home now, my darling, where we belong.'

Mrs A put a finger to his cheek, and laughed as he turned to try and suckle it.

'I can't see anything red in his eyes, can you?' Nikki asked.

Mrs A shook her head. 'Not at all,' she replied, 'he's a very healthy and handsome little boy, with the most beautiful clear blue eyes, and very definitely the smelliest bottom in all of Bristol.'

Laughing, Nikki went to drag his changing mat from behind the sofa, feeling so tired now that she wasn't quite sure how she was managing to stay on her feet.

However, when she finally crawled into bed later, after a delicious spag bol, followed by a lovely long bath with Zac, she suddenly came wide awake. She knew it was because she was afraid Zac would have trouble breathing again, which was why he was in his Moses basket on the bed right next to her. But maybe that wasn't such a good idea, because if she turned over in her sleep and knocked the basket off . . .

Getting up again, she went to lie him down in his cot, placing him on his back with no blankets or toys anywhere near his face. But then she was afraid he might get cold, so she went downstairs to turn up the heating.

As it turned out he slept peacefully throughout the night, but Nikki knew it was going to be a while before she would be able to sleep easily again.

The rest of the week sped by as Nikki, tired though she was, used what energy she had to pick up her life where she'd left off, continuing her lists ready for the move, taking Zac up to the Factory to see all his friends, and sorting out a selection of her best articles for Spence to look at when he came home.

On Wednesday she went to her stretch class while the landlord showed his prospective new tenants round the house. Whether they liked it or not she had no idea, because they'd gone by the time she returned home, but Mr Farrell had left a note telling her he'd get the lock repaired on the front door. She hadn't actually realised it was faulty, and when she tried it, it seemed fine to her, but if he'd discovered a problem then it was good that he was fixing it.

By the weekend she was more than ready to see Spence, and he was clearly as keen to see her, because he couldn't stop kissing and hugging her when he came in the door, and made her laugh with how eager he was to make love as soon as Zac went off to sleep. Luckily, David had gone straight to his mother's and since neither Kristin nor Dan were down for the weekend, they had the place to themselves until lunchtime on Saturday, which was when David turned up with the newly-rented van.

They spent the rest of the day loading it up, while Zac bleated happily in his cot, apparently fascinated by the new Happy Safari mobile Spence had rigged up like an umbrella.

'He hasn't coughed once since I've been back,' Spence commented proudly, as they wheeled him up to the Factory on Saturday night.

'He's definitely over it now,' Nikki said confidently. 'Mrs A says he's doing just great.'

'But you're still not sleeping too well?'

'It's getting better. Last night was easier, because you were there, so tonight should be OK too.'

'I wonder when we're going to hear about the blood test,' he remarked.

'We should have by now,' she replied, stifling a yawn, 'but I'm telling myself that no news is good news.'

'Are you sure you want to go out?' he asked, pulling her in closer to keep her under the umbrella. 'We can always grab a pizza and take it home.'

'Actually, why don't we have one drink with the others, and then do that?' she replied. 'There's a Roland Joffe film on later that I've never seen, and it's such a horrible night, we don't really want to be out for long, do we?'

'Not if you don't want to,' he assured her.

When they got to the Factory most of their crowd were already there. Since David had gone on ahead to order, a couple of four-pint jugs of No. 7 were waiting on the table between the red sofas, along with a mix of tapas and an orange juice for Nikki. Zac was fast asleep, so they left him in his buggy, parked next to Spence, apparently oblivious to the loud music and torrent of voices rising and falling like a roaring tide around him.

Once they were settled it seemed easier to stay than to leave, and since there weren't going to be many more nights when they could all get together like this, both Nikki and Spence decided to make the most of it. At one stage, when Gabriella's 'Sweet about Me' came over the speakers, Nikki even found the energy to get up and dance, which was something she hadn't done in ages, she realised, when she slumped breathlessly back in her seat. But it had felt really good, and even better was the way the tension of the past ten days was finally starting to unfurl.

She was in such a great mood that when she saw Terri Walker over the other side of the room with a small group of people she was tempted to go across and say hi. However, it probably wasn't a great idea while Spence was there, and besides, she wasn't really feeling quite so inclined to befriend her now, maybe because she was still getting over the scare they'd been through with Zac, or maybe because a draining tiredness was starting to swallow her up.

It was Monday morning, just after ten thirty, when Mr Pearce's secretary rang Nikki on her mobile. Nikki was in the middle of ironing Zac's tiny vests, a task she adored, but when she realised who was on the line she put the iron aside and closed her eyes, bracing herself for the blood-test results. *Please God, please, please, please, let everything be all right.*

'I'm calling,' the secretary explained, 'because Mr Pearce would like to have a chat with you and your husband.'

Nikki's heart missed a beat. 'Is . . . Is there a problem?' she asked, her voice barely more than a croak.

'I'm afraid I don't know what it's about,' the secretary replied, 'you'll need to talk to Mr Pearce.'

'It's about Zac's test results, though?' Nikki insisted. There was a buzzing in her head, a swoop and drone of fear that made her words seem like leaves swirling in a vicious storm.

'The doctor will explain everything, I'm just ringing to set up an appointment.'

Nikki was feeling sick and trying to make herself think. Spence was in London, she was here. Could she go alone? Did she want to? 'How urgent is it?' she asked.

'I think the doctor would like to see you sometime this week,' came the reply.

Nikki's insides went into free fall as her hand went to her mouth to stifle a gasp. That soon? They must have found a tumour on Zac's eye. He was going to go blind. They needed to operate on his brain. 'Spencer's away at the moment,' she heard herself say. 'Can I . . . Could I bring someone else with me?' Mrs A would surely say yes if she asked.

'I think Mr Pearce would like to see you both.'

Nikki was forcing herself to stay calm, but it was hard,

almost impossible. 'Uh, um, I'll have to call him and ring you back,' she said.

'OK. Let me give you the number for our direct line.'

After jotting it down in a scrawl she barely recognised as her own, Nikki said, 'Can you tell me when Mr Pearce is free?' If she could give Spence a day and time he'd be sure to move things around so he could make it.

'I can offer you two thirty tomorrow,' the secretary answered, 'or four o'clock on Thursday.'

It couldn't be that urgent if they were suggesting Thursday, Nikki tried telling herself. They weren't about to rush him in and cut him open. However, she knew she'd go insane if she had to wait that long. 'Can you book us in for tomorrow?' she asked. Whatever else Spence was doing, he'd have to put it on hold. Zac must come first.

Spence didn't even hesitate when she told him. 'Of course,' he agreed, sounding as afraid as she was. 'No question. Did they give you any idea what the results showed?'

'No, she said we have to speak to the doctor.' She pressed a hand over her mouth as she looked at Zac. 'Oh my God, Spence, what if . . .'

'Don't go there,' he cried. 'Let's just wait and see what he says.'

'If it was anything serious, he'd tell us to come in right away, wouldn't he?' Nikki said, needing to drag some reassurance from somewhere.

'Definitely,' Spence replied with confidence.

'Actually, the secretary didn't even tell me to take Zac. So perhaps it's about something we're doing wrong and he wants to give us some advice.'

Though Spence sounded doubtful, he said, 'Could be, but I think we should take him anyway. Who's going to look after him otherwise?'

'I wasn't meaning we should leave him behind, only that if they didn't specifically say they wanted to see him . . .' She was grasping at straws, and they were already turning into thin air. 'When are you going to come?' she asked shakily.

'Tonight if I can. I'll call as soon as I've managed to change things round.'

Mrs Adani was sitting in her car outside the Health Park on Downton Road in Knowle West. Her hand was gripping the phone tightly as she waited for Mr Pearce's secretary to put her through to the paediatrician.

When his voice came down the line, using her Christian name, Pallavi, to greet her, she automatically responded by using his. 'Hello Anton, what can I do for you?' she asked, managing to sound cheerful when she was actually extremely anxious. The call had to be about Zac, because he was the only baby she had under Anton Pearce at the moment.

However, as she listened to what he was telling her she began to frown in confusion. 'I've never heard of it,' she said.

'It's very rare,' he told her, 'apart from amongst a certain section of the Jewish community. Is either of the Jameses Jewish?'

She shook her head. 'Not that I know of,' she replied, wondering if Spence with his dubious parentage might be, but whether he was or not, the test results were still the same. 'What's the prognosis?' she asked.

When he told her, she felt as if all the blood was draining from her veins.

'I'd like you to be here tomorrow when I speak to them,' he said. 'They're coming in at two thirty.'

'Of course,' she murmured, and after the call ended she dropped the phone in her lap and covered her face with her hands.

In London, Spence was frantically trying to change his schedule around so he could leave that night, but it wasn't proving easy.

Then Nikki rang and said, 'I think you should come tomorrow.'

'But . . .'

'No, listen, we've got no idea what the paediatrician's going to tell us yet, and it might be better if you take some time off after we see him, rather than before.'

Though he could see the sense in that, he wasn't happy about her being alone tonight.

'I'll be fine,' she insisted. 'Honestly. And if I'm not, I can always call Mrs A.'

'You should do that anyway,' he told her.

'I have, but she must be with someone, so I left a message.'

'Hello dear,' Mrs A said when Nikki answered the phone later in the day. 'I would have called earlier, but I've had a very full schedule this afternoon. How are you?' Her eyes closed at the disingenuousness of the question, but it was imperative that she sounded as normal as possible.

'OK, I think,' Nikki answered. 'You got my message about having to see Mr Pearce tomorrow?'

'I did, and I'll be there myself, so I don't want you to worry . . .'

'Do you know what it's about?' Nikki broke in.

Mrs A hated lying, but it wasn't her place to break the news, especially when she knew so little about the condition. 'He wants to go over the blood-test results with you,' she prevaricated. 'He'll explain everything . . .'

'But has he told you what's wrong?'

'He's going to explain things to me at the same time,' she answered, avoiding the question again. 'This is normal practice, so . . .' She broke off as Zac started to cry in the background.

'I think he's picking up on my nerves,' Nikki told her.

'Probably, but isn't it time for his tea?'

'Yes, it is.' Then, 'Do you . . .?'

Mrs A waited, knowing and fearing what was coming.

'Well, I was wondering if you might be able to come over tonight.'

As her heart split with guilt and shame at having to lie again, Mrs A said, 'My dear, I would if I could, but I am hosting a Bible-study group this evening, and it's too late to start ringing round.' It would be too hard for them to spend any time together before they saw Mr Pearce – she couldn't tell Nikki anything, and holding back would only make matters worse.

'It's OK,' Nikki said. 'I understand. I just . . . No, it doesn't matter. I'll see you there tomorrow, then.'

'Yes,' Mrs A whispered, 'yes, you will.'

Nikki was waiting at the station with Zac when Spence's train came in the following day.

They were too tense to greet one another with their usual warmth, just a peck on the cheek, before Spence peeped into Zac's buggy to see him staring up at the furry animals dangling from his Jungle Pals arch.

'He can definitely see,' he declared.

Nikki nodded. Her face was pale and pinched, but knowing how afraid Spence was too, she attempted a smile.

Taking control of the buggy, Spence led the way to find a taxi. Mrs A would have taken them, but she was already at the hospital on other business, so she'd offered to drive them home afterwards. No buses today – apart from anything else, in their anxiety they might have got on the wrong one.

The sky over Temple Meads was a thick grey sludge of cloud, almost the same shade as the grand old station itself. There were no glimmers of sunlight to lend some warmth to the day, or promises of any to come later on.

Fortunately there weren't many people around so they didn't have to wait long at the taxi rank.

Twenty minutes later they were at the hospital, riding up in the lift, silent and rigid with dread. There was nothing to say, and even if there were, they were too afraid to force any words through the cracks in the strain of holding themselves together.

Mr Pearce's secretary was a stout, friendly-looking woman, who greeted them with a smile that made Nikki's heart beat with hope. She wouldn't have smiled like that if the news was bad.

'Mr Pearce is already here,' she told them, 'and Mrs Adani.'

As she opened the door to the inner office Spence went ahead with Zac, and Nikki followed, her feet feeling awkward and heavy, while her head was pounding with fear.

Mr Pearce got up from his desk, and Mrs A, looking as crisp and elegant as ever in a sage-green trouser suit, came forward to help with the buggy.

Nikki took the hand Mr Pearce was offering. He seemed different in this setting, she thought, but couldn't exactly say how. His greying hair and whiskery eyebrows were the same, as was the warmth of his smile . . .

He was smiling, so there was no need to be this afraid.

After shaking Spence's hand, Mr Pearce offered them a seat.

The office wasn't large, and its window looked out on to another medical building rising to the same height next door, but there was a homeliness to it, mainly due to the photographs of children on the walls – patients, or his own? Nikki wondered – and the toys piled up in one corner.

As she and Spence perched on the two chairs facing the desk, Mr Pearce returned to his own, and Mrs Adani to the one she'd pulled up at an angle.

'We brought Zac,' Spence said, keeping a hand on the bar of the buggy. 'I guess that was the right thing to do?'

Mr Pearce smiled as he nodded. 'How is he?' he asked. 'Cough gone?'

'He seems really well now,' Nikki said, eagerly. Or was it pathetically? She didn't know, nor did she care. She just wanted this to be over.

'Good. Good,' Mr Pearce said, and folding his hands together he fixed them with his frank grey eyes.

As she looked back, Nikki felt a hot knife of dread starting to slice her apart. She didn't want to be here any more. She wanted to go home, wind back the clock, find a place that was safe and secure where no one could reach her and Zac.

'I've had the results of Zac's blood test,' Mr Pearce began. He was watching them closely, knowing that the only way to deal with this was to come to the point as quickly as possible, but it wasn't going to be easy, because these situations never were. 'It was the red spot in his right eye that enabled us to isolate what the problem could be,' he continued, 'and I'm very sorry to have to tell you that he has a genetic disorder known as Tay-Sachs disease.'

Even though she'd never heard of it, a slow paralysis began descending over Nikki's brain.

'What . . . What is it?' Spence stammered, his hands bunching in iron-hard fists. 'I mean, is it serious?'

Pearce's eyes went to his. 'It means he's missing a vital enzyme called hexosaminidase A,' he told him. 'Hex-A is easier,' he added, knowing they'd never remember the longer word, much less be able to pronounce it. 'Without this enzyme a fatty substance collects in the nerve cells of the brain, which will eventually start to cause progressive destruction of the central nervous system.'

Nikki wasn't listening. She couldn't allow herself to, because this was all nonsense and none of it was happening.

Spence's voice sounded strangled and rough as he said, 'Does that mean . . .? Is he going to . . .?'

Mr Pearce looked at him directly. 'Yes, I'm afraid he is going to die,' he said. He had to use the word, or the reality wouldn't kick in, and as tragic as it was, he had to make sure it did.

As Nikki reeled off into another world, Spence shot to his feet. 'No!' he cried savagely. 'You've got it wrong. Look at him. He's perfectly healthy.'

'I know he seems that way now,' Mr Pearce conceded, 'and indeed he is a very lively and alert young fellow, but that's because the symptoms don't usually appear until the child is around six months old. The only reason the disease has come to light now is, as I mentioned, because of the cherry-red spot we detected in his right eye. This is the first sign of the disease, which is a very rare . . .'

'But how did he get it?' Spence demanded, dragging his hands frantically through his hair. 'Is it something we did? There's got to be some kind of treatment for it, right?'

Mr Pearce's expression remained gentle and calm. 'It's a genetic disorder,' he repeated, 'which means he's inherited it . . .'

'But he can't have,' Spence shot back. 'Look at us. We're perfectly all right.'

'Indeed, but you don't have to be suffering the disease yourself to be a carrier.'

'So is it me? Am I the one who's done this to him?' His voice, his entire being was ragged with guilt.

'You both have to be carriers,' Mr Pearce replied.

Beside him, Mrs A's heart was heavier than she could bear. She'd been dreading this almost as much as if Zac were her own, and seeing the way Nikki was trying to detach herself from the horror was making her want to go and wrap her in her arms and tell her everything would be all right. But how could she, when it wouldn't?

'Tell me,' Mr Pearce said to Spence, 'is either of you Jewish?'

Spence looked at him in confusion. 'No, but what's that got to do with anything?' he demanded.

'Tay-Sachs disease is very rare in the general population,' Mr Pearce answered, 'but amongst Ashkenazi Jews there is a very high incidence.'

Spence only stared at him, barely even knowing what an Ashkenazi Jew was, never mind how a disease common to them had come to be in his son. Then, remembering the prognosis, he felt his head swim with panic and his eyes burn with tears. 'You have to do something,' he choked. 'You can't just let him . . .' He couldn't say the word, he just couldn't.

'I promise, we will do everything we can to alleviate the symptoms when the time comes,' Mr Pearce assured him, 'and you will receive special counselling to help you . . .'

'We don't *want counselling*,' Spence raged. 'We want our son.'

Mr Pearce's expression was one of profound regret.

'No!' Spence yelled, banging a hand on the desk. 'You have to do something. If it was your son you'd find a way. Is it money you want? We'll find it.'

'I'm afraid no amount of money is going to help him,' Pearce said softly, hating himself for having to dash even that wildest of hopes. 'There is an expectancy that some form of gene therapy will reverse the disorder at some point in the future, but I'm afraid medical science isn't there yet.'

Suddenly Nikki spoke. 'How long will he live?' she asked, her eyes as glassy and blank as her tone.

Pearce regarded her carefully. She was in shock, of course, but he suspected she was also in denial and he needed somehow to try and bring her out of it, because not until she accepted what was happening would she be able to deal with it. 'Until he's four, maybe five,' he answered.

Spence's head fell into his hands as he started to sob.

Pearce watched Mrs Adani go to comfort him, his own heart aching for the young man's pain, but at least the tears confirmed he was taking it in. The mother, on the other hand, was clearly still blocking. 'When Zac's around six months old,' he went on, addressing Nikki, 'you will start to notice a slowdown in his development, and a loss of peripheral vision.'

Nikki's face remained stony.

'By the time he reaches two he will very probably be experiencing recurrent seizures and his mental function will be severely diminished. His motoring skills will be affected, making him unable to crawl or sit up. He'll lose the ability . . .'

Nikki got to her feet. 'I think we should go now,' she said to Spence.

Spence looked up at her, his face ravaged with tears.

'Please, we're here to help you,' Pearce told her. 'I understand this has been a terrible shock . . .'

'Yes, it has,' she agreed, 'but it's all right, because I'm not going to let him die. He's my son, so I will make sure he lives,' and walking round Spence to the buggy, she turned it towards the door.

'Don't leave like this,' Pearce urged, getting up from his chair. 'We need to discuss . . .'

'I'd rather go home now, thank you,' Nikki told him. 'Come on Spence, it's almost time for Zac's feed.'

As she opened the door to push the buggy through, Spence, clearly not knowing what else to do, got up to follow, while Mrs A went to grab her bag. Quickly jotting something on a Post-it she handed it to Spence, together with her car keys. 'This is the number of my parking space,' she told him. 'I will be coming right behind you.'

Spence took it, and Mrs A watched with an expression that conveyed all the sorrow she was feeling as they left. Then, turning to Mr Pearce, she said, 'I must go with them, but perhaps we can meet again tomorrow. I have many questions to ask.'

'Of course,' he replied. 'My main concern right now though, is the mother. She obviously heard everything I said, but she's not processing it.'

'I agree. So what can I do about that?'

Going back to his desk, he wrote on the same Post-it pad.

'This website will give you some basic information about the disease,' he said handing it over. 'Have a look at it, and try to talk things through with her. It could be a good idea to get her to look at it too before she goes searching the Internet herself, because most do these days. Try to make sure you, or someone else is with her when she does, because it contains some difficult reading.'

'Thank you,' she said, slipping the Post-it into her bag.

'I've already contacted social services,' he told her. 'There's a lot of backup we can offer in these cases, if she's willing to take it.'

'And treatment for the baby?'

He shook his head. 'At the moment, he is like any other healthy infant his age, so there is nothing to treat. Later, when things have started to sink in and settle down a little, we can start discussing how to control the symptoms when they begin.'

'And you're absolutely sure there's no hope?' she said, her voice cracking with the strain.

'I'm sorry,' he said softly. 'You're welcome to seek a second opinion, of course, but I'm afraid the diagnosis will still be the same.'

Chapter Thirteen

No one spoke throughout the drive home. Neither Spence nor Mrs A could find words to reach Nikki, whose silence seemed to generate a power all of its own. She stared out of the window seeing nothing, feeling even less and hearing only the hum of the engine and the faintest whisper of Zac snoring.

When they reached the house she went in first, carrying Zac in both arms, while Spence brought in the buggy and Mrs A went to park further down the street. By the time Mrs A came back Nikki had put the kettle on and Spence was standing in the middle of the sitting room, clearly at a total loss.

Going to give his hand a reassuring squeeze, Mrs A said, 'When you are ready we should sit down and talk.'

He swallowed dryly and gave a distracted nod of his head.

Understanding that it was too soon to expect much response from either of them, she went into the kitchen to find Nikki still holding Zac while dropping tea bags into cups. There was a stiffness about her that made her seem so vulnerable and fragile that Mrs A thought she might break if she as much as touched her.

'Why don't you let me do that?' she offered.

'It's OK, I can manage,' Nikki said hoarsely.

Mrs A went on watching her, understanding she had to tread very gently, yet hardly knowing which way to go. 'Shall I take Zac?' she ventured. 'He's probably too warm in his coat.'

To her surprise Nikki handed him over, almost as though she'd been waiting for the suggestion, then she went to fetch some milk from the fridge.

Leaving her for the moment, Mrs A took Zac in to his father and placed him gently in Spence's arms. She could tell from the way Spence's eyes closed how hard he was finding this, to a point that he was almost afraid to touch his son, but it was so important that he did. Zac needed his parents now more than he ever had.

To her relief Spence pulled Zac to him and gave a sob as he pressed a kiss to his head. 'Take off his coat,' she advised, 'and play with him.'

When Spence looked at her she could see how close he was to coming apart. 'You can do it,' she whispered, and after patting his arm, she returned to the kitchen to find the kettle boiling on the stove and Nikki staring into space.

After turning off the gas, Mrs A forced her own emotions aside and went to stand in front of Nikki, placing her hands on her arms, as though in some way it might help to hold her together. 'We need to talk about what the doctor told you,' she said.

Neither Nikki's head nor eyes moved. It wasn't even clear if she'd heard.

'Nikki?' Mrs A prompted.

'Why?' Nikki asked dully. 'What's there to say? He's got this Tay whatever it is, and there's nothing they can do.'

Mrs A's heart flooded with the pain Nikki was trying so hard to reject. She had to give herself a moment before she said, 'There are things you will be able to do to help him . . .'

'I don't want to discuss it,' Nikki interrupted, and tried to turn away.

Mrs A let her go. 'I understand you're in shock now,' she said, 'but the sooner you face up to what is happening . . .'

'What do you want from me?' Nikki suddenly cried, her voice cracking with emotion. 'Tears? Hysterics? Is that what you're looking for? Well that's not going to help him, is it? You heard what the doctor said, nothing is, so what good are my tears going to do?'

'They will help you to release some of the tension you have inside.'

Nikki turned her head away.

Mrs A's eyes shone with pity, but deciding she'd pressed

hard enough for now, she let her be and started to make the tea.

'He needs feeding,' Nikki suddenly announced, and moments later she'd taken Zac roughly from Spence and was heading up the stairs.

Going into the sitting room, Mrs A found Spence on the sofa with his head in his hands. 'Here,' she said, passing him a cup of tea.

He looked up, seeming not to know what it was, then his hand came up and took it. 'Thanks,' he said. His voice was shredded and frail. He took a sip, then glanced up again. 'I'm sorry about Nik,' he said. 'It's all a bit . . .'

'Ssh, you don't have to apologise to me,' Mrs A told him.

They sat quietly for a while, listening to the sound of Nikki moving around upstairs and Zac crying until, presumably, he started to feed, because everything fell silent.

'She's a good mum,' Spence said, almost defensively.

Mrs A nodded. 'And you're a good dad.'

He shook his head. 'I shouldn't have lost it like that, back there in the office.'

'It was a very normal reaction.'

He looked down, as though not wanting to be excused, and Mrs A understood that he might welcome her anger or condemnation simply to have something else to deal with.

'I am concerned about Nikki,' she said. 'We must not be letting her bottle this up. Perhaps not today, but sooner rather than later, she has to face what is happening and discuss it.'

He continued to stare down at his tea. 'I guess you're right,' he said after a while, 'but who can blame her for not wanting to?'

Mrs A's eyes were full of sadness. 'No one,' she replied, 'but it will be better for her, and for Zac, if she speaks to the people who can help her through this. I am not only talking about you and me, but about the professionals who are trained to give support in cases like this.'

Spence turned his head away. 'I know you mean well, Mrs A,' he said, 'but I don't want to think of us as "a case like this". Nikki won't, either.'

Understanding perfectly, Mrs A reached into her bag and pulled out the website address Mr Pearce had given her, but didn't hand it over. 'When are you thinking of going back to London?' she asked.

Spence glanced at her briefly, then shook his head. 'No idea.' He hadn't even considered it. He took a sip of his tea, then hung his head again. 'I don't understand why this is happening to us,' he said, brokenly. 'I mean, we're not those kind of Jewish people he talked about, so how come we're carrying the gene?'

Having done an Internet search herself last night, Mrs A was able to say, 'It's not only the Ashkenazi Jews who carry the gene, it can occur in anyone, it's just much more prevalent in them.' She'd had no way of calculating the odds of two British Caucasians being carriers, but she did know that in the general population about one out of every three hundred and twenty thousand babies was born with Tay-Sachs, whereas one in thirty Ashkenazi Jews was a carrier. It was why Jewish women were screened for this during pregnancy, whereas it simply didn't come up as an issue for someone like Nikki.

'I know both your parents died when you were young,' she said tentatively, 'but do you think there's any chance . . .'

'They weren't Jewish,' he broke in. 'I mean, I suppose the jury's always out about my dad, but even if he was, what difference would it make now? It's too late to do anything about it.'

Having to concede the point, Mrs A showed him the Post-it she was holding. 'This is a website Mr Pearce recommended. It'll tell you all about the condition and how you'll be able to help Zac through it.'

He glanced at the note, then let it slide through his hand to the floor.

'When you're ready, we can look at it together, if you like,' she offered.

He didn't respond, and she could see that his mind was drifting elsewhere. 'I should go up and see if she's all right,' he said.

Mrs A smiled. 'Take her some tea,' she suggested, 'and sit with her if she wants you to.'

He got to his feet and ran a shaky hand through his hair. 'What are you going to do?' he asked as she stood up too.

'Whatever you would like me to do,' she replied. 'I can stay, or I will go home and you can always reach me by phone.'

He took a moment to think about it. 'Will you stay for a while?' he asked.

'Of course.' She gave him a reassuring smile, guessing that he didn't want to be alone if Nikki wouldn't talk to him. 'I'll go and make her a fresh cup.'

Nikki looked up as Spence came into the bedroom. She was sitting on the bed with Zac, her legs stretched out in front of her, her back resting on a bank of pillows as she fed him.

'Hi,' she said, her voice drifting ghostlike in the semi-darkness.

'Hi,' he answered. 'I brought you some tea.' He put it on the side table and stood looking down at Zac.

She could tell that he didn't know what to say or do, and whatever he decided she knew it wouldn't be right. 'Why don't you sit down?' she said.

Doing so, he took her free hand and wound his fingers round hers.

'How are you feeling?' she asked. She didn't want him to be hurting like this. He didn't deserve it. Neither of them did.

'OK, I think,' he answered, then gave a mirthless laugh. 'Actually, bloody terrible,' he confessed. 'How about you?'

She looked down as Zac let go of her nipple. 'Is that it?' she asked tenderly. 'No more?'

By way of answer Zac turned his head away.

Spence's smile was contorted by grief. 'Sometimes it's like he actually understands,' he said.

Nikki's eyes stayed down. 'I know. He's a clever little thing, aren't you, my darling?' and raising Zac up she kissed him on the cheek, the way she always did, before settling him on her shoulder to start winding him. Then, realising Spence might not have held him since they'd left Mr Pearce's office, she said, 'Would you like to do it?'

His eyes suddenly flooded with tears. 'I don't . . . I think
. . . I mean, yes, if it's OK,' he said brokenly.

Feeling a lump forming in her own throat, she passed Zac
over, and put a hand on Spence's cheek. 'It'll be all right,'
she said softly.

He couldn't answer, because he knew it wouldn't, and
unlike her he wasn't able to pretend.

'Is Mrs A still downstairs?' she asked.

Spence was gazing at Zac as he nodded.

'I should go and apologise for the way I snapped at her.'

His eyes came to hers. 'I think she understood.'

'I'm sure, but she's been so good to us . . . I shouldn't have
. . . I didn't mean to upset her. Will you be OK here, while I
go down?'

'Of course.'

Putting her arms round them both she held them tightly
for a moment, then got up from the bed to go downstairs.

After she'd gone Spence sat in the fading light, holding
Zac against his chest, loving him with all his might and
wanting desperately to carry him off to a place where no one
and nothing could hurt him. He listened to him snuffling
and gurgling, and felt his little heart beating against his, and
it was tearing him apart. They'd only had him six weeks, but
every day their love for him had doubled. He was everything to them now. He filled their world in a way nothing
else ever could. He was a miracle, a blessing, a true gift from
God. That was what they'd thought, but it seemed God's
gifts could come with a curse, because even as they were
sitting here together, Zac's tiny cells weren't functioning the
way they should. Was Spence to blame? Had his mother
slept with someone who'd passed on this terrible gene? The
man he'd called Dad hadn't been Jewish, but he was
contaminated in other ways that Spence never allowed
himself to think about.

He had no answers, all he knew was that something was
happening to Zac that he couldn't even begin to understand.
It was hard, almost impossible to believe, when he seemed
so normal. Maybe the doctor had got it wrong. Blood tests
were always getting mixed up, everyone knew that, you
heard stories all the time, and since he and Nikki had no

Jewish ancestry, or none that he knew of, maybe they should ask the doctor to do another test.

He became so engrossed in his determination to challenge the diagnosis that it was a while before he realised Zac had drifted off to sleep. All the angry edges of his heart melted as he gazed down at the tender little face with the long dark lashes, button nose and sweet rosebud mouth. This couldn't be happening. It wasn't real, because it was making no sense at all.

After a while he got carefully up from the bed and carried him towards the window. How could the world out there still look the same, when the world in here had changed so completely?

Mrs A was in the kitchen and Spence was still upstairs with Zac when they heard Nikki starting to scream.

'No! *No, no, no.*'

All but dropping Zac into his cot, Spence dashed across the bedroom and began taking the stairs four at a time.

When he got to the sitting room he found Nikki on her knees, sobbing as though her heart was tearing apart. Mrs A was beside her, vigorously rubbing her back.

'What happened?' Spence demanded, dropping to his knees.

'Oh Spence!' Nikki wailed helplessly. 'Please, don't let it be true. I can't stand it. I just can't stand it.'

Gathering her into his arms as she shuddered and gasped with pain, he looked at Mrs A, who nodded towards the computer.

'The . . . the . . . website,' Nikki gasped. 'It says . . . Oh God, Spence, what are we going to do? We can't let it happen.'

Going to the table where her laptop was still displaying the site Mr Pearce had recommended, Spence tried to read the screen, but he was too panicked to take it in. His eyes wouldn't focus, or his brain wouldn't register. *Loss of co-ordination . . . Inability to swallow . . . Breathing problems . . .*

Then he connected with the words that he knew must have finally tipped Nikki over the edge.

Eventually the affected child becomes blind, mentally retarded, paralysed and unresponsive to his or her environment.

'You shouldn't have looked at it,' Spence told Nikki a while later, his voice rough with emotion as he continued to rock her in his arms. The words were still crucifying him, but he had to try to be strong for her, even if he couldn't for himself. 'It was too soon.'

Though the worst of the storm had passed now, Nikki was still shuddering and shivering and trying hard to catch her breath. Her eyes were bloodshot and sore, her whole face was ravaged by confusion and grief.

'That's what I tried to tell her,' Mrs A said, looking almost as stricken. 'Tomorrow, or the next day, maybe . . .'

'I had to know,' Nikki interrupted raggedly. 'I can't explain it. It just came over me.' She tried to blow her nose, but she was still racked by dry, wrenching sobs. 'Something is wrong with us,' she said to Spence, 'we've got some wicked, evil gene and we've passed it on . . . passed it . . .' Her voice fell into the chasm of horror that kept opening up inside her.

Spence tightened his embrace and buried his face in her hair. 'We have to get a second opinion,' he said forcefully. 'I was thinking, maybe there's been a mix-up with the results. It happens, doesn't it?'

His expression was so intense that Mrs A could only nod. 'Yes, it does,' she conceded, because it was true, it did, and she was already praying that maybe it had this time. 'I will speak with Mr Pearce,' she told them. 'I can draw the blood myself, if you are willing, and I will also take it to the laboratories where I know one of the technicians. That way it cannot be mislaid or confused with somebody else's.'

Nikki's eyes were starting to burn with hope as she looked at her. 'Yes, please do that,' she said. 'If you have your things with you now . . .'

'I don't,' Mrs A said, 'but you can bring him to the Health Park tomorrow. We will do it there.'

Nikki turned to Spence. 'There has been a mistake,' she told him, sounding heartbreakingly sure. 'I just know it. None of what we read applies to us. We're not even Jewish, much less Ashka-whatever it is.'

'Ashkenazi,' Mrs A supplied. Then, because she'd read up on that too last night, she was able to tell them that most

Jewish people were Ashkenazi. 'It is not a small sect, as I thought when I first heard of it,' she said. 'It is what around eighty per cent of Jews are.'

Spence and Nikki looked at each other.

'But it is not only Jewish people who are prone to carrying this mutated gene,' Mrs A went on, feeling she must give them the benefit of all she'd discovered. 'There is a certain district of Quebec in Canada where a high incidence of carriers has been found. It is the same for Cajun people from Louisiana in the United States, and an Amish order in Pennsylvania.'

Again Spence and Nikki looked at each other. 'I don't even know anyone from Quebec or those other places,' Nikki said.

Spence shook his head. 'Me neither. But who can say who my mother knew?'

Nikki turned to Mrs A. 'My parents are British,' she assured her, 'and they're definitely Christian, not Jewish or Amish or anything else. So you see, I can't be carrying this gene, even if Spence is, and it says it has to be both of us. Zac's blood must have got mixed up with someone else's.'

Mrs A nodded and made her smile as comforting as she could. 'It is the correct thing to ensure that a mistake has not been made,' she agreed, 'so that is what we will do. Bring Zac early in the morning, and we shall try to get the results by the end of the day.'

Having been thrown this thread of a lifeline, both Spence and Nikki grabbed it in a way that enabled them to get a little more sleep than they otherwise might have that night, and they even managed a piece of toast between them for breakfast in the morning. They didn't discuss how fragile, or maybe even futile their hope was, they simply clung to it, and were still clinging on tight when Mrs A crooked Zac's little elbow to draw his blood at the clinic.

When she'd finished, Spence and Nikki took him home to begin the terrible wait. Mrs A hadn't been able to promise that her friend at the labs would be able to deliver a result today, but they were all hopeful, and dreading, that he might.

'If it turns out that he does have it,' Nikki said towards the middle of the afternoon, 'then I won't be able to move to London at the weekend.'

Though Spence looked at her, he was barely comprehending what she was saying.

'I don't want him to be amongst strangers,' she went on. 'Mrs A knows him and loves him . . .'

'He's going to be all right,' Spence broke in gruffly.

'I know,' she said, 'I'm just saying . . .' She faltered as another gulf of horror opened up and sucked in her heart. She took a breath, as though to recover it. 'You're right, he's going to be OK,' she growled, in defiance of her fear.

Spence's mobile rang and they both leapt out of their skin. His face was completely white as he looked at Nikki, then checking who it was his eyes closed with frustration and relief. 'David,' he said, and clicked on.

'I've just spoken to Mum,' David told him, the tremor in his voice conveying his shock. 'Jesus, Spence, you should have rung last night. I'd have come straight down there.'

'Thanks mate,' Spence said, 'but we need you to keep things going with the film. Have you told Drake yet?'

'No, but he's worried. We all were when we didn't hear from you.'

Spence's eyes returned to Nikki. 'Don't say anything to anyone yet,' he told David. 'We're waiting to hear from your mum about the second test results.'

'I know, she said.' There was a moment before David continued. 'I don't know what you think about God,' he said in a voice that was thick with emotion, 'but I'm going to pray for you, Spence. I'm going to ask that guy up there to make sure it's all a terrible mistake. I know Mum's doing the same.'

Suddenly Spence was too tense to continue the conversation.

Taking the phone, Nikki said, 'David, it's me. We're OK, and Zac's just great. We know there was a mix-up, but we need to have it confirmed.'

'Of course,' David said. 'I'm seeing Dan later, shall I tell him what's happening?'

In spite of the way she'd made herself sound, Nikki was too traumatised to keep it up for long, or to think very quickly. 'Uh, I don't know,' she mumbled. 'Things might change between then and now . . . But OK, yes, tell him, because it'll be too hard for you to keep it to yourself, and anyway, it'll probably be good news by then.'

'Definitely, it will,' David assured her.

After ringing off she put the phone back on the arm of the sofa next to Spence and went to sit on the floor beside Zac's Moses basket, where he was fitfully dozing. As time ticked on the silence in the house deepened and broadened, surrounding them in a way that seemed to isolate them from the rest of the world. They were on an island, in another dimension, suspended in purgatory.

Eventually the light began to fade, and as though sensing his parent's tension Zac started to fret. He wouldn't feed, and his screams seemed louder than they ever had before when Nikki tried to change him.

Spence took over and Zac calmed down for a while, but then he was crying again, harsh, repetitive squalls of anguish. Nikki put her hands over her ears, unable to bear it. Spence rocked him back and forth, pacing up and down, until racked with guilt, Nikki took him and did what she could to soothe him.

It appeared to be what he wanted, because his wailing finally ebbed, but his little body continued to shudder in the aftermath of distress. It made her think of the seizures to come and her head turned away, as though avoiding a blow.

'It's going to be all right,' she murmured against his silky cheek. 'You don't have to worry. Mummy and Daddy are here and we're going to keep you safe from all the nasty things in the world.'

'Nikki, stop,' Spence growled. 'We don't know that yet. Maybe we should be thinking of how we're going to deal with it if it is confirmed.'

'It won't be,' she said vehemently.

'But what if it is?'

She clutched Zac to her and squeezed him so tightly that he started to cry again. 'I'm sorry, I'm sorry,' she wept, resting her cheek against his. Then she suddenly laughed, a harsh desperate sound that wasn't like her at all. 'You rascal,' she scolded, 'you might not be able to speak yet, but you definitely know how to get your message across.'

Zac blinked once or twice and arched an eyebrow.

'Look at him,' Nikki choked. 'You're right, he knows what we're saying.'

Spence came over to hug them both.

'If it is bad news,' Nikki said into his shoulder, 'then I think you should go back to London and continue with the film.'

'For God's sake, Nik!'

'I mean it,' she said, sitting back on her heels to look at him. 'If it is this Tay-Sachs thing, and there's nothing we can do, then you have to carry on working, otherwise how will we survive?'

He put up a hand as though to block her. 'Don't let's talk about this now,' he said. 'We can make those decisions once we know what's happening.'

They seemed to veer between extremes; first she was positive, then it was his turn.

His phone rang again and they looked at one another, so cold with fear this time that neither of them could move.

'It won't be her,' Nikki said. 'And even if it is, it'll be good news.'

He nodded, and pulled a hand over his face.

'Shall I answer?' she offered.

Taking a deep breath, he blew it out quickly and snatched up the phone. He didn't say hello because he couldn't get the word past his dread.

'Spence, are you there?' Mrs A asked.

His insides turned rigid. 'Yes, I'm here,' he whispered. He looked at Nikki, and reading his expression she bunched her hands at her mouth.

'I am very sorry, Spence,' Mrs A said softly, 'but there has not been a mistake.'

The words came to him from the bottom of a pit he couldn't see or feel. He was falling, drowning, and the phone slipped from his hand.

'Oh God no,' Nikki cried. 'Please, no!'

Spence sank to his knees.

Nikki grabbed the phone. 'Mrs A,' she sobbed. 'It's good news, right?'

'Oh Nikki,' Mrs A murmured.

'Tell me it's good news,' Nikki begged.

'I want to, really I do.'

Nikki opened her mouth to scream. She could feel the words erupting from the raging denial inside her. *No! No! I won't let you do this. It's wrong. He's not sick. Anyone can see that.* Everything was swimming and tilting, moving away from her then coming back like a monstrous force to smother and destroy her. Spence was crouched on the floor, his head buried under his hands. She could hear him sobbing, but it seemed to be happening a long way away. She looked at Zac and clutched her hands to her face.

His eyes were open, he was watching her.

Her heart twisted so painfully it was like a knife in her chest.

She dropped the phone and scooped him up in her arms, pressing him to her as though she could absorb him back into her womb.

Somewhere deep inside her a single word was beginning to work its way to the surface, pushed on by all the neediness and despair she was feeling. *Mummy, Mummy*, she could hear herself crying, as though she was still a child. She couldn't do this, she just couldn't. Her parents had to make it all go away.

She felt Zac's little body in her arms and remembered that she was a mummy too. It was up to her to make all this go away for him. 'You're not going to suffer,' she whispered raggedly. 'I won't let you, because I'm going to keep you safe, I promise. Do you hear me, my darling? I'm going to protect you from everything they're saying because it's not true, so you mustn't listen. It's all nonsense and Mummy is going to make it all go away.'

Chapter Fourteen

Mrs Adani was staring at David and Danny in confusion. 'What do you mean, the house was empty?' she said.

'There wasn't anyone there,' Danny told her. 'The shutters were closed, and there was no furniture in the hall that I could see. There used to be, because I remember it. I mean, I can't tell you what it was, but I know there was some there.'

Mrs A blinked slowly as her imagination struggled for a place to go. Having sought David and Danny's opinion on whether she should contact Mr and Mrs Grant, she'd now learned from Danny that they were no longer at their address in Bath.

The three of them were in Mrs A's kitchen on Somerset Road, where she was in the middle of preparing a chicken biryani to take over to Spence and Nikki. She'd provided most of their meals these last few days, knowing that if she didn't they probably wouldn't eat, and they needed to keep up their strength. However, on the whole, Spence seemed to be coping, if breaking down every few hours could be called coping, but at least he was facing up to what was happening and even starting to research what they could do to help Zac when the time came.

Nikki, on the other hand, was worrying Mrs A quite a lot, because while on one level she seemed to be accepting what was happening, on another she was giving all the signs of still being in denial. She wouldn't discuss Zac's condition with anyone, least of all the community paediatrician or support groups who'd tried to get in touch. She wouldn't even speak to Mr Pearce on the phone when he called, and he'd tried several times during the course of the week.

It was the weekend now, and David and Danny had arrived last night, distraught and desperate to do whatever they could to help. It was clear from looking at them that they were more than a little hung-over this morning, and it was Mrs A's guess that Spence was too. It would do no harm for him to let go, considering the enormity of the blow he'd suffered.

'So what next?' David prompted, going to take two cans of Cobra from the fridge and passing one to Dan. 'Shall we go over to Bath again to see if they've come back?'

Mrs A returned to her cooking. Being busy with her hands usually helped her to think. Ever since Zac's second blood-test results had proved positive, she'd been of the opinion that more than anything over the coming days and months Nikki would need her parents. Of course she would always be there for her, but in her experience no one could ever really take the place of a mother, or father, in a crisis. It was true, Nikki and her parents hadn't spoken in a while, but that wasn't to say nothing could be done to repair their differences. Secretly, Mrs A was confounded, because she found it very hard to comprehend how anyone could block out their own child the way the Grants seemed to have done with Nikki, particularly when they must know that their grandchild was in the world by now. All the same, she felt certain that if they were made aware of what their daughter was going through, they would be eager to do everything they could to help her.

'I am presuming you have tried Mr Grant's office,' she said, stirring raisins into the rice and chicken she was bringing to the boil.

'Spence did,' Danny answered, 'and the secretary said she didn't know when he'd be back.'

'Have you talked to Spence about contacting her parents?' David asked her, while helping himself to one of her spicy crackers.

'No, not yet,' she confessed. 'I was going to bring it up yesterday, but Nikki was there and she's very . . . I don't know, it is hard to put into words. How did she seem to you?'

David and Dan exchanged glances. 'Distant, I'd say,'

David answered. 'Like she's not really connecting with anything you're saying.'

Danny agreed. 'But she's taking it in, because she'll say something later that proves it. It's just that she doesn't seem to engage at the time you're saying it.'

Mrs A nodded. 'Yes, this is how I have found her to be,' she said. 'And sometimes I watch her with Zac and it is as though . . . Well, I think maybe she is trying to use the power of her love to heal him.'

David's eyebrows rose. 'That can't be a bad thing,' he said, 'if you believe in miracles.'

'Which I do,' she confirmed, 'and I hope Nikki does too, because they can happen. However, in the meantime, we must do everything we can to give her and Spence all the support they need. They won't accept it from professional outsiders at the moment, which is why I am even more convinced that we must contact her parents.'

'So how are we going to find them?' Danny asked.

'And do you think we should tell Spence we're trying?' David added. 'Personally, I do, just in case he thinks it's a bad idea.'

'As he was wanting to tell them about the baby's birth, I don't think he will,' Mrs A pointed out, 'but you are right, we should consult him before we go any further.'

Spence and Nikki were lying on the bed with Zac between them, tickling his toes and laughing at the little noises he was making.

'He definitely smiled just now,' Spence said.

'It was when you drew circles on his belly,' Nikki agreed.

Doing it again, Spence chuckled as Zac kicked his legs and bunched his fists at his mouth. The next second a little fountain of pee was heading Spence's way.

'I swear he saves this up for me,' Spence cried, rolling back as Nikki grabbed a towel.

Laughing, Nikki wrapped Zac up and carried him into the bathroom. 'Now, what would you like to do today?' she said, as she sat on the toilet to start sponging him down. 'It's not as cold as yesterday, so we could go to the park. Or we can pop up to the Factory to see your friends. I think you'd like that, wouldn't you? Oh, I know, why don't we go to the park first, then to the Factory?' She dropped her voice to a whisper. 'Daddy's got a mega hangover today because he drank too much vodka last night, so we have to treat him gently.'

Zac burped, then yawned.

Smiling, Nikki said, 'I hope you don't get drunk when you're all grown up, my lad. Well, not often anyway, because I suppose everyone does sometimes. I used to, before I was pregnant with you, and I expect I will again when I'm not breastfeeding any more. Not the way I used to, though, because I'll still have you to look after, and I won't want to set a bad example. And we definitely won't want to be like Daddy's parents, who were drunk most of the time. They neglected Daddy terribly when he was little, you know, which is a horrible thing to do, so we have to take care of him now and make sure he knows how much we love him. He's going back to London on Sunday to carry on setting up his film. He's going to be a very important director one day and we'll be so proud of him that he'll forget all about the way his mummy and daddy let him down, because we'll be all that matters to him. You might even have brothers and sisters by then. Would you like that?'

Out on the landing Spence's heart was fracturing into a thousand pieces. It wasn't only the way she was talking about a future for Zac, it was because she didn't seem to have realised yet that the chances of them having any more children when they were both carrying this gene were next to nil. Or maybe she had realised, but was choosing to ignore that too.

Hearing his mobile ringing, he went back into the bedroom and scooped it up from the bed. Seeing it was David he clicked on.

'Hey,' David said, 'can you talk?'

Spence glanced towards the bathroom. 'I'll go downstairs,' he said, and a couple of minutes later he was in the kitchen with the door closed. 'What is it?' he asked.

'Mum wants to know how you'd feel about her trying to contact Nikki's parents.'

Spence's eyes closed as a wash of relief and hope went through him. They might not have any answers or cures, but if they could help Nikki through this, he only wished he could reach them right now. 'I guess you've told her we don't know where they are,' he said.

'Yes, but she says she'll be able to find them.'

'How?'

'He wants to know how,' David said to his mother.

'There are records we can check,' Spence heard her reply, 'and I will ask Mr Pearce to explain to Mr Grant's secretary that it is an emergency, so she must tell us where he is, if she knows.'

'OK,' Spence said. 'Yeah, ask her to do it.' He heard Nikki singing to Zac as she carried him down the stairs. 'The sooner, the better,' he added and quickly rang off.

'Ah, here he is,' Nikki said to Zac as she brought him into the kitchen. 'Who was that on the phone?' she asked Spence.

'Just David,' he replied.

Carrying on past him, she tugged open the door of the washing machine to start unloading the laundry that had just finished spinning.

'Why don't I do that?' Spence offered. 'Or I can take the baby, either way.'

Nikki looked down at Zac. 'Do you want to go to Daddy?' she asked him. 'Let me see, he's having a think about it, and the answer is . . . yes, he does,' and turning round she handed him over. 'I keep meaning to ask,' she said, 'are you taking the digital camera to London with you?'

'Uh, I'm not sure,' he answered, deciding not to remind her that the plan had been to move everything, lock, stock and barrel, today, so they could have at least one day together in the new house before he went back to work. 'Why?'

'I want to take some more shots of Zac,' she answered, shaking out one of his Babygros and dropping it into the basket.

Knowing he couldn't get involved in that, he left her to it and took Zac into the sitting room. He was aware of the way Nikki was still keeping a journal, writing to Zac as though he was going to be around in years to come to read it, and it was killing him. He didn't know what to do to shake her out of it. There again, he wasn't entirely sure he needed to, because just when he was thinking she'd gone into total

230

denial, she'd start breaking down, saying how unbearable their situation was.

He didn't know where he was with her, and was almost afraid to say anything in case he struck a wrong note, which was why no mention had been made yet of how long she wanted to stay here in Bristol. However, he'd already contacted Mr Farrell to explain the situation and to ask him not to relet the house for the time being. Now, with two rents to pay, both here and in London, he wasn't sure how they were going to survive, especially if David ended up ditching Kristin, which was looking more likely by the day. Maybe they should continue shacking up at Dan's place, but it was so small and with three of them there . . .

No, they should go ahead with the move, he decided, because he still had some funds left from the second-unit stuff he'd shot for Drake back in November. True, there wasn't much, because, as he was discovering all the time, babies didn't come cheap, but provided they were careful there should be enough to keep both places going at least for a couple of months. Whether Nikki would feel ready to come to London then was anyone's guess, and he certainly wasn't going to push it now, understanding why she wanted to stay put. In fact, he wanted her to stay here, with Mrs A close by, and other people she knew, because in London she'd be alone with Zac during the day, with no one to turn to if she needed help.

Taking out his mobile as it rang again, he saw it was Kristin and clicked on. 'Hey,' he said, 'what news?'

'I can come,' she told him. 'I'll get the train down tomorrow and stay with Nikki till Wednesday. I have to be back in London then, but Dan said he might be able to take a couple of days off to be with her till you get back at the weekend.'

'Great,' he said, wanting to hug her. 'Thanks. I really appreciate it.'

'I just wish I was there now,' Kristin said with feeling. 'I had to finish the shoot though, I mean it would have been really unprofessional if I'd just walked, but knowing Nikki she'll understand that.'

'Of course,' he assured her. 'Ring when you know what

time you're arriving and someone will come and get you from the station.'

'OK. You're taking all my stuff to London, are you?' she asked tentatively.

'I think it's already in the van,' he told her, hoping he was right. *Please David don't chuck her now*, he implored inwardly, *because we really need her.*

'Great, thanks. How's Nikki?'

He glanced towards the kitchen, but she'd gone into the conservatory to load the washing into the tumble dryer. 'To be honest, I'm not sure,' he answered. 'Up and down, I guess. I'll be interested to hear what you think after you've spent a few days with her.'

'No problem. When I spoke to Dan just now he said Mrs A was going to try to contact her parents.'

'That's right. With any luck she'll succeed, because right now we could do with all the support we can get, both moral and financial.'

When it came time to leave the next day, Spence had never felt more wretched in his life. With most of his belongings in the van and a job and new house waiting for him in London, it was as though he was abandoning the two people he loved most in the world. The night before, he'd come very close to calling Drake to tell him he'd have to find another director. It was Nikki who'd reminded him how important it was to keep the connection going, even if he wasn't being paid very much this time around.

'He can put other jobs your way that will earn you bigger money,' she'd pointed out, her tone as rational and wise as his own was tormented and tragic. 'And once all this is . . . Well, it'll be easier to pick up the pieces if we have something to move on to.'

It was the closest she'd come to admitting that Zac wasn't going to be around in a few years, and it told him that somewhere, on some level she knew what was happening. It was a relief, but he still wished she'd find a way to talk about it more openly.

Now, as he wrapped her tightly in his arms, Nikki said, 'I'll see you next weekend.'

Just like that, as though it were any normal parting. He couldn't help feeling hurt. 'Are you sure you're going to be . . .'

'Everything's cool,' she assured him. 'Kristin's here, and Mrs A is at the end of the phone.'

'You'll call if you need to, won't you? It doesn't matter what time it is, or where I am.'

'I promise.' Her eyes were so lucid and blue, her smile almost too beautiful to bear. For one heart-stopping moment he felt as though he was seeing her for the first, or maybe it was the last time. Then he pushed the unsettling thought aside, trying to stop himself reading even more tragedy into their lives than they already had.

David came to embrace her, squeezing her hard. 'You know where Mum is,' he reminded her. 'You can call her any time of the day or night.'

Nikki smiled. 'Zac's not ill,' she reminded him, 'so please stop worrying.'

It was true, Zac wasn't, yet. It was her they were all worried about.

Danny was next, and it was all he could do to keep himself together as he held her close. 'I'll be here late Wednesday afternoon,' he promised, 'and I'll stay till Spence gets back on Friday.'

'Cool,' she said. 'Zac will look forward to seeing you and I'll make us something delicious to eat, or I expect Mrs A will.' She gave a laugh. 'She's so busy cooking these days maybe she should open a restaurant. What do you think, David? Should your mum open a restaurant?'

David smiled. The words were said light-heartedly, but somehow they were hitting a wrong note, and making him feel more anxious about her than ever. This wasn't Nikki.

In the end, with Kristin holding the baby at the front door, and Nikki standing at the gate waving, David drove off up the road, while Spence looked over his shoulder waving too. Squashed in between them, Dan was struggling to hold back his tears.

'It's good that Kristin's there,' David said as they turned the corner. 'Girls are better at coping than we are.'

'That's right,' Danny agreed.

'Yes,' Spence said. 'Yes they are.'

He wanted to ask David what his plans were regarding Kristin, but for the moment he was struggling too hard with his emotions to say very much. Why was God doing this to them, he was crying inside. How could he be so cruel to such an innocent little soul? What good could ever come from making a child suffer the way Zac would have to before he eventually died? What purpose was there in putting anyone through the agony of watching him?

His eyes closed as they turned out of Beauley Road to start driving along the cut. Maybe Zac's destiny was all the proof he needed that there was no god, and if there was no god, why shouldn't they take the matter of life and death into their own hands? Because there were laws to stop them? Or because they wouldn't have the courage to go that far?

These crazy thoughts had been going around in his head for days. He'd never dare to speak them aloud, because he didn't mean them, he just couldn't help thinking them.

Chapter Fifteen

It was Tuesday afternoon and Mrs Adani had just left her Vauxhall Corsa in the underground car park beneath Waitrose in Bath to begin walking over Pulteney Bridge to the address Danny had given her for Mr and Mrs Grant.

Though Mr Pearce had made some progress with Mr Grant's secretary yesterday, it was only to learn that the investment brokerage company Mr Grant used to own had gone into receivership, and that the secretary was only there answering phones until the end of the month. Apparently she hadn't heard from Mr Grant for several weeks, but if he did ring in she'd promised to give him the message to call Mr Pearce.

There were other avenues Mrs Adani intended to explore if she got nowhere today, such as the Land Registry to find out if the Grants still owned the house, and the electoral roll to see if their name cropped up anywhere else in the city. However, she wanted to pay a visit to the empty house herself before taking things any further.

When she reached it she found, to her surprise, that all the shutters were open, giving the distinct impression of someone being inside. Having already suspected that the Grants had just been away for a while when Danny had come, she decided this probably confirmed it.

Hooking her bag higher on to her shoulder, she pushed open the gate and knocked on the front door.

'I'll go!' she heard a voice shout from inside, and a moment later a very attractive young woman with a copious mane of blonde hair and a very pregnant belly was regarding her in friendly surprise. 'Hello,' she said. 'I'm guessing you're not the plumber.'

Mrs A smiled. 'That is correct,' she told her. 'My name is Mrs Adani. I am looking for Mr and Mrs Grant.'

The woman frowned for a moment, then her lovely face lit up again. 'Oh, you mean the people who lived here before?' she said. 'That's right, their name was Grant.'

Mrs A regarded her carefully. 'Do you know where they have moved to?' she asked.

The woman frowned again, this time more warily than thoughtfully.

'I am wanting to give them some news of their daughter,' Mrs A explained.

The woman nodded slowly, seeming to assess the verity of this. In the end, apparently deciding Mrs A looked trustworthy, she said, 'I think they ran into some financial trouble, actually, but you didn't hear that from me, OK? All I know for sure is that we bought the house from them about a month ago, and we haven't heard from them since. Well, why would we, we didn't know them? However, I'm sure they left a forwarding address which I think I should be able to put my hands on. We're still in a bit of a muddle after the move,' she explained, turning back inside.

Leaving the door open as she picked her way through an obstacle course of boxes, she began riffling around in a desk drawer halfway along the hall. 'Ah, here it is,' she declared, pulling out a small white business card. 'I'll jot it down for you.'

A few moments later she was handing over a scrap of paper, saying, 'I'm afraid they didn't leave a phone number, but it's a Bath address, and I don't think it's too far from here. Would you like me to check the A–Z for you? Or maybe you know Bennett Street. It's up towards the Royal Crescent, I think.'

'I have my own map, thank you,' Mrs A told her, patting her bag. 'You have been most helpful. I wish you luck with the little one,' she added, nodding towards the eight-month bump.

The woman beamed happily. 'He's due in three weeks,' she confided. 'It's our first.'

Thinking of Nikki and how proudly expectant she'd been a couple of months ago, Mrs A smiled kindly, and after thanking the woman again she turned back into the street.

Luckily it wasn't raining today, and the wind had dropped after a very gusty night, so she was able to consult her street map without too much difficulty. Finding Bennett Street to be just off The Circus, which was indeed in the same vicinity as the Royal Crescent, she set off on the twenty-or-so-minute walk.

Though she generally enjoyed a stroll through the historic city, her pace was quicker today, and her thoughts more focused on Nikki than on the splendid architecture she was passing. She'd called round to see her that morning, in half a mind to tell her where she was going, but in the end she'd decided not to. It would be more sensible to discover Mr and Mrs Grant's whereabouts first, and if she wasn't able to manage that today there was no point upsetting Nikki by telling her that they seemed to have disappeared.

However, they hadn't, because when Mrs A arrived at the address she'd been given, the Grants' name was beside one of the bells. Apparently this grand house in the middle of a Georgian terrace had been divided into flats.

After giving the bell a firm press she began going over what she intended to say, feeling slightly anxious now, partly because of what she'd heard about Nikki's parents – though she knew children often exaggerated when criticising their parents – but also because of how difficult the meeting was likely to be even if they did turn out to be friendly.

A woman's voice came down the intercom, asking who was there.

Mrs A stepped forward. 'My name is Mrs Adani,' she said. 'I am a friend of Nikki Grant.'

The silence that followed left Mrs A wondering what reaction she had stirred, and whether the woman – Mrs Grant? – was considering coming down to the street to check what sort of person this unexpected visitor might be before letting her in.

In the end the voice said, 'We're on the first floor,' and a buzzer sounded, releasing the door.

The hallway was freshly painted, the stairs were wide and carpeted and each tread was comfortably low. Everything about the place, from the glossy black front door, to the watercolours on the walls, to the artistically carved banisters, spoke to Mrs A of wealth and privilege. Certainly not somewhere she would expect to find people experiencing financial difficulties, but then, remembering the grand house on Great Pulteney Street, she supposed everything was relative.

On reaching the first landing she was about to knock on the only door when it opened, and a smartly dressed woman with intense blue-grey eyes and a slightly harassed expression said, 'Hello. I'm sorry, I didn't quite catch your name.'

Mrs A smiled as she repeated it. 'And you are Mrs Grant?' she said politely.

'I am, yes. I . . . You said you're a friend of Nicola's. Is she all right?'

'She's fine,' Mrs A assured her. 'I'm her health visitor, as well as a friend, so I thought I should come because . . . Well, I'm not sure if you are aware that you have a grandson now. His name is Zac and he is a very lovely little boy.'

Though Mrs Grant's eyes appeared to soften, the colour rising in her cheeks showed her embarrassment at being told this by a stranger. 'Is he . . .? How . . .?' She seemed unsure what to ask.

Deciding she must come to the point, Mrs A said, 'I am afraid that I have some very sad news about him.'

Alarm sharpened Mrs Grant's features. 'I thought you said he was a lovely little boy,' she reminded her.

'Oh, he is, most certainly,' Mrs A confirmed, 'but unfortunately it has been discovered that he has a very rare condition.'

Mrs Grant's face started to drain. 'What do you mean? What kind of condition?' she asked, almost as though Mrs A might be responsible for whatever it was.

Mrs A held her gaze. 'If you do not mind me saying so, I do not feel that this is something we should be discussing on the stairs.'

Seeming only now to realise she'd forgotten her manners, Mrs Grant immediately stepped back through the door. 'No, no of course not,' she said, gesturing for Mrs A to come in.

'I'm sorry. Please go through. Second door on the right.'

Following the instruction Mrs A found herself in a spacious, elegant sitting room with two tall sash windows overlooking the street, and an eclectic collection of antique furnishings that appeared to owe rather more to show than comfort. 'Oh,' she said, startled, as a tall man with a hawkish face rose up from one of the chairs. He was casually dressed in corduroy trousers and a grey pullover, and was in need of a shave.

'This is Mrs Adani,' Mrs Grant informed him. 'Nicola's health visitor. Apparently the baby has a . . . a condition.'

Mr Grant's close-set eyes darkened with concern as they returned to Mrs Adani. 'This is a very distressing thing to hear,' he said sombrely. 'Would you care to sit down?'

Going to perch on the edge of the chair he indicated, Mrs A bunched her hands on top of her bag as Mr and Mrs Grant sat down too. She was trying to find a resemblance to Nikki in one of them, but neither was much like her, except perhaps the mother, around her mouth. If she'd smile it might be easier to tell, but Mrs A had to concede there was little to smile about today.

'So, what is the condition?' Mr Grant asked, his tone somewhat gentler than Mrs A had been led to expect.

'It is called Tay-Sachs disease,' she replied.

The Grants looked at one another blankly. Apparently neither had ever heard of it. 'Is it serious?' Mrs Grant asked.

'Yes, I am afraid so,' Mrs A replied. 'It is a degenerative condition that there is no cure for.'

Mrs Grant gasped as she clasped a hand to her mouth.

Seeming equally upset, Mr Grant said, 'Has she sought proper advice, or a second opinion?'

'Yes, she has. I am sorry to say that it was confirmed.'

Mrs Grant rose to her feet, appearing both distressed and distracted. 'This disease,' she said, 'how did he get it? How does it happen?'

'It is an autosomal recessive disorder,' Mrs A told her.

'You mean he inherited it?' Mrs Grant looked suddenly angry. 'I knew no good would come of her relationship with that boy, and now look what he's done, given her a child that's . . .'

'Please excuse me,' Mrs A interrupted gently, 'the mutated gene must be present in both parents for this to have occurred, so your daughter is a carrier too.'

Mrs Grant's eyes dilated with shock, then immediately turned hostile. 'Are you trying to say that we have this gene too?' she demanded.

Mrs A said nothing, letting her work it out for herself. She wondered if the worst part for Nikki's mother, for the moment, was finding out that she might share any type of gene at all with the likes of Spencer James and his family, never mind one so malignant.

In the end Mrs Grant turned to her husband, who appeared to have been stunned into silence. Seeming irritated, she said, 'Jeremy, will you please say something?'

His head came up, but before he could speak Adele Grant turned back to Mrs A.

'Why didn't Nicola come to tell us this herself?' she demanded.

'Why do you think?' her husband cut in. 'She's still angry with us . . .'

'But she needs us,' Adele protested, 'so it's ridiculous to send a messenger . . .'

'Actually, she doesn't know I'm here,' Mrs A admitted.

Seeming not to hear, Grant said, 'Does she need money? I'm afraid to say she's too late if she does.'

'For heaven's sake, not everything's about money,' Adele snapped.

He continued as though his wife hadn't spoken. 'This flat and what you see around you belongs to friends. We can barely even afford the rent.'

'My husband has lost everything during this economic downturn,' Adele went on crossly, as though trying to dispense with the issue before Grant allowed it to take over. 'It's been a very difficult time.'

'I'm afraid our experiences these past few months have all been about demands for money we no longer have,' Grant continued.

'There are other forms of support besides financial,' Mrs A pointed out, as gently as she could, 'such as emotional and parental.'

'Yes, yes, of course,' Mrs Grant said hurriedly, 'but I still wonder why she didn't pick up the phone, or come to see us herself. She must have known we'd want to help.'

Taking a quick decision not to mention that Danny and Spence had tried to get in touch after the baby was born, since it didn't actually answer the question, Mrs A said, again, 'Actually, Nikki doesn't know I am here, and I am not sure how she was going to come to see you when you were not letting her know that you had changed your address.'

Mr Grant blinked with surprise. 'But I sent her an email,' he protested. 'It contained everything, our new address and phone numbers, why we were having to move. Everything.'

'She has never mentioned this email,' Mrs A told him. 'May I ask when you sent it?'

'A week or so before Christmas. We never received a reply, so we knew she was still angry with us.'

'We asked her to come and see us before the baby was born so we could explain what had happened to her father's business,' Adele continued, 'but she stormed out before we had the chance to. She was very upset, and in retrospect I can see we handled things badly. We should have waited to tell her what we'd found out about her boyfriend. I wanted to, but you,' she said to her husband, 'insisted on putting it first, to get it out of the way, you said.'

Mrs A's eyes moved from one to the other. 'May I, if it is not too impertinent, ask what you told her about her boyfriend?'

Again Adele glanced at her husband, her expression showing as much unease as anger. 'We . . . That is, my husband, hired a private investigator to look into Spencer James's background. What we discovered . . .' She swallowed dryly. 'It turned out that his father was a convicted . . . paedophile. We thought Nicola should be told, in case her boyfriend might have inherited . . . In case he might in some way . . .' As her voice fractured she put her hands over her face. 'It seems he's passed on something just as terrible,' she said wretchedly.

'It could have been his mother,' Mrs A reminded her, still inwardly reeling at the revelation. This was something she'd never heard about Spence's father, making her wonder if Spence himself knew. If he did, she could hardly blame him for keeping it a secret.

Adele inhaled deeply, trying to gather herself together. 'If she doesn't know you're here,' she said, 'maybe she doesn't . . . What can we do?' she finished helplessly.

'That will be up to you,' Mrs A replied. 'I understand now why Nikki hasn't contacted you herself. She's afraid of what you'll say to Spence if you see him. Do you happen to know if he's aware of his father's conviction?'

Adele shook her head. 'But it's hardly the issue now, is it?'

'No,' Mrs A agreed, and getting to her feet, she said, 'I will leave it for you to decide when and how you make contact with your daughter, but if I may be so bold, I would advise you to assure her that you are not going to cause any difficulties over the matter of Spence's father. As you said, it really isn't the issue now.'

As she walked to the door neither of them moved. Clearly shock was making them slow with their manners.

'Before you go,' Mrs Grant said, 'please tell us the name of the condition again.'

Mrs A turned round. 'It is called Tay-Sachs disease,' she said. 'It does not normally become evident until a child is around six months old, but Zac had some breathing problems one night and was taken to hospital. They discovered it then.'

Mrs Grant swallowed. 'What . . . what kind of disease is it?' she asked. 'I mean, how does it manifest itself?'

Taking a pen and notepad from her bag, Mrs A wrote down the Web address Mr Pearce had given her. 'This will tell you all about it,' she said, tearing out the page and handing it over. 'You will find that it is most prevalent in Jewish people, and a certain order of Amish, as well as . . .' She stopped as she noticed that Mrs Grant's face had suddenly drained of colour.

Coming forward, as though to shield his wife, Grant said, 'Thank you for coming, Mrs . . .'

'Adani.'

He nodded. 'I take it Nicola is still living at the same address in Bristol?'

'Yes, she is,' Mrs A confirmed, and not at all sure what

had happened in those final minutes, she followed him to the door.

The instant Grant returned to the drawing room Adele cried, 'I always said we should have told her.'

His expression turned to astonishment. 'But, Adele, it was you who didn't want her to know.'

Her hands flew to her head as she struggled to deal with this fresh horror that was erupting around them. 'That poor baby,' she gasped. 'Oh God, to think we could have . . .' She broke off, unable to go on.

'Could have what?' he prompted.

'You know what I'm talking about,' she raged. 'We're responsible for . . .'

'How could we possibly have known anything like this would happen?' he broke in angrily. 'I've never even heard of the disease until today. Have you?'

She shook her head. 'What are we going to do?' she implored, her words as helpless as the despair in her heart.

He only looked at her, his eyes darkening with shadows of an inner torment impossible for him to express. 'I don't know,' he said huskily. 'I really don't know.'

'It seems they have been going through some difficult times,' Mrs A was telling Spence on the phone as she walked back to her car. 'They have sold the house and are living in a friend's flat.'

'And they were proposing to tell their daughter they'd moved when, exactly?' he demanded furiously.

'They say they sent an email, just before Christmas.'

'But they . . . Oh, God, it must have been the one she deleted.'

'I see. Has she ever told you that she went to see them around that time?'

He sounded surprised and baffled as he said, 'No. Why? Did she?'

'It would seem so, but they had another falling out, which is presumably why she deleted their email.'

'But why didn't she tell me she'd gone?' he murmured.

Deciding it wasn't her place to answer that with the full

243

truth, Mrs A said, 'Probably because she didn't want to worry you.'

'But that's just . . .'

'Getting back to the real point of my visit,' Mrs A interjected, 'they were very upset to hear about Zac.'

'Well, at least it shows they're human. So what are they going to do?'

Mrs A was thoughtful as she said, 'I cannot be sure about this, but I think . . . Well, maybe that they have more to tell than they revealed to me.'

There was a beat before Spence said, 'What does that mean?'

'Mrs Grant seemed very upset when I mentioned the principal carriers of the gene.'

Again Spence fell silent. 'Is this going to end up with you thinking she's Jewish, or Amish?' he said doubtfully. 'Or French Canadian?'

'To be honest, I'm not sure what to think,' she admitted.

'We have to remember who we're talking about here,' Spence said. 'Mr Grant the banker, or investment manager anyway. Almost everyone in his world is Jewish, so maybe he's the one hiding his roots.'

'But why would he do that?'

'God knows, all I know is that my son has an incurable disease because of some bastard inherited gene, and if one of them knew they might be a carrier then they've virtually condemned him to death by not speaking up.'

Understanding his rage, Mrs A didn't remind him of his own parents' responsibility, because now wasn't the time, and besides, he'd had no one to ask. He was looking for someone to blame, and that too was understandable, when he was suffering such pain. 'The question now,' she said, 'is whether or not I tell Nikki I've been to see them.'

'No, let me speak to her first,' he decided. 'If they upset her the last time she saw them . . . I want to find out what that was about, why she went, and why she never said anything. If they . . . Hang on . . .' His voice was muffled as he spoke to someone his end, then coming back on the line, he said, 'I have to go, but thanks, Mrs A, for going over there. I'll talk to Nikki and get back to you.'

Nikki and Kristin were lying on the sitting-room floor with Zac, laughing at his baby attempts to secure their attention. He'd definitely perfected the art of letting out a joyous sort of scream to bring his mother's face down for a kiss, so that he could grab her hair. And he could blow bubbles and kick his legs, which generally entertained the world at large and made all sorts of people ooh and aah.

As they played, Kristin was loving the way he gripped her finger and wouldn't let go. He really seemed to enjoy it. 'He's so sweet and gorgeous,' she laughed, gazing down at him. *It's impossible to believe there's anything wrong with him,* she was thinking.

'He's a rascal and a tiger,' Nikki told him playfully, and leaned down to blow a raspberry on his belly.

As she watched her, Kristin felt a tumult of emotions churning inside her. She had no idea how Nikki could act so normally in the face of what was happening, but she kept telling herself that if Nikki could, then she could too. She wasn't sure whether she wished Nikki would talk about it or not, and she definitely didn't know how to bring it up herself. Two whole days had gone by, and neither of them had mentioned it at all. It was weird, kind of scary in a way. Nikki wasn't discussing it with Spence on the phone either, from what Kristin could tell, because she often overheard their calls. It was almost surreal the way Nikki spoke to him, as though everything was cool and normal.

They'd had a bit of a row last night, though, something to do with Nikki going to see her parents and not telling him.

'It was no big deal,' Nikki had cried. 'They just got into their controlling thing again, so I walked out.'

Kristin hadn't heard Spence's reply, but then Nikki said, 'Please, Spence, I don't want to talk about them. I'm sorry I didn't tell you, but let's leave it now, OK? It's not important.'

Apparently Spence had let it drop, because by the time the call ended Nikki was talking softly again, and after she rang off she carried on in her usual way, as though no cross words had been spoken, and nothing at all was wrong in her world.

It was weird watching her be her normal self, when Kristin knew that inside she had to be in a terrible state.

Anyone would be in her position, but she never let it show. It was all bottled up, and the only way she seemed to have changed, as far as Kristin could make out, was that she was no longer easy to talk to. Kristin didn't even know how to bring up the subject of David, and whether Nikki had spoken to him the way she'd promised. If she had, she might have forgotten about it with all that was going on, so maybe she needed a prompt. And if she hadn't . . . Well, it might remind her to do it the next time she saw him. The trouble was finding the words.

'You know what I wish?' Nikki said, drawing circles around Zac's tiny chest. 'I wish he could go now, before all those horrible things start happening to him.'

Kristin went very still. Her eyes came up to Nikki's face. This was the first allusion she'd made to Zac's condition, and though Kristin could understand where she was coming from it was still a bit of an odd thing to wish. 'You don't mean that, right?' she said.

Nikki shrugged. 'I don't know,' she admitted. 'I mean, how would you feel if he was yours? You've read the stuff on the Internet, would you really want him to spend the next four years suffering like that?'

Kristin wasn't quite sure what to say to that, because no, of course she wouldn't, but on the other hand Nikki was so strange at the moment that there was no knowing how she might take anything she said.

'Do you think it would be kinder to let him go now,' Nikki said, 'or to allow him to go through losing his sight and hearing, never be able to talk or walk or even sit up? He'll struggle to breathe and swallow. He'll cling on to a life that has no quality at all, because apparently God has the say about when we die.' She paused to wipe the drool from Zac's hands. 'I don't know if there is a god,' she went on, 'but I do know that no animal has to suffer like that. So tell me, Kris, would you wish it on your child?'

Not sure she was really up to something this deep, but wanting desperately to be as supportive as she could, Kristin said, 'You didn't wish it on Zac, Nikki. It just happened. You know, it's the way things are, and you can't change them.'

'But I can,' Nikki argued.

Kristin was watching her closely, but Nikki's head didn't come up so she couldn't read her face.

'The way I see it,' Nikki continued, 'is I have a choice. I can either let my son – my *healthy* son – turn into a vegetable that feels terrible pain and distress, or I can let him go with dignity and no pain. What would you do if you were me?'

'Oh Nikki, don't,' Kristin protested. 'I mean, I understand how hard this is for you, but what you're saying . . . If I'm reading you correctly . . .'

'You are,' Nikki told her. 'What you're thinking now is exactly what I'm thinking.'

Kristin's face drained. 'But it's against the law, Nik,' she protested.

'I know that, but how long would I have to serve? Five, six years? Ten, fifteen at the most? However long, it has to be worth it, doesn't it? Anything to save him from going through all that misery fate has in store. Why should I allow that to happen if I don't have to? Wouldn't it be cruel of me to sit back and do nothing when I could spare him all that? He's my son, so why shouldn't I have as much say over what happens to him as something as random as fate, or God, or destiny, or all that other bollocks that's going on out there?'

As emotional and irrational as she was sounding, she was making a lot of sense too, so Kristin didn't know what to say.

'There's only one thing stopping me,' Nikki said, lifting Zac into her arms.

Kristin looked at her, hardly daring to breathe.

'I don't have the courage to do it,' Nikki said, and burying her face in Zac's neck she started to cry.

Chapter Sixteen

The following afternoon Danny arrived to stay with Nikki until the weekend, when Spence was due back. How much longer they'd be able to keep an eye on her like this was hard to say, but with everyone's schedules starting to become more demanding they all knew it couldn't be for much longer. What would happen then, when they were finally forced to leave her on her own, none of them liked to think about; they simply remained hopeful that Nikki would suddenly return to her old self, and they wouldn't have to worry quite so much about her.

Before leaving, Kristin managed to take Danny aside to warn him about the way Nikki's mind was working. 'I honestly don't think she'll do anything,' she whispered behind the closed door of the kitchen, 'but I thought I should tell you what she said, you know, just in case.'

Danny's face had turned pale; his eyes were dark with worry as he tried to think what to do. 'Have you told Mrs A?' he asked.

'No, she hasn't been round since yesterday morning, but she's coming later, so I think you should tell her.'

Danny nodded. 'How has Nikki been otherwise?'

Kristin shrugged. 'It's hard to put into words, like she's there, but not, if you know what I mean. She cried yesterday, but not for long. It's like she can't, or just won't let herself.' She watched Danny's face as he absorbed this, and her concern for Nikki slipped into second place as she wondered if she dared to broach the subject of David with him.

'How's everything at the house?' she ventured. 'Are you guys settling in OK?'

Danny's eyes came briefly to hers. 'More or less,' he answered. 'None of us have been there much, so there's still a lot of unpacking to do.'

Anxious about where her own possessions might have been stored, she said, 'I can probably make a start on it over the weekend. Is David going to be there, do you know?'

Danny shrugged. 'He said something about coming here last night, but I don't know what he's decided.'

Suspecting that if David knew she was going to be around in London he'd firm up his plans to come to Bristol, Kristin struggled to keep the emotion from her voice as she said, 'OK, I'll give him a call.' She glanced at her watch to try and hide her tears. 'I should be going now or I'll miss the train. Give Mrs A my love when she comes, and if there's anything you want me to do for you in London just let me know.'

After she'd gone Danny remained where he was in the kitchen, sunk in all kinds of emotions he really didn't want to deal with right now. He wondered how Kristin was going to take it when she found her belongings in the single bedroom. Maybe not as hard as when she discovered his in one of the double rooms with David's. Though he might not be Kristin's number one fan, he still felt really bad about keeping things from her, but what could he do when it wasn't his place to tell her? It was David's, and Danny understood how difficult he was finding it coming out to everyone, especially when he'd been struggling against his natural instincts for so long. Still, at least they'd told Spence now, who'd been as cool about it as Danny was sure Nikki would be when he got round to telling her.

Now definitely wasn't the right time for that, though, because Mrs A had just let herself in the front door, and though Danny and Spence felt confident she'd be able to handle David's homosexuality, David kept reminding them that she was a devout Catholic for whom an act of love between two men was unnatural at best, and a sin against God at worst.

'Hi,' Danny said, going to greet her with a hug. 'I didn't realise you had a key.'

'The door was open,' she told him, taking off her coat, 'but I think it would be a good idea for me to have one. So, how are you, my dear?'

'I'm cool,' he answered, silently hoping she would go on liking him once she found out.

She cocked her head curiously as she regarded him. 'Is that a new earring?' she asked. 'I don't think I've seen it before.'

He smiled. 'You're scary sometimes with the things you notice,' he teased, thankful she had no way of knowing it was a gift from David.

She chuckled and patted his hand. 'And don't you forget it,' she told him playfully. 'Now, where are my charges? It is the day to give Zac his check to see how he is progressing.'

Hating the way he wondered what the point was when they all knew it would make no difference to Zac's future now, Danny said, 'I need to have a quiet word with you about something Nikki said to Kristin.'

Mrs A's eyebrows rose.

'Not now,' he whispered, hearing Nikki on the landing, and looking up he smiled as she came down the stairs wearing her boots and a bobble hat, and carrying Zac in a pale blue fleecy blanket.

'What are you two whispering about?' she asked, eyeing them suspiciously. Then, seeming to lose interest, 'There's a late stretch class, due to start in ten minutes so I'll have to hurry.'

Mrs A made to take Zac, but Nikki turned away. 'He's coming with me,' she said. 'He could do with some air, and he likes being around the other children.'

Mrs A's arms fell to her sides. 'It's his check-up day,' she reminded her.

'I know, but we don't need to bother with all that any more, do we?' Nikki said, in a tone that was more dismissive than bitter. 'It's not as if it's going to matter in a few months, so don't let's fuss him.'

Mrs A's eyes flicked to Danny. 'OK,' she said, apparently deciding not to argue for now, 'we'll leave it for today, but I will need to carry on giving him his regular checks.'

Seeming either not to have heard, or choosing to ignore it,

Nikki snuggled Zac into his buggy and reached for her coat. 'We'll be back in just over an hour,' she told Danny. Then to Mrs A, 'Thanks for coming in. The biryani was delicious, by the way. One of your best.'

With Kristin's warning still ringing in his ears, Danny stooped to pull the blanket aside, needing to check Zac was OK. To his relief he was awake and alert, and Danny immediately felt dreadful for thinking the worst.

After Nikki had gone, he made Mrs A a cup of tea and they went into the sitting room while he passed on what Kristin had told him.

Though Mrs A's face showed a marked concern, in her typical matter-of-fact way she said, 'It is very natural for her to be having those thoughts, any mother would in her shoes. In fact, I think it would be very unusual if she didn't, because a child's suffering is much worse than your own.'

Though he was ready to accept that, Danny said, 'She's not right though, is she? I mean, she's definitely not herself.'

'That would be too much to expect at this stage,' Mrs A told him. 'It will take some time for her to come to terms with what the future has in store, and it is understandable for her to try to shut it out.'

'Yet she talked about it just now in a way that was . . . I don't know, almost callous.'

Mrs A nodded. 'She is trying to avoid her emotions in order to cope,' she said. 'Every now and again she allows them in, but I think it is going to be a gradual process and we must allow her to do it her way, until she is ready to confront the full force of the truth.' She took a sip of her tea, then replaced the cup in the saucer. 'Do you know if her parents have been in touch?' she asked.

He shook his head. 'I have to presume not, or Kristin would have mentioned it. From what Spence told me about your meeting with them, I thought they might have been by now.'

'Mm, me too,' she agreed. 'I just wonder . . . Something got to them when I mentioned the Jewish and Amish connection. I wonder if that's what's holding them back.'

Danny shrugged, having no suggestions to offer. 'Are you thinking of contacting them again?' he asked.

She nodded pensively. 'I might, but I'll talk it over with Spence first.'

Dear Zac, Nikki wrote in her journal the next day, *You are being quite naughty at the moment, crying a lot and refusing to eat. I don't blame you, because it's how I feel too, except I don't cry and I try to eat. I know you're afraid, we both are, but I've already promised not to let you suffer and I swear I won't let you down. I've been thinking, when the time is right, we should go to a place where everything is the way it should be and nothing can hurt you. I'll be able to keep you safe there and I'll always be with you. I'm not sure if Daddy will come with us, it is a hard question to ask and I haven't managed to find the right words yet. He'll probably be shocked, but he loves us very much, so I think he would rather be with us than stay here alone.*

Sometimes all this feels like a dream. I wish it was, so I could wake up and find everything the way it was before you were taken to hospital. I keep thinking back to how happy we were just two short weeks ago, and it feels like another lifetime. I suppose it was. The world has fallen out of kilter. It's not somewhere we belong, or I can relate to any more. Everything seems strange, or blurred, or warped out of shape. Sometimes, when I hear people talking, their voices are slow and garbled, as though they're speaking to me from under water. Or perhaps it's me who's in the water, trying to listen, wanting to take in what they're saying, but I can't because I'm drowning.

I wonder if you'll remember any of this when you're older. I still imagine you growing up, because it's my way of freeing you . . . I'm sure if I send you telepathic images of how you will be at six, then sixteen, then twenty-six, you will see yourself too, strong and handsome, a sportsman maybe, or a lawyer, or a film director like Daddy. There's no reason why life has to be played out on the mundane level of reality. Our minds can easily take us to other places, or dimensions, where everything is happening the way we want it to. This is how we protect ourselves from a fate, or a being like God, that allows us to have no say or control over what's happening to us in this world. We can transport ourselves beyond its reach as often as we like, and we can even stay there if we choose to. I think we shall, but we have to give Daddy the chance to come with us, so until I speak to him about it we will stay where we are, because nothing bad is happening to us yet.

Looking up from her book as Zac snuffled and shifted in his cot, Nikki sat staring at nothing for a while, aware of thoughts flitting through her mind like birds busying about but failing to perch. Or flocking in too fast and creating an impenetrable blackness. Yesterday she'd written that it was as though a glass wall had gone up between her and Zac and the rest of the world, and it was. She could see and hear everything, but she never really let it in. Air filled her lungs but not too deeply, her limbs moved but not fluidly any more.

She'd filled a whole notebook this past week with long, rambling thoughts that didn't necessarily make any more sense than those she'd written now – it was simply something she felt compelled to do, often while Zac was sleeping, as though she could write her way into his dreams. It might seem crazy to some, but what did that matter? She wasn't sure anything did any more, which was defeatist and sad, but nevertheless true.

Once Zac had gone, what future would there be for her and Spence? She'd read enough about the genes they were carrying to know that it wasn't possible for them to have more children, but would they want to after this? The foetus could be screened, but what if it proved positive? It would mean an abortion, and then they would have killed another innocent child.

All this went round and round in her mind, hour after hour, day after day. One minute she wanted to end it all, the next she felt ready to fight. She'd get through this, though, she was sure of it, she simply hadn't worked out yet which route to take.

She was writing in her journal again the following day when she heard Spence come in downstairs. He was earlier than expected, which would normally have pleased her and made her run down to greet him, but she still had a lot of thoughts she needed to get out, so she continued to write until he came upstairs to find her.

'Hi,' he said from the bedroom door. 'What are you doing?'

She closed her book. 'Just writing stuff down. Is David with you?'

'He's gone to his mum's, he'll be here later.'

She seemed to have no more to say, so he went to look at Zac. 'How long's he been asleep?' he asked, putting a finger to Zac's cheek.

'I'm not sure, but it's probably time he woke up.'

Lifting him into his arms, Spence inhaled the warm, baby scent of him, and closed his eyes as the purity of him stole through his heart.

Nikki watched them, trying to connect with what she was feeling. It was there, but it seemed frozen inside her, or trapped the other side of the glass wall.

'Are you going to come down?' he asked.

'In a minute,' she answered. 'You can take him if you like. He probably needs changing.' She picked up her pen.

Leaving her to carry on with a task that, from what he'd been hearing, seemed to be bordering on an obsession lately, he took Zac down to the sitting room, where Danny was watching E! News.

'She still writing?' Danny asked.

Spence nodded.

Even to Danny, who loved Nikki almost as much as he did, Spence didn't want to admit how much he'd been dreading coming home tonight, but it was the truth. As the week had worn on and he'd become more and more engrossed in the film, the release, the escape, that working had provided had made him increasingly reluctant to return to reality. His feelings hadn't been helped by how unpredictable Nikki was each time he rang, one minute sounding distant, cut off, as though she was trying to push him out of their lives, the next as though she needed him so desperately that she couldn't go another hour without him. His conscience was constantly on the rack, tearing him apart for not thinking about her every minute of the day, and making him feel unprofessional for wishing the movie to hell so he could be with his son.

When it had come time to leave today, he'd been assailed by an almost overpowering urge to get on a train to anywhere but here. He hated himself for it, but in extreme and irrational moments he almost wished Zac had already gone, because he didn't know how he was going to stand the next four or five months watching him develop like any normal child, while knowing it was just an illusion – a trick, a wicked, tasteless joke that nature was playing on them all, with no redemption or mercy to follow.

'You look all in,' Danny told him. 'I guess it's been a tough week.'

'Fairly,' Spence admitted, and sinking down on the sofa he began bringing Zac gently awake, while thinking how easy it would be to hold the blanket over his little face now, and . . .

'I'm sorry,' he sobbed, as Danny came to take Zac. 'I just don't . . . I guess I . . .'

'It's OK,' Danny soothed. 'You're tired and this is the first time you've seen him all week, so it's brought it all back.'

Spence nodded and tried to swallow his tears. 'Much good I'm going to be to anyone if I carry on like this,' he said. 'I leave her to cope without me all week, then as soon as I get back . . .' He shook his head in despair. 'If she'd just talk to me,' he choked in frustration, 'if she'd let me know what's going on in her head I might be able to help her, or at least feel as though I'm doing something worthwhile, but she shuts herself away inside . . . How long's she been up there now?'

'Most of the afternoon,' Danny answered, rocking Zac back and forth as he started to wake up.

'She was like it with Kristin too, and now she doesn't want Mrs A to give him his regular checks . . . For God's sake, doesn't she realise it's not all about her? I have feelings too, and Zac needs to be taken care of as if he were normal, because right now he is.'

'Ssh, ssh,' Danny cooed as Zac started to fret. 'I expect you're hungry, little man, and I'm sorry there's nothing I can give you.'

'How much longer is she going to stay up there?' Spence growled angrily, slamming his fists into the sofa.

'Just calm down,' Danny advised. 'She'll be here the instant she hears him crying, and if you two are going to start rowing I won't be able to leave you.'

Remembering that Danny and David were going to have dinner with Danny's parents tonight, Spence did his best to crush his frustration. This was a big deal for Dan, since he'd never taken anyone home before, and probably even bigger for his mum and dad, who, to Dan's amazement, hadn't objected when he'd told them that the friend he was bringing was male.

Having met Danny's folks on a few occasions, Spence could just imagine the flap they were getting themselves into now, but all he could really think about was how much he wished that his only concern for Zac was that he might grow up to be gay.

What a godsend, a true blessing, that would be.

The following afternoon Nikki was in the bedroom again, staring vacantly into space as she sat on the floor with her back resting against Zac's cot, and her notebook on her lap. There was a pen in her hand, but she hadn't written anything for a while now.

She could hear the rain beating against the window, and imagined it bouncing off the pavements, filling the gutters and battering umbrellas as her neighbours went about their day. Who were they really, these people? What were their lives like? Did they all have families, or were some of them alone? If they were, she wished to scoop them up in her arms to make them feel wanted and safe. It saddened her deeply to think of their isolation and rejection. She felt connected to them, whoever they were. She could feel their loneliness as though it was her own, and she wanted to help heal it.

Her thoughts drifted on to David and Dan. They were a couple now, which was great. She hadn't felt surprised when Spence told her, only happy for them, and sad for Kristin. They'd come back late from Danny's parents last night, then slept in this morning. When they finally got up they'd persuaded Spence to go to the Factory to catch up with the old crowd. She hadn't felt like going, Zac seemed to have a bit of a cold, so she'd stayed here to take care of him.

Spence was back now. She'd heard him come in about

half an hour ago, but Dan and David hadn't returned with him. The place was strangely quiet, almost as though it was holding its breath. She imagined Spence was on his computer. He'd have a lot of work to do, and emails to send. But then he was coming up the stairs and into the room. She looked up and her heart jolted with confusion as he swung his bag down from the top of the wardrobe and began packing. 'What are you doing?' she asked, pushing her voice past the prison of her throat. 'I thought you were here until tomorrow.'

'No,' he said shortly. His look, his manner, his whole demeanour was taut and closed off. Frustration was boiling inside him, anger was beating at his heart. Then suddenly he exploded. 'I can't take any more of this,' he cried. 'It's driving me crazy. I can't talk to you, you won't talk to me . . . I have to get out of here . . .'

The words came at her like stones. 'Spence! No! Wait!' she gulped, starting to get up. 'You can't go. You can't just leave me.'

'Why? You don't need me. You don't need anyone . . . All you do is sit there writing in that damned book, pretending he's going to grow up, talking to him as though everything's going to be all right . . . Well, I can't do that. He's going to die, Nikki. You have to face it . . .'

The glass wall was shattering, falling in dangerous, lethal shards all the way through her. 'I know that,' she choked desperately. 'But I . . . Spence, no! Don't go!' she panicked as he turned to the door.

'I have to.' His voice was shredding with grief as he turned back. 'I'm not strong enough to do this, Nikki. I just don't have it in me to watch him die and feel you slipping away at the same time. I'm not . . .'

'He's your son!' she cried as he ran down the stairs. 'You can't just walk out on him! Oh God, Spence, please,' she implored over the banister as he unhooked his coat. 'Don't leave me. I can't do this alone.'

'I'm sorry,' he sobbed, and pulling open the door he disappeared into the driving rain.

Nikki was halfway down the stairs, going after him, when she heard Zac crying. Dashing back to the bedroom, she scooped him into her arms. 'It's all right,' she rasped through the grief and fear that was tearing her apart. 'Everything's cool. Mummy's here.'

Zac went on screaming, louder than he ever had before, as though on some level he sensed what was happening.

She carried him to the window, but there was no sign of Spence.

'He can't go,' she choked, hardly aware of the tears on her cheeks. 'We need him. Oh God, Spence,' she gasped, her voice a tormented wail of anguish and despair. 'Spence, come back, please, please.'

Zac was still crying, loud staccato bursts that sliced through her ears. She looked down at him and didn't know what to do. His face was red and angry, tears were soaking his cheeks. 'I'm sorry,' she wept, as she kissed him. 'I'm really sorry.'

She went to lie down with him and unfastened her bra. To her relief he took the nipple and started to feed, while she continued to cry, her shoulders jerking with the force of her sobs. She didn't know what to do, or where to turn. Where were her parents? Mrs A had told them about Zac, so why hadn't they come? It didn't make any sense. Surely they wouldn't leave her to cope with this alone? Horror and fear began cleaving ruthlessly through her. She wanted to leave too, but she couldn't. For her there was no way out. She was all Zac had and she must do everything she could to protect him, even knowing that in the end she would fail.

She looked at her mobile on the floor as it started to ring. Danny's photo came up. She couldn't reach it, but she didn't want to talk to him anyway. She just wanted Spence to come back and their lives to be the way they were, before everything had fallen apart.

An hour later she was still on the bed with Zac, watching him as he looked up at her. What was it going to be like when he couldn't see any more, or hear? How hard was it going to be when he struggled to breathe and to swallow, when his tiny limbs lost their power to move and his brain stopped functioning? She didn't think she could stand it, she knew she couldn't, yet somehow she'd have to.

She was only dimly aware of the front door opening and

closing, and footsteps on the stairs. Somewhere in the back of her mind she was thinking it might be Kristin, or David and Dan. *Please let it be Spence,* she begged silently. *Please, please.*

'Hey,' he said from the doorway.

Her heart turned over so hard it hurt. She looked up at him and loved him with such an intensity she almost couldn't bear it. His hair was wet, his face showed all the anguish and suffering that was crushing both their hearts.

'I'm sorry,' he said huskily, coming to sit with her.

'It's OK,' she whispered, reaching for his hand. 'You came back, that's all that matters.'

He pulled her and Zac into his arms and held them in a way that was as encompassing as it was binding. 'I'm sorry,' he said, over and over. 'I don't know what . . . I just lost it, but I swear it'll never happen again.'

'It was my fault,' she insisted, pulling back to look at him. 'I was pushing you away . . . Oh God, Spence, I'm sorry . . . This is . . . It's so hard . . .'

'I know, but we'll get through it,' he told her.

She nodded, seeming to take strength from the light shining in his eyes. 'I'm going to try harder,' she promised. 'It was just . . . I've been so afraid to go forward . . . It was like, if I stayed where I was then none of it would happen. I know that sounds crazy . . .' Her eyes were tragic and pleading as she gazed at him. 'You won't ever leave us, will you?' she said brokenly.

'Never,' he vowed. 'My life wouldn't be worth anything without you. Or you,' he added with a shaky smile as he looked down at Zac. 'We're going to be here for you, my wonderful, special boy. No matter what happens, or how difficult it might get, I swear I'll never let you down. Or you,' he said to Nikki. 'I will never, *ever* walk out on you like that again.'

Chapter Seventeen

Saying goodbye to one another on Sunday was much harder than Spence and Nikki had ever found it before, and yet, in a way, it was easier too. After spending the rest of Saturday and most of that morning talking, and often crying, together, they'd felt the bond they shared tightening in a way that they were certain would provide the strength they needed to sustain them while they were apart.

'Are you sure you're going to be OK on your own?' he murmured against her hair as they hugged one another hard before he left.

'I'll be fine,' she promised. 'I'm really going to miss you, but you'll be back next weekend and we'll speak every day.' She smiled up at him. 'You can tell me all about the shoot and how it's going,' she said. 'I'm going to live vicariously through you for a while.'

He brushed a hand over her face. 'Will you think about leaving here and coming to London soon?' he asked softly.

Though her insides shrank from the prospect, she knew she had to sooner or later, so she nodded and said, 'I'll speak to Mr Pearce and Mrs A to see if there's someone they can put me in touch with up there.'

'And you'll contact one of the support groups this week?' he prompted, reminding her of their agreement.

'Definitely. I just have to find one in this country. They must exist. If not, maybe we could go to the States to talk to people there.'

'Whatever works,' he replied. 'As long as we're doing everything we can to help him, and ourselves, I think we'll be able to cope.'

Loving him more than ever, she went up on tiptoe to kiss

him. 'You'd better go,' she told him, 'you've got a big day ahead of you tomorrow, so you don't want to be late getting back.'

Remembering what was waiting for him at the London house, he groaned and sighed with dismay. 'I just hope Dan and David have sorted things out with Kristin by the time I get there,' he said. 'How did she sound the last time you spoke to her?'

Nikki grimaced. 'Angry, hurt, all the things you'd expect, but for the moment, at least, she seems to want to stay in the house. It won't be easy for her living *and* working with David over the next couple of weeks, though.'

'That's what I was afraid of,' Spence responded, 'so let's hope they stay professional and keep the personal stuff till after we wrap.' Then, going to lift Zac from his makeshift bed on the sofa, he kissed him softly on the head. 'I want you to take care of Mummy,' he whispered gently, 'and be a good boy. No more crying and getting yourself into a state, OK?'

Zac's mouth formed a tiny O that made them both melt, and as a little bubble emerged they laughed over sobs of pride and despair. Taking out his phone, Spence quickly captured the image and set it to replace the previous week's home screen.

'You could always record his screams and use them as a ringtone,' Nikki suggested mischievously.

He raised one eyebrow. 'Think I'll pass on that,' he said drily, and pulling them both into one final hug, he handed Zac over and picked up his holdall. 'No, stay here in the warm,' he said, as Nikki started to follow him to the door. 'I'll call when I get to the station.'

'Loads will have happened between now and then,' she teased, 'so don't forget.'

Laughing, and feeling confident at last that she really would be all right on her own, he gave her an affectionate wink and left.

After he'd gone Nikki laid Zac down again and set about clearing the place up, since no one had done anything all weekend. There was a sink full of washing-up, and the Sunday papers were all over the floor, along with Zac's toys, half a dozen or more empty coffee cups and a toppled pile of DVDs. She hadn't got very far by the time Spence rang to let her know he was on the train, and almost as soon as she'd finished speaking to him Kristin called for the third time that day, needing to vent some more.

'Tell me honestly,' she cried down the line, 'did you know? Is that why you wouldn't speak to him for me?'

'Kris, I had a lot of other things on my mind,' Nikki reminded her.

'That still doesn't mean you didn't know, so why didn't you tell me? As my closest friend you should have done the decent thing . . .'

'Kristin, I didn't *know*,' Nikki cut in forcefully. 'OK, I had my suspicions, but it wasn't my place to tell you.'

'How can you say that when you owe it to me to be truthful and supportive? If I'd known what was happening I might have been able to stop it.'

'Kris, David being gay isn't something you can stop.'

'Of course he's not *gay*. I should know, I've been going out with him for long enough, and if you were any sort of friend you'd be on the phone to Danny right now telling him to back off.'

Bristling, Nikki said, 'Kristin, you have to get over this. Your relationship with David's never been that close anyway, or not the way I saw it, so I don't know why you're getting yourself so worked up . . .'

'Listen to you,' Kristin cried hotly, 'you think you know everything. Well, for the record, David and I were every bit as close as you and Spence, and if Danny hadn't come along . . .'

'Danny and David were friends before any of us knew you,' Nikki reminded her. 'Now, I'm sorry, I have to go. Zac's going to need feeding any minute, and I want to . . .'

'It's OK, I know you couldn't care less about the way I'm feeling, but just remember, I'm the friend who was there for you last week, so if you can't do the same for me, well, at least I know where I stand.'

'Oh, Kris, don't be like that,' Nikki groaned. 'I really appreciated you coming, honestly I did, but there's nothing I can say that's going to change David's mind.'

'How do you know unless you try?'

'I just do, but OK, if you want to discuss it some more then go ahead. I'm listening.'

'Are you sure?' Kristin asked, sounding much meeker now. 'I mean, if you don't have the time . . .'

'Tell me again what David said when you saw him.'

As Kristin went right back to the beginning, adding even more details than she had during her past three phone calls, Nikki sank into a corner of the sofa to listen, like a dutiful friend.

By the time Kristin finally rang off, Nikki had managed to feed and change Zac and even put him to bed. Thankfully he fell asleep almost straight away, and she was so tired herself by then that she decided to leave the clearing up till tomorrow and have an early night too.

As she snuggled under the duvet and turned out the light she felt the familiar dread of what was happening starting to swoop through the darkness, like a physical force intent on smothering her. It was always there, lurking like a predator, stealing her joy, her sleep, her rational thinking, the very beats from her heart. She was determined to fight it off with constant reminders that Zac hadn't even started to go downhill yet, so she must treasure every day she had with him now and stop scaring herself half to death with thoughts of the future, but it was never easy.

In spite of being so tired, it was gone midnight before she finally bested the demons and fell asleep, but by two she was awake again with Zac screaming the way he had the night before, though whether in fury, or pain, or hunger, she had no idea. He wouldn't feed, nor would he settle for any longer than an hour at a stretch.

By morning she was fraying with helplessness and worry. He was still fractious, but at least he'd taken some milk, which decided her against calling Mrs A. All babies went through periods of crying for reasons no one could determine, she reminded herself, and other mothers coped, so she could too. However, most other mothers didn't have a child who'd been diagnosed with a terminal illness, and even if the symptoms weren't supposed to kick in yet, how did she know if his distress wasn't in some way related?

In the end, after spending the entire morning trying to calm him down, she got on the phone to Mrs A to explain what was happening.

'Don't worry,' Mrs A told her, 'my day's quite full, but I'll come over as soon as I can.'

By the time she arrived Nikki was ready to climb the walls with frustration and tiredness. 'He just won't stop,' she wept, as she passed the squalling bundle to Mrs A. 'I don't know what's wrong with him. He's never been like this before.'

'Ssh, ssh,' Mrs A soothed, rocking him back and forth, 'what is it, mm? Tummyache? Or are you just a bit out of sorts?'

Zac went on crying, so Mrs A carried out all the usual checks, seeming unfazed by the noise he was making. 'I don't think he's in any pain,' she said, as Nikki put her hands over her ears.

'So why won't he stop?'

'I'm afraid this is probably just a phase he's going through, but if he's still like it in the morning, pop him round to the surgery. Dr Merton's on tomorrow. I know you like him better than Dr Mills.'

'And what do I do in the meantime?' Nikki asked helplessly.

'Try taking him out for a walk. The buggy will probably lull him off to sleep. If that doesn't work, ring me again and I'll come round later to take him out in the car. That usually does the trick.'

She was right about the buggy because it did work, but only for as long as Nikki was pushing Zac around. As soon as she got home and lifted him out he started crying, and she was simply too tired to take him out again. So, true to her word, Mrs A came back and took them all for a drive. Luckily the rain had gone off, but it was rush hour, so it was stop, start, stop, start, until they reached the outskirts of the city. Within minutes of being on an open road both Zac and Nikki were fast asleep and stayed that way for the entire journey to Wells and back. At Nikki's front door, Mrs A gently woke her.

To Nikki's unutterable relief Zac barely came awake

when she changed him for bed, so she laid him down without feeding him, so needful of more sleep herself that she all but passed out as soon as her head hit the pillow.

An hour later Zac was yelling and getting himself into a terrible state.

Remembering he was hungry, Nikki put him to the breast and he immediately clamped on, sucking greedily. She started to doze, and was almost completely asleep again when she was dragged back by more urgent screaming. Forcing herself up from the bed, she began pacing up and down with him. Up and down, up and down. She mumbled nursery rhymes and rubbed his back, gave him more milk and put him into the bed with her. He slept then, but it was less than an hour before he was crying again.

The doctor gave her an appointment for ten thirty the next morning, and by the time she got there Zac was fast asleep. He continued to sleep right through his examination, and he didn't wake up and start crying again until they got home. Nikki was so frazzled by now that she wanted to scream and even shake him, anything to make him stop, but he wouldn't, and no one seemed to know what was wrong with him.

In despair Nikki rang Mrs A again, who promised to come as soon as she could. Minutes after she rang off Zac stopped crying. He lay in his Moses basket gazing up her with sore, wet eyes and a flush to his cheeks that made him look so sweet that she had to wipe away her own tears.

'You're such a bad boy,' she said gently. 'I know it's not your fault, but I wish you could tell me what's wrong.'

He gurgled and smacked his lips, then after a series of funny little whimpers he went off to sleep.

Continuing to gaze down at him, Nikki wasn't sure whether she wanted to laugh or continue to cry. In her exhausted state she barely had the energy for either.

Though she wanted nothing more than to sink on to the sofa and from there to oblivion, she looked around at the mess in the room, and could only imagine what kind of state she was in too. Did she care? The answer was no, not right now. All that mattered was being able to put her head on a pillow and close her eyes while she could.

Gathering up a throw she wrapped it around herself and within minutes, maybe it was seconds, she was all but dead to the world.

Then her mobile rang, snagging her from the depths and reeling her back again.

Forcing her eyes open, she saw it was Spence, and flopped out an arm to scoop the phone up from the floor. Had it been anyone else she'd have ignored it, but she'd promised to call after seeing the doctor, so he'd be worried that he hadn't heard from her. 'Hey,' she said, trying to sound more awake than she was.

'Hey, everything OK?'

'Great. Nothing wrong with him, apparently. It's just a phase. He's asleep now.'

'You sound as though you were too.'

'I was.'

'Sorry, I should have thought.'

'It's OK. How's it going your end?'

'Good. David's doing a relight at the moment, so I thought I'd give you a call. Go back to sleep now. Ring when you wake up.'

Barely able to say goodbye, she rang off, let the phone drop to the floor and was just snuggling back under the throw when someone knocked on the door. Somewhere, in the cobwebby corners of her mind, she remembered Mrs A saying she'd call round later, so she'd better answer or Mrs A would worry. Dragging herself to her feet, she rubbed her hands over her face in an effort to bring herself round, and after sending a silent prayer of thanks that Zac was still sleeping peacefully she went to let Mrs A in.

'We really must give you a key,' she was saying, while stifling a yawn, as she opened the door. 'Spence was meant to be getting one cut . . .' She stopped, feeling suddenly confused and disoriented as she registered who was standing there.

Her head started to spin.

Was she still dreaming?

'Mum. Dad,' she said. They looked so out of place here that she couldn't quite make herself believe it was them.

'Can we come in?' her father asked.

Her heart gave an odd sort of beat. He looked . . . different. Older, and strangely shrunken. Then she remembered noticing that he'd lost weight the last time she saw him.

'We heard . . .' her mother said. 'We've come because . . .'

Nikki's eyes went to her. It wasn't like her mother to be hesitant. Her face was pale and there was something in her expression that made Nikki feel uneasy. Where was the relief she should be feeling that they'd finally come? Maybe it was too late. They'd taken too long.

She stood aside to let them pass, then, recalling what a dreadful mess the place was in, she had to stop herself pushing them out again. They'd take the chaos as evidence that she couldn't cope. They'd assume she was falling apart, sinking into a depression, tearing herself to shreds for the mistake she'd made of having a baby in the first place. It was what her mother had predicted, and the instant she walked into the sitting room she'd pronounce herself right.

She might even say I told you so.

Then Nikki's heart thudded a terrible beat as she remembered the bigger truth, the devastating, unthinkable reality of what was happening to Zac. Compared to that, nothing else mattered at all.

She watched her mother look around the sitting room, taking it all in, and wanted to plead with her not to judge. Why did she have to come now, on today of all days, when Nikki was feeling so useless and wrung out? She couldn't get a grip on what was going on inside her. Nothing was happening the way she'd expected it to.

She tensed as her mother approached the basket where Zac was sleeping. She couldn't see her face, she only saw the way her mother's hand went to her throat and heard the strangled cry of . . . what? Joy? Pride? Shame for not having wanted him? Horror of what was awaiting him? What was she thinking?

She watched her father go to peer over her mother's shoulder. It was as though he wanted to see his grandson, but was afraid of getting too close. Any other grandfather might scoop the baby up in his arms and feel pride oozing from every pore. Why couldn't he?

'Would you like some tea?' she heard herself offer. They liked tea, but she didn't like them. She loved them and she was glad they were here, even though she knew they couldn't make everything all right the way they always used to. This was something her father couldn't control.

She wondered how much they knew about Tay-Sachs. They were all victims of this rogue gene, now. More than anything else it was binding them together – her, Spence, his parents, her parents, they must all be carriers, at least one of hers must, and one of Spence's.

She wondered which one of hers it might be.

Her father looked ill.

'You look tired,' her mother told her. There was no smugness in her tone, only concern, and suddenly Nikki wanted to cry.

'Having a young baby does that to you,' Nikki said, trying to make light of it. Then, because she wanted them to know something of how Zac had been before the cruel disease had robbed her of her dreams, she said, 'He started off so perfectly, sleeping most of the night, feeding easily, but it turns out he was lulling us into a false sense of security.'

Her mother smiled. 'They do that,' she said, as though she knew all about babies, when she'd only had one.

Nikki looked into her eyes, then had to turn away before she started blurting out words that probably wouldn't make any sense. Quickly clearing a space for them to sit down, she said, 'I'll go and boil the kettle.'

'It's OK,' her mother said. 'We don't want any tea. We . . .' Her eyes flicked to her husband. '. . . came to see how you are.' She turned to look at Zac again, while her father kept his eyes on her.

'We have something to tell you,' he said quietly. 'So shall we . . .?'

'Sit down?' her mother finished.

Nikki had heard that people who'd been married a long time began and ended each other's sentences.

Knit one, purl one.

Granny May had taught her that. She suddenly wanted Granny May now. She felt safe, while for some reason her parents didn't.

Tiredness was getting the better of her, making everything seem dreamlike to the point of surreal.

As they sat down her mother looked around the room again, apparently taking in the dirty dishes and discarded nappies mixed up with newspapers and DVDs.

Her father seemed uncomfortable, too big for the armchair. *We have something to tell you*, he'd said, and remembering the last time he'd uttered those words she felt her defences start to rise. Then suddenly an uncontrollable rage was surging through her over the way her father had delved into Spence's life and tried to suggest that he might be like his dead father, who might not even be his father at all. If they spoke one word against Spence today . . . She wouldn't let them. Suddenly she wanted them to go. Most of all, though, she wanted to attack them for giving her the gene that was going to kill her son. It would be good to blame them, because she hated them, but at the same time she loved them, and was so glad they were here that she wanted to throw her arms around them. They'd come. At last.

She looked at her father again and saw the man who'd always been there for her, who'd thought she was the best thing that had ever happened to him, who wanted to make her world the most perfect place in every way.

She wondered what it was like to be a parent who'd given everything to a child for more than eighteen years, only for that child to say that she didn't care what they wanted, she was going her own way.

It must be a whole lot worse than being a parent whose child hadn't slept for three nights and two days in a row.

But not worse than being a parent whose child had Tay-Sachs.

'It looks as though you could do with some help,' her mother commented, still absorbing the mess.

Nikki's eyes went to hers. Was that a criticism? Was she harbouring some sort of satisfaction for being proved right? Nikki couldn't cope. She'd been abandoned by her friends. The baby was going to die, his father was nowhere to be seen . . . His father, the son of a paedophile. Why had they dug into Spence's past like that? Why couldn't they at least have met him first? Were they here to try and take her away from him?

Suddenly she was on her feet, and before she could stop them words were streaming out of her, angry, bitter and accusatory. 'It's only in your world that people have *help*,' she cried. 'In mine we can't afford cleaners or dailies or whatever the hell you call them. But at least we have our priorities right. For me my child comes first, and he always will. So don't you dare come here looking down your nose at me and my home . . .' Her voice started to fracture. 'I want you to go,' she managed to shout. 'Please leave, now. I'm not interested in what you have to tell me, just like you're not interested in me.'

'Nicola, please try to calm down,' her father said quietly.

'Don't speak to me like that,' Nikki screamed.

Her mother rose to her feet. 'She's overwrought and exhausted,' she said to her husband. 'We can't achieve anything today. She needs to sleep.'

'Yes, that's it, go!' Nikki yelled as they started to the door. 'Don't bother to help me clean this place up, I know it's beneath you to touch anything that might belong to Spence, or even to your own grandson. No, don't!' she shouted as her mother tried to take hold of her. 'Just go. You're not welcome here, so don't even think about coming back. You don't have a daughter or a grandson any more, do you hear me? It should make you happy, because you never wanted me in the first place. I'm the one who ruined your life, remember?'

Her mother's face was stricken. 'I understand we picked a bad time,' she said, 'but we love you, Nicola, and we want to help in any . . .'

Nikki's hands were over her ears. 'Leave me alone,' she raged. 'I don't want you here any more. Just go.'

Nikki was still sobbing when Mrs A arrived half an hour later.

After letting her in Nikki returned to the sofa and hugged Zac to her as though he was all that mattered in the world, and actually he was. She'd been holding him that way since her parents had left, needing to feel the comfort of his tiny

270

body and the unbreakable bond they shared. Why wasn't it like that between her and her mother? Or was it, and she'd somehow lost the feel of it?

Mrs A went to make her a cup of tea, then sat holding Zac as Nikki told her what had happened.

'I know I shouldn't have exploded like that,' she sniffed at the end, 'but I couldn't help it. I was so tired and everything started crowding in on me. I thought they were going to say something horrid about Spence, or try to take me away from him . . .'

Mrs A smiled understandingly. 'Did they mention him at all?' she asked, watching Zac's velvety blue eyes darting around the room, probably searching for his mother whose voice he could hear, but he'd know it wasn't who was holding him.

Nikki shook her head and looked at Zac. 'They didn't even ask if they could pick Zac up,' she said, feeling herself veering close to the edge again. 'I wanted them to come so much, and now I wish they hadn't.' She lifted her eyes to Mrs A's. 'Do you think I overreacted? I did, didn't I?'

Sitting back with Zac and settling him more comfortably, Mrs A said, 'It is very hard to think clearly when you've had little sleep, and I'm sure your parents understood that.'

Nikki felt worried and guilty as she wondered if they had. From what her mother had said she'd seemed to understand, but she wished she could have the time over again so she could at least try to give them a chance.

'When I went to see them,' Mrs A said carefully, 'they told me what they'd found out about Spence's family.'

The sluggish grittiness in Nikki's head seemed to join with the heaviness in her heart as she looked up. 'You mean, about his father?' she said, wondering if she was going to be sick, or pass out.

Mrs A nodded. 'I take it you still haven't mentioned this to Spence.'

Nikki shook her head. 'He might not know, and if he doesn't . . . Even if he does, they shouldn't have done it. It was horrible, and when they tried to suggest he could be like it . . . How can they even think it, when they've never even met him?'

Mrs A's eyes were sad. 'I agree, it is misguided,' she said, 'but what they did . . . I know it might not have been the best way to show it, but I have no doubt it was done out of concern and love for you.'

'That still doesn't make it right.'

Unable to dispute that, Mrs A let it go and said, 'Did they tell you that they have been experiencing some difficult times?'

Nikki felt her mouth turn dry.

'Apparently your father has lost his business,' Mrs A continued, 'and they've been forced to sell their home.'

Nikki's head started to throb. 'So where are they living?' she asked hoarsely. 'Where were they when you saw them?'

'They're still in Bath, but at a friend's place that they are renting.'

Nikki looked away, unable to imagine her father being anything but wealthy and successful, and yet it would explain why he'd looked, and even sounded, so . . . diminished. Then she realised, all this time later, why the drawing room at home had seemed different when she was there. Things had been missing. They must have sold their paintings and antiques, but it still hadn't been enough to save the house. 'So that's what they came to tell me,' she murmured, feeling worse than ever now for the way she'd shouted at them.

'Possibly,' Mrs A agreed, 'but I also think they wanted to see their grandson.'

At that Nikki's heart hardened a little. 'I told you, they didn't even ask if they could pick him up.'

'Perhaps they didn't want to disturb him, if he was sleeping.'

Nikki had totally shredded the tissue she was holding, so she dropped it and reached for another. 'I think they came because they wanted me to know that they can't help me, because they don't have any money.'

'There are other ways of offering support,' Mrs A reminded her.

'Not with my parents. To them money means everything – and status.'

'You know them better than I do,' Mrs A conceded, 'but I

think it will be easier for you to be a little more objective after you have had some sleep. So I will stay here tonight, I think.'

By the time Spence came home at the weekend Nikki had been blessed with the luxury of only one full night's sleep, which was when Mrs A had stayed over, but at least she'd been managing to catnap occasionally, sometimes for as long as a couple of hours.

Even so, she was tired and scratchy, and it didn't help much when Spence took himself off to David and Kristin's old room halfway through Friday night, saying he had to get some sleep or he wouldn't be fit for filming again on Monday.

On Saturday morning he came downstairs looking refreshed and raring to go. One look at Nikki was enough to warn him not to suggest doing anything that might involve her having to leave the house.

'I know, why don't I take him up to the Factory, while you catch up on some sleep?' he said, lifting a bawling Zac out of his basket. 'I don't know about you, my son, but I'm famished.'

'So am I,' Nikki informed him, 'but it's OK, you go out while I stay here and clean the place up.'

Spence glanced over his shoulder at her. 'Is that you asking me to do the housework?' he said.

'It would help if someone did.'

'So I work all week, sometimes fifteen or sixteen hours a day, then I have to come home and put a pinny on? Ain't going to happen.'

Nikki saw red. 'Then maybe you shouldn't bother coming home,' she yelled.

Immediately backing down, he said, 'OK, sorry, handled that badly. I just don't want us spending what little time we have doing laundry and hoovering and all that crap. We need to have some fun. Zac, my boy, what is the problem? Waaah, waaah, waaah. You've got to stop.'

Nikki watched as Zac's wailing started to subside until he was looking at his daddy, teary-eyed, but apparently happy, as he made a grab for Spence's face. It seemed

Spence had some kind of magic charm that was eluding her. Stifling a stab of envy, in spite of feeling relieved, she said, 'My parents came here on Tuesday.'

Spence turned round in surprise. 'And you're only telling me now?' he said.

She shrugged.

'What happened?'

'Nothing. They didn't stay long. I . . . I practically threw them out.'

Frowning with concern, he settled Zac more cosily and came to raise her chin so he could look into her eyes. 'What did they say to you?' he asked.

'I didn't give them much chance to say anything,' she admitted. 'I hadn't slept . . . The place was a mess . . . My mother said something about it, and suddenly I went off on one. I couldn't seem to stop myself. I was afraid they were going to say something about you, or try to make me go home with them and shut you out. I didn't realise, until Mrs A told me later, that they've lost everything. They're not even living in the house any more. I think that's what they came to tell me.'

Pulling her to him, he pressed a kiss to the top of her head. 'Do you want to go and see them?' he asked. 'I don't mind taking you, or I'll look after Zac while you're gone.'

After giving it some thought, she shook her head. 'Not yet,' she answered. 'I'm still too tired, and I don't want it to take up our weekend.'

'OK, but if you change your mind . . .'

Wandering over to the sofa, she began picking up Zac's discarded clothes and folding them. 'Are David and Dan coming this weekend?' she asked, deliberately changing the subject, because she couldn't work out how she was feeling about the possibility of seeing her parents, or what else to say about them.

Spence regarded her in surprise. 'I told you on the phone,' he said, 'there's a Derek Jarman retrospective in London this weekend, so they're staying in town.'

She remembered now, and realising how much Spence would have liked to go too she felt guilty for dragging him here, and annoyed all over again. However, she managed not to let it show, saying instead, 'It would be great if you could take him up to the Factory. Thanks.'

With Zac resting on one shoulder, Spence came to kiss her on the cheek. 'Use the time to sleep,' he told her gently, 'and I'll give you a hand with everything else when I get back.'

It was around three in the afternoon when the roar of the vacuum dragged her out of a bizarre and slightly scary dream where she was trying to pull Zac back to earth as he floated like a bubble around her.

Spence laughed when she told him about it. 'See,' he said to Zac, 'you can fly, so how's that for special powers?'

Nikki looked at Zac, and her heart dissolved to see how contented and sleepy he seemed. 'Did you use some of the expressed milk?' she asked Spence.

'Yep, and he took to it like a dream. Which isn't to say he went floating off into space, the way he did in Mummy's weirdy head space . . . Hey, are you all right?' he said as Nikki started to sway.

Leaning into him as he held her up she waited for the dizziness to pass, then smiled as her tummy let out a monster roar. 'I can't remember when I last ate,' she confessed.

Spence's eyes widened. 'Then just as well we picked up some Clark's pies while we were out, wasn't it Zac?' he said, as though Zac was listening. 'We thought Mummy might like one, but if she's that hungry, we'd better let her have two.'

Laughing, Nikki said, 'Right now I could eat six and still have room for more.'

Spence pulled a face. 'That's not going to leave any for us,' he informed Zac, 'but no problem, we're all full up anyway. So, my darling,' he said to Nikki, 'if you'd like to go and put your feet up in the sitting room, we'll bring you a double helping of pie, and a pudding of your choice to follow.'

'Mm, let me see, what shall it be,' she pondered. 'Tiramisu, apple crumble, cheesecake . . .'

'How about a delicious chocolate eclair?' Spence offered. 'We don't have one,' he muttered in an aside to Zac, 'but we can have it here by the time she's finished the pie.'

Loving the light-heartedness as much as she did Spence

for trying to coax her into it, Nikki went to do as she was told, and loved him all over again when she saw how much tidier the place was.

After she'd eaten two whole pies she could barely move she felt so full, but luckily she didn't have to because Zac was zizzing away in his basket, and Spence was at the computer checking his emails. When he'd finished she patted the sofa next to her, an invitation for him to come and tell her all about his week.

It was only when he launched into it that she realised how eager he'd been to discuss it, because he became so animated that she could only wish that she was able to feel herself being swept up in it. However, it felt like another world, somewhere she might have visited once, but had almost forgotten. Though she presumed she still longed to be a part of it, she wasn't feeling the same kind of pull she once did. Nor was she any closer to moving to London than she'd been a week ago, and if things continued the way they were she knew that wouldn't change. She simply didn't have the energy to pack up what was left here and set it all up again in a new place, where she knew no one, and had no idea where anything was, in spite of how mad she'd been about the house. Nor had she even attempted to speak to Mrs A or Mr Pearce about finding a new health visitor and paediatrician. She guessed she'd have to tell Spence that at some point, but until he asked she decided not to bring it up.

Fortunately he didn't ask, maybe because he already sensed what her answer would be, or maybe because it was easier for him right now not to have her there when he came home at night. Or not to have a crying baby, anyway. Except Zac seemed to behave so much better when Spence was around.

When they went to bed that night Nikki found herself unable to sleep again, even though Zac seemed quite settled and Spence took no time at all to drop off. She'd been trying to broach the subject of her parents' visit again, but since she still wasn't clear about what she wanted to say, she'd never quite found the words. All she knew was that she was very mixed up about things, and because she hadn't managed to catch up on enough sleep yet to deal more rationally with her emotions, it probably wouldn't be a good idea to see them again until she had. Nevertheless, it hurt that they hadn't made another attempt to contact her. Why, she wondered, as she lay staring into the darkness. She knew they all loved one another, in some ways perhaps too much, so why were they all finding it so difficult to deal with one another?

Chapter Eighteen

'He seems a lot better now,' Nikki was saying to Mrs A the following Wednesday. 'He slept really well on Saturday, and for most of the night on Sunday.'

Mrs A held him up, smiling with pleasure. 'You're a good boy,' she told him cheerily. 'And I'm glad to say Mummy's looking more like herself this morning.'

'Probably because I managed to shower and wash my hair before you got here,' Nikki informed her, wishing she felt as bright as she apparently looked. Why was her head still so clogged, and her body feeling so heavy? 'He didn't do so well last night, but at least he went down again – eventually.'

They both turned round as someone knocked on the door.

'Are you expecting anyone?' Mrs A asked.

Nikki shook her head, and her heart started to pound as she thought of her parents. They'd come unannounced last time, so maybe they had again.

Since Mrs A was about to weigh Zac, Nikki left her to it and went out into the hall. There was no window to see who was waiting outside, so she swung the door wide, prepared to be more welcoming than she had the last time.

To her amazement she found Terri Walker standing on the step in her royal blue coat and long black boots.

'Hello,' Terri said, her pallid complexion colouring slightly as she met Nikki's startled gaze. 'I don't mean to bother you, but . . .' She shrugged, and blushed more deeply. 'Well, I heard about your little boy and I wondered . . . I just wanted to say if there's anything I can do . . .'

Still thrown at finding her there, but touched all the same, Nikki said, 'Thank you, that's really kind of you.' She glanced back over her shoulder. 'Uh, I'd invite you in,' she said, 'but he's with the health visitor at the moment.'

'Oh, no problem,' Terri assured her, already backing away. 'I don't want to push myself on you or anything, it was just to say, you know, if you need a friend, someone to chat to, or to take him off your hands for a couple of hours . . . I only live round the corner. Or, I'm about to start work at the Hen and Chicken, and I'll be there most days.'

Nikki thanked her again, and watched her walk out of the gate, feeling dismayed at herself for thinking how unlikely it was that she'd ever hand Zac over to someone who was little more than a stranger – especially one who couldn't have children of her own. She hated that sort of prejudice, but it seemed she was as guilty of it as anyone.

After closing the door she returned to the sitting room to tell Mrs A who it had been, but she was speaking to someone on her mobile while attempting to fasten Zac's nappy with one hand, and by the time she'd finished her call she was in a hurry to get away.

'Sorry, I'm running a bit late today,' she said, as she hugged Nikki goodbye. 'He's put on a whole pound since last week, so he's doing very well indeed.'

Feeling her pride go off like a damp rocket, Nikki looked down at Zac and began sinking into a swamp of despair. She knew she'd never loved anyone as much as she loved him, and that she'd do everything she could to give his little life as much quality as she was able, but knowing she was powerless to change the course of the next few years seemed to make a mockery of all her maternal instincts.

As he started to grizzle she lifted him up and held his face to hers while rocking him back and forth. He usually liked that, but today he remained tetchy until she gave him some more milk. It wasn't his feed time, but what difference did it make? Why not give him anything he wanted whenever he wanted it? There weren't going to be many other ways to spoil him during the short time he'd be with them.

When he decided he was full she hoisted him up to start

winding him, then spent the next hour or more pacing up and down trying to stop him crying. Just when she'd thought he was over the worst of his phase, as Mrs A called it, here it was, back with a vengeance. He must be distressed, or in pain, or maybe he just didn't like her, because to her mind his wails seemed louder and angrier when she was holding him than they did with anyone else. It seemed so unfair on them both that they had to suffer like this, especially when there was going to be no point to it in the end. From here on it would be all struggle and almost no joy until finally he died. How could they live a normal life with so much uncertainty and heartbreak holding them back all the time? She couldn't even bring herself to go and join Spence in London, so how long would it be before Spence started moving on without them?

Realising a long build-up of tiredness was as responsible for making her gloomy as her dread of the future, she decided that as soon as she'd settled Zac down she must try to make contact with a support group. It was the only way she'd get through this, to seek advice from someone who'd been there before, or it was going to drag her down to a place from which she might never escape.

In the end, he took so long to go off, that by the time she laid him in his basket and stood over him, willing him not to wake up again, she felt so weary and downcast that she wondered if she ought to get some sleep too. However, a wayward shred of energy, like the last live wire in a broken cable, pushed her to the computer, where she called up the website Mr Pearce had recommended.

As she sat watching the home page download, she suddenly realised she could go no further. No matter how desperately she might need help, she was too exhausted to search for it now, so getting up from the chair she took herself upstairs to lie down. She might write in her journal, she was thinking as she walked into the bedroom like a zombie, because sometimes when she spilled all her random and frightened thoughts on to the page she felt calmer afterwards, and even a little stronger. She wouldn't do it in a letter to Zac, she'd simply date it, then let her hand follow the direction of her mind.

However, only minutes after she'd opened her book her eyelids started to droop, and not long after that she was falling like Alice down the rabbit hole into a strange and bottomless sleep.

She woke with a start an hour later, coming out of a dream in which she was running through pitch darkness, knowing that at any moment she was going to crash into something terrible and nothing would ever be the same again. The effect of it was still with her, making her disoriented and shaky. Nothing was feeling right – everything seemed to be slipping away, vanishing into a darkness that was so consuming and endless that there would never be any escaping it.

Forcing herself up from the bed, she looked down as her book fell with a thud to the floor. Leaving it, she went to check Zac in his cot, then remembering she'd left him downstairs she picked the book up and took it down with her.

The instant she walked into the sitting room she sensed something wasn't right. Then she looked at Zac's basket and her heart stopped dead.

At first she thought he wasn't there, but then she saw a tiny hand peeping out from under the blanket that was *covering his face*.

Panic-stricken, she threw herself to her knees, ripped it back and grabbed him between her hands. He didn't seem to be breathing. She'd left him alone and somehow the blanket . . . *No, no, no, no!*

Desperately, she began blowing into his mouth, then realising she needed help she snatched up her mobile and fumbled in 999. 'It's my baby,' she shouted at the operator. 'He's not breathing. I think he's . . . Oh my God, I think I've killed him.'

The operator's voice was steady, but urgent. 'Please listen to me,' she said firmly. 'I need your name and address. We'll get a rapid response vehicle there right away.'

Nikki mumbled the words, then threw the phone aside. She had to save him. She must make him start breathing again.

Seizing his little body, she forced open his mouth and tried inflating his lungs again. *He's going to be all right*, she was telling herself fiercely. *Any second now he'll start breathing with me.*

She was still blowing into his mouth, with tears streaming down her face, when a paramedic turned up six minutes later.

'I think he's going to be all right,' she told him, looking up at him in terror.

The paramedic's eyes were on Zac as he whipped a bag and mask from his kit to take over the resuscitation. 'An ambulance is on its way,' he said, and after sliding a tube into Zac's throat he tore open the Babygro. Using two fingers on Zac's tiny chest, he began pumping.

Nikki stood over him, shaking uncontrollably, her hands bunched at her mouth, her heart using all its might to will Zac's to beat.

Somewhere, at a distance, she could hear the sound of sirens. Then two more paramedics were in the room. One of them eased her aside while the other attached a monitor to Zac's limp little body.

'No activity,' one of them murmured, and Nikki wanted to scream.

One of them was filling a needle. Nikki gasped as he jabbed it hard into the bone below Zac's knee.

'OK, let's get him to emergency,' someone said, and scooping Zac into his arms he began running with him to the door.

Nikki went after them, leaving everything behind. She didn't notice the crowd gathering outside, or the police car turning into the street, she only saw Zac disappearing into the back of the ambulance and the hand that reached out to pull her in too.

The sirens started up immediately, and as the vehicle drove away the efforts to revive Zac continued.

At the hospital he was whisked straight into emergency where the paediatrician who'd saved his life before was already waiting.

He can do it again, Nikki cried urgently to herself. *He will, because he has to.*

One of the paramedics was saying something about adrenalin.

The doctor was listening while attaching Zac to another monitor.

A nurse came to put an arm round Nikki. 'They'll do everything they can,' she said, trying to lead her away. 'He's in the best hands.'

The monitor flatlined.

'*No!*' Nikki screamed, wrenching herself free. '*Please, no.*'

The nurse quickly grabbed her while the doctor attempted further cardiac compressions.

'You have to save him,' Nikki begged. 'Please. Don't let him die.'

The rescue attempt continued. They all seemed so big and frightening, towering over Zac's tiny body. She couldn't see him, but they were going to save him, she knew it.

Several more minutes ticked by, until finally the doctor stepped away from the bed and gave a brief shake of his head to the others. He turned to Nikki, his pale eyes filled with regret.

Zac was no longer with them.

Nikki stared at him. 'No!' she cried, as the world started to shift from under her. 'He can't be . . . *No, he can't!*' she screamed as the doctor came to put an arm around her. '*Please,*' she begged, '*please* . . . You have to bring him back.'

'Is there someone you can call?' the doctor asked a few minutes later.

Nikki looked at him blankly.

They were in a small room somewhere off the emergency ward. She vaguely remembered walking here, passing fish tanks and toys and a sign that said 'Breast Feeding Room Available'. She hadn't seemed able to take much in then, but there was a small clarity in her mind now, like a paler haziness in a blanket of fog.

She looked around and noticed the walls were all different colours. Red and yellow and pink and green . . . A rainbow.

'Here you are,' a nurse said.

Nikki looked up, then watched the nurse put a cup of tea on the table in front of her. She lifted a hand, but let it drop again. Everything was dislocated and unreal. She shouldn't be here. These people were strangers . . .

The doctor repeated his question.

'Do you have a phone?' the nurse asked.

Nikki shook her head. She hadn't brought anything with her. *Zac! Zac! Where are you?* she was shouting inside. Could he see her, wherever he was? Did he need her? Was he trying to reach her? A terrible urgency swept through her. She must go to him . . .

The doctor fished a mobile from his pocket. 'Here,' he said, handing it over.

Nikki took it, but did nothing. She didn't know any numbers to dial.

'Drink some tea,' the nurse advised.

Obediently Nikki picked up the cup, and after taking a sip she felt the warm liquid running through her like a pain. 'It's my fault,' she whispered, 'I know it is, but I didn't mean it to happen.'

'Sssh,' the nurse soothed. 'You mustn't blame yourself.'

Nikki's eyes were hollow as she looked at her. Somewhere deep inside she could feel a need that was stronger than she'd ever known in her life.

Opening up the phone she pressed in her parents' number and waited for the connection. After three rings she was diverted to a recording telling her that the number was no longer in service. Then she remembered they'd moved, and maybe that was a good thing, because she was no longer sure she wanted to speak them after all.

She wanted Spence, more than anything in the world, but she hadn't memorised his number.

'I have to go home,' she said.

'I think someone should come to get you,' the doctor advised. 'Let me make the call for you.'

Nikki looked at him. 'Do you know Mrs Adani?' she asked, feeling momentarily lifted by the thought of Mrs A. 'She's a health visitor.'

'No,' he replied, 'but if it's who you'd like us to ring . . .'

'I can't remember any numbers,' Nikki explained.

'Don't worry, I'll find it,' the nurse assured her, and after squeezing her hand she slipped quietly from the room.

Nikki looked at the doctor. 'Did you remember him?' she

asked. 'We brought him in about three weeks ago when he couldn't breathe.'

The doctor nodded. 'Yes, I remember,' he told her.

Nikki's eyes drifted. She began searching for the end of the rainbow. 'He was going to die anyway,' she said huskily. 'Did you know that?'

'You're in shock,' he said gently.

Her lifeless gaze came back to his. 'He had Tay-Sachs,' she told him. 'He was diagnosed just after you saved his life.' Her face started to crumple. 'Maybe it's better he went now, like this,' she said. 'It was quicker . . . Do you think he suffered?'

Putting a hand over hers, he said, 'We'll know more once they've done a post-mortem, but I think it's unlikely.'

'Where will they do that?' she asked.

'Probably at Great Ormond Street, in London.'

She frowned. 'Why so far away?'

'It's where all our paediatric pathology cases are taken,' he replied.

Her mouth turned dry. *Paediatric pathology*. But it was all right, this was a dream. She'd wake up in a minute. 'Can I go with him?' she asked shakily.

'That probably wouldn't be a good idea. The best thing now is for you to be with your family. Do you have a husband? Parents?'

As she started to answer, tears welled up in her eyes and spilled on to her cheeks. 'I can't remember their numbers,' she choked.

'It's OK,' he assured her.

They sat quietly for a while until the nurse returned to tell them that Mrs Adani was on her way.

Nikki whispered a thank you.

Quite suddenly she felt so cold it was as though an arctic wind had blown into the room. She started to shiver so hard that it was as though her bones, her teeth, her very soul, were rattling inside her.

'I'll get a blanket,' the nurse said quickly.

The doctor put an arm round her and tried to keep her warm until the nurse came back with a soft pink shawl.

Soon after that Mrs A arrived.

Though her face was stricken and tear-stained, comfort radiated from her in a way that stole through to Nikki as she embraced her. 'Oh, my dear, my dear,' she murmured, holding her close as Nikki started to cry. 'My poor girl,' she soothed, stroking her hair.

'I didn't mean it,' Nikki sobbed. 'I only thought . . . I didn't mean . . .'

'I know, I know,' Mrs A said, fighting back more tears of her own. 'It is a terrible tragedy, but perhaps it is also a blessing.'

Nikki pulled her head back and sniffed as she tried to stop crying. 'I have to tell Spence,' she said, but even the thought of it caused her to break down again. 'He'll be filming,' she choked, burying her face in Mrs A's shoulder. 'His phone might be turned off . . .'

'Don't you worry about that,' Mrs A told her, 'I'll find a way to get through to him.' She looked at the doctor. 'Can I take her home now?' she asked.

He was starting to reply when the door opened and a tall woman with neat fair hair and a dark grey trouser suit under a fawn raincoat apologised for interrupting.

'Are you Nicola Grant?' she asked, looking at Nikki.

Nikki nodded as her eyes moved past the woman to a pale-skinned man with brown spiky hair and round-framed glasses, who was standing behind her.

'I'm Detective Sergeant Helen McAllister,' the woman explained, showing her badge. 'And this is DC Oliver Freeman. We're from the Child Protection Team.' It wasn't what the unit was called these days, but Helen McAllister wasn't in the habit of introducing herself to a recently bereaved mother as an officer from the Child Abuse Investigation Team. 'Could we have a few words? Please.'

Nikki's eyes went nervously to Mrs A, who seemed to be drawing herself up defensively. 'She has only just lost her child,' she informed Helen McAllister. 'Can't it wait?'

'It won't take long,' the detective promised. Her expression was too bland to read, but her manner was respectful.

'I'll leave you to it,' the doctor said.

'Actually, I'd like to speak to you too,' she told him, 'so if you're going off duty . . .'

'I'll be here for another six hours,' he assured her.

After he'd gone Helen McAllister gestured for Nikki to sit down again. 'I'm very sorry for your loss,' she said, pulling up a chair.

Nikki swallowed and pressed her fingers to her mouth to stop herself crying again. It all felt so surreal. She couldn't understand why she hadn't woken up yet.

'In cases of sudden death,' McAllister said gently, 'the police are automatically called in. Did you know that?'

Nikki nodded, but she hadn't known.

'So perhaps you could give me an idea of what happened leading up to the time you realised your baby was in trouble,' McAllister said.

After a few broken attempts to begin, Nikki finally managed to describe how she'd fed Zac, then spent an hour or more trying to get him off to sleep.

'Were you on your own with him?' McAllister asked.

Nikki nodded. 'I was then. Mrs A had been round earlier to give him his check.'

McAllister glanced at the health visitor. 'Where's the baby's father?' she asked. 'Does he live with you?'

Nikki's face turned paler than ever. She still hadn't told Spence. He was going about his day, loving being a director, and a dad. He had no idea what was happening here. 'He's in London, filming,' she said shakily. 'I haven't . . . I haven't spoken to him yet.'

Mrs A slipped a comforting arm around her.

McAllister's eyes were still on Nikki. 'So how did you get the baby off to sleep in the end?' she asked.

Nikki's shoulders jerked as she sobbed. 'I rocked him and walked up and down. He kept crying. It's been hard to make him stop lately.'

McAllister appeared to understand. 'So how did you make him stop?' she asked softly.

Mrs A shifted uncomfortably. She'd seen too many grief-stricken parents talk themselves on to the wrong side of the law, without realising what they were doing, to let this continue the way it was going. 'I don't think you should question her any more,' she said. 'It is too soon after the shock. Her mind cannot be very clear.'

McAllister was still watching Nikki. 'What do you say?' she asked. 'Is your mind clear? Do you remember putting your baby down to sleep?'

Nikki seemed confused, but she nodded. 'I put him in his basket,' she said. 'Then I . . . I felt tired myself, so I went upstairs to lie down.'

'Did you fall asleep?'

Nikki nodded.

'For how long?'

'I'm not sure.'

'And when you woke up? What did you do then?'

'I went downstairs to check on Zac, and he was . . . He was . . . I couldn't see him . . .' She buried her face in her hands. 'I know it might be for the best,' she choked, 'but I didn't want him to die. I thought I did . . .'

'That is enough,' Mrs A cut in firmly. 'You can see how distressed she is. She is not thinking about what she is saying, so please leave her alone now.'

McAllister seemed about to object, then apparently thinking better of it she got to her feet. After offering her condolences again she gestured for Freeman to follow her and left the room.

Nikki turned to Mrs A. By now the last few words had registered and her eyes were widening with alarm. 'Do they think . . . Oh my God, they think I . . .' she spluttered. 'They think I killed him.'

Mrs A grabbed her hands and held them firmly. 'Whatever they think, we know you didn't,' she told her forcefully, 'so don't worry, everything will be straightened out. Now, as soon as we can I think we must go home.'

'Can I . . .? Do you think they'll let me see him?' Nikki asked.

'Of course,' Mrs A assured her. 'I'll go and find the doctor.'

During the hour since this case had landed on her desk DS Helen McAllister had already learned quite a lot about the dead baby, Zac James, and his mother Nicola Grant. For instance she knew about the call Nicola had made to the emergency services, what had been said, and how long it had taken the RRV to get there. She'd also managed to locate one of the responding paramedics, who'd talked her through his part in the attempted resuscitation. Then she'd spoken to the duty paediatrician who'd pronounced life extinct.

What was interesting her the most, for the moment, however, was the rare disease she'd just found out about. She'd look it up on the Internet as soon as she got back to the office, but from the little the emergency doctor had been able to tell her, being no specialist himself, it seemed the condition was irreversible and fatal.

'The consultant's lecturing in Birmingham today,' DC Freeman told her, closing up his phone. 'His secretary's going to get in touch and ask him to call.'

McAllister nodded, then put up a hand to stop him as she got through to the coroner's office. After passing on the requisite details to start proceedings for a forensic post-mortem, she said, 'I'll be attending myself, so I'd appreciate a call back as soon as you can give me a time.'

After ringing off she looked pensively at Freeman, whose green eyes were magnified by their prescription lenses. 'Have you contacted the community paediatrician?' she asked.

'He's on his way.'

'Social services?'

'Same.'

'OK. I take it someone's at the house? We don't want anyone going in there disturbing anything at this stage.'

'I'll check, but I'm pretty sure there's a uniform outside.'

'Good. Do you know if anyone's spoken to the father yet?'

He shook his head.

'Do we have any reason to think he's anywhere other than where she says he is?'

'None, so far.'

'Right.' She took another moment to think. 'Looks like a lot's going to hang on this post-mortem,' she murmured, and opening up her phone again she put a call through to her inspector to update him on what she'd learned so far.

*

Nikki's hands were bunched at her mouth as she stared down at Zac's dear little face. She almost regretted coming now, and yet, in a way, it was helping her to see him looking peaceful, as though he was sleeping. He still bore the marks of the attempts to revive him, and she wondered what his eyes would be like if she pulled back the lids. She wanted to scoop him up in her arms and hold him tightly, but she was afraid if she did she'd never let him go. She wanted him back. She didn't care how ill he was going to be, or that he would die in the end anyway, she wanted her baby back in her arms.

Feeling Mrs A's hand on her shoulder, she understood they had to leave now, so, somehow stifling the screams inside her, she leaned forward to press a gentle kiss to Zac's forehead. *This was the last time she'd ever kiss him and she just couldn't bear it.*

As they walked back to the Rainbow Room, where they'd been asked to wait until the police were ready to come home with them, Nikki could feel the bond with Zac, stronger and more unbreakable than ever, as though it was pulling her back to where she'd left him. It wasn't right that he was there. He'd be afraid on his own. He should be with her.

'Ah, it's David,' Mrs A said, as her mobile vibrated. 'You go on in and sit down while I talk to him.'

Obediently Nikki went into the room and tried to make herself stop screaming inside. *Zac. Zac. I'm sorry. I shouldn't have left you downstairs on your own. Oh my God, it's my fault. He'd be here now if I hadn't left him alone.*

She wondered what Mrs A was saying to David, and how he was taking the news. Her heart cleaved in two as she thought of Spence and how he was going to react when he found out that his son was dead. It wasn't supposed to have happened now. They were going to live in London together. Everything was planned.

The door opened and Mrs A came in.

'David's going to take Spence to one side to tell him,' she said.

Nikki nodded. Her eyes were puffy and scared, her hands were clenching and unclenching as though she didn't know what to do with them. 'What did David say?' she asked.

'He was very shocked and upset,' Mrs A replied. 'I think

Spence will call back on this number,' she added, and handing the phone to Nikki she removed the hospital shawl from her shoulders and covered her with a blanket that she'd fetched from the car. 'How are you feeling?' she asked.

Nikki shook her head. 'I don't know. Afraid, I think, and . . .' She swallowed hard. 'I thought sometimes that I wanted him to die now, before . . . but I didn't. Not really. That's being selfish though, isn't it, because he would have had a horrible life, and now I keep thinking, maybe there is a god after all.'

'You can be sure of it,' Mrs A assured her.

Nikki's eyes welled up again. 'I'm going to miss him so much,' she said, brokenly, 'and I feel so guilty for leaving him on his own, and for thinking the way I am. I really loved him, you know that, don't you?'

'Of course I do. We all did. His time with us might have been short, but you did everything you could to be the best mother in the world. I feel very proud of you, but please, you must take care now what you say to the police. Like the detective told you, a sudden death is something they have to investigate, and you do not want to be giving them the wrong impression.'

Nikki's heart lurched as she thought back over what she'd already said, then she jumped as the phone started to vibrate. Seeing it was Spence, she looked at Mrs A, her eyes showing how afraid she was.

Taking the phone, Mrs A clicked on, then passed it back.

'Hello,' Nikki said faintly.

'Nik! Oh my God!' Spence cried. 'David told me, but . . . How did it . . .? Are you OK?'

'I think so,' she managed. 'I don't know. It happened so fast.'

'Where are you now?'

'Still at the hospital with Mrs A. The police want to come home with us.'

'What?' he said, sounding stunned. Then, in a voice that betrayed how close he was to breaking down, he said, 'I'm leaving now. David's coming with me.'

'What about the film?'

'I don't know. I can't think about it . . . I'll be there as soon as I can, so hold on, OK? Everything's going to be fine.'

As she rang off she wondered why he'd said that, because her arms felt so empty and her heart so shredded that she couldn't imagine how anything would ever be fine again.

Chapter Nineteen

When Nikki and Mrs A returned home it was to find a uniformed police officer stationed outside the house, which was awful enough, but when they went inside to discover the place exactly as Nikki had left it – Zac's bedding strewn across the floor and his basket on its side – Nikki sank to her knees as deep, heart-wrenching sobs began tearing from her. 'Zac,' she cried desperately. 'I want him back, Mrs A. Please, please, bring him back.'

Mrs A gathered her into her arms while DS McAllister kept at a discreet distance in the hall, watching and waiting until the worst of the despair had passed.

'I need to feed him,' Nikki said, her voice thick with pain and confusion. 'I'm soaked . . . I . . . Oh God, Mrs A, I don't know what to do.'

'Ssh, ssh,' Mrs A soothed, dabbing away the tears as DS McAllister stepped into the room.

'I understand how difficult this is for you,' McAllister said kindly, 'but I have to ask you to keep the baby's bedding . . . It's only procedure,' she added hastily, as Nikki looked about to panic. 'As soon as we have the autopsy results . . .'

'What do you think I'm going to do with it?' Nikki sobbed. 'They belong to my son. I can't just throw it away.'

McAllister's expression showed only sympathy as she said, 'Of course not.'

Nikki's hands went to her face. 'I'm sorry,' she choked, 'I just . . . I want him back, and look at me . . .' Her front was saturated with all the milk that had leaked from her breasts.

'We need to express,' Mrs A told her gently. She looked at McAllister. 'Is that permissible?' she asked, seeming unsure.

McAllister nodded, and deciding to leave them to it she returned to her car. There were other things she could do for now, such as finding out more about this fatal condition.

After the detective had gone Nikki allowed Mrs A to help her express the milk, and though the process was excruciating, she somehow forced her way through it, and even started to drift into a state of exhaustion towards the end. Then an image of Zac's tiny body, shut up in its cold, sterile morgue drawer, flashed in her mind, and she came brutally awake again. 'Oh God, oh God,' she gulped, seeming unable to get any air.

'Sssh,' Mrs A whispered, 'just take it slowly . . . Breathe . . . That's right . . . In and out, in and out . . . Good girl,' and once the panic had subsided she rested Nikki's head on her shoulder, holding her like a child as she continued trying to come to terms with what had happened.

'I'd like you to eat something, if you can,' Mrs A said when Nikki sat forward a while later.

Nikki shook her head. Her mouth was too dry, her stomach still churning in terrible knots. 'I keep asking myself how the blanket got over his face,' she said huskily.

Mrs A's smile was sad. 'It happens sometimes when they kick,' she replied.

Nikki knew that, but if she'd been there she could have folded it back again. Her head went down, as though pulled there by the weight of guilt in her heart. All mothers slept at the same time as their babies, so she shouldn't torment herself like this, but how was she ever going to stop when she knew what she'd been thinking only that morning? She'd wished Zac dead, not only to set him free, but to set herself free too. How selfish and wicked was that?

Sitting forward, she buried her face in her knees and clasped her hands over her head. Even if it was wrong, on one distant but lucid level she couldn't help feeling glad that he was free, but at the same time she wanted him back so much it was as though someone had torn out her heart. She wasn't sure how she was going to function in the days and weeks to come, she only knew that right now, this minute, she would give anything in the world to be with him, wherever he was.

It was some time later that she realised she must have fallen asleep, because when she opened her eyes Mrs A had gone. She could hear her moving around upstairs, and guessing she was packing up Zac's things she felt such a ferocious longing sweep through her that it took every ounce of willpower she possessed not to run up there and stop her.

Telling herself that she should go and help, or at least change her clothes, she forced herself to her feet, and after a wave of dizziness had passed she was about to start up the stairs when she heard a car pull up outside.

Please let it be Spence, she begged silently, and going to the window she saw a taxi driving away as David came in through the gate. There was the sound of a key in the front door and moments later she was in Spence's arms, being held so tightly that they could barely draw breath to sob, or speak, or do anything more than cling together as though without the strength of each other they would fall completely apart.

That night, needing to see his son one last time, Spence went to the mortuary with David while Mrs A and Nikki waited at home. Nikki simply couldn't bring herself to go there again. If it were possible, she'd rather block the entire last twenty-four hours from her mind so she could remember Zac looking healthy and alive, kicking around on the bed, or lying sweetly in her arms waving his funny little fists as he took in the world.

When Spence returned, he helped her through the awfulness of expressing more milk, and when it was done they lay quietly on the bed together, looking at photographs and holding one another close as tears of pure grief streamed down their cheeks. In the end Nikki took one of the Valium the emergency paediatrician had prescribed for her and managed to sleep for most of the night. Spence did too, which made him feel guilty and ashamed when he woke up in the morning. He couldn't understand how he'd been able to shut off like it was any other night.

By mid-morning Danny and Kristin had joined them, clearly as shocked and upset as everyone else. Since there was nothing anyone could do until they knew the autopsy results, they simply sat around poring over yet more photographs, and talking and crying, occasionally even laughing, particularly when they recalled Zac's favourite party trick. Friends and neighbours dropped in to offer their condolences, and though everyone's kindness and support went some way towards easing Nikki's wrenching sense of loss, the moments of overwhelming longing were starting to become more intense as the hours ticked by.

Towards the middle of the afternoon she went upstairs to search for her journal while Spence walked up to North Street with Danny and David, partly to get some air, but also to pick up some pizzas because none of them had eaten all day.

'Are you OK?' Kristin asked, coming into the bedroom to find Nikki on her knees next to the bed. 'Can I help you find something?'

Nikki looked puzzled as she gazed around the room. 'I know I had it yesterday morning,' she said, 'but it's not here.' Realising Kristin didn't know what she was talking about, she told her, then pulled her mobile from the pocket of her jeans as it rang. Seeing it was one of their friends from the Factory, no doubt ringing to offer sympathy, she let it go through to voicemail and tried to remember what she'd been doing.

Going to sit on the edge of the bed, Kristin said, 'I guess you'll be moving up to London now.'

Nikki's eyes came to hers. Though she'd heard the words, and even understood them, she didn't want to respond, because she couldn't bring herself to think that far ahead. It would seem disloyal to Zac, as though she was glad he was out of the way so she could get on with her life, and that was so far from the truth that she could feel tears stinging her eyes even to think it.

'Oh, I'm sorry,' Kristin cried. 'That was really stupid of me. Obviously it's too soon to be talking about that.'

Nikki sank back on her knees and used a sleeve to dry her cheeks.

A few minutes passed while they sat staring at nothing. Then Kristin said, 'Are you going to have him buried or cremated?'

Nikki took an unsteady breath. 'Spence is making the decision,' she answered.

Kristin nodded. 'Do you have any idea when you'll get the body back?' she asked.

A searing wretchedness burned through Nikki's heart. These questions were too hard, but she had to face them, so she forced herself to say, 'No, not yet. I'm . . . We're not sure who to ask.'

Since Kristin didn't know either, they lapsed into silence again, until Kristin started to cry. 'I'm sorry,' she wailed, 'it's just that I keep thinking that it's the best for him, and then I feel terrible. He was so sweet and lovely and we all really adored him. It's so strange without him.'

Nikki's gaze was distant; she didn't know what to say.

Wiping her tears with her fingers, Kristin said, 'So what did the police ask you, yesterday?'

Nikki's eyes went to her, then moved away again. 'Just what happened,' she replied, feeling her stomach clench with unease. She couldn't remember much of what she'd said now, but they must surely have realised how emotional she was when she'd answered their questions. They'd be dealing with people in the same sort of situation all the time, so they'd know better than anyone how easily things came out the wrong way when someone was in shock.

'So what did happen?' Kristin pressed. 'I mean, I know you came upstairs to lie down, but . . .'

Nikki got to her feet. 'I don't want to talk about it again,' she said. 'I just want to find my journal.'

There were times when DS Helen McAllister actively detested her job. True, there was never much fun to be had dealing with victims of child abuse. Taking down the creeps and monsters who thought they could get away with torturing and even killing defenceless children, though, did bring a certain sense of satisfaction to her world. However, when it came to cases like the one she was faced with now, she often wished she'd pursued a career with Disney if she was so mad about kids – or taken up teaching kindergarten, even nursing, anything that might have allowed her to back off from the reality of someone's genuine tragedy.

She was in her car now, driving back from London where she'd spent the past four hours observing the forensic autopsy of Zac James. Another part of her job that she wasn't too struck on, but the law required the investigating officer to be present for the purposes of identity and continuity, so she'd had no choice. She could have sent Oliver Freeman, but big girl that he was, he generally chucked up at the first slice, which didn't exactly get things off to a rollicking start.

As she waited for him to answer his mobile phone she used the steering-wheel controls to flip through radio stations, searching for a traffic update. It was still only four o'clock, so roadworks and weather permitting she should be back in Bristol by five thirty, six at the latest.

At last Freeman picked up, but he was clearly still speaking on the other line, because she could hear him thanking whoever it was and saying he'd get back as soon as he had some news. 'Sarge,' he said, finally giving her his attention. 'How did it go with the PM?'

In another world she might have just spent the day in Downing Street, in theirs he was talking about a laboratory for dead bodies and pickled brains. Come to think of it . . . 'Blood in the nose and lungs,' she answered, moving past the analogy, 'retinal bleeds, torn fraenulum, bruising on cheeks . . . In other words, the prof was pretty certain that our baby was deliberately smothered.'

'Oh,' Freeman murmured. 'So nothing to do with his Tay-Sachs thing?'

'Apparently not,' she replied. 'The prof was pretty definite about that, so given that Nikki Grant admits she was in the house alone at the time, and that we've got a record of her 999 call, plus a motive that might send any mother in the same direction, I think you know what I'm going to say.'

'Yes, Sarge,' he replied, sounding about as thrilled by the next step as she felt. 'I'll go myself,' he told her. 'Her local nick's at Broadbury Road. Do you want me to see if I can get her in there?'

McAllister tried not to groan. 'Unless you can find us a suite at the Hotel du Vin,' she quipped. 'And make sure someone picks up the baby's bedding, along with anything else they think might be relevant. CSI are going to love us,' she went on, 'getting them out on a night when they might miss themselves on telly. They won't get much from the scene of course, with the amount of people going in and out of there . . .'

'Always the problem with babies, Sarge,' Freeman told her, as if for some reason this had escaped her during a fourteen-year career.

'Yes, Ollie,' she said, knowing he hated being called that. 'Go gently with our perp,' she added, 'she's still a bereaved mother, remember,' and before he could remind her that he already knew that, she rang off.

Nikki was lying on the bed with Spence, searching through the bewilderment and pain in his eyes as though trying to connect with what else might be going on in his mind. Though they'd talked, a lot, sharing memories of the past seven weeks as though they'd filled as many years, she wanted, needed, to understand some of the complexities of his emotions, maybe so she could reach him in ways she never had before. Already it was as though he had become her lifeline, and perhaps she was his too. This experience, the joy of having Zac, the love they'd shared, the hopes and dreams that had been dashed on the rocks even before his death, would always bind them together.

'What are you thinking about?' he asked softly. His voice was nasal from so much crying.

She smiled. 'I was wondering the same about you,' she replied.

It was as though they'd fallen into a small pocket of time that was standing still, while the rest of the world went on its way.

He sighed tiredly and rolled on to his back. 'Do you think it's too soon to call the coroner's office?' he asked. 'Will they know the results yet?'

Feeling a dryness spreading through her throat, she lay back too and stared blindly up at the ceiling.

'I hate this waiting,' he growled. 'It's just prolonging the agony. I mean, what are they expecting to find?'

'They have to do it,' she said, repeating what she'd been told.

'But why? He had breathing problems before . . .' He jerked himself up and swung his legs off the bed. 'It was a cot death,' he growled, as though trying to convince himself, or her, she wasn't sure which.

Nikki closed her eyes. She was trying not to get caught up in his fear and frustration, but her own was so close to the surface that she could feel it starting to break through.

'Nik, I'm sorry,' he said suddenly, 'but I have to ask you this. Did you . . .? I mean, is there any way . . .?' He turned to her, his eyes shadowed with pain and doubt. 'I wouldn't blame you if you did,' he told her earnestly. 'God knows I thought about doing it myself . . .'

Realising what he was asking her, Nikki felt her control slipping away. 'It happened the way I told you,' she cried desperately, more tears starting down her cheeks. 'I could never have hurt him, and if you think I did . . .' She felt so wretched she could hardly force any more words out. 'Then you don't know me at all,' she finished brokenly.

'I'm sorry, I'm sorry,' he groaned, gathering her into his arms as she started to sob. 'I know you couldn't, I just . . . I guess it's because of what went on in my mind. And we have to admit, however much we're going to miss him it has to be better for him like this.'

'I know,' she wept, 'but it's still a terrible thing to think.' She looked up at him. 'I swear, if I could have yesterday all over again,' she said, 'I'd never have left him downstairs on his own, because if I'd been there I'd have seen the blanket fall on his face . . . I could have saved him, but I was so tired and he was sleeping so peacefully . . .' She gasped for breath. 'He must have had another attack, the way he did before, and I wasn't there . . .' She couldn't bear it, it hurt too much even to think of it. 'He was struggling on his own and there was no one to help him,' she choked. 'It's all my fault and I know I'll never forgive myself, even if he has been spared the horrible life he'd have had.'

Pulling her even closer, as though to absorb her pain, he

felt his own tears starting again as he said, 'It's not your fault. You were a great mum. Even Mrs A says so, and she should know.'

Hearing someone knock at the front door downstairs, they listened quietly as David went to find out who it was, then looked at one another curiously when they heard a voice neither of them recognised.

David told whoever it was to come in, and Nikki felt her heart rising into her throat as, moments later, David began climbing the stairs. Then he was in the bedroom doorway looking at her with his big, soulful eyes as he said, 'It's the police. They want to speak to you.'

A rush of panic swept in like a blow. 'Just me, or both of us?' Nikki asked shakily.

'He asked for you.'

'It's OK, I'll come too,' Spence told her. 'They're probably here to give us the results.'

Getting up from the bed, Nikki pressed her palms to her cheeks, willing herself to stay strong. 'It'll be fine,' she said to Spence, as much to bolster herself as him.

'Of course,' he assured her, taking her hand. They followed David down the stairs.

DC Freeman and another detective were standing in front of the fireplace when Spence and Nikki walked into the room. Freeman's hands were clasped loosely in front of him, his glasses reflecting the overhead light so they couldn't see his eyes. His colleague was slightly behind him, so it wasn't possible to see his expression either. David, Danny and Kristin were sitting down, their faces as pale as Nikki's, as, like her, they seemed to hold their breath.

Freeman cleared his throat. 'Is there somewhere private we can talk?' he asked.

Nikki looked thrown and alarmed. 'I . . . Uh . . . Only the kitchen, but it's . . .'

'Please tell us what you've come to say,' Spence urged. 'We're amongst friends. We have nothing to hide.'

Freeman seemed hesitant, but in the end he turned back to Nikki and said, 'Are you Nicola Grant?'

Confused, because he already knew she was, Nikki said, 'Yes.'

'What is your date of birth?' he asked.

She glanced at Spence to see if he might understand what was happening, but he appeared equally bemused. 'The fourteenth of July nineteen eighty-eight,' she said.

Freeman took a step forward. They could see his eyes now, big and round and tinged with something that looked like regret. 'Nicola Grant,' he said solemnly, 'I am arresting you for the murder of Zac James . . .'

Nikki shrank back in horror. 'No!' she cried. 'I didn't do it. You can't arrest me . . .'

Spence was holding her and shouting at them to leave her alone.

The other man stepped forward, as though to restrain Spence.

David and Danny were on their feet; Kristin was frozen in shock.

Freeman was still speaking. '. . . you do not have to say anything, but it may harm your defence if you do not mention when questioned something which you later rely on in court. Anything you do say may be given in evidence.'

Nikki's eyes were bulging, aghast. Her head was spinning; her heart was beating too fast. 'You can't do this,' she told him brokenly. 'I'm his mother, I would never hurt him.'

'I must remind you that you're under caution,' Freeman said, 'so it would be advisable not to say any more.'

Nikki suddenly wanted to scream and run, tear at his face, do anything to make him stop, but she could only listen to him telling the others that the house needed to be searched, so they must find somewhere else to stay.

'What evidence do you have?' Spence suddenly blurted as Nikki was led to the door. 'You can't arrest her without proof.'

Freeman turned to him. 'You're the baby's father?' he said.

Spence nodded.

'Then I'm sorry to tell you that the autopsy has shown a consistency with deliberate smothering.'

Nikki felt as though she was drowning. Or maybe she was going to throw up. 'I swear I didn't do anything wrong,' she mumbled huskily. 'I know I said some things yesterday, but . . .'

'I have to stop you,' he said, reminding her again that she was under caution.

Making a superhuman effort to pull herself together, even though she was trembling violently, she said to Spence, 'It's all right. We can get this sorted . . .'

'Where are you taking her?' David thought to ask.

'To the station at Broadbury Road,' Freeman replied.

'What about a lawyer?' Spence demanded. 'She has the right to one.'

'Do you have one?' Freeman asked Nikki.

Her eyes were dark pools of fear as she shook her head.

'Then one will be provided,' he assured her, and after waiting for her to put on her coat he led her outside, where the CSI team was waiting to turn the house into a crime scene, and a couple of uniforms were gearing up ready to take contact details and preliminary statements from Spence and his friends.

Chapter Twenty

It was pitch dark by the time DC Freeman pulled up outside Broadbury Road police station where he'd been told to come in through the front office, due to some security repair works going on at the back. Since the forecourt was full of white vans and police vehicles, he parked his car in the street, muttering something about hoping the wheels would still be on it when he came back, and got out to open the rear door for Nikki.

As she stood up a blast of icy wind caused her to stagger. Freeman steadied her, then kept a hand on her elbow as he took her across the road. The other detective stayed in the car, talking to someone on the phone.

Though terrified beyond anything she could bear, Nikki was doing her best not to connect with her feelings, or think about where this might end, or she knew she'd never get through it. She simply kept her eyes fixed on the two-storey building ahead with its redbrick and white-panelled exterior, trying not to see it for what it actually was. It was merely a place she passed from time to time, one she'd hardly noticed until now, because it was just there, like a school, or a church, or a shop she had no reason to enter. She knew of it by reputation, though, because it often featured in the local press as the station where thugs and criminals were taken following arrest for aggravated robbery, or grievous bodily harm, or worse.

Realising she was in the final category, a band of horror closed round her chest. This couldn't be happening, it just couldn't, and yet it was. She wished she could die. She'd be with Zac then, and no one would be able to harm either of them ever again.

The front office was bedlam as two uniformed officers struggled with a pair of angry women apparently hell-bent on tearing each other apart, while behind the desk the duty sergeant was shouting to make himself heard as he dealt with an elderly couple who were shouting back.

Nikki kept her head down as she went through, pausing when she reached a door for Freeman to use a swipe card to release it. After ushering her in ahead of him, he steered her through a tight grid of corridors to the custody area at the back of the station.

The custody sergeant was busy checking someone else in, so they were forced to wait, like trapped animals in a warren of dingy walls and concrete floors. Eventually Freeman took her into a sort of cubicle with secure doors either side, wood and glass-panel walls, and a high counter that kept the custody sergeant apart from his visitors.

The next few minutes passed in a daze of short questions and equally brief answers as she was asked if she understood why she was there, and her rights were explained to her. At the end she was directed to sign an electronic pad which the custody sergeant pushed towards her. She had nothing for them to confiscate, no laces in her ankle boots, no belt or jewellery and nothing in her pockets apart from a crumpled tissue and an unused nappy sack. Seeing it, she felt herself collapsing inside, and as she brought it to her face she started to cry. This time forty-eight hours ago she'd still had Zac and none of this was happening. It seemed such a short, yet such a long time ago.

'It's OK,' Freeman murmured, doing his best to comfort her. 'I know this is hard.'

'I didn't kill him,' she choked. 'I swear I didn't.'

Freeman turned to the custody sergeant. 'Is the doc here yet?'

'On his way,' the sergeant answered.

To Nikki, Freeman said, 'Someone's going to help you with the milk. He'll probably give you an injection.'

Nikki could hardly see or hear him, she was sobbing so hard. She tried taking gulps of air to bring herself back under control, but it wasn't easy when everything in her was so rigid with fear.

'Has she got a brief?' the custody sergeant asked.

'No,' Freeman answered, 'we need to organise one.'

'OK, you can get on to that while I go on processing her.'

From there everything seemed to plunge deeper and deeper into a living hell as her fingerprints were taken, then her photograph, then her DNA. She was told she could keep her clothes, which made her shrink inside, since it had never occurred to her that they might be taken away.

Then she was led to a cell. As she stepped through the door disbelief and panic welled up inside her. How could this be happening? She'd only just lost her baby and now they were doing this to her. They were like automatons with no sense of right and wrong, simply programmed to go about their duty with no understanding or feelings, just a blind adherence to protocol and process.

'The duty solicitor's on her way,' Freeman told her, 'and the doctor's just arrived.'

Nikki heard herself whisper a thank you. It sounded like someone else trying to use her voice.

Freeman was talking to the sergeant again, saying something about constant watch and CPS and Helen McAllister. The words were sliding over her like stones as she stood like a crumbling rock, taking in the starkness of the walls around her, the thin PVC mattress on a concrete slab of a bunk and the stainless steel toilet with no seat or privacy. Then the massive steel door was closing, and as the clang resonated through her like a physical jolt she wanted to scream and beg them to let her out again.

She sat down on the bunk, shivering and still shuddering with the occasional sob. Everything in her was trying to reject this madness, as though it was something physical that she could hold at bay, or hide from, or maybe even fight if she only knew how. Her only weapon was the truth, but she'd already told it and no one was listening. Instead they'd brought her here, locked the door and left her powerless to walk away. It was this stealing of her freedom, the inability to reason with anyone and make them believe her, that was frightening her more and more as each second passed. What terrible sin had she committed to be punished like this? Whatever it was, surely nothing could be bad enough to warrant losing her son, then being blamed for his death. She'd loved him more than her own life, and wanted him so much now that her arms, her whole body, ached with the need to hold him.

Feeling another onrush of panic she forced herself away from it, understanding on some distant level that if she was to help herself at all, she must try to stay calm and think straight. She hadn't done anything wrong, so, terrifying as all this was, she had to keep reminding herself that they were only doing their job. The fact that they thought Zac had been smothered was appalling, but it was a mistake, and in its way an understandable one, because the blanket had been over his face. No one had put it there, though, it was simply the result of him kicking as he struggled to breathe.

As the thought of his final moments emerged with a terrible clarity she felt herself breaking apart again. She hadn't been there for him, and she should have been, and now she had to live with her failure for the rest of her life.

She wondered where he was now. Had the pathologist treated him gently? Her hands came up as though to block out the images of him being cut apart. She couldn't let her imagination go that way or she'd end up screaming, or throwing herself against the walls, or doing something that would make them think she was insane. It was already bad enough that they thought she'd hurt her son. If they decided she was crazy too, God only knew where she might end up.

The sound of the door being unlocked penetrated her fear and her heart started to thud. Then hope sprang up like a flame inside her. They'd realised their mistake, they were letting her go.

'The doctor's here,' the custody sergeant told her. 'We'll take you to the medical room.'

As more fear overcame her she drew back against the wall, hugging her knees to her breasts as though to protect them. The milk was for Zac. If she allowed them to make it stop, it would be like letting him down again. Even though she knew that made no sense, it was how she felt. She didn't want them to touch her.

The sergeant came to squat down in front of her. His eyes

were kind, his voice was understanding as he said, 'It'll be for the best.'

Though somewhere deep inside she knew he was right, it was still a long time before she could make herself move and go with him.

When the doctor had finished she returned, almost zombielike, to the cell, and after that she had little sense of how many minutes or hours passed. She only knew that by the time she was taken to an interview room she was too afraid to feel any more hope. She kept thinking of the way Spence had doubted her, and if he did, then how on earth was she going to stop other people feeling the same way?

The interview room was just like those she'd seen on episodes of *The Bill*, small and dingy with no windows and a single table with a few chairs scattered around. She thought of the scenes Kristin had acted out in a setting like this, and wondered if she'd had any idea what it was like to be in such a place for real. She'd given a good performance, but that was all it was, a performance. When she'd finished she'd been able to walk away, and had probably laughed with the actors playing the detectives who'd just been treated to her fabricated wrath.

Where was Kristin now? Where were Spence and the others? What were they doing?

She was alone in the interview room for a while before the door opened, and a fat-faced woman with an unruly mop of auburn hair put her head round.

'Nicola Grant?' she asked.

Nikki cleared her throat. 'Yes,' she answered.

The woman looked relieved, and coming into the room she hefted a briefcase on to the table and shrugged off her coat. 'Maria Townsend,' she told her. 'I'm here to represent you.'

Nikki watched her shoot open the clips on her briefcase and remove a large yellow lined pad which she placed on the table, along with a couple of pens and a mobile phone.

'Have you given a statement yet?' Townsend asked as she sat down.

'No,' Nikki replied. 'No one's asked for one.'

Townsend looked baffled, then rolling her eyes she said,

'Sorry, I was thinking of something else. It's all go tonight, and I was . . . Well, never mind about that. So, you're here because they think you smothered your baby? Is that right?'

Nikki swallowed.

'So, did you?'

Nikki's eyes widened. 'No,' she replied.

Townsend's smile was brief, but friendly. 'Then you have nothing to worry about,' she declared, and after making a few notes on her pad, she sat back in her chair and looked up again. 'OK, talk me through what happened,' she said, 'from when you last saw your baby alive to when DC Freeman came to arrest you.'

Daring to take heart from Maria Townsend's apparent certainty that she had nothing to worry about, Nikki cleared her throat again and managed to find her voice.

The events might have taken less time in the telling had Maria Townsend not stopped to take an urgent phone call in the middle of it all, and the fact that Nikki had to repeat a couple of things made her start wondering if she wasn't explaining it well, or if the solicitor was paying sufficient attention.

Eventually Townsend stopped making notes, and after punching a quick text into her mobile, she said, 'Right, well, I think we're ready to talk to DS McAllister now.' She glanced at her watch. 'With any luck we'll be out of here in twenty minutes. An hour tops.'

As it turned out she couldn't have been more wrong, because it was evident from the moment DS McAllister came into the room, with a scowl of impatience directed at Townsend, that she was not going to be rushed.

After unwrapping two fresh cassette tapes, she slotted them into the recorder on the table, identified herself, then asked Nikki and Townsend to do the same. She then made sure Nikki was aware of her rights, a laborious process that got Townsend glancing at her watch and making a slight performance out of folding her arms.

Ignoring her, McAllister began by asking Nikki to describe what had happened on the morning of Zac's death, starting from the time she got up. Nikki told her, trying to be as clear and accurate as she could, and listening respectfully whenever McAllister interjected a question or comment. Yes, Zac had been crying a lot that morning, she admitted. Yes, she had felt tired and a bit down in the dumps. No, she wasn't suffering from post-natal depression.

'Is that a medical opinion, or your own?' McAllister wanted to know.

Nikki was thrown. 'My own, I suppose,' she replied. 'I was just feeling a bit low that morning. I hadn't had much sleep, and it's hard to keep your spirits up when you know . . . Well, when I knew that Zac was never going to be like other children.'

Townsend frowned. 'Why not?' she wanted to know.

McAllister looked at her coldly. 'The baby had a condition known as Tay-Sachs disease,' she answered, her tone making it plain that she took a dim view of a lawyer who had not managed to ascertain this crucial piece of information for herself.

'What the heck is that when it's at home?' Townsend demanded.

'Look it up on the Internet,' McAllister told her, and turning back to Nikki she said, 'After you found out about Zac's condition, did you ever think to yourself that it would be better if he died now, before he had to suffer what was in store for him?'

Nikki's face drained as her mouth turned dry. 'Well, I . . . It wasn't that I . . .'

'It would be an understandable reaction,' McAllister sympathised.

Nikki's heart was starting to pound. 'Yes, but I would never have done it,' she said earnestly. 'If you'd ever been in my shoes you would know that you'd do anything to spare your child something like that, but . . .'

'Anything?' McAllister echoed. 'Such as putting a blanket over his face?'

'No,' Nikki cried. 'That's not what I meant. You asked if I ever thought about it, and the honest answer's yes, I did, but I could never have hurt him, no matter how desperate I was to save him from that horrible disease.'

McAllister sat back in her chair. 'You were in the house alone yesterday morning?' she said, making it a question.

Nikki nodded.

'For the record Nicola Grant nodded a yes,' McAllister said, for the tape.

'Mrs Adani, my health visitor, came about ten,' Nikki told her.

'And will Mrs Adani's records show that the baby was in good health when she saw him?'

Nikki's eyes were shining with sincerity as she said, 'They should, because she told me he'd put on a pound and he was doing really well.'

McAllister nodded. 'What time did Mrs Adani leave the house?'

Nikki thought. 'I'm not really sure. About half past ten, I think.'

McAllister made a note on the pad in front of her, then said, 'So what did you do after she left?'

'I fed Zac and tried to get him off to sleep. It took quite a long time, because he wouldn't settle.'

'Was he crying?'

'Yes.'

'Would you say he was in much distress?'

'I think so. No one could find anything to cause it, but lately he's been crying a lot. When I first had him, he hardly cried at all.' It was difficult talking about Zac at the beginning, before it had started to go horribly wrong, but she mustn't allow herself to break down.

'Were all the right medical checks given?'

'Yes. Mrs Adani is very thorough, and we saw the doctor too. They said it was just a phase he was going through and it would probably pass.'

'But it didn't?'

'No, well, it hadn't really been going on all that long.'

'It just seemed a long time, because you were tired and worried and very upset by the diagnosis you'd received?'

Nikki started to nod, then a look of fear crept into her eyes. 'I know what you're trying to imply,' she said, 'but you're wrong.'

'What am I trying to imply?'

'That I couldn't take any more, so I . . . I . . .' Her head went down, she couldn't say the words.

'But you've told us you were in the house alone when it happened,' McAllister reminded her, 'so who else could have done it?'

Nikki's head came up. 'Nobody did it,' she cried. 'He had breathing problems before and we had to rush him to emergency. It must have happened again when the blanket fell over his face . . . That's how it was when I found him.'

McAllister regarded her closely, either assessing the quality of the statement or waiting for Nikki to say more, it was hard to tell which. 'Let me explain to you in layman's terms,' McAllister said, 'what the paediatric pathologist found when he examined your baby. Apart from blood in his lungs, nose, and eyes, there was a torn ligament in his neck and a bruise on his cheek. I think you'll probably agree, the weight of a blanket cannot cause those kinds of injuries.'

Nikki was staring at her in horror. 'No, but I . . . It could have happened when I was trying to revive him.'

'The internal injuries are not consistent with that,' McAllister told her, wondering when Townsend might care to join in. 'Someone held the blanket over his face.'

'It wasn't me,' Nikki cried. 'I know I was there on my own, but I was asleep . . . It was how I found him, I swear it.' They'd got it wrong. There couldn't have been any blood or bruising, because no one had killed Zac.

'Who else has keys to the house?' McAllister asked.

Nikki tried to make herself think. 'All of us who live there, and the landlord.'

'Might any of your friends have loaned their keys to someone?'

Nikki shook her head. 'I don't think so. I . . . Oh yes, David gave his to his mother. She's Mrs Adani, my health visitor, but I think she gave them back again.'

McAllister made another note, then continued. 'OK, so you say you found him under the blanket. Was he still breathing when you pulled it back?'

Nikki's heart skipped a beat. She didn't know the answer to that. 'I, um . . . I'm not sure. He just didn't look right, so I started trying to revive him, then I rang 999 and . . .'

'Why did you tell the operator you'd killed him?' McAllister interrupted.

Nikki's insides folded. 'I . . . I don't know. I mean, I was upset . . . I'd been thinking about . . .'

'My client was under a lot of strain at that point,' Townsend finally interjected, 'and we all know how mothers blame themselves in situations where they weren't to blame at all.'

McAllister cast her a chilly glance, and was about to continue when Nikki cried, 'I thought I was supposed to be innocent until proven guilty, and you're treating me like . . .'

'That's for the courts,' McAllister interrupted, not unkindly. 'Here we work on presumptions, and I'm afraid, Nicola, that I can only presume you either reached the end of your tether yesterday morning, or maybe you'd planned for a while to save your son from his fate . . .'

'That's not true,' Nikki protested. 'I admit I didn't want him to go through it, but when the time came I would still have loved him and done everything I could to make his life bearable.'

McAllister was regarding her with narrowed eyes. 'Which is very easy to say, now that you won't be put to the test,' she commented.

'It's true!'

Sitting forward, McAllister bunched her hands on her notepad and looked Nikki straight in the eye. 'For what it's worth, now I've learned something about the disease, I can understand why you did it . . .'

'But I didn't!'

'. . . and I'm pretty sure a judge would too, so if you give us a full confession there's every chance . . .'

'But I can't confess to something I didn't do,' Nikki cried, her voice coming from the depths of a confused and terrible fear.

McAllister pursed her lips as she continued to regard her, then suddenly clicking off the tapes she removed them and started to pack them away.

'Can I take it my client is free to go?' Maria Townsend demanded.

McAllister looked up. 'No, Maria, you cannot,' she retorted, and gathering up the tapes and her notebook she swept from the room.

'Don't worry,' Townsend said confidently to Nikki. 'I've been here a hundred times before. It'll be all right.'

DC Freeman was in the custody area when McAllister came out of the interview room.

'Did you find us an office?' she asked, flipping open her phone to check for messages.

'Right behind you,' he replied, pointing to where the Crown Prosecution lawyer was generally to be found during the day.

After informing her long-suffering husband that she was still at Broadbury Road, McAllister put her phone away again and followed Freeman into the office, where she slumped into a chair and propped her feet on the desk. She looked and felt very ready to go home.

'The baby's father and the housemates have moved over to an address in Totterdown,' Freeman informed her. 'It belongs to the health visitor, who's also the mother of one of the friends.'

McAllister nodded. 'Has anyone taken statements from them yet?'

'Yep, they're being photocopied as we speak, and they're all willing to make themselves available for further questioning if required. Most helpful. CSI have done their stuff at the house, and her health records should be with us by noon.'

'The baby's too?'

'Yep.' He opened a file and passed over a floppy red book. 'His personal health record,' he explained, as if she hadn't seen a thousand of them before.

'Anything unusual?' she asked, flipping through it.

'No. According to that he was developing like any normal baby.'

'Which he would, according to what we've read about Tay-Sachs.' Sighing, she closed it and pushed it back across the desk. 'She's still claiming she didn't do it,' she told him, 'and I have to hand it to her, she sounds pretty convincing.'

'They usually do,' he commented. 'Think Huntley and that lowlife from Dewsbury, what was her name?'

'She deserves to be forgotten,' McAllister responded, 'and

314

you're right, we've seen more Oscar-worthy performances in here than we ever do on our tellies, but I'm also thinking Angela Cannings and Sally Clark, who turned out to be telling the truth.'

'We're not talking cot death here,' he reminded her.

'Nevertheless, I don't want to rush into charging her at least until I've read all the statements, and the alibis have checked out.'

'Understood,' he said, 'but here's something else you might find interesting,' and opening his file again he slid a black PVC notebook across the desk.

It didn't take McAllister long to work out that it was some kind of journal, and simply from the couple of pages she read, she could tell that it was going to provide some of the most damning evidence of all against Nicola Grant.

'Has this been photocopied?' she asked.

'Yep. And there are two more like it, both full, so if you're short of some bedtime reading . . .'

'Very droll,' she commented, and getting to her feet she pushed the interview tapes towards him. 'Do the necessary with those,' she told him, and winced as some drunk started mouthing off in the custody area. 'We can hold her up to twenty-four hours without charge, but unless someone else comes forward with a confession, or one of those alibis doesn't check out, by this time tomorrow my guess is, she's going to find herself in Eastwood Park.'

Chapter Twenty-One

'I can't stand this, not knowing,' Spence was growling as he paced up and down Mrs A's kitchen. 'It's half killing me thinking of her in that place, surrounded by drunks and scumbags. We don't even know if they got her a lawyer.'

'They said they would,' David reminded him. 'And I think they have to.'

'But is he, or she, any good? That's what I want to know.'

'At least she won't have to share a cell,' Kristin pointed out. 'I mean, they don't on *The Bill*, and the writers do loads of research to make things as accurate as they can.'

Spence shot her a look that made her wish she hadn't spoken. Then, bunching his fists to his head, he let out another growl of frustration.

However, Kristin was right about the cell, so at least he didn't have to worry about Nikki rubbing up against the dregs of humanity in a physical sense. Nevertheless, the idea of her being locked up anywhere, terrified out of her mind, grieving for Zac, and probably not having managed a minute of sleep all night, wasn't one he was handling very well at all. God knew, he'd barely slept himself, nor had Danny who'd shared the guest room with him, and when they'd come downstairs to rummage around for something to drink in the early hours of the morning they'd found Mrs A and David sitting at the table sipping tea.

It was where they were now, at the table, with Kristin and Danny, watching Spence tear himself up with frustration and fear.

'I just don't know how anyone could think she did it,' he ranted, 'except I, fucking idiot – sorry, Mrs A – idiot that I am, had to go and ask her yesterday if she had. What the hell was I thinking? We all know she'd never hurt a fly, let alone her own son, so how could I even let it enter my head?'

'You have to stop beating yourself up like this,' David told him. 'It's not going to help her, and it won't do you any good either. We have to think of something positive we can do.'

Mrs A rose to her feet. 'I have to go to the office this morning,' she said. 'My manager is coming to collect my records and take them to the police.' She looked at Spence. 'While I'm there, I will make some enquiries about the body, and when we might have it back. We will need to arrange the funeral.'

As her words twisted through him Spence put a fist to his head again and pressed in hard, as though to silence the clamouring horror going on in his mind.

After Mrs A had gone the rest of them remained where they were, each steeped in their growing concerns, and in Kristin's case a mounting sense of guilt over what she'd told the police in her statement. Except it would have been wrong to lie, so she'd had to tell them about the chat she'd had with Nikki when Nikki had said she wished Zac would die now. Of course, it didn't mean she'd brought that about, but she'd said she would if she had the courage, so maybe something had happened to help her find it. How was anyone to know, when she'd been there on her own that morning? Anything could have happened to make her flip. Or maybe she'd been planning it . . . Whatever, the point was she hadn't wanted Zac to go through that horrible illness, and no one could blame her for that, plus having him was really screwing up her life in other ways. Anyway, whatever the others wanted to believe, in their hearts they must all know that there was a good chance Nikki had smothered Zac and was now regretting it and trying to get out of it.

Rising from his chair Danny walked over to the window, where he stared blindly out at the pond full of goldfish, and the tumbling view of the city below. He knew he should be on his way back to London by now, but there was no question of him leaving while Nikki was still being held by the police, even if it meant he ended up losing his job. She'd always been there for him, so there wasn't a chance in hell of him letting her down now, even though he barely knew what to do.

After a while, he said, 'Do we know if anyone's told her parents yet?'

Breaking from their reveries, everyone looked at him.

Feeling their eyes on his back, he turned round. 'I just thought . . . I mean, Zac was their grandson, and she's their daughter . . .'

They all looked at Spence, but it was David who said, 'Do any of us know how to get hold of them?' As they each shook their head he reached for his phone. 'I'll give Mum a call,' he said, 'at least she knows where they live, even if she doesn't have a number.'

'Maybe Mrs A's the one who should tell them,' Danny suggested. 'Or you, Kris?'

Kristin almost recoiled. 'Why me?' she cried. 'I've only ever met them once, and that was ages ago. They probably won't have the first idea who I am now.'

'Even if they haven't you're still a white, middle-class girl, which, for them, has got to be better than hearing it from the gay, the Indian or the druggie.'

Kristin's eyes moved from one to the other. 'I'm sorry, I just don't think it's my place,' she told them. 'You're a lot closer to Nikki than I am, Danny. You've known her longer and your parents live in the same city.'

Danny skewed her a look. 'Like what's that got to do with anything?' he asked sarcastically.

'It should be me,' Spence piped up.

'Actually,' David said, 'I think Danny's right, it should be Mum. You're under a lot of pressure, Spence, so you don't need all their shit if they start going off on one . . .' He broke off as Spence's mobile started to ring.

Grabbing it, Spence saw it was Drake. Crushing the disappointment that it wasn't Nikki, he clicked on.

'How are you doing down there?' Drake wanted to know. 'Any news on the autopsy yet?'

Bracing himself, Spence said, 'There's . . . It's not good. They seem to think Nikki might have . . .' He swallowed hard. 'They arrested her last night.'

'Jesus Christ,' Drake murmured in horror. 'Has she got herself a lawyer?'

'I think the police arranged one. We haven't been able to speak to her yet, so . . .' He took a quick breath. 'Listen, with the way things are, you know, with the funeral and all this other stuff now, I can't see me being able to come back to London for a while. I'm really sorry to let you down . . .'

'Put it out of your head,' Drake said firmly. 'Val's been itching to make her directorial debut, so looks like she's about to get her big chance, unless . . . What about David and Kristin? Are they staying with you?'

Spence's eyes went to David. 'It's Drake,' he told him, 'he wants to know your plans.'

Reaching for the phone, David said, 'Drake, I'm really sorry, man, but I can't leave Spence in the lurch. There's too much going down now.'

'I understand,' Drake responded. 'I can always ask Scott or Francis to stand in for you. Kristin's a different story, though, so can you give me some idea what she's intending to do?'

'She's here. I'll put her on,' David replied, and passing the phone to Kristin he said, 'He can work out replacements for me and Spence, but if you're not there the whole thing's going to fall apart.'

Kristin's eyes became battlegrounds for importance and unease as she looked at him. 'What shall I do?' she whispered. 'Is it going to seem really terrible if I go back while Nikki's in all this trouble? I mean, if I'm being professional, which I ought to be . . .'

Spence said, 'Right now, carrying on with the film is the best thing you can do for all of us. That way David and I won't feel so bad about letting everyone down.'

Kristin almost smiled with relief. 'You're right,' she declared, and taking the phone she said to Drake, 'I'll be on the next train to London, so I should be ready for make-up by midday.'

'Good girl,' Drake murmured. 'Can you put Spence back on?'

'I'm here,' Spence said, as Kristin hurried from the room to start packing.

'I want you to keep in touch,' Drake told him. 'Let me know if there's anything I can do, OK?'

'Thanks,' Spence said. 'I really appreciate that.'

After he'd rung off Danny returned them to the subject of Nikki's parents. 'They have to be told about Zac,' he said decisively, 'but I think we should try to find out from Nikki how much else she wants them to know at this stage.'

Spence nodded. 'You're right,' he said, 'because if the cops realise they're making a mistake and end up letting her go today, there won't be any reason for her parents to get involved in all that.'

'So how do we ask her?' David pondered. 'If they won't let anyone see her . . .'

'We'll have to find out who the lawyer is,' Spence said.

'Or,' Danny chipped in, 'we could take some clean clothes to the police station and ask if we can give them to her.'

Spence and David looked at one other. It sounded like a plan.

'Even if they say we can't see her,' Danny ran on, 'she'll probably need some clothes anyway, because she didn't take anything with her last night.'

'There's only one problem,' Spence pointed out, 'they might not let us into the house to get some.'

'Then we buy some,' David declared. 'We can call into the Broadwalk shopping centre on our way.'

Spence was on his feet. 'OK, let's hit the road,' he said, raring to go now he finally had something constructive to do.

As they reached the front door David said, 'You two go on, I need to talk to Kristin before she goes back to London. I'll meet you at the cop shop.'

Spence was already on his way through the front gate, so out of earshot as Danny murmured to David, 'Is this going to be about what I think it is?'

David nodded. 'Have you ever told Spence about the chat Nikki had with Kristin?'

'No way,' Danny whispered.

'Then keep it that way, at least until I've found out what she told them in her statement. If she blabbed that conversation then Nikki could be well and truly screwed.'

Nikki was sitting on the bunk in her cell, her back resting against the wall, a battered copy of an old Ludlum novel open but unread on her lap. The policewoman who'd brought her breakfast had said, 'We don't have much of a library here, but this one's quite good, and I think all the pages are there.'

Nikki had thanked her politely, then watched her leave, still not quite able to believe that she couldn't leave too.

The policewoman had looked back through the trap door and given her a *buck yourself up, it'll be all right* kind of smile, so Nikki had smiled too. She kept thinking if she was nice to people, and respectful, they'd come to realise that she wasn't the type of person who'd murder her baby, so they could let her go. It was absurd, because she knew things didn't work like that, but being difficult and abusive, the way she'd heard others being through the night, wasn't going to help her either.

She hadn't eaten the cornflakes and bread roll she'd been given, or drunk the coffee. Now wasn't the time to go back on caffeine, much as she might like to. An attack of diarrhoea would have been bad enough at the best of times; when she had only a few squares of Izal for cleanliness and a spyhole opposite the toilet to monitor her every move, it wasn't a further piece of hell she wanted to explore.

She had no idea what was happening now, or even what time it might be. She guessed it was still morning, because no one had brought her any lunch yet. She wouldn't eat it when they did. Her mouth was too dry, and her insides too tense to be able to cope with food. However, she seemed to have the panic under better control now, after exhausting herself with so much of it during the night. She'd dozed for an hour or two around dawn, and when she'd woken she'd discovered the rational, sensible Nikki trying to push her way past the demons. She wasn't going to help herself by allowing her imagination free rein, this Nikki kept telling her. She must stay focused and strong, and never forget that she'd done nothing wrong, so she had nothing to fear. This was England, where justice was for everyone, and where mistakes made in autopsies were quickly discovered so that all the false assumptions and misconceptions could be corrected and filed away.

With a beat of optimism she told herself that it was probably a second autopsy that was causing this delay. Somehow she'd managed to convince DS McAllister last night that she was telling the truth, so the detective had either asked for a second opinion on the results, or maybe she'd ordered another post-mortem altogether. If she had, then any minute now the door could swing open and someone would be there to tell her that the initial findings had either been misinterpreted or mixed up with someone else's, and she was free to go home.

However, as time ticked on, the only sounds she could hear were the banging and clanking of other cell doors, the jangle of keys and occasional raising of voices – and footsteps that came and went, but never stopped for her.

DS McAllister was back at Broadbury Road police station after spending the morning at her desk going through updates of the other cases she was involved in, most of which would be stomach-churning to the average joe. They weren't particularly edifying to her either, but at least they weren't exercising her conscience the way Nicola Grant's case was managing to. She felt sorry for the girl, and wished there was something she could do to help her, but the law was the law, and no matter how understandable the motive, no one could be allowed to get away with the murder of an innocent child, even if the child was destined to die anyway.

Looking up as Freeman came into the interview room they'd been allocated, she leaned back in her chair and said, 'So all the alibis check out?'

He nodded confirmation. 'The friends were in London on a film set; the health visitor was in some regular meeting with social services and no one else, except the landlord, has access to the house.'

'And someone's spoken to the landlord?'

'We're still waiting to hear back, but he's in Spain, went last Friday, so I think we can rule him out.'

'No sign of breaking and entering?'

Freeman shook his head.

McAllister sighed and looked down at the file again. 'So, when we put the autopsy results together with our girl's admissions, first to the 999 operator, then to the emergency paediatrician, then to me, plus her entries in her journal and the statement from . . . What was her name?'

'Kristin Lyle,' Freeman supplied.

McAllister found it in the pile. 'Right here we have a case for premeditation,' she said, scanning the statement again. '"I wish he could die now before all those horrible things start happening to him . . . I don't know if there's a god, but I do know that no animal has to suffer like that. He's my son, so why shouldn't I have as much say in what happens to him as something as random as fate . . ."' McAllister grimaced as she shook her head.

'The CPS isn't going to have much problem signing off on this,' Freeman informed her.

McAllister looked up as a uniform put his head round the door.

'Sorry to interrupt,' he said, 'but we've got a couple of Nicola Grant's friends in the front office. One of them's the baby's father. They've brought some clothes, and they're asking if they can see her.'

McAllister glanced at Freeman. 'Go and have a chat with them and I'll take this to the CPS,' she said. 'Is he around?' she asked the uniform.

'In his office the last time I saw him,' the uniform replied.

Freeman was on his feet. 'So what do I tell them?'

McAllister's heart sank as she said, 'Thank them for the clothes and tell them if they want to see her they should go to the magistrates' court later today, because she's about to be charged.'

'No!' Spence raged. 'You can't charge her with something she didn't do. I'm not going to let it happen.'

'I understand your frustration,' Freeman told him, 'but I'm afraid all the evidence . . .'

'What evidence? You don't have anything . . .'

'The post-mortem results . . .'

'. . . are crap. They don't mean anything, because I'm telling you she didn't smother him. No one did.'

'That's not what the pathologist concluded. The findings were consistent with . . .'

'I don't give a fuck what they're consistent with, I'm telling you she didn't do it. Ask anyone who knows her, she doesn't have it in her to hurt anyone, least of all her own child.'

Freeman's tone remained sympathetic as he said, 'Once again I have to tell you that the evidence against her is overwhelming.'

'Can we at least give her the clothes?' Danny said, looking up from his mobile where he'd just read a text from David.

Freeman took the bag Danny was holding out and looked inside.

Danny said, 'They're all brand new, some underwear, a pair of jeans and a top. There's some deodorant and a hairbrush too.'

After he'd finished checking, Freeman said, 'If there's court time available she'll appear this afternoon.'

Spence looked as though he'd been punched. 'Then what?' he asked.

'That'll be up to the magistrates,' Freeman replied, and scrunching the bag under one arm he used his swipe card to go back into the secure depths of the station.

Spence turned to Danny.

'There's something I have to tell you,' Danny said. 'Let's find the nearest pub. I'll text David to meet us there.'

Nikki was staring at the custody sergeant, watching his lips move as he spoke, hearing his words and feeling such a bewildering sense of dislocation that it was a while before she heard herself shouting at him to stop.

Except she didn't move a muscle, or utter a word. She only stood looking at him, tears streaming down her face as she told herself this was her punishment for the terrible thoughts she'd had about Zac.

'. . . you are charged with the murder of Zac Jeremy James, aged seven weeks,' the sergeant was saying, 'in that you held a blanket over his face and exerted enough pressure to stop him from breathing.'

Nikki felt stifled too, by guilt and horror and the dread of what was going to happen to her now.

The sergeant asked if she understood the charge.

She tried to answer, but her throat was locked tight. Her head was fuzzed with a strange white noise, her eyes were burning. It was as though she'd crossed over into a dark and frightening world where nothing good would ever happen, and no one had the time or inclination to listen to what she was saying.

She heard them talking about the magistrates' court and calling up the 'Reliance people' to take her down there. Someone mentioned Maria Townsend, and something about new clothes. She started to feel dizzy, but it was as though the world was whirling and she was standing still, or being sucked into a void that no one else could see. She wanted to disappear, turn into nothing, become an empty space that wasn't required to think or speak or feel any more.

She didn't understand why they hadn't discovered their mistake by now. What had gone wrong? Why were they going ahead with this when she was innocent? She hadn't killed him, so they couldn't prove she had. But they seemed to think they could and now she was trapped in here with no way out, and no one to turn to who could make a difference.

As sobs tore from her heart she cried out for her parents, but they weren't here. They didn't know what was happening to her and she didn't know how to get in touch with them.

Spence was staring at David and Danny in disbelief. They were in a pub not far from the police station, where David had met up with them a few minutes ago.

'And you're saying Kristin told the police about this conversation?' he demanded, his tone so rough that both Danny and David realised Kristin was fortunate not to be there.

'She didn't take long to admit it when I asked her,' David told him. 'She clearly feels really bad about it.'

Spence's eyes were cold. 'And you know she's telling the truth, because?'

David glanced awkwardly at Danny.

'When she first told me about it,' Danny said, 'she was really upset and . . . Not that I'm defending what she did,' he added hastily, 'I just . . . Well, I don't think she'd lie about something like that.'

'Well, you better hope she did,' Spence growled, and snatching out his mobile he punched in Kristin's number.

She answered on the second ring.

'What the hell were you thinking?' he raged. 'You had to know how your statement was going to look . . .'

'I'm sorry, I really am,' she broke in desperately, 'but it was what she said, and I couldn't lie . . .'

'You didn't have to tell them either,' he roared. 'You realise what you've done, don't you? Because of what you told them, they're charging her with murder.'

'Oh my God!' Kristin sounded horrified. 'They can't . . . But Spence, it's not my fault. I didn't make her say those things, and you have to face it, I mean, I know you don't want to, but you have to admit there is a chance she did it.'

Spence's face turned white. 'I don't ever want to hear you say that again,' he snarled. 'You've known her long enough . . .'

'She was under a lot of pressure,' she cried. 'Everything was going wrong with the baby, she couldn't come to London, her career was falling to bits . . .'

'Jesus Christ, what is it with you?' Spence seethed. 'Are you trying to send her down, or something, because that's what's going to happen if you carry on like that. Sure she was under pressure, but that doesn't mean she hurt him, and for you to think she did, or even might have, tells me what a fucking lousy friend you are, when she's always stood by you . . .'

'I'm on her side,' Kristin protested helplessly. 'I don't want anything bad to happen to her, I swear I don't, but when they asked me about her state of mind leading up to it all I didn't have a choice, I had to tell them what she said.'

'No! You could have told them she was under strain, that she was worried, unhappy because of the diagnosis, eager to come to London, you could have told them any of those things, and left it at that. Instead, you've well and truly screwed up her chances of ever being able to get out of this.

Well, I hope you're ready for what's going to happen next, because you're going to have to stand up and face her across a courtroom, and when you do, I want you to remember the part you've played in putting her where she is, because were it not for you, she probably *wouldn't be there,'* and clicking off the line he slammed the phone so hard on the table that the battery fell out and all the glasses jumped.

Realising now was no time to remind Spence that the post-mortem results were far more damning than anything Kristin might have said, Danny and David maintained a discreet silence until eventually Spence said, 'I want Kristin out of the house by the time I get back there. As far as I'm concerned she's dead.'

No one argued as he downed the rest of his pint.

'Come on,' he said, 'we need to make contact with the lawyer to find out when she's in front of the magistrate.'

Nikki was in the back of DS McAllister's car. Apparently she'd been charged too late in the day to be picked up by the Reliance van that generally transported prisoners to court, so the detectives were taking her instead. There had been some discussion about whether or not to handcuff her for the journey, but McAllister had brushed it aside, reminding everyone that she was a first offender with no history of bolting or violence. So now Nikki was sitting beside DC Freeman, buckled tightly into her seat, child locks securing the door beside her to prevent her from trying to jump out.

She was wearing the new clothes Spence had brought, a pair of pale blue jeans that were a size too big, a warm blue fleecy top and fresh underwear and socks. He'd even thought to add a hairbrush and deodorant, or maybe that was Danny's doing. It would be more like Danny to think of the extras, but whoever it was, knowing that they'd considered her needs, and had cared enough to bring them to the station was such a boost to her morale that she only wished she could tell them.

As they drove alongside the cut where roadworks were holding everything up, tears rolled silently from Nikki's eyes as she looked out at the world she knew well, and saw it as a place that was strangely disorienting. She felt like a ghost moving by unseen, a visitor from another time, who no longer lived there. It was too hard to grasp the reality of what was happening, and yet it was as stark and uncompromising as the towering office blocks and riverside walkways. Her eyes dropped to her hands as they tightened around the bag her new clothes had arrived in. It contained her old ones now that needed washing.

She wondered if Spence would come to the court, and found herself dreading it as much as she longed for it. Thinking of him was almost as difficult as thinking of Zac. It swamped her with such an overwhelming sense of longing that it was as though everything in her was trying to wrench free of its roots to go to him. She'd never felt so much love or despair. She wanted to believe he could make everything all right, or at least that he'd be there for her, and this gesture of the clothes told her he was. However, knowing that he'd doubted her, if only for a moment, was still haunting her every thought. Each time she went back over the last two days she found herself slipping into a state so bewilderingly surreal that she'd even begun to doubt herself. Had she sleepwalked downstairs to the baby? Maybe she'd smothered him and somehow managed to blank it from her mind. She'd been having memory lapses over the last few months, so had she done it, then forgotten it? It felt like madness even to think it, but they kept insisting someone had done it, and if she'd been the only one in the house, even she could see why they believed it must have been her.

By the time they reached the courts on Marlborough Street a fine drizzle was dampening the chill March air. She watched an electric shutter door roll open, and felt a choking sense of claustrophobia and despair as DS McAllister eased the car forward into a vehicle dock. After the shutter door was securely closed again, DC Freeman came round to release Nikki from the back of the car.

'Thought there might have been some press around,' she heard him comment to DS McAllister.

Nikki didn't catch McAllister's reply, because her face was buried in her hands as she started to pray in a way she never had before in her life. It hadn't even crossed her mind that the media might take an interest in her case; all she'd allowed herself to consider was the mistake the police were making and how soon it might be cleared up. Everything else was just a process that had to be gone through, an experience that she might even use as research one day, but now, to think that her case might be tried in the press as well as in court . . . *She couldn't stand it. She just couldn't.* Something or someone had to make this stop, because she wasn't capable of taking any more.

McAllister and Freeman led her into a basement area not unlike the custody suite she'd just come from. The officers were wearing different uniforms, though, with badges that read *Reliance Custodial Services*. She was checked in, and her bag was allocated a number that matched the cell to which a Reliance officer escorted her. They passed other cells, with steel bars for doors that allowed the prisoner to see out, and Nikki to see in. Some were empty, but others contained offenders waiting for the prison van to come and collect them. Nikki wasn't aware of that, though, she only knew that they were catcalling and jeering in a language she barely recognised as English – and that the place stank of sweat and urine and something nauseatingly sweet.

Her cell was number six. It had the same steel gate of a door as the others, a single concrete bunk with mattress, and a toilet enclosed by a half wall. As the Reliance officer turned the key she looked at him with eyes that couldn't quite understand why, or how he could do this. He ignored her and walked back to the desk where McAllister and Freeman were both talking on their mobile phones.

As the other prisoners continued shouting and swearing Nikki blocked her ears, needing somehow to try and displace herself. She couldn't be here, she was somewhere else, where people weren't bragging about their crimes, or slagging off their lawyers or threatening one another. The clamour of their voices, the stench of their bodies were coming at her in bursts, like brief awakenings in the midst of a dream.

A nightmare.

That was all this was, a terrible, crazy nightmare that would be over as soon as she could make herself wake up.

Long, awful minutes ticked by. Was this going to be her life from now on? Moving from one cell to another, assailed and abused by other prisoners, no one ever believing anything she said? Her eyes closed as the horrifying spectre of prison life started to loom. She buried her head deeply into her arms, as though blocking it out could stop it becoming real. For a few brief moments she tried to make some sense of it all, but then she shied away from that too. There was no sense to this, because even when she tried to make some, what resulted was a three-dimensional picture of guilt.

She'd been the only one there, she had the motive and the opportunity, so it had to be her. And if everyone said it was, then maybe they were right.

Except they *weren't*.

She started at the clatter of keys and looked up to see the Reliance man was back.

'Your brief's here,' he told her.

Getting to her feet, Nikki followed him past the other cells again, trying not to hear the cackles and guffaws and disgusting names the occupants were calling her. Even so, they were sinking into her like claws, injecting her with the poisons of fear and panic and self-loathing.

Maria Townsend was standing with her back to the interview-room door as Nikki came in. Turning round, she glanced at her watch. 'Hi, how are you?' she said. 'Sorry, I got delayed. They're about to take you up, so we don't have much time to talk, but it's OK, nothing's changed since I saw you last night.'

'Yes it has,' Nikki said, incredulously. 'They've charged me with . . . They've . . .' She took a quick gulp of air. 'You said I had nothing to worry about.'

'You haven't if you didn't do it,' Townsend asserted with a smile. 'I take it you're still saying you didn't?'

'Of course I am. Why would I admit to something I didn't do?'

Townsend's eyebrows rose. 'It's a way of getting a lighter sentence,' she informed her, 'which is something you might want to consider further down the road. For now, though, you don't have to say anything. Just leave it all to me, and we'll have you out of here in no time.'

Once again Maria Townsend couldn't have been more wrong, because as the evidence of Nikki's guilt was presented to the magistrates even Nikki could see why no one would believe her. The biggest shock of all came when the prosecutor read from her journal, since she hadn't even known the police had taken it. Then he recited extracts from Kristin's statement, and Nikki could hardly believe her ears.

Kristin had told them all that?

It got even worse when the prosecutor claimed that not only was she a flight risk, but she should be remanded in custody to prevent her causing any harm to herself.

Nikki's head started to spin. When had she ever said or done anything to justify such a concern? This man, this total stranger, was making up lies to stop her from going free. Why? What purpose would it serve? What did he stand to gain from doing this to her?

They were still talking, the lawyers, the magistrates, all strangers, deciding her fate, and in spite of the screaming inside her, she wasn't allowed to say a word. She was aware of Spence and the others somewhere behind her, feeling their presence almost as if they were touching her, but she dared not turn round. Instead she continued to stare wild-eyed at the dour-faced individuals who had somehow taken charge of her world.

They stood up, and as the lawyers began talking to one another, Spence shouted, 'No! I'm not letting you get away with this.'

Nikki looked down as the man standing next to her held out a set of handcuffs.

'She didn't kill him,' Spence yelled. 'Take me if you have to take someone. Just don't do this to her.'

Her eyes went to the Reliance officer who was clasping the handcuffs around her wrists. His head was down, so all she could see were bristly whorls of greying hair and the red tips of his ears. Then he was leading her from the court, towards the staircase they'd climbed a lifetime ago. She turned to look at Spence, but their eyes barely had a chance to connect before she was being ushered through a door.

'I didn't do it,' she shouted, hoping he would hear.

'I *know*,' he shouted back, and she almost sobbed with relief.

The force behind the word told her that at least he believed her, but there was no time to think about it now. She was on her way back to the bowels of the courts, and in spite of missing the words that had condemned her, it was clear she wasn't going home.

Instead she was going to prison, where people who'd committed real crimes and despised anyone who'd harmed a child were housed.

Another silent scream began curling itself from the very depths of her, powered by more terror than she'd ever felt in her life, but when it reached her throat all that came out were two small words, and even they were no more than a whisper.

'You know, I've been meaning to ask about that,' Townsend said, coming up behind her, 'where are your parents? You could . . . What?' she said, as the Reliance man spoke to her.

'I was saying, your client's in luck,' he told her. 'The van's outside and it's only got one place left, so no waiting.'

'Well, there's a blessing in disguise,' Townsend muttered. Then, to Nikki, 'They'll return your belongings now, so you can take them with you.'

Nikki only looked at her.

'It'll be all right,' Townsend told her, almost cheerfully. 'Do you have any money?'

Nikki shook her head.

Townsend rolled her eyes. 'We should have thought of this earlier,' she declared, as though Nikki could have known it was a requirement. 'Still, no worries. As a remand prisoner you can have visits every day, so get someone to bring a few pounds. It'll help with the phone, and other little things while you're in there. Oh, and it might be best if you ask to go on the rule when you get there, which means you'll be segregated from the other prisoners. Probably wise, when we consider what you're going in for. Ah, at last, I've been waiting for this call,' and clicking on her mobile she turned away.

Nikki stared at the way her coat strained over her back. She wasn't sure what she wanted to say, or ask. All she knew was that whatever it was, there was no point, because even her lawyer wasn't listening.

Chapter Twenty-Two

Spence's expression was a mask of anger and frustration as he left the court, walking purposefully, as though he knew exactly where he was going and what needed to be done.

'That lawyer was worse than useless,' David declared, as the doors swung closed behind them. 'She hardly said a word in Nikki's defence.'

'That's why we have to find her another,' Spence answered shortly, and came to a sudden stop at the kerb as a bus sped past.

'Do you know someone?' Danny asked.

'Even if I did, which I don't,' Spence replied, 'we can't afford one, but I know someone who can.'

Danny glanced at David. 'You mean her parents?' David asked.

'Exactly,' Spence confirmed, as they started to cross the road. 'I need you to get their address from your mother so I can go over there first thing tomorrow. Meantime, we go online to find out what we can about Eastwood Park and their visiting hours.' Flipping open his mobile as it rang, he barked, 'Hello.'

As he listened he continued for a few more steps, then slowed to a halt as his face started to drain.

'What is it?' Danny cried in alarm.

Spence put up a hand, continued to listen, then, as his face grew paler still, he said, 'I'll get back to you,' and ringing off he stared at the others in horrified disbelief.

'Who was it?' David prompted.

Spence still couldn't get his head round what he'd just heard.

'Spence, tell us what it is,' Danny urged. 'We're in this together, remember?'

Spence's eyes went to him. 'It was the coroner's office,' he finally managed. 'Apparently Zac's body is back . . .' He took a breath. 'They can release it for burial, but his . . . His brain is still in London.'

Danny's mouth fell open in shock.

'They're saying it has to stay in the pathology lab until the trial is over,' Spence continued, 'so do we want to bury Zac without his brain, or should they hang on to the body until the brain can be released too?'

'Jesus Christ,' David murmured, looking as appalled as he felt.

Spence closed his eyes as though to ward off any more crucifying images of his son's tiny body and the state it must now be in.

'What happens to the brain if you go for the burial without it?' Danny asked after a while.

Spence shook his head. 'I didn't ask. I suppose I should before I mention it to Nikki.'

Danny and David looked at him helplessly. He didn't have to voice how unwilling he was to bring this up with her now, nor did he have to explain how sick the call had made him. It was there between them all, a force without words, a decision that no parent should ever have to make.

In the end Spence turned round to look at the magistrates' court, seeming almost as though he might go back. 'Knowing she's still in there,' he growled impotently, 'and I can't get to her . . . It makes me want to stampede the place and get her out.'

Danny put a comforting hand on his shoulder as David said, 'What matters now is doing everything we can to get her a good lawyer,' and taking out his mobile, he pressed to connect to his mother.

Until now Nikki had had no idea what a prison van was like. If she'd been asked to guess she supposed she'd have imagined prisoners sitting on long bench seats behind a thick wire screen, possibly bullet-proof glass, and probably each one shackled to the next.

It was nothing like that at all.

The back of the van she was travelling in was divided into six micro-cells, three on one side of a central corridor, and three on the other. They were so small that there was barely room to turn around, and her knees practically touched the opposite wall when she sat down in the moulded metal seat. After the guard had removed her handcuffs, and before he'd locked her in, he'd explained that there was a trapdoor overhead for the police or fire brigade to haul her out, in case of emergency.

Every time she thought this ordeal couldn't get any worse, it did.

She knew they were on the A38 now, heading north, because she'd seen a sign a while ago. The window was heavily tinted, but she guessed that was to prevent people looking in, rather than prisoners from gazing out. An odd sort of courtesy that probably wasn't one at all.

In her mind she'd stopped being who she really was, instead she'd begun playing a part, like an actor who mustn't look at the cameras or try to contact the crew. She simply had to trust they were there, capturing images of the van as it sped through the countryside, carrying its cargo of players in their roles of security guards and grave and petty offenders. Some of the prisoners, jammed like sardines in their steel cans, were bellowing lines from a script Nikki hadn't seen, in a language she knew but never used. At times the words were so foul they churned her stomach, and the shrieking laughter was so piercing it made her wince. Her expressions and reactions were a part of the film. They weren't real, either. They would stop as soon as the director called cut.

She stared hard at the passing landscape, willing herself to stay in character, even though she wasn't sure who she was supposed to be. She was accused of murder, which made her a serious offender, but it wasn't how she felt, because she was trying to stop herself feeling anything now. If she fell out of character, she must try to be an observer of her own life, a detached mind watching an obedient body entering the prison system like a cadaver being sucked into a grave.

Maria Townsend's parting words swooped in ominous echoes through the confusion in her mind. 'Go on the rule . . . you'll be segregated . . . wise when we consider what you're going in for.' What did 'the rule' mean? Who should she ask? What was segregation like? Presumably better than being amongst those who considered it their role in the movie, or in life, to inflict their own kind of punishment on inmates who harmed their children.

Inmates.

She was an inmate now. Unconvicted, but nevertheless incarcerated. Remanded in custody awaiting trial for the killing of her baby son.

Grief and panic started to rise like an explosion inside her, but she quickly pushed it down again and returned her gaze to the window. Everything was passing in a blur, fields, trees, cottages, garden centres, pubs . . . The crew was out there, the cameras were rolling.

They were turning now, heading down another road which ran through a drab housing estate. She saw a sign for HMP Eastwood Park, and as the van slowed she realised they'd arrived. She wanted to run and never stop, but her space was so small she couldn't even take a step. All she could see through the window were high fences with rolls of vicious barbed wire across the top and a CCTV camera pointing her way. It reminded her of the role she was supposed to be playing, but as the minutes ticked by and the van trundled forward again, her attempts at fantasy began draining away like water from a sink, leaving her in the cold, stark grip of unthinkable reality.

The van came to a stop, but it was a while before the Reliance officers began unloading their consignment. For Nikki it couldn't be long enough, but all too soon someone was unlocking her door, and as she stood up the Reliance man held out the handcuffs. A moment later her wrists were in steel bands and she was being led through the van, out into the late afternoon chill and in through a door to a bleak, strip-lit office where two uniformed wardens were waiting to take her in.

Suddenly her terror was so great that she wanted to be sick, and she might have been had one of the officers not stepped forward to put a hand on her arm. She was a young woman with scraped-back blonde hair and a kindly smile.

'Your first time?' she asked.

Nikki's throat was too dry to speak, so she only nodded. Friendliness was the last thing she'd expected – it didn't fit with anything at all she'd ever heard about prisons.

'We'll get you checked in as quickly as possible,' the officer said, glancing over her shoulder as the phone started to ring.

The other officer picked it up, while the young blonde woman flipped a page on her clipboard and said, 'OK, name and date of birth.'

Nikki answered in a husky, respectful voice.

After writing it down the officer went on to the next question. 'Why are you here?'

Nikki started to sway, and her eyes filled with tears as she said brokenly, 'They think I killed my baby, but I didn't.'

The officer glanced up, gave her a small smile and was about to continue when Nikki said, 'My lawyer told me to ask if I can go on the rule. I don't know what that is, but . . .'

The officer was frowning now, but her tone wasn't hostile as she said, 'It's Rule 43 of the prison code, which entitles you to segregation if that's what you want.' She glanced down at the form. 'Yeah, maybe it's a good idea for you,' she decided, and turning to her colleague who'd just finished on the phone, she said, 'We've got a Rule 43 here, do you want to deal with it?'

'On it,' the other one said and picked up the phone again.

Continuing the check-in, the blonde officer said, 'Next of kin?'

Nikki stumbled in her thoughts, knowing it had to be her parents, but wanting it to be Spence. In the end she said, 'My boyfriend is the closest to me. Can I . . .'

'It has to be family,' the officer told her. 'If you have any.'

Nikki swallowed. 'Then it's my father,' she said. 'Jeremy Grant.'

The officer asked her to spell it. 'Contact details?' she asked.

Nikki's throat was closing.

'Phone number, address?' the officer prompted.

'I – I don't know,' Nikki managed. 'But I think I can find out.'

Apparently unfazed by this, the officer quickly filled out the rest of the form, signed it at the bottom, then allocated Nikki a number. 'So, what do we have here?' she said, putting the form aside and picking up the sealed bag the Reliance officer had dumped on the desk when he'd brought Nikki in. After rummaging through, she noted its contents on another form, added a few more ticks or comments, then pointed to a door, saying, 'You'll get your welcome pack as soon as you've been searched, so go through there and wait. You'll be called when it's your turn.'

Feeling an icy fear spreading through her veins, Nikki started through to the next room, suspecting this was going to be her first face-to-face encounter with other inmates. She was right, because two women were already in the holding room, one stretched out on a bench, the other slouched on a facing bunk, chin on her chest, and hands stuffed deeply into her pockets. When she glanced up Nikki quickly looked away, judging it best to avoid any eye contact unless it was invited.

Deciding to keep as distant as she could, she perched on the edge of a chair just inside the door. Then she began trying to cast her mind into the safe haven of other waiting rooms she'd been in, like doctors' and dentists', but they made her think of her mother, and because the need for her parents was so intense she had to bring her thoughts back to the present or she knew she would cry. She should have told them straight away what had happened to Zac. They'd have come, in her heart she knew it, but she hadn't given them the chance.

She glanced up as the door opened and a different officer checked her list before saying, 'Nicola Grant?'

The supine woman opened her eyes. 'We got some favouritism going on here?' she growled.

The officer appeared amused. 'Never imagined you being in a hurry to join us, Gina,' she responded.

The woman gave a grunt of disgust and closed her eyes again.

The officer nodded at Nikki, who rose to her feet and followed her into another room where her fingerprints were taken, then she was handed a terry dressing gown and told to strip down to her bra and pants.

Starting to shake now, as much with dread as with cold, Nikki unfastened her jeans and let them slide to the floor. Then she hiked the fleecy sweater over her head and wrapped herself in the dressing gown, clutching it tightly in front of her and trying to steel herself for an internal search, front and back, to check she wasn't carrying drugs. She desperately wanted to refuse, but she had no rights now, so she had no choice but to endure it.

'OK, drop the top of the robe to your waist,' the officer told her.

Doing as she was told, Nikki stared at nothing as the officer walked around her, asking her to lift each arm, then the bottom of her bra cups to see if anything fell out, before saying, 'Are you breastfeeding?'

'I was,' Nikki replied. 'A doctor gave me an injection to dry up the milk.'

The officer noted this down, then said, 'Right, top back on, and raise the bottom of the robe to your waist.'

Once again the officer walked around her, asking her to lift one leg, then the other, before instructing her to stretch the elastic in her panties so that anything hidden there would fall out.

'You'll do,' the officer told her. 'Shower's over there. You'll find a clean tracksuit, towel and some flip-flops on one of the shelves, together with a welcome pack. Don't be long, we've got four more to process yet.'

Disrobing quickly, Nikki stepped into the shower. At first the water was lukewarm, but then it turned hot and the sensation was so comforting that she'd have stayed there all night if she could.

However, mindful of her instruction to be swift, she'd barely finished soaping herself when she stepped out again and grabbed the nearest towel. A navy tracksuit fell on to the wet floor, along with a pair of large brown flip-flops, but she wasn't about to make an issue out of size or condition. She wasn't even sure if she was meant to put them on yet, so deciding to dress in her jeans and fleecy top again, mainly because it made her feel close to Spence, she pushed her feet back into her trainers and gathered up the prison-issue items.

A few minutes later another officer came to find her. This one was bullish and chunky, and wearing a huge bunch of keys that jangled and clanked over her hip as she walked. 'Grant?' she barked.

'Yes,' Nikki replied.

'Follow me.'

Nikki fell in behind her, still clutching the tracksuit, towel, flip-flops and welcome pack, which she hadn't looked in yet. The officer's shoes squeaked on the concrete floor, while her meaty thighs in their grey nylon slacks hissed together as she waddled from one iron gate to another, unlocking and locking as they went, making sure the sinister clang when she closed a gate echoed through the stark stone corridors. Then they entered a door labelled A Wing, and the noise and stench hit Nikki like a physical blow.

'So you're on the rule,' the officer stated coldly.

Nikki's heart tensed with fear as she nodded. She could tell this officer wasn't one she could look to for protection.

As though to confirm it, the woman treated her to a scathing look, then kicking open a door she jerked her head towards it for Nikki to go in.

Half expecting to be kicked too as she passed, Nikki entered the cell and forced herself to keep breathing. It wasn't anywhere near as bad as those she'd been in at the police station and court. This one was a dull white colour, with a proper bed hugging one wall, a cupboard at the foot of the bed with a small TV on top, a sink attached to the opposite wall, a toilet and a barred window at a low enough level to see through.

Trying to convince herself that it was better than sleeping on the street, she turned back to the door in time to have it slammed shut in her face. She jumped and stared at it in panic. As the key ground in the lock she wanted to throw herself against it, to scream and rant that they had to let her out, but instead she forced herself to take several more deep breaths before dropping what she was carrying on to the bed.

She had to find a way of dealing with this, or she would go under. If she could, she must stop herself thinking about Spence and Zac and what might be happening outside, and try to stay focused on what was in front of her now. For the moment it was simply the task of unfolding the limp duvet and sheets to make up her bed, so she made herself start to do it.

When she'd finished she picked up the welcome pack to inspect its contents: a small tube of toothpaste, a folding toothbrush, a double sachet of shampoo, a flannel, a bar of soap and a small pouch of tobacco with papers to roll cigarettes. There was also a bar of chocolate and two cellophane-wrapped ginger biscuits.

She wasn't hungry, but maybe she would be in the night, so she stowed the food away in the cupboard, pushed the tracksuit and flip-flops in after it and picked up the remote control for the TV.

Suddenly the walls seemed to be closing in on her, and as though all the air was escaping from the cell she started to panic and gulp. She couldn't stay in here. She just couldn't. She wanted Spence and her parents. She needed her baby, to feel him in her arms and know he was safe. Why was God punishing her like this? He must know she hadn't harmed Zac. She might have thought about it, but she'd never, ever have done it.

'Please God, please, please, please,' she sobbed as she sank to her knees next to the bed. 'I'll do anything, *anything*, just please don't make me stay here.'

Spence and the others were crammed into Mr Adani's study, where they'd been busy on the Internet and phone since arriving back from court. Apart from all the other vital information they'd managed to find out, they were now certain that Nikki was eligible for legal aid if her parents didn't come through with the money to pay a good lawyer. But the Grants had to do this, Spence was determined about that. Mrs A was going to drive him over to their flat in the morning, then he'd go to see Nikki in the afternoon. He'd already requested a visit, and because she was only on remand he had every confidence it would be granted. David was currently downloading directions on how to get to Eastwood Park by bus, because Mrs A was due to go through Nikki's health records with the police in the afternoon, and Danny was ringing round everyone they knew to see if anyone could put them in touch with a brilliant lawyer who'd be prepared to take on Nikki's case as soon as they had the funds.

Spence was about to go and talk to Mrs A, who was in the kitchen making up food parcels to take to Nikki, when his mobile sprang into life.

'Hey,' he said shortly.

'Hey,' Nikki said softly, 'it's me.'

His tension unravelled so fast he almost swayed. 'Nik! Thank God,' he gasped. 'Are you OK?'

The others immediately turned in his direction.

'I've been in better hotels,' Nikki quipped, but her voice was frail and nasal from so much crying. 'They gave me a chip-and-pin thing for the phone, but it won't last long, so I . . .'

'That's OK. I'm coming there tomorrow. We can talk then. Just tell me, is there anything you need that I can bring?'

'Um, a writing pad and some pencils? A few books to read, you know the kind of thing I like. And a photo of Zac. The one with you where he looks as though he's going to kiss you.'

Feeling his heart contract, Spence said, 'Consider it done. Anything else?'

'Some money for the phone.'

'No problem. And listen, we're going to get you a better lawyer, OK? We're working on it right now . . .'

'So you really believe I didn't do it?'

'I *know* you didn't,' he growled, 'but if we're going to believe the police then we have to accept that someone did, so we have to find a good lawyer. I'm going to see your parents in the morning . . . Please tell me you're cool with that.'

She didn't answer right away.

'Nik! Are you still there?'

'Yes,' she said. 'They'll want to help, I know they will. Just tell them . . . Tell them I'm sorry I didn't call when I first knew about Zac, but I was . . .' Her voice fell apart as she started to sob. 'Oh God, Spence, it's so awful in here. I don't think I can stand it.'

'We're going to get you out,' he said fiercely.

She started to reply, but whatever she'd been about to say was lost as the connection failed.

The following morning, at Spence's insistence, Danny returned to London where he was scheduled for the weekend shift.

'If you don't go, you could lose your job,' Spence pointed out, 'and we need someone to keep paying the rent while all this is going on.'

Unable to argue with that, and already sensing his manager's patience wearing thin, Danny agreed to go, but not before making them promise they'd keep in touch every step of the way.

After dropping Danny off at the station Mrs A steered the car out of the concourse, listening quietly as David said to Spence, 'You know, if this doesn't work out with Nikki's parents, you could always try to talking to Drake about raising some cash.'

Spence nodded, while staring ahead to where the traffic was merging on to the Bath Road. 'I've been thinking the same thing,' he admitted, 'but he's been so good to us already, and you know what legal fees are like. We can't ask him to cough for an unlimited amount when we've got no idea how, or when, we can pay it back.'

'He might be able to put us on to a good lawyer, though,' David pointed out. 'I mean one that does legal aid.'

'Bristol isn't his neck of the woods, but I guess there's no harm in asking, if it does come to it.'

'I'll give him a call while you're talking to the parents,' David said, 'it could be a fallback, if nothing else.'

'And I will be ringing Mr Adani in India,' Mrs A informed him. 'I told him last night all about what was happening and he reminded me that he knows very many people in the area from the legal profession, because sometimes he is asked to appear in court as an expert witness. He says he is going to make some calls, so I will be finding out if he has any news.'

Giving her hand a squeeze, Spence said, 'I don't know how any of us would manage without you, Mrs A.'

'Oh, don't be saying silly things now,' she scolded. 'This is a serious situation and everyone is doing their best to help.'

'We just have to hope her parents will too,' David commented, voicing everyone's thoughts, though no one could imagine they wouldn't.

It was almost ten o'clock by the time they turned into Bennett Street, and though there was no way in the world Spence was going to back out of this, he had to admit to feeling a certain trepidation, considering everything he'd heard about the Grants. However, he didn't doubt that they loved their daughter, so at least they were on the same page over that, and he couldn't believe they'd allow their antipathy towards him to stand in the way of helping her now.

As they pulled up outside the grand Georgian terrace Mrs A switched off the engine and turned to Spence, regarding him with wide, worried eyes. She'd wanted to tell him last night what the Grants had found out about his father, but after Nikki's call he'd been so distressed himself that she simply hadn't been able to add to the burden of what he was already suffering. If she could be certain that he already knew, it might have been easier, but she couldn't, and now wasn't the time to tell him, either. She could only hope that the Grants wouldn't bring it up themselves, though once they realised why he was there, she felt sure they'd be too upset about Zac and Nikki to bother about something as trivial as Spence's relatives.

'Remember,' she said gently as he glanced up at the house, 'you are going to be telling them that they've lost their grandson, so give them a moment to absorb the shock before you tell them what's happened to Nikki.'

Spence swallowed dryly.

'They only met Zac once, for five minutes,' David pointed out.

'Nevertheless, he was still part of their family,' his mother responded.

'What am I going to do if they refuse to let me in?' Spence said. 'Besides beat the door down?'

'Try first,' Mrs A advised, 'and if there is a problem I will see if they are more willing to speak to me.'

Spence looked up at the house again, then, taking a deep breath, he said, 'Right, here goes,' and pushing open the car door, he stepped out into the path of a man and his dog. 'Excuse me,' he mumbled, and after ruffling the dog's head, he went to ring the Grants' bell.

A few moments later a gruff male voice came over the intercom asking who was there.

'It's Spencer James, Nikki's partner,' Spence replied. 'I need to talk to you, sir.' Hopefully the respect would stand him in enough good stead at least to be let in through the door.

To his relief it seemed to work, because the buzzer sounded to release the door and he was being told to come to the first floor.

When he got there Mr Grant was waiting, his eyes not quite as stern as Spence had imagined them to be, but his mouth was grim, and the unkemptness of his hair and unshaven chin came as a bit of a surprise. On closer inspection his shoulders seemed vaguely stooped, giving him the air of someone who'd had the stuffing knocked out of him, which, if what Spence had heard was true, he probably had. How the mighty had fallen during these difficult times, he was thinking, which didn't do much to bolster his confidence of a fruitful outcome to this meeting.

'Hello, sir,' he said, holding out a hand to shake. 'I hope I haven't come at an inconvenient time, but we don't have a phone number for you.'

Grant took the hand in a firm enough grip. 'My wife should be back any minute,' he said. 'She's just popped into town.'

'I see,' Spence responded, not sure yet whether it was a good or bad thing that she wasn't there now, and wondering if he was going to be kept on the landing.

'You'd better come in,' Grant said, and standing aside for Spence to pass, he closed the door. 'Through there,' he said, pointing the way.

Noting the grandeur of the place, Spence knew already that he was going to take it very badly if Grant tried to back away from his responsibilities. OK, he might have hit hard times and this place might be rented, but it must be costing a packet nevertheless, and he'd never believe that someone in Grant's position couldn't lay their hands on a sizeable stash in an emergency.

'So,' Grant said, gesturing for Spence to sit down, 'I suppose we were always destined to meet one day. I'm now intrigued to learn why it's today.'

Though his manner wasn't cold, exactly, it wasn't particularly friendly either, but Spence was determined not to let the man under his skin when much more important issues were at stake than his pride. 'I'm afraid,' he began, 'that I have some sad news about Zac.'

Though Grant's expression didn't alter particularly, he seemed to stiffen, and Spence sensed a change in him that he couldn't quite fathom. Maybe it was guilt and embarrassment for the way he'd shunned his daughter and grandson.

'He died three days ago,' Spence said, digging his nails into his palm to try to relocate the pain.

Grant blinked, then took a step back as though he'd been struck.

'I'm sorry to break it to you . . .' Spence stopped at the sound of a key going in the front door. He looked at Grant, but the man seemed not to have heard. 'I think . . . I guess that must be your wife coming back,' he said.

When Adele Grant came into the sitting room to find a stranger with her husband, her eyes dilated with surprise. 'Hello,' she said, looking curiously from Spence to her husband and back again. 'Are we . . .?'

'I'm Spencer James,' Spence told her, holding out a hand to shake.

Though clearly thrown, and even vaguely reluctant, she took the hand. 'Jeremy?' she said, looking at her husband, who had sunk into a chair.

Spence swallowed. 'I'm afraid I've just had to break some bad news to him,' he said.

Panic flared in Adele's eyes. 'Oh my God. Something's happened to Nikki.'

347

Realising his mistake, Spence said, 'No. She's fine. I mean
. . .' He started again. 'It's Zac. He died three days ago.'

Adele froze in horror. 'But I thought this disease . . .'

'It wasn't the Tay-Sachs,' Spence told her. 'It was . . . Uh, I
think you'd better sit down.'

Doing as he said, Adele kept her eyes fixed on him, as
though afraid he might run away, or do something crazy
like hit them, or smash up their home. 'Did it have
something to do with his condition?' she asked.

Bracing himself, Spence said, 'No, it was . . . Well, the
police think he was smothered.'

Adele blinked. She seemed confused. 'Are you saying
someone . . .?'

Spence nodded. 'Actually, it's worse than that,' he went
on, 'because they think Nikki did it, and they've arrested
her.'

Adele gave a cry of shock, as Grant dropped his head in
his hands. 'No, no, no,' he mumbled. 'We can't take any
more.'

'They can't be serious,' Adele protested. 'She would never
. . . Why do they think that?'

'Because she was the only one in the house at the time.'

Adele was shaking her head. 'It's not possible,' she
insisted. 'They've got it wrong. My daughter would never
harm anyone, least of all her own child.'

'I know,' Spence said, 'but she's been remanded in
custody, and she's got the world's worst lawyer, so I was
hoping . . . I've come here to ask you to do something to help
her.'

'We don't have any money,' Grant told him brokenly.

Ignoring him, Adele said, 'Are you sure she was in the
house alone? Where were you when it happened?'

Taken aback, Spence said, 'I was in London.'

'Have the police checked that out?'

Hardly able to credit the bluntness, Spence said, 'As far as
I know, yes they have.'

'So did you give yourself an alibi and get someone else to
do it for you? I imagine you have the necessary contacts.'

Spence gaped at her in amazement. 'What the hell are you
on?' he cried. 'This is my son you're talking about, and no

matter how sick he was, or how much he might have to suffer, there's no way in the world I'd ever have set up something like that. And even if I had, do you seriously think I'd do it in a way to let Nikki take the rap?'

No longer seeming certain of anything, Adele said, 'It would save your skin and free you up to go and live whatever life you have planned for yourself, while my daughter serves a prison sentence for something she didn't do.'

Spence was only just controlling his temper. 'Listen,' he growled, 'I don't care what you think of me, all that matters here is that Nikki is in Eastwood Park and I – we – need to get her out.'

'And how do you propose we do that?' Grant asked pathetically.

'She needs a decent lawyer,' Spence told him. 'She qualifies for legal aid, but as her father I was hoping you'd be willing to pay for the best.'

At that, Grant looked defeated again. 'I'm afraid that's not possible,' he said shakily. 'We've had to sell our house and most of our assets as it is, thanks to this economic catastrophe, and we're still in debt.'

Spence's fists were clenching. 'And you expect me to believe that?' he demanded.

Adele stiffened. 'Frankly, we don't care what you believe,' she informed him.

'So you're saying you can't help your own daughter, even though she's never needed you more?' Spence challenged.

Adele flushed. 'Of course that's not what we're saying. If we had the funds they'd be hers, but we don't.'

'Do you know what, I don't believe you,' he said frankly, 'because I know how people like you operate. You've got something squirrelled away . . .'

Adele's expression turned icy. 'You don't know the first thing about people like us,' she spat. 'How could you, when your mother was a prostitute and your father a paedophile?'

Spence went white. His head started to spin. 'How . . . How do you know about that?' he stammered.

'It wasn't difficult. We made some enquiries and . . .'

'Does Nikki know? Oh my God, that's what you fell out over, before Christmas. It's why she won't see you . . .'

'I hope you're proud of the way you've come between us and our only child,' Adele cut in nastily. 'We never wanted her to get involved with you, and now look what's happened. She's . . .'

'Adele, stop,' her husband interjected. 'He's right. All that matters is Nicola and getting her out of that place.'

She turned to him. 'And how are we going to do that when . . .'

Grant's hand went up. 'Thank you for coming, young man,' he said to Spence. 'You don't need to worry any more. We'll sort out what's to be done about our daughter.'

'She's my responsibility too,' Spence cried. 'You're not using this to cut me out of her life. I won't let you. Nor will she.'

'She will if she has to choose between you and her liberty,' Adele threw at him.

At that Spence looked as though he might hit her. 'Don't you dare make her choose,' he warned.

'Adele! Enough,' her husband barked as she started to respond. 'You're losing sight of what's at stake. It's not about this boy and his background. It's about our grandson, and our daughter and her freedom.'

Adele's eyes closed as the horror of it seemed to shudder through her again, bringing her back to her senses. 'You're right. I'm sorry,' she whispered, though whether to Spence or her husband wasn't clear.

'If you don't mind, my wife and I need to discuss this,' Grant said to Spence.

'Don't worry, I'm going,' Spence told him. 'I can see myself out.'

Seconds later he was slamming the front door behind him and charging angrily down the stairs.

David's face fell the instant he saw Spence's expression. 'Jesus, don't tell me they're not going to help,' he protested, as Spence sank into the car.

'I don't know what they're going to do,' Spence answered, 'but whatever it is, her father's insisting he doesn't have any money.'

'Well, I'm glad to say I have some good news,' Mrs Adani told him. 'Mr Adani has been in touch with a very important

350

lawyer in Bristol who he has worked with on several occasions. His name is Jolyon Crane and he has made an appointment for you to see him at his office first thing on Monday morning, before he goes into court.'

Spence turned to her in amazement, then his eyes flooded with tears as he scooped her into his arms. 'I told you we'd never manage without you,' he said, 'now do you believe me?'

She was smiling. 'It is Mr Adani you must thank for this,' she reminded him. 'He is sending you his best wishes and wants you to know that if he can help in any other way we must certainly call him.'

'And the lawyer, is he OK about doing it on legal aid?'

'Mr Adani says that should not be a problem, but you will need to discuss it with Mr Crane when you see him.'

'Here,' David said, handing over his BlackBerry which was connected to the Internet, 'Jolyon Crane's credentials. Senior spartner of his firm; president of Bristol Law Society; twenty years' experience defending murder, manslaughter, rape and robbery . . . There's loads there. I'm telling you, if we can get him on our side, then Dad's pulled one mega rabbit out of the hat with this one.'

Mrs A was smiling proudly. 'Dear Rajan,' she said, 'even when he is far away he is with us. Now, I must be getting you young men back to Bristol, or I will be late for my afternoon appointment.'

'And I have to see Nikki,' Spence reminded them. 'Just thank God – and Mr A – that I have some good news to give her, because relying on her parents . . . Well, I guess I'd better start working out what I'm going to tell her about them.'

Chapter Twenty-Three

Adele Grant was pacing the sitting room, so agitated she couldn't make herself stop. 'You must know someone,' she shouted at her husband for the umpteenth time. 'All those years managing people's finances, surely to God one of them was a lawyer.'

'There were several,' Grant conceded as he scoured his address book, 'but we've all lost a lot of money, Adele, and I'm sure I don't need to remind you that most are blaming me. It won't be easy to ask them to help us out now, especially when we can't pay them.'

'But we can sell the bonds you kept back in case of emergency, because if this isn't one, I don't know what is.'

At that, Grant's shoulders seemed to slump.

'Oh my God,' she murmured. 'Please, Jeremy, don't tell me they've gone too. How? When?'

He raised a shaking hand to dab the tears from his eyes. 'All we have left of any value,' he said, 'is your car.'

Reeling, she dropped her head in her hands. Then, suddenly realising he was struggling for breath, she ran to him. 'Jeremy, what is it?' she cried.

'I'm . . . I'm all right,' he gasped.

'Is it your heart? Do you have any pain?'

'It's fine . . . It's . . . passing.'

She grabbed his hands. 'Shall I call an ambulance?'

He shook his head. 'We have to get this sorted out,' he reminded her. 'I'll . . . see about selling your car.'

Needing to deal with this first, she said, 'Sit quietly for a moment. Do you feel faint? Is there something I can get you?'

His eyes closed as he sank back in his chair. His skin looked grey and old, his cheeks were wet with tears.

'It's all been too much,' she choked, as tears streamed down her face too. 'The stress, the way people have blamed you, and now this with Nicola . . .'

'It's all right,' he said, patting her hand. 'Just let me sit for a moment.'

Fear was still driving her. 'I'll bring you some tea, shall I?' she offered. 'Or whisky?'

It was a while before he said, 'Whisky would be nice.'

Going to the drinks trolley, she emptied the last of the Glenfiddich into a tumbler and brought it to him.

After taking a sip, a hint of life seemed to return to his pallor. 'We treated that boy badly,' he told her. 'He's lost his son and we . . .'

'Oh Jeremy, don't,' she said wretchedly. 'I know I shouldn't have said those things. I wasn't thinking straight, and I feel so ashamed now. He's trying to help her, and I was so . . .'

'Do we know how to reach him?'

She shook her head. 'Only through Nicola, and how are we going to get hold of her while she's where she is?'

'She must be allowed visits.'

'But will she want to see us? If he tells her what I said to him, how I threw his father's crime in his face . . .'

'From the way he behaved he seems more concerned about her than what you said.' He tried to sit forward, then winced as another pain shot through his chest.

'Jeremy, you have to let me get a doctor.'

'I'm fine. Don't fuss. Now pass me my address book again, please.'

Picking it up, she placed it in his hand and sat on the arm of a chair watching him as he continued to go through it. 'Whatever happens, we can't let her go to trial,' she suddenly blurted. 'If she does, everything will come out and . . .'

'Ssh,' he said, cutting her off. 'It's not going to help us at all if you start thinking that way.'

Nikki was walking beside the blonde prison officer who'd checked her in yesterday, keeping her head up but eyes down as they made their way to the visitors' hall. Being on the rule meant that she didn't go anywhere unescorted, even to the phone last night, but it didn't stop the other inmates shouting abuse in her wake.

She was trying not to listen, but the names they were calling her as she passed their cells were making her feel sick and ashamed, even though she knew she was neither a nonce nor a pervert, nor a baby-killer.

'I'm never sure whether the rule's the right way to go,' the officer, whose name was Jen, commented, after telling someone called Serena to wash out her mouth. Serena. It was such a gentle, feminine name, Nikki was thinking, as she waited for Jen to unlock another gate. It conjured images of nymphs and sylphs, or elegant women with gentle smiles. Certainly not someone with clacking false teeth, badly dyed ginger hair and vigorously tattooed arms, who'd just called her a cunt of a sick bitch.

'You see,' Jen continued, standing back for Nikki to pass through, 'this way everyone gets to find out what you did, and if you end up being found guilty then you'll probably have to serve your whole sentence shacked up on your own. Now, I understand that the druggies and lowlife you get in here aren't the kind of company you'd go looking for in the normal course of events, but not everyone's like that. There are other mercy killers too, and fraudsters who are pretty harmless really, and women whose husbands you'd help push over a cliff if you had to put up with them. You know what I mean? Are you married, Nikki?'

'No,' Nikki answered, looking away as Jen locked the gate, apparently not noticing the gestures of those who were watching. A finger slicing across a throat; a hand stuffed between legs; a fist pressed up against a face. 'We've got plans to, though,' she said, as they turned to walk on. She had to put those women out of her mind, pretend they weren't there, and thank God they didn't have visitors today, or a way of getting to her while she was in her cell.

'Reckon he'll wait that long then, do you?' Jen asked, with no malice, only interest.

Nikki didn't have to answer, because Jen's radio squawked into life.

The prisoners who had visitors today were already in the

hall, so Nikki wasn't having to walk there with them. However, knowing she'd have to sit amongst them when she arrived was unnerving her badly. The hard-core aggressors were back in the cells, she reminded herself firmly. The rest seemed more interested in their own lives than in anyone else's.

'You're a cool cat, I'll give you that,' Jen remarked, as she stuffed her radio back in its holster. 'You've got manners and class written all over you, and I like that. Mind you, it's what's giving that lot back there the gyp. I mean, they don't like bad things happening to kids, that goes without saying, no one does, but from what I hear it was a good thing you did to yours, not a bad one.'

'It wasn't good and I didn't do it,' Nikki told her.

Jen cast her a look. 'If I had a fiver for every time I've heard that, I'd be living on the French Riviera with a swimming pool in the back garden and a fuck-off Merc parked outside,' she said, 'and I've only been here three years.'

Knowing there was no point protesting her innocence again, Nikki kept quiet as Jen wittered on until they reached the visitors' hall, where she was handed over to the duty officers.

The place was packed with prisoners on one side of the tables, and visitors the other. Some were in groups, and there were lots of children running around, or playing in the designated area at the back. The noise was deafening, but Nikki heard Spence call her name at the same instant her eyes found him. He was sitting near the back, next to the window, his quirky, handsome face looking both worried and relieved to see her. Though all she wanted was to run to him and hold him until their arms couldn't take any more, she'd been warned that any sudden moves or overt displays of emotion were not allowed. So she picked her way down the line as swiftly as she could, and grabbed his hands as though she was afraid he might slip away.

'Hey,' he murmured, gazing searchingly into her eyes. 'Are you OK?'

'I am now,' she answered, drinking in every beloved feature of his face. 'Are you?'

'I'm cool, but worried about you being in this place. How are they treating you?'

She shrugged. 'It's OK.' She didn't want to get into the name-calling and extra protection, since it would only worry him more.

'Shall we sit down?' he said.

Keeping hold of his hands, Nikki sank into the chair opposite his and continued to gaze at him as though twenty-four days, rather than twenty-four hours, had passed since she'd last seen him.

'I left the photo and notebook and stuff at the gate,' he told her. 'They wouldn't let me hand it over myself. And Mrs A's made up some meals for you too. As a remand prisoner, you're allowed them. I don't know if you know that. They just have to be reheated. It'll be a lot better than the rubbish they're serving up here, I bet.'

Nikki gave a smile. 'It's a lot better than you get anywhere,' she reminded him, hoping that having this privilege wasn't going to cause her any problems with the kitchen staff, or envy amongst the inmates.

'You're right about that,' he agreed. Then, wrapping his hands around hers, he sat even closer to her as he said, 'I've got some good news. Mr A has put us in touch with a top lawyer in Bristol. I've made an appointment with him for first thing Monday morning to talk about your case. He's the real business, Nik. We've been reading about him on the Internet, and I reckon if anyone can get this sorted, he can.'

An uneasy hope began trickling into Nikki's heart. 'That's fantastic,' she told him, 'but how are we going to pay him? Have you seen my parents?'

Spence's eyes dropped. 'Yeah, I have,' he admitted. 'They're definitely there for you, I'm sure about that, but I don't know where they are financially. It's OK, though. The brief Mr A's put us in touch with is probably going to take us on legal aid.'

'So what did my parents say?' Nikki pressed, tightening her grip on his hands.

He raised his eyes to hers.

'Oh my God,' she choked. 'They told you about your dad, didn't they?'

'It doesn't matter,' he assured her. 'I'm just sorry you had to find out about him that way. It should have been me who told you.'

'I understand why you didn't,' she said, moving closer to him. 'And even if that man was your dad, I know with all my heart that you're not like that.'

Spence's smile was weak, but grateful. 'Definitely not,' he said. 'But don't let's talk about him any more. He's not relevant in any way to what's happening now.'

Unable to let it go just like that, Nikki gazed directly into his eyes as she said, 'It never changed the way I feel about you. Not even for an instant.'

Spence visibly swallowed. 'If you make me cry in front of everyone here . . .' he warned.

Nikki laughed, as her own eyes filled with tears. 'So tell me about this lawyer you've found,' she said, knowing she'd have to deal with the issue of her parents at a later date.

'His name's Jolyon Crane,' he told her. 'Mr A's obviously got some pull with this guy, and what I'm hoping he's going to say on Monday is that we need an independent expert to check the autopsy results. He might even insist on a second one being done, who knows? The point is, I'm still not convinced Zac was smothered the way they're making out he was. I mean, I know it might have looked like he was, but they're getting stuff wrong all the time. The news is full of it, and if we can get some other evidence . . .'

'I think we can,' Nikki broke in eagerly. 'I've been going over and over it in my mind and if the autopsy results turn out to be right, well, there's something I didn't tell the police when they interviewed me, because I forgot all about it until last night. It happened about three weeks ago, when I was at one of my stretch classes. Mr Farrell brought someone round to look at the house, and when I got back he'd left a note saying he'd repair the lock on the front door. I didn't know anything was wrong with it, but he must have had a reason for saying something was, so maybe . . . Well, what I'm thinking is, if the door didn't shut properly after Mrs A left and I didn't notice . . .' She was looking at him desperately, hoping with all her heart that this meagre straw might be enough to save her.

'Meaning that if the door was open then anyone could have come in?' Spence said, warming to the theory. 'We have to get hold of Mr Farrell to find out why he thought there was a problem, because this is exactly the kind of thing the lawyer is going to need to know when I see him.'

'Don't you think you should tell the police too?' Nikki prompted.

'I expect the lawyer will do that. Let me talk to him and get some advice. Oh Nik,' he said, squeezing her hands so tightly it hurt. 'Everything's going to be all right, I just know it. We'll get you out of here and once all this is behind us . . .' His voice caught on a rush of emotion, but a moment later, realising their visiting time was about to come to an end, he was sober again as he said, in too much of a rush, 'I got a call about Zac's body yesterday. They're ready to release it for burial, but . . .' He broke off as he realised there was no reason to tell her about the brain yet, because things might change now they had a decent lawyer coming on board. 'I'll tell them that we might be going for a second opinion,' he said, 'so not to do anything yet.'

'Does that mean he's back in Bristol?' Nikki asked, her eyes dimming with grief.

He nodded.

'Have you seen him?'

'No. I thought . . . Well, maybe it's best not to now.'

She swallowed hard and nodded. 'I guess you're right,' she whispered. 'God, it's so hard to believe that this time four days ago he was still with us. So much has happened since then.'

'I know, and a lot more needs to for us to get this sorted, but we will, Nik, I promise. I still don't believe anyone killed him, but if they did, and that's a big if, we have to find out who it was, because I know in my heart it wasn't you.'

Her eyes went down as tears spilled on to her cheeks.

'We're going to get you out of here,' he repeated fiercely. 'I'd like to think it might even be as soon as Monday. Do you think you can stand it till then?'

With an ironic smile hovering over her unsteady lips, her gaze came back to his. 'Less than an hour ago I was terrified I might be here for ten years or more,' she said, 'so I think I can manage a few more days.' She looked around at the other women, who were all engrossed in their own visits. Some, or even one of them, might be grieving for a lost child too, and if anyone could understand how they felt . . . 'I might even manage to make some friends,' she whispered, wondering if she'd dare to venture out of segregation. 'A lot of people in here have had really bad starts in life, you can tell, and not everyone has it in them to rise above it, the way you did.'

Spence's eyes closed in mock despair. 'One day,' he said, 'you'll learn that you haven't been put on this earth to save the rest of mankind. All you have to think about now, Nik, is you and me, and what we're going to do once all this is behind us.'

She attempted a smile. 'And it will be, won't it, Spence?' she said, clutching his hands. 'Sooner, rather than later, because I didn't do it. Honest to God. I swear on both our lives . . .'

He put a finger gently to her lips. 'I know,' he whispered, 'so you don't have to keep trying to convince me.'

Chapter Twenty-Four

On Monday morning Spence arrived outside Jolyon Crane's office fifteen minutes earlier than expected. However, the main door was already open, so he pushed through and climbed the stairs to reception. The building was as old and full of character as a Dickensian curiosity shop, as was most of the legal district of Bristol. Knowing that here he was at the heart of things lent even more confidence to Spence's step. This place was the business – if anyone could help Nikki then it had to be someone who carried clout around here, and as far as he could make out Jolyon Crane carried more than most.

Finding no one in reception he looked around, saw a bell to press, and after a few minutes heard a heavy tread coming down the stairs.

'Ah, you must be Spencer James,' a burly, grey-suited man with piercing eyes and a ready smile declared as he came into the room.

Spence took the hand the man was offering. 'And I know you're Mr Crane,' he responded, 'because I saw your picture on the Internet.'

Jolyon Crane chuckled. 'So you've been checking me out, and so you should,' he said. 'Now, let's go up to my office. I have to be in a pre-trial meeting at nine, but it's only across the street, so we have a good hour which should be ample time to kick things off.'

'Actually,' Spence said, following him up the creaking stairs, 'I saw Nikki on Saturday and I have some extra information that the police don't know about yet.'

Crane was clearly interested as he cast a glance back over his shoulder. 'Then I'd like to hear it,' he replied. 'I believe I have some information that you will want to hear, too. Through there,' he said, directing Spence into a shadowy hallway that led into a bright and spacious office with a huge oak desk at its centre, two tall sash windows over-looking the Crown courts across the street, and stacks of files and books hiding the walls. 'Do take a seat,' he said, as he closed the door. 'I'm afraid I can't offer you a coffee, because I haven't made any yet, but . . .'

'I'm cool,' Spence assured him. 'I just want to be sure that you're OK with taking this on legal aid, because we don't have the kind of funds . . .'

Crane waved a hand. 'The accounts department will sort that out with you,' he told him, 'what we need to focus on is this.' He held up a pile of documents tied together with pink string. 'Nicola's case notes,' he explained. 'I had them sent over from Maria Townsend's office on Saturday.' He regarded Spence from under lowered lids. 'I regret to say that not all lawyers offer as good a service as they should, and duty solicitors are often hard pressed, but I'll go no further with that. What I will expand on, however, are the several things that jumped out at me while I was reading through the file. First, though, tell me about the extra information you have.'

Spence sat forward in his chair. 'It's about the front door of our house,' he said, trying to keep his excitement in check. 'A few weeks ago the landlord found a problem with the lock. I've tried it myself, now we've been allowed back in, and I can see what he means. Sometimes the latch sticks and it doesn't close properly. I mean, it looks closed, because it's a sticky door, but if you give it a push it'll just come open.'

Crane's eyes were widening with approval. 'Well, that could explain how the first paramedic got in,' he com-mented, 'because there's nothing in either his or Nicola's statements to tell us who opened the door when he arrived. Has she ever told you she did?'

Spence's heart began thudding as he shook his head. 'She's never mentioned it,' he answered.

'I'm also concerned by the fact that there appear to be no statements from the neighbours,' Crane informed him, 'so we have no idea if anyone saw anything suspicious that morning.'

Spence's eyes sparked with hope. He didn't want to get too carried away yet, though, so trying a bit of caution he said, 'Wouldn't someone have come forward if they had?'

'Not necessarily, which is why I think you need to speak to your neighbours.'

'Me?' Spence cried.

Crane smiled. 'Legal-aid funding doesn't go far,' he told him, 'and our schedules here are fairly full, but I'm going to assign a clerk to the case to advise you when necessary, and she'll report back to me at the end of each day.'

Needing to be sure he was understanding this correctly, Spence said, 'So like, you want me to carry out an investigation?'

'In so far as you can. Not everyone will want to talk to you, of course, and since you don't have the same powers as the police your success might be limited, but it's certainly worth trying, wouldn't you say?'

Spence was already itching to get started. 'Absolutely,' he agreed. 'Shall I go now?'

Crane chuckled as he shook his head. 'I have more to tell you,' he said. 'Based on the lack of statements from neighbours, the confusion concerning how the paramedic gained access to the house, *and* the faulty door, I'm going to try to get a bail application before a judge sometime this morning. If we're successful Nicola could be released today.'

Spence's eyes opened wide. 'This is fantastic,' he cried. 'Oh God, I can't thank you enough, Mr Crane, because she didn't do it. I swear she didn't, and I think this is starting to prove it.'

Crane raised a cautionary hand. 'There's still a long way to go,' he warned, 'and it wouldn't be advisable to go rushing in to your neighbours bombarding them with questions until you've worked out what to ask. Take it gently, explain why you're there – because the police didn't come themselves – and that you're hopeful they might be able to shed some light on certain anomalies that have arisen.'

Spence was focusing hard on the words. '"Certain anomalies that have arisen,"' he repeated, memorising it. 'Do we tell the police about the lock?'

'Certainly. I'll get Felicity on to that as soon as she arrives. She's the clerk I'm going to assign to your case.'

'Cool. Felicity. Uh, just one other thing, if you're going to be in court all morning, on another case, how are you going to be able to deal with this one?'

'This kind of bail application can go to a judge's chambers,' Crane explained, 'and shouldn't take long to process, so I'll be able to step out to take care of it. We'll need to get the CPS down to the courts, but let me worry about that. Felicity or I will phone you as soon as there's any news.'

Spence sprang to his feet and stuck out a hand. 'Thanks so much for this,' he said earnestly. 'I only wish I could tell Nikki about it, because she was sounding really nervous when she rang last night, and quite low. I think she's afraid to get her hopes up in case things don't work out.'

'It won't be easy for her being in a place like that,' Crane sympathised, 'but if we're successful the ordeal should be over by three, which is the time she has to be picked up by, or she'll be in for another night. Don't forget to leave us your number,' he added, pushing a notepad and pen across the desk.

After jotting it down, Spence thanked him again and had just reached the door when Crane said, 'Remember, if we do get her out she'll be on bail and certain conditions will apply.'

'Whatever, we'll stick to them,' Spence assured him, and with a cheery salute he took the stairs in record time back down to the street.

'David,' he said, as soon as he made the connection, 'we're about to become detectives, and we need to find out what your mother's doing this afternoon to see if she can be on standby to take us out to the prison.'

'You're kidding,' David cried. 'What's happened?'

'I'll tell you when I get there. If your mum's not free, speak to Rufus at the Factory. He said we could borrow his car any time, if he's not using it. All we have to pay for is the petrol.'

By midday Spence and David were back at the house after an intensely frustrating morning. They had talked to as many neighbours as they could, asking if any of them had seen or heard anything unusual or suspicious around the time Zac died.

No one had, but being as fond of Nikki as most of them were, everyone wanted to know how she was and to pass on their condolences again.

'The devil was at work in those genes,' one old soul said bleakly.

'Got a real soft spot for that girl,' said another. 'Always has a smile on her face and goes out of her way to help carry my shopping. Can't imagine her doing anything to hurt her kiddie. Lovely little chap he was.'

The only good news, which actually had the potential of being brilliant, was that the paramedic, whom David had managed to get hold of by phone, had confirmed that the front door was open when he'd arrived.

'I assumed she'd opened it ready for me to come in,' he'd said in his gruff West Country burr, 'but I can't swear that happened, because I didn't see it. All I know is, it was open when I got there.'

'That's everything we need to know,' David told him jubilantly. 'Is it OK if we pass this on to the police?'

'Of course. I'll tell them the same if they ask.'

Though it didn't resolve whether or not anyone else had entered the house between Mrs A leaving and the paramedic arriving, it was something to report to Jolyon Crane, or his clerk, when one or the other of them rang.

The call came from Jolyon himself just before midday.

'OK, you can pick her up this afternoon,' he announced with no preamble. 'She'll be told all her bail conditions before they release her, but remember to be there before three or she won't be allowed out until tomorrow.'

'We'll be there,' Spence assured him, wanting to cheer the triumph while hardly able to believe how fast things were happening now a decent lawyer was on board. 'And Mr Crane?' he added, his voice deep with feeling. 'Thank you.'

'I hope you're still saying that at the end of all this,' Crane told him darkly. 'Any luck with the neighbours?'

'Not yet, but we're staying on it.'

'Good, and get your landlord to confirm in writing the date he realised there was something wrong with the lock.'

'Will do. The paramedic says the door was definitely open when he got here, so we need to find out from Nikki now whether or not she opened it herself.'

'A crucial question,' Crane commented, 'because if she did it's not going to help us. However, if she didn't, the whole thing is going to be thrown wide open, if you'll pardon the pun. So, good luck picking her up. I'll call you around five this evening, when I'm back in the office.'

Nikki was sitting on her bed, manically filling up the notebook Spence had brought with him, detailing everything that had happened over the last five days. Describing Zac's death had been so heart-wrenching that she'd barely been able to see the page through her tears as she wrote. Even now, as she moved on to the shock of her arrest, and being held in police custody, she was still yearning for her baby boy, wanting to hold him in her arms and rock him gently till he slept. She started to write him a letter, the way she always used to, telling him about the detectives and the court, but knowing he'd never read it now, she lost heart and let her pen go.

Minutes later she was writing again, knowing that if she didn't the anxiety that had kept her awake for most of the night would descend on her again.

Please God let Spence and the lawyer get me out of here, she wrote frantically. *I have to go home. I can't stay here any more.*

She looked around at the walls and the window, the toilet, the cupboard and TV, and felt them closing in on her as though to crush all the hope in her heart. She picked up Zac's photo, but it hurt so much to look at him that she closed her eyes and took several deep breaths, trying to bring her fear under control. Everything was going to be fine. They'd check the front door, find out she was telling the truth that it was faulty, and then they'd have to accept that *if* Zac had been smothered there was a chance someone else had done it. The question of who would have to come later; all that mattered for now was leaving this place and going home.

She thought of Spence and wished there was a way of contacting him to find out what was happening. This waiting, the not knowing, was beyond endurance. Far, far worse, though, were the fears that had swamped her during the night, when she'd imagined herself here for years and years, rotting away like a forgotten relic while Spence got on with his life. Even if he waited, she knew things could never be the same between them again. They'd be strangers by the time she got out. She'd be another person, nothing like the Nikki he'd known and loved. But he'd have found someone else by then, another writer maybe, or an actress, someone who didn't carry the cruel gene that would have destroyed Zac's innocent little life. He'd be sure to have children who were normal and healthy, and be surrounded by friends who loved and admired him as much as she, Danny and David did now.

It's not going to happen like that, she told herself brokenly. *You're going to be let out of here and one day all this will seem like nothing more than a terrible dream.*

It was a moment before she realised the door to her cell was being unlocked. Her eyes darted to it. The key was grating. Her heart started to thud and churn. It was still only midday, but there could be news already.

For several bewildering moments nothing happened. There were no sounds from outside, and no one was coming in. Deciding to check what was happening, she started to move forward, but then the door swung open and her heart froze into a block of abject terror. Serena with her biker's arms and spiky orange hair was standing there, a smirk of pure malice exposing her big clacking teeth. Behind her two more women, as mean-looking and large, came to stand either side of her.

Nikki's heart was charging with panic. Who had let them in? They'd used a key, so it had to be one of the officers, which meant there was no point screaming for help.

'Thought you might be interested to find out what we do to scum like you,' Serena snarled, planting her tattooed hands on her bulging hips.

Nikki only looked at her, her eyes so wide with terror they might have burst from her head.

Serena took a step forward. 'What we do,' she said, 'is the

same as you did to that kiddie of yours. Do you know what I mean?'

Nikki shrank back against the wall.

'Do you know what I mean?' Serena demanded again.

Somehow Nikki shook her head. She was trembling so hard she couldn't speak, and her bowels were starting to melt. She could smell the women now, their tobacco breath and unwashed bodies. What were they going to do to her? *Please God help me.*

'OK, girls, she's ours,' Serena barked, and before Nikki could move they were pinning her to the bed, one of them squatting on her legs, the other gripping her arms, while Serena grabbed a pillow and jammed it over her face.

Nikki tried to gulp for air, but couldn't.

'Getting the feel of what it was like for him now?' one of Serena's friends growled.

Nikki was trying desperately to fight them off, but they were so heavy she could barely move. Panic thundered through her, making her want to buck and scream, but the sound was deadened by the pillow, and her hips were trapped by dead weights.

There was nothing she could do. She was trying to breathe but it was impossible. They were stifling her and no one was going to stop them. Her lungs were on fire, her head was bursting.

This was what it had been like for Zac.

Oh dear God. His terror and fight became her own. She could see him and hear him, feel the agony of her muscles ripping apart . . .

No air. No escape.

They weren't letting her go.

The darkness was strobing with colour, her head was going to explode.

The weight on her face was immense. The pain was crushing.

It was an eternity, yet no time at all, before she started to lose consciousness. At a distance she was aware of the fight draining from her limbs, as the darkness began to swirl.

There was a creeping numbness.

No more air. No more panic. Only darkness and echoes and then . . . nothing at all.

Chapter Twenty-Five

Since Mrs A was using her car, Spence and David had taken Rufus up on his offer and borrowed his. By two o'clock they were approaching the prison, with no precise idea of what time Nikki would come out, only knowing it would be before three.

'I should have thought to bring her some fresh clothes,' Spence said, as David drove through a dreary housing estate and into the prison car park, which wasn't much more than a churned-up field.

'She won't be able to change into them here,' David pointed out. 'Champagne would have been a better idea, but we didn't think of that either.'

'We'll have some at the Factory tonight,' Spence decided. 'Or no, maybe we should save it till we get the entire case thrown out, because it will be, I just know it.'

'Me too,' David said confidently.

Being too agitated to stay in the car, Spence got out and began to walk towards the prison. 'I wonder where she'll come out,' he said, as David joined him. 'Let's take a look around, see what's what.'

As they left the car park their eyes were fixed on the random cluster of sage-green buildings opposite, tucked in behind a barrage of towering fences topped with barbed wire, and watchful closed-circuit TVs.

'It's hard getting your head round the fact that she's in there,' David muttered, as they hunched against the cold.

'Not for much longer,' Spence reminded him.

Though they knew already that there were no visiting hours on Mondays, they stopped to read the sign at the visitors' gate.

'She's sure to come out here,' Spence decided. 'There doesn't seem to be another exit anywhere.'

David was looking past him. 'God, what do you reckon that place is?' he said, nodding towards a gothic monstrosity perched like Count Dracula's pile in the trees at the top of a nearby hill.

'No idea,' Spence mumbled, 'but I wouldn't want to go there after dark.'

David shivered, then took out his mobile as it started to ring. 'Dan,' he said when he answered.

'Is she out yet?' Danny wanted to know.

'No, but we're at the prison.'

'OK. Tell her I need to hear her as soon as you put a phone in her hand.'

'Will do.'

'How's Spence?'

David glanced in Spence's direction. 'Bit nervous, but he's doing OK.'

'Tell him it's all going to work out. I can't stop now, but I'll speak to you all later.'

After ringing off, David went to stand beside Spence outside the visitor's gate. The fences around them were totally solid, preventing anyone from seeing in or out. There was a small hatch in one of the gates, but it was firmly closed, and there were no sounds to be heard coming from the other side.

As the minutes ticked on, a chill wind began scooping debris from the gutters, scattering it over the road like macabre confetti. The bare branches of trees tilted towards the skyline like skeletal fingers. The place was as bleak and silent as a forgotten grave.

By three o'clock Spence was ready to start hammering on the gate. 'Something's happened,' he decided, trying not to panic, 'and no one's bothered to tell us.'

David wished he could offer some reassurance, but the deadline was passing with nothing and no one coming in or out.

'This is ridiculous,' Spence cried, snapping open his phone. 'I'm going to call this Felicity person, see what she knows.'

After punching in the number he began pacing as he waited for a connection. David watched his face, sharing his stress and wanting to rage and hammer at the gate for him, as if it would do any good.

'Felicity?' Spence barked into the phone. 'It's Spencer James. Yeah, we're at the prison, but nothing's happening. I know . . . I . . .'

'Spence, hang on,' David broke in. 'Look. The gate's opening.'

Spence spun round, and as the gate swung wide a prison officer with scraped-back blonde hair appeared, clearly expecting to see them.

Spence closed up his phone. His heartbeat was thickening in a way that was filling him with dread. What was going on? Where was Nikki?

Then suddenly she was there, her face as colourless as the sky, and her eyes seeming swollen and bruised. The instant she saw Spence she broke into a run and didn't stop until she was safely in his arms.

'Oh thank God, thank God,' Spence cried, over and over, as he held her and David hugged them both. 'I was beginning to think . . . I don't know what the hell I was thinking. Are you OK?'

'I'm fine,' she whispered. 'There was . . . I . . . It doesn't matter.' She didn't need to tell him she'd only just been released from health care. It was over now, she was alive, he was here, so was David and all she wanted was to go on holding them, or to spin and twirl and swoop her way like a bird over the countryside, to lap up her freedom as though it was as tangible and precious as Spence himself.

'So what we need to know, Nik,' Spence was saying as David drove them home, 'is did you open the door to the first paramedic?'

Nikki blinked as she tried to remember, then, connecting with the importance of the question, her haunted eyes became alert. 'No,' she answered, 'I didn't. Why? Is he saying it was open when he got there? It must have been, because I know I didn't let him in.'

Almost coming apart with relief, Spence said, 'You're

absolutely sure you didn't run to the door after you dialled 999, then go back again?' He knew he needed to be a hundred per cent certain.

'Completely. I've been writing everything down, exactly as it happened, because I thought it might help in some way, and I know I didn't open the door. I swear I never left Zac, not even for a second.'

'And you didn't notice the door was open when you went up for a rest, or when you came down again?'

'No. If I had, I'd have closed it, wouldn't I?'

'Of course.'

'We've spoken to most of the neighbours,' David told her, 'and no one seems to have seen or heard anything around that time. Obviously, some weren't home, so we're going to try and talk to them tonight. You won't be surprised to hear that the grumpy old git across the street wouldn't let us in.'

Nikki caught his eye in the mirror. 'Actually, if anyone saw anything it'll be him,' she stated. 'He never misses a trick, stuck behind those revolting nets like some wizened old dwarf with a monster grudge. Who went to see him? If it was you, David, you know what he's like, he'd never answer the door to a foreigner, and as far as he's concerned that's what you are.'

'We went together,' Spence told her. 'And you're right, he started going off about Pakis, the way he does, the racist bastard, so we just left.'

Nikki was thinking fast. 'I'll go over there when we get back,' she decided. 'I'll tell him if he doesn't speak to me he'll have to speak to the police, that might get his door open for once in his life.'

She was both right and wrong when, less than thirty minutes later, she went to bang on Gladstone's worn front door. Spence hovered by the gate.

'Who is it?' he shouted from inside, as if he didn't know – he must have seen them coming.

Playing his game, she said, 'It's Nikki Grant from across the street. I need to speak to you.'

'Well I don't need to speak to you, so go away.'

'Mr Gladstone, I've been accused of killing my baby and

it isn't true. So if you saw anyone outside our house the day he died . . .'

'You've always got Pakis and queers going in and out of there,' he snarled.

Biting back her anger, she said, 'That's not what I'm asking. Did you see anyone who's not normally there? Or even if . . .'

'There was someone in a blue coat,' he growled. 'Now go away.'

Nikki's eyes rounded as she stared at the door. Her mind was working so fast now that she was struggling to keep hold of the threads. Of course, Terri Walker. Everything had been so chaotic and stressful that day that she'd forgotten Terri had called round, earlier, while Mrs A was there. 'Mr Gladstone,' she shouted, banging again. 'Wait. What time did you see this person?'

'How am I supposed to know? Do you think I look at my watch every time you have a visitor?'

'This is very important,' she told him. 'Please, try to remember. What time was it when . . .'

'About an hour after the Paki woman went,' he shouted. 'Now get lost and leave me alone.'

Nikki turned back to Spence, still standing by the gate. He seemed almost ghostlike in the twilight. 'Did you hear any of that?' she asked.

'Some. Obviously it's meaning something to you.'

'We have to call the police,' she said, going to join him. 'They need to talk to him now, because I think he saw that girl, Terri Walker, come to the house after Mrs A left. She was definitely there before, but I didn't let her in. Maybe she came back.'

DS McAllister was at the house Nikki Grant shared with her friends, staring at the girl in a way that wasn't quite hostile, but wasn't entirely friendly, either. She'd come herself because she'd heard from the CPS that Nikki had been released on bail due to some oversights in the investigation, and she didn't want anyone else taking the case over yet. She'd have words with her superiors later to remind them that this was the sort of thing that happened when budgets were so tight that a case had to be wrapped up the instant it was looking provable. For now she wanted to get to the bottom of this.

Nikki was saying, 'I know it looked as though I did it, and I know I definitely didn't help myself with the things I said, so you can't be blamed for jumping to the conclusions you did, but . . .'

'Stop,' McAllister said, putting up a hand, 'let's get back to this neighbour of yours. You say he saw a woman in a blue coat come to the house . . .'

'That's right. If it's who I think it is, her name's Terri Walker and she came earlier that morning, while Mrs Adani was here, but I didn't let her in.'

'Why didn't you tell us this before?'

'Because I'd forgotten. Everything was so . . .'

'OK. Why did she come?'

'She said she'd heard about Zac and she wanted to know if there was anything she could do.'

'Did she say anything to make you think she might intend him any harm?'

'No, but . . .'

'So what else did she say?'

'Just that she was about to start a job at the Hen and Chicken, which is up the road here . . .'

'I know where it is.'

'. . . and if I needed a friend, or someone to take care of Zac, I should let her know.'

McAllister was puzzled. 'And based on that, you think she came back here an hour or so later and smothered your baby. Why would she do that?'

'I don't know. I mean, I've been told that she can't have children of her own and her husband's left her . . . Maybe she got angry because I didn't let her in . . .'

'Nikki, I want to help you here,' McAllister interrupted, 'because the last thing I want is anyone going down for a crime they didn't commit, but what you're telling me . . .'

'He said it was someone in a blue coat,' Spence cut in, 'and this woman always wears a blue coat. She picked up Zac once, at one of Nikki's stretch classes, without asking for permission.'

'Look, I don't want to accuse someone of doing something they didn't do either,' Nikki said, 'but . . .'

'. . .you should at least speak to her,' Spence finished.

McAllister nodded. The trouble with liking a suspect was how hard it made it to remain objective. 'Do you know where she lives?' she asked.

'Luckwell Road,' Nikki told her. 'I don't know the number, but . . .'

'I can find it,' McAllister interrupted. Then, getting to her feet, her eyes narrowed as she looked at Nikki. 'I heard what happened at the prison today,' she said. 'Are you all right?'

Nikki shot an anxious look Spence's way. 'Yeah, it was nothing,' she said.

Cynically, McAllister raised an eyebrow. 'The Serena treatment is never nothing,' she told her, 'but it might help to know that the officer who opened the door has been suspended.'

Actually, it did help, Nikki realised, but that was either behind her now, or for another day. What mattered at this moment was finding out if Terri Walker really had come back to the house that morning.

Once outside on the street DS McAllister made a couple of calls, got the house number for Terri Walker, and decided she might as well go and see if this potential monster with an infertility issue was at home.

Ten minutes of talking to Terri, and a short stroll up to the Hen and Chicken, was all it took to convince McAllister that Terri in a blue coat, red anorak, or even a luminous pink poncho hadn't gone back to Nikki Grant's house that day.

'She started her shift bang on half past ten,' the pub landlord confirmed, 'and she didn't leave here again till gone three. I know, because I was showing her the ropes, and I didn't leave the bar myself except to have a pee, and she'd have to be pretty fast if she was going to be out of here and back in that time. So, what's she supposed to have done? Please don't tell me I need to sack her, because she's got a five-star rating as far as I'm concerned. My missus can vouch for her too, because she was in the bar that day, having one of her book-club meetings.'

'I think you can keep her on the payroll,' McAllister said, and after downing her bitter lemon she told him someone might be back to take a statement later, and left.

Now she was standing in front of Mr Gladstone's lively-looking gaff, rapping at the door and wondering when it had last seen a lick of paint.

It wasn't long before he shouted, 'Who is it?' sounding like Steptoe on downers.

'Police, open up,' she shouted back.

'Fuck off,' he told her.

Charming, she thought. 'If you don't open the door it'll get broken down and we'll leave you to freeze,' she informed him, making a mental note to check if social services had him in their sights.

'She told me she wasn't going to call the police,' he snarled, sounding seriously pissed off.

'Well, happy Christmas, I'm here. Now open up, Mr Gladstone, before my goodwill runs out.'

It didn't take all that long, but the instant the door opened the stench that came out was so bad it knocked her back a clear two steps.

Wishing she'd sent Freeman, who usually ponged like a lavender bag himself, she forced herself not to mask her nose with her scarf. Showing her badge, she said, 'You told Nicola Grant you saw someone in a blue coat going into her house on the day her baby died. First, why didn't you come forward with that information before . . .'

'Because no one ever asked,' he grunted. 'And I didn't say coat, I said car. It was someone in a blue car. They were out there after the Paki woman left, and before the ambulance turned up.'

McAllister took a pause. 'Car, not coat,' she said, needing to be clear.

'Are you all deaf?' he snarled.

'No, I don't stink either,' she said, unable to resist it. 'What kind of car?' she persisted.

'How am I supposed to know?'

'Big, small, hatchback, saloon?'

'It was a Merc. Two doors.'

Her eyebrows went up. 'Have you ever seen it round here before?'

'I don't know. Maybe. A week or so ago.'

'Did you see who got out?'

'No.'

'So how do you know if it was anything to do with Nicola Grant?'

'I don't. I never said I did. I'm just telling you I saw the car that morning, all right?'

'And I don't suppose you noted the registration number.'

'That's your job, not mine.'

She smiled sweetly. 'Thank you,' she said. 'My colleague will be round tomorrow to take a statement from you. His name's Oliver Freeman, I think you'll like him. You're not planning on going anywhere in the meantime, I take it.'

'Fuck off,' he told her again.

And she almost laughed.

Nikki turned away from DS McAllister, pressing her hands to her cheeks.

'So it couldn't have been Terri Walker,' Spence said unnecessarily.

McAllister shook her head. 'She'll be interviewed again, but her alibi's rock solid, and . . .'

'No, don't interview her again,' Nikki protested. 'I feel terrible enough that we thought it might have been her. Was she very upset?'

'I don't think it's the best thing that's ever happened to her,' McAllister admitted, 'but I'll go round there tomorrow and explain the mistake in person. Hopefully it'll go some way . . .'

'I should be the one to do that,' Nikki cut in.

'No, you should be telling me if you know anyone who owns a blue two-door Mercedes.'

Nikki's face was pale as she looked at Spence.

'I don't think we do,' he answered.

'Nikki?' McAllister prompted.

Nikki shook her head. 'There's no one . . . I've never noticed one on this street before.'

McAllister got to her feet. 'Well, give it some thought,' she said. 'I'll be back in the morning to talk to you again.'

After seeing her to the door, Spence came back into the room, frowning in confusion. 'Nik, what's going on?' he said. 'I can tell when you're . . .'

'My mother has a light blue vintage Mercedes,' she told him, and as the horror of what she was saying curled round her heart, she pushed a fist to her mouth. 'It has to be a coincidence,' she said shakily. 'I mean, it can't be . . . She wouldn't . . .'

Spence only looked at her, his face as ashen as hers.

She turned away from him, then back again. 'Can you remember where they live?' she asked.

'I think so,' he replied hoarsely, still stunned by the conclusion they had both reached.

She picked up her bag, then went to fetch her coat.

'I take it we're going over there,' he said, coming after her.

'We have to,' she answered, and handing him the keys to Rufus's car she led the way outside.

Chapter Twenty-Six

The lights were on in the first-floor flat when Spence and Nikki turned into Bennett Street, showing that someone was probably at home, but the curtains were drawn so it wasn't possible to see in.

As Spence turned off the engine, Nikki stayed where she was, trying to steel herself for what might lie ahead. Apart from being horribly nervous, she couldn't be sure whether she was afraid, or simply still too dumbfounded to know what was really going on in her head. The instant McAllister had mentioned the blue Mercedes she'd thought of her mother, but during the journey here she'd weighed the coincidence, the likelihood, the reasons why, and couldn't seem to make anything work.

'Are you sure you want to do this?' Spence asked.

Nikki looked up at the window again. 'We have to,' she said, her voice faltering slightly. She turned to look at him. In the glow of the street light his eyes were dark hollows in his pallid skin. 'I keep thinking,' she said. 'I can't . . . I mean . . .'

'We need to find out if it really was her car,' he reminded her gently.

Accepting he was right, she took a deep breath and pushed open the door.

Once he'd joined her on the street, she reached for his hand, then went to press the bell next to her parents' name. It felt oddly disorienting coming to a place where they lived that she had never been a part of, as though they'd become dislocated in a dream, or perhaps she was going to find they weren't here at all.

'Hello?' a voice said through the intercom.

Feeling a jolt in her heart, Nikki leaned forward and said, 'Mum, it's me.'

There was a moment's silence before her mother said, '*Nicola*? I thought . . . Oh my goodness. Come in, come in,' and the door buzzed open.

After glancing at Spence, Nikki stepped into the hall first, and blinked as a light flooded the stairwell. 'Up here, first floor,' her mother called out. 'Are you all right? Your boyfriend said you were . . .'

'I'm all right,' Nikki told her. 'Spence is with me.'

Since her mother didn't voice an objection, Nikki kept hold of Spence's hand as they climbed the stairs. She found Adele waiting at the door, clearly agitated and relieved, and was there something else in her eyes, a hint of defensiveness, fear, regret? Nikki's heart was in her throat.

'Let me see you,' Adele implored, reaching for Nikki's hand. 'What were they thinking of, putting you in that place?'

'I'm fine,' Nikki assured her, easing her hand free. 'They made a mistake, but I think they know that now.'

'I should hope so,' her mother replied.

As Nikki looked at her mother she was trying to imagine her coming into the house that day, finding Zac asleep in his basket . . . Her mind veered away from what came next. She couldn't believe it. Her mother could be cold and judgemental at times, bigoted, snooty, even cruel with words, but Nikki couldn't make herself believe she'd ever go so far as to . . . She just wouldn't.

Adele's eyes moved to Spence. She seemed awkward and unsure of herself, spots of colour staining her cheeks. 'I'm . . . glad you came,' she told him. 'When you were here last . . . I owe you an apology for the things . . .'

Spence put up a hand to stop her. 'I'm cool,' he said. It wasn't the issue.

Swallowing, and trying to force a brightness, Adele turned back to Nikki. 'Come in,' she said warmly, standing aside. 'Are you sure you're all right? It's terrible, dreadful, to think of what you've been through . . . My poor girl . . .'

Nikki was only half listening as she walked into the hall, taking in paintings she'd never seen before, and the furniture that must belong to someone else. Her parents had become strangers, she was thinking. These past few months had opened up a chasm between them that seemed unbridgeable, and she didn't want it to be like this. She didn't want to lose them, but if the car had been her mother's, there would be no going back. 'Where's Dad?' she asked, making towards a room with a light on.

'He's taking a bath, but I've told him you're here. Can I get you anything? Sit down, sit down.'

Nikki went to stand in front of the fireplace, and briefly met Spence's eyes as he came to join her. Whatever chasm there was in the room, she knew he was on her side of it, and would always be there for her to hold on to.

Her mother was appearing nervous now, and lost for something to say, which wasn't a state Nikki had seen her in often. Oddly, she wanted to comfort her, as though it would make all the horrible suspicions go away, but until she asked the question . . .

'I'm sorry you didn't get our change of address,' her mother blurted, glancing briefly at Spence. 'We sent it, but I think it must have gone astray, because your friend Mrs Adani told us . . . Well, at least you know where we are now.' She gave an awkward smile. 'I expect you've heard that things haven't been going well for Dad,' she continued, her eyes seeming to plead understanding. 'His health has suffered a bit because of it . . .'

'Mum,' Nikki broke in, 'did you come to see me last Wednesday?' Her fists were so tight and her heart pounding so fiercely she almost couldn't hear her own voice.

Adele Grant's expression showed only surprise, with perhaps a trace of confusion. 'No,' she answered. 'We came the week before. You must remember that . . .'

'I do,' Nikki confirmed, 'but a neighbour saw a blue Mercedes outside our house last Wednesday around the time Zac . . . died.' Her insides were reeling away from the horror of what she was saying, but the strength of Spence standing beside her was keeping her steady.

Adele still seemed perplexed. 'I don't understand,' she said. 'Are you . . .?' She stopped and her eyes dilated with shock as she registered the meaning of the question. 'Oh my

God, Nicola, you can't think I hurt your baby. Please, *please* don't tell me you think that . . .'

'Were you there last Wednesday?' Spence asked.

Adele's eyes flicked to him, then back to Nikki. 'No,' she answered forcefully. 'Oh dear God . . .' She spun round as her husband came into the room. 'Jeremy, Nicola's here,' she said, apparently forgetting she'd already told him.

Grant's face was sallow and strained, and his eyes were shadowed, as though he hadn't slept in a while. 'Nicola,' he said, in a voice that was so weary it seemed an effort to get the word out. Nevertheless, he looked pleased she was there.

'Hello Dad,' she said, her insides turning liquid with fear to see how worn and defeated he was.

'I've been trying to get some money together for you,' he told her, 'but I see they've let you out now.'

'On bail,' she explained. Then, 'Dad, are you all right?'

'Yes, yes, I'm fine,' he assured her.

Nikki glanced at Spence, then at her mother.

'Jeremy, Nicola's come to ask us if we went to see her last Wednesday,' Adele told him. 'Apparently someone saw a blue Mercedes outside the house around the time the baby . . .' It seemed she couldn't bring herself to say the word.

Grant's eyes went from her to Nikki, and then to Spence.

'I was in the shop,' Adele reminded him, 'where I always am on Wednesdays, and you were . . . Where were you, darling?'

Grant's eyes were glassy, he seemed to be looking at no one now.

'Jeremy,' Adele pressed, starting to look scared, 'where were you last . . .' She gave a sob and covered her mouth.

Nikki was so horrified she could only stare at her father as her mother said, 'Jeremy, please tell me . . . Oh my God,' she gasped. 'Jeremy, did you go over there?'

Grant couldn't look at her.

'Oh my God, you did, didn't you?' Adele cried.

Nikki was still staring at him, willing him to deny it, but he didn't. Suddenly she couldn't take it any more, and launching herself at him, she pounded him with her fists. 'How could you?' she raged, tears of fury and hatred and denial rushing down her cheeks. 'He was a baby. Your grandson. How could you do anything to hurt him?'

Grant stood like a statue, letting her blows rain over him.

'Why did you do it?' Nikki sobbed. 'What made you think you could get away with it?'

Grant flinched at she struck his face.

'Answer me,' she yelled. 'Why did you do it? He was a defenceless baby. *Answer me,*' she screamed. 'Don't just stand there . . . Oh God,' she choked as Spence came to take her in his arms. She turned to him, sobbing so hard she could barely stand. 'He killed my baby,' she wept. 'He killed my baby.'

Adele was wringing her hands, unable, or unwilling, to grasp the enormity of what was happening. Surely to God Jeremy hadn't done this terrible thing. He just wouldn't, but why wasn't he defending himself? 'For God's sake, say something,' she implored. 'Please tell me you didn't hurt that baby.'

Nikki turned round to look at him, her breath still coming in gulps, as she used her wrists to try and dry her eyes.

Spence's eyes were burning with menace as he waited for the man to respond. Were he not Nikki's father he knew he'd have beaten him to a pulp by now.

'Surely you didn't go over there intending to hurt him,' Adele pleaded, racked by the horror of this unbelievable possibility.

Grant shook his head. 'No, I came to see you,' he told Nikki. 'I wanted . . . It was . . . There are things your mother and I have never told you,' he finally managed, 'and when we heard what was wrong with the baby . . . I . . . I thought it was time you knew the truth.'

'Oh Jeremy,' Adele choked, pressing her hands to her mouth.

'Your mother didn't want you to know,' he continued, 'she said it wouldn't make a difference, and I don't suppose it would have, but I . . .' His voice fell away as he raised an unsteady hand to his head. 'I thought you needed to understand how it could have happened, why you are carrying that gene, so I came to tell you.'

Adele turned to Nikki, who was watching them with tormented eyes. 'It's not . . . I didn't mean . . .'

'Just tell me what it is,' Nikki cried.

Adele turned back to her husband. He looked so frail and broken that he might have been about to collapse. 'You're not up to this now,' she told him. 'Why don't I . . .?'

He nodded. 'Yes, you tell her,' he said.

There was a moment when nothing seemed to happen at all, then Adele nodded, as though finally accepting she had no choice, and swallowing hard she forced herself to face Nikki and Spence. 'This won't be easy, for any of us,' she told them, 'but I want you to know, Nicola, that I regret with all my heart . . .' She dashed a tear from her cheek. 'I've made a lot of mistakes . . . I wish I'd . . .' As the words eluded her, Jeremy came to put a hand on her shoulder, and she reached up to grasp it. 'I don't know where to begin,' she confessed.

Seeming stronger, or perhaps less scattered in his mind, Grant said, 'I used to have a partner, many years ago. His name was Matthew. Matthew Cairns. He is your real father, Nicola. I adopted you when you were a few months old.'

Nikki felt suddenly unsteadied, as though the world was starting to spin and break apart. She saw her mother drop her head in her hands and felt Spence tightening his arm around her, but nothing was reaching her. Everything was an illusion. Her father wasn't her father. This man, whom she'd loved all her life, whom she'd fought with and defied, trusted, laughed with and tried but failed to please, wasn't even related to her – and he'd smothered her son. A huge, desperate sob erupted from the core of her. She wasn't sure she could take any more.

Then her mother, apparently finding her voice now that her husband had opened the way, was saying, 'Matthew died when I was seven months pregnant with you. We were married, but it . . . It wasn't a good marriage. He was . . . He liked to drink and became violent when he did. I thought when I became pregnant that he'd stop, but if anything it seemed to make him worse. His frustrations would get the better of him and everyone would be blamed for the way his life was turning out. He was desperate to become a writer. It was a passion with him, an obsession, but everything he submitted ended up being rejected. Time after time. It drove him crazy. He just couldn't cope with it. The fact that his and Dad's . . .' she looked awkwardly at Grant, 'partnership was starting to take off didn't seem to make a difference. He was good with people, everyone liked him and wanted to put their business his way, but then the terrible black moods would come over him and he'd reach for the vodka. He didn't want to be a stockbroker, he hated it, even though he had a talent for it, and the more successful he became the more he resented it. He stopped caring about his clients, lost them money and even started to abuse them when they rang up to complain. He was always drunk when that happened, and neither Jeremy, nor his parents, who he'd always been close to, could persuade him to take his life back under control.'

As her head swam with images of a man in anguish and torment, a man she'd never know now, Nikki said, 'Is he . . . I take it he was Jewish?' Her voice was husky and shredded with confusion.

Her mother's eyes filled with tears as she nodded. 'His family were lovely people,' she said. 'They tried so hard to help him, but it wasn't what he wanted, so he stopped going to see them. Then he gave up the office too. He just stayed at home, writing and writing, then he'd throw it all in my face when I came back at night. He seemed to think it was my fault that everything was going wrong for him, and when he ripped up his work it was as though he was doing it to punish me.'

She took a breath, then forced herself to continue. 'The first time I ended up in hospital it wasn't too serious, a cracked rib and some bruising. The second time my injuries were enough for them to keep me in overnight. The police became involved because he turned up on the ward, drunk, and threatening to cut the baby out of me.' She swallowed hard, as the memory of it opened all the old wounds. 'He was arrested,' she said shakily, 'and they put a restraining order on him to try and stop him coming near me again. I . . . used to love him, when we were first together, there was a lot about him to love then, but by the time the courts imposed the order I was terrified of him. It was affecting my work, badly, but the senior partners at my firm tried to be understanding. I'd always wanted to be a lawyer, and they were convinced I'd make a good one. I just had to get out of my marriage, and to a place where I could feel safe.

'Your father,' she glanced at Jeremy again, 'he . . . He was a great support to me during that time, in some ways my only support, but Matthew's parents cared too. They were very good to me, but once Matthew realised they were still seeing me, he decided I was turning everyone against him. I was so afraid of what he might do to me, and you, that when Jeremy suggested I go to stay with him for a while, I agreed.

'I knew if Matthew found out it would probably tip him over the edge, but I was so scared that I'd have gone anywhere with anyone as long as they were willing to protect me. Of course, Matthew did find out, and he immediately assumed Jeremy and I were having an affair. We weren't, but . . . It wasn't that Matthew wanted me himself, I think he was beyond wanting anyone by then, he just couldn't stand the thought of losing me to the man who was doing so well when his own life was falling apart. For him, it was another rejection he couldn't deal with, something else that made him feel worthless and gave him even more reason to drink.

'Then one night he must have waited outside Jeremy's apartment block for someone to come out so he could slip in. I'd never have let him in myself, even with Jeremy there, which he was that night. The instant we heard a bang on the front door we knew it was him. He began shouting and kicking and making such a scene, that Jeremy had no choice but to go and try to calm him down. As soon as he opened the door Matthew punched him in the face and barged his way past. He began rampaging through the flat, telling me to come out from wherever I was. I was hiding in the bedroom, so I didn't see him grab a kitchen knife, I only knew he had it when I heard Jeremy shouting at him to put it down.

'As soon as I heard that I ran to the phone, but I didn't even have a chance to pick it up before Matthew burst in through the door. I tried to get away from him, but I was trapped behind the bed. The next thing I knew Jeremy was there, dragging him off me, and then . . . Then . . . There was blood everywhere. At first I thought it was Jeremy who'd been stabbed, it might even have been me . . . but then Matthew sank to his knees and as he rolled over I saw the knife in his chest. He was looking at me, his eyes were open and . . .' She bunched her hands to her mouth. 'I couldn't bear to look at him, so Jeremy took me out of the room and sat me down in the kitchen while he washed the blood from us both. I don't think I heard him the first time he told me what we had to do, and even when I did I don't remember . . . I don't know what I was thinking.'

'Do you understand why you have to say it was you who stabbed him?' Jeremy asked, using a wet cloth to dab the blood from her cheeks.

Adele was shaking too hard to nod, but yes, she thought she understood.

'He has a history of violent attacks,' Jeremy reminded her. 'There's a restraining order out against him. We'll tell them how he forced his way in here. We'll say that he and I were fighting, and you were so afraid he'd kill me, or you, that you ran into the kitchen and grabbed a knife. Everyone will understand why you did it. You were trying to protect us, but more importantly you had to protect the baby. He threatened to kill it once in front of witnesses, so even the police will say that you had good reason to be afraid. So now, we have to go back into the bedroom and you have to put your hand around the handle of the knife. OK?'

Adele shuddered and drew back. 'No, don't make me do that, please,' she begged.

'I know you don't want to, and I wish you didn't have to, but if they find out it was me . . . Adele, they'll send me to prison, and all I was doing was protecting you. He was out of control. You saw him, you'd never have been able to fight him off yourself, so I had to do something. It was the only solution, the only way I could make him stop. I saved you, and the baby, so please, Adele, save me now. If you say you did it, they'll understand that you didn't have a choice. It was self-defence. I'll swear that was the case, and there won't be any reason for anyone to think it didn't happen that way. Please Adele, do this for me. No, not just for me, for the baby too, because I can give you a good life, both of you. I'll take care of you

from now on and make sure nothing bad ever happens to you again. All you have to do is come back in there with me and put your hand on the knife.'

Adele was shaking almost as much now as she had then. 'So I went into the room where Matthew was lying in a pool of his own blood and wrapped my hand round the knife.'

Nikki had stopped breathing. Her eyes were round with horror. She could see the scenario, almost as clearly as if she'd been there herself, and yet it was frighteningly surreal. The people her mother was speaking about were her parents, all three of them, but they felt like strangers. Nothing was coming together. Everything was fractured and crazy, and she seemed to be falling through the cracks.

'When the police came,' Adele went on, 'I let Jeremy do all the talking. Everyone assumed I was in shock, and I was. It didn't occur to me that we were doing anything wrong, because I really had been terrified Matthew would kill me, and I couldn't let Jeremy go to prison for protecting me. So taking the blame myself seemed the only, the *right* thing to do.'

She took another unsteady breath. 'After that, everything happened more or less the way Jeremy said it would. There were a lot of questions, obviously, there was even some talk about charging me with manslaughter, but we had a good lawyer and in the end it went away. Everyone was on our side, they understood, even Matthew's family, but they were so devastated at losing their son, especially that way, that they couldn't bring themselves to see me any more. It wasn't that they blamed me, and I don't blame them now, because who would want to continue a relationship with someone who'd killed their son?'

As the words reverberated around them, Nikki's and Spence's eyes went to her father. He was looking so shattered and guilt-stricken that, in spite of everything, Nikki couldn't help feeling sorry for him. Could she and Spence continue a relationship with him, now he'd killed their son? Right now it was hard to imagine, but there was so much to assimilate that it was impossible to know how any of them were going to go forward from here.

'I was so traumatised by what had happened,' Adele continued, 'that everyone started to worry that I'd lose the baby. The doctor ordered me to stay at home until after you were born, and I didn't argue. My confidence was already in shreds, so I couldn't have done my job anyway. Jeremy went on taking care of me, making sure I wanted for nothing, except counselling, because of course we couldn't risk that. Granny May came to help look after me, and she and Jeremy were kinder to me than I could remember anyone ever being. And because I wasn't going out any more it wasn't long before they became the centre of my world. I stopped wanting to be a lawyer, I didn't even want to keep up with my friends. I only wanted to be safe at home, waiting for Jeremy to come back and you to be born. I thought once you arrived that everything would be all right again, but it wasn't. I loved you and wanted you, but I couldn't convince myself that I deserved you . . . It was as though I really had killed Matthew. I was blaming myself, and punishing myself. Granny May was wonderful, but really it was Jeremy who took over feeding and changing you, bathing you and putting you to bed. I'd watch him and long to do it myself, but I was afraid that if I let my feelings show something would happen to take you from me.'

Racked by the tragedy in her mother's voice, and the desperate confusion that had forced its way between her and her baby, Nikki could only wish, for her mother's sake, that there was a way to turn back time so she could have a second chance.

'When Jeremy asked me to marry him,' Adele said, 'it seemed the most natural thing to do, and when he offered to adopt you that seemed right too. After all, we were already living with him, and because I no longer had the heart to pursue a career of my own, I agreed with him when he suggested that I stay at home to concentrate on being a full-time mother. He couldn't have children of his own, it was the reason his first wife left him, so he wanted to give you, us, everything he could, and how could I not be happy for him to do that? And I was happy, in so far as I could be, because by then I loved him. It was years before I realised we were trapped inside the lie we'd told. It was binding us together more tightly than our marriage vows. Not that I wanted to get out, but it's caused as much bitterness between us as it has pain, and every time I thought I wanted my freedom I'd remember what had happened, and what he'd done for you. I knew he wasn't always the easiest of fathers, but I never doubted that he loved you, or that you loved him. What always broke my heart, though, was that you and I were never as close as I wanted us to be. I kept telling myself you knew how much I loved you, so I didn't have to say it, and if I didn't say it, no one would hear, so no one would spoil it. It's only been since I started going for therapy in recent months that I've come to a place where I can begin to acknowledge my mistakes. The trouble is, I'm still not sure what I can do to repair them.'

She looked at her husband. He was standing motionlessly in the doorway, his glazed eyes staring at nothing. It wasn't even clear if he was taking in everything his wife was saying.

'I expect you're starting to understand now,' she said to Nikki, 'why your father and I reacted the way we did when you said you wanted to be a writer. It was a reminder of whose daughter you really were, and therefore of the terrible thing we had done. Then when your friend Mrs Adani came to tell us about the baby . . .' Her voice was swallowed by emotion. 'We'd never heard of the disease before, but when she mentioned the Jewish connection . . . It was another reminder of Matthew, and I just didn't know what to do. Telling you about him wasn't going to change anything for the baby, it was already too late for that, and I'm not even sure that if you'd known about Matthew before getting pregnant, you'd have realised there could be a danger. I wouldn't have been able to tell you, because it wasn't something I knew about, but maybe, if I'd kept some contact going with your grandparents . . . They'd never mentioned it to me when I was pregnant, but I'm not Jewish, so I guess they presumed I was clear. If that's right, then I can't see why they'd have said anything to you either, because I'm presuming your boyfriend isn't Jewish?'

Spence's expression was showing very little as he shook

his head. As far as he knew, anyway, and besides, what did it matter now?

'I don't think there's anything we could have done,' Adele went on, 'even if you'd decided to tell us you were pregnant when you first found out, because we truly didn't know. Of course, we'd have tried to persuade you not to go through with it, but not for that reason, for the ones I tried to give you at the time. You see, I know what it means to give up your dreams, and to watch your life go off in a direction you'd never imagined and one you couldn't turn back from. You didn't seem to understand that having a baby would change things for you, because it always does. If I hadn't had you, maybe I'd have found the confidence to go back to work, who knows? It doesn't really matter any more. All that is important now is you, and what you do with your life.' Her hand was trembling badly as she pressed it to her head. 'You have to understand that in spite of how it might have seemed to you at times, I've only ever wanted the best for you, and that's never going to change. I'd give anything for you not to have gone through what you have, and I wish to God there was some way I could change it, or at least create an understanding between us, because I'd like to think we can go forward from here in a way that's . . . I don't want to lose you, because you mean more to me than my own life, but the lies, the secrets and now this . . .' She wiped more tears from her face and looked helplessly towards her husband, the man who'd killed her daughter's father and son. How was Nicola ever going to forgive that? No one could.

Grant remained silent and unmoving, seeming almost to have slipped into a trance.

'Did you go to Nicola's intending to do what you did?' Adele asked him hoarsely.

He shook his head. 'No, of course not,' he replied.

'Was it because he was Matthew's grandson?'

His eyes came to hers, and he shook his head again.

'Then why?' she implored. 'He was just a baby. He had no way of defending himself . . .'

'I didn't,' Grant broke in roughly. 'It wasn't . . .' He wiped an unsteady hand over his face.

'You have to tell us what happened,' she insisted.

He nodded, and tried several times to clear his throat. 'When I . . . When I got to the house,' he began, 'I knocked on the door, but no one answered. I tried again, and the second time the door came open. I went inside and I . . . I could hear him breathing right away . . . I wasn't sure what it was at first, but when I found him in the sitting room . . . He was gasping . . . Struggling . . . I started to pick him up, intending to help him, then I remembered what kind of life he was facing and I . . . I thought of how horrible it was going to be for him, and what it would do to Nicola, how hard it would be for her tied to a child who . . . who wouldn't be able to function, and to what end? All her precious youth was going to be wasted on trying to make him better, and it would never happen. I didn't want her to suffer like that so I . . .' His voice dipped to little more than a whisper. 'I picked up the blanket and . . . I don't know how long I held it there, but I'm sure it was only seconds before I realised what I was doing and I . . . I couldn't do it. I thought I could, but . . .' His eyes went to Nikki. 'When I left, I was certain he was still breathing . . . I could hear him . . .'

'Why didn't you call me?' Nikki cried.

He shook his head. 'I didn't know where you were. I thought you'd gone out and left him, or . . . I don't know what I was thinking. I was so appalled by what I'd tried to do that I didn't know . . . It was . . . Oh God, I'm sorry, I'm sorry,' he gasped, as he started to break down. 'I didn't mean to hurt him . . . I wish I'd never gone over there . . .'

Nikki's stricken eyes went to Spence, whose face was chalk-white. She could sense the pent-up violence knotted inside him, and understood it.

'All these years,' her father went on, 'I've thought of you as my own, Nicola. You mean more to me than anything, but then the reminders that you're Matthew's began. You wanted to write . . . I might have been able to bring myself to support it, but your mother couldn't. She still bears the scars of the time she spent with him. The nightmares haven't stopped, but they became less frequent until we found out about the Tay-Sachs. I couldn't bear the thought of you both suffering any more because of him . . . And then to know that the baby would, too. I wanted to put an end to it all, and in those moments when I was with . . . When I . . . But I couldn't do it . . . I swear . . .' His breathing was becoming more laboured now, and as he clutched a hand to his chest Nikki and her mother started forward.

'Jeremy?' Adele cried. 'What is it?'

'It's all right,' he rasped. 'I'm fine. Just . . . It's OK.'

Somehow suppressing his fury, Spence came to lead him to a chair. 'Sit down,' he said, almost wishing he had it in him to walk away and let the man suffer – which was what he'd done to Zac.

As he sank into the chair Grant thanked Spence, then looked at his wife. 'You'd better call the police,' he told her.

Adele's face turned ashen.

'Let's get it over with,' he said quietly.

Adele looked at Nikki.

'Young man, please bring me the phone,' Grant said to Spence.

Spence looked around the room.

'No, wait,' Nikki cried as Spence went to pick up a handset. 'Let's just think about this . . .'

'We have to clear your name,' her father told her, still sounding breathless. 'I let your mother take the blame for me once, I'm not going to let you . . .' He coughed and put a hand to his chest again. 'The phone,' he said to Spence.

Nikki was shaking her head. 'No,' she said firmly, 'not yet. I have some things to say first.'

As they all looked at her she went to sit on the edge of a sofa, resting her hands in fists on her knees, and fixing her eyes on her father. When Spence seemed as though he might come to sit with her, she gestured for him to stay where he was, then waited for her mother to sit down too.

By the time she'd finished speaking Spence had left to wait outside in the car, and her father, unable to stop coughing after more than an hour of arguing, had gone to lie down. 'She's your daughter, Adele,' he'd reminded his wife. 'I don't care how you do it, just make her see sense.'

Only Nikki and her mother were left in the room now, and there was still much to be said between them, but they were both too exhausted to find many more words.

Adele's eyes were heavy and deeply baffled as she regarded her daughter. 'Is it because you realise what it'll do to him . . .'

'. . . if he's charged and stands trial,' Nikki finished. 'Yes, in part, but I'm thinking about Zac, too, and my real father . . . And you.'

Adele shook her head slowly. 'You won't have heard the last of this, you know that, don't you?'

Nikki rose to her feet. 'Spence will be waiting outside,' she said, and without saying goodbye she left.

Chapter Twenty-Seven

Mrs Adani was waiting outside Temple Meads station when David came through from the platforms, an overnight bag slung across one shoulder, his camera case over the other. It was an exquisite April day, almost like summer it was so warm, even this early in the morning. It had poured down during the night, though, so the cobbles were glistening wetly in the sudden burst of sunshine and the blossoming trees were dripping petals like raindrops. The freshness of the air, the whole feel of the day made it believable that spring had arrived.

Watching David walking towards her, Mrs A's soft brown eyes glowed with maternal pride – he really was a handsome lad, she was thinking, though she knew she wasn't supposed to say so herself. Things were working out well for him in London, he'd barely had a day free since the beginning of March, shooting for commercials or second units, and, more recently, another short film written and directed by Val Fleming, one of the industry's new rising stars. After David had abandoned Val's first film to support Nikki and Spence during their loss, he'd felt certain no one at Drake's company would want to give him a second chance, but luckily that hadn't been the case. Not that he was working exclusively for Drake and his protégés, but those projects took up so much of his time that he might as well be doing so.

'Hey, Mum,' he said, tugging open the rear passenger door to dump his bags on the back seat. 'Everything cool?'

'Everything's cool,' she assured him, as he slipped in beside her and planted a kiss on her cheek. 'You must have got up very early this morning.'

'Tell me about it,' he yawned, 'but I couldn't afford to be late, could I? So, how's tricks?'

Sliding the car into gear, she reversed out of her parking space to start down the station concourse and join the early morning traffic. 'Tricks are fairly normal,' she told him, 'but they'll change when Dad comes home next week.'

David smothered another yawn. 'Bet you've really missed him,' he commented.

She certainly had. 'Very much,' she replied, 'but it was necessary for him to be with his mother.'

'And secretly you're not sorry the old boot's finally kicked the bucket.' He laughed. 'Hey, that works . . . Boot, kicking . . .'

'That is a very wicked thing to say,' Mrs A chided. 'I am happy for your grandmother that her soul is now with her Maker.'

David grinned. 'Yeah, right,' he said. 'So, did Dad mind that you didn't go over for the funeral?'

'I think he would have liked me to be there, but he understood why it wasn't possible.'

At that David's expression sobered, since he knew only too well why. Apart from anything else, it was the reason he'd spent all of Tuesday here in Bristol, and was back again today.

Turning his attention to his mobile, he began sending a text. 'Just to let everyone know I've arrived,' he explained. 'Have you seen anyone yet this morning?'

'Only Danny. He didn't come with me to the station, because he had some work to do on the computer, but he's promised to have breakfast ready for when we get back.'

'Cool,' David nodded. 'It was good of you to let him stay last night.'

Mrs A smiled, and brought the car to a stop at a set of red lights. Since she could sense that her son was steeling himself to broach a subject that would be difficult for them both, she let the silence run, hoping it might help him, even though, if the truth were told, she'd rather not have gone there. However, she didn't want him to feel that he had to keep his secret from her.

Her intuition proved right, because as she pulled away

from the lights to join the Wells Road, David said, 'Mum, about Dan . . .'

When he stopped, she waited for him to find the words, but it seemed he couldn't, so she said, 'He's a very good friend to you, and I am always happy for him to come and stay.'

David glanced at her awkwardly, his unshaven cheeks flushed hot with embarrassment. 'But you know we're . . .'

'Yes, I know,' she said gently, 'so, shall we leave it at that?'

David continued to stare at her, trying to read her face. 'You're Catholic,' he reminded her.

'This I am aware of,' she reminded him.

'So, doesn't it, well, bother you?'

She glanced over at him, and wished she could have held his beloved face between her hands as she said, 'I admit it is not what I would have chosen for you, but what is much more important to me is that you are happy and healthy, and that you have a goodness in your soul that I know will take you to heaven.'

David's expression turned wry. 'Now, why do I feel as though I'm about to sprout wings and float off through the ozone?' he joked. Then he shrugged. 'Hey, wings, fairies and all that . . .'

Mrs A laughed. 'You are most irreverent,' she told him, 'but I am so pleased to see you that I will let it pass. However, I will ask you to let me break this news to your father.'

'Oh, be my guest,' David responded, all generosity. 'Nanette and Diana know, by the way, and they're cool with it.'

'That is good,' she said, suspecting that her daughters would be cool with just about anything their younger brother did, they loved him so much.

'So,' he said, turning to look out of the window, 'D-Day has arrived at last. I don't suppose you've spoken to Nikki yet this morning.'

Mrs A shook her head. 'It was too early when I left the house, but I think she'll have a lot to be dealing with, so I am sure she is already awake.'

'Do you think I should call?'

'If you've sent a text, letting her know you're here, that will probably be enough for now.'

He stared down at his mobile, imagining Nikki and Spence at the house they'd all shared in Bemmie, and where Nikki and Spence still were, all these weeks after they should have moved to London.

'Did her parents stay over last night?' he asked.

'They've been there all week, so I expect they did.'

David's expression was turning more solemn by the second. 'This has got to be a major nightmare for them,' he commented.

'Yes, indeed,' Mrs A agreed, 'but I think the real nightmare will begin when the jury return their verdict today, presuming it happens today.'

Unable to argue with that, David closed his eyes and sent a silent prayer to God that everything went the right way, because if it didn't, he couldn't even bring himself to think about what it might mean.

'Ah, here you are,' Nikki said, finding her father in the sitting room already wearing his coat. 'Are you OK?'

Though his face was yellowed and haggard, and his eyes appeared permanently misted these days, he seemed to have rallied since his bout of anxiety during the night. 'I'll be glad when today's over,' he admitted.

Giving his arm a comforting squeeze, she forced down her own nerves and went out to the hall, where Spence was helping her mother on with her coat. 'What time's the taxi supposed to be here?' she asked, reaching for her own.

'Nine,' he replied. 'The lawyers want us there by half past.'

Though she already knew that, she nodded anyway, and slipped on the navy, double-breasted suit jacket that belonged to her mother. It was smart and sober, which was how they'd agreed they should all present themselves during this critical week.

Adele's complexion, and the circles round her eyes, showed how badly she'd slept these last few nights. 'Thank you,' she whispered to Spence, as he passed her scarf. They'd become surprisingly close during these last few weeks, and though nothing had ever been said, Nikki knew that her mother's liking and respect for Spence for his loyalty and support continued to grow by the day.

'It'll be all right,' Nikki said confidently as her father came to join them. 'I promise, it'll be fine.'

The way he looked at her showed how fragile he was inside, and she almost couldn't bear it. 'If it doesn't go the way . . .'

'It will,' she broke in firmly. 'It has to,' and turning to her mother she gave her a hug.

Though Adele might normally have given a quick hug back, this morning she held on to Nikki so tightly that in the end Nikki started to laugh to stop herself crying. 'That must be the taxi,' she said, as a car tooted its horn outside.

Spence had been ferrying them to and from the court in her mother's four-year-old Fiesta all week – the Mercedes had long gone to help pay the legal fees – but they'd decided between them last night that today wouldn't be a day for anyone to drive. Though there wasn't much left in the pot now, there was enough to spring for a couple of taxis – and even a celebratory dinner should everything, by some miracle, go in their favour.

As the driver pulled away from the house, with Spence in front and Nikki behind with her parents, the three of them clutching hands, she prayed with all her might that all four of them would return tonight.

The journey into the centre of Bristol took a full half-hour, mainly thanks to rush-hour traffic and roadworks. They travelled in silence since no one wanted to discuss the case with a stranger in the car, but none of them had much to say anyway. The outcome was in the hands of the jury now, or it would be as soon as the lawyers had finished their closing arguments.

Hearing the wheeze of her father's chest, Nikki turned to look at him, afraid he might be suffering more than he was admitting. He gave her a small nod, as though saying he was all right, but she was worried anyway, because the strain of this trial, coming on top of losing his home, business and virtually all his capital, had really taken its toll. During the past two months he'd been rushed to hospital twice, both times with suspected heart attacks, which, fortunately, had turned out to be nothing more serious than panic attacks caused by stress. However, the doctors had warned him that his blood pressure remained a problem, and his weight was dropping too, since he was finding it difficult to eat.

As usual the court was surrounded by press when they arrived, local and national, because the case had attracted a lot of attention. The lawyers had advised them not to watch the news themselves, or to take any papers, because the sensationalist style of reporting wouldn't prove helpful to their understanding of what was happening, or to their morale.

So, keeping their heads down as usual, they pushed their way through the crowd, Nikki holding tightly to Spence's hand, and Adele to Jeremy's, ignoring all questions and cameras until they were inside the court building. A security officer was waiting to scan their bags and coats before allowing them into the central hall.

Jolyon Crane arrived minutes later, and after greeting them all with a shake of the hand and a reassuring smile, he led them to an interview room on the first floor where they'd started each day this week. It wasn't large, but there was enough room round the table to seat eight people, and flasks of tea and coffee were laid out on a tray that one of Jolyon's assistants made sure was prepared each morning before their meeting got under way.

Jolyon spent the first few minutes going over the events of the day before, explaining the importance of Mrs Adani's evidence, and why, even though she'd been called by the prosecution, her evaluation of Zac's health and the circumstances at his home was so vital to the defence. Then Adam Monk, their barrister, came in, already wigged and gowned and looking his usual solemn self. However, there was a watchfulness behind the sobriety of his expression that had given Nikki confidence in him from the start. Her father had felt buoyed by Monk's manner too, since it was crisp, but not patronising, and his command of the English language regularly impressed them all. In fact, as the week had progressed, Jeremy's respect for the younger man had grown almost to a point of hero worship, which, in its way, had been quite touching for Nikki to watch. However, she couldn't help wondering how her father might be feeling about the barrister by the end of the day.

After talking them through what was likely to happen over the next couple of hours, Monk took Jolyon Crane aside to discuss the closing statement they'd spent until the early hours preparing. Then Jolyon, who was acting as Monk's junior, went off to the robing room, leaving his clerk to hand out coffees in an attempt to quell mounting nerves.

At nine forty-five the doors to the court opened and everyone started filing in. Once again the press and public galleries quickly filled to capacity, and the lawyers' benches were soon populated by many advocates in black robes and curled wigs, or dark suits and white shirts. For the moment the judge's bench was empty, but the magnificent crest behind it was as regal and intimidating as the man himself, the Right Honourable Sir Mark Ledell CBE. Adam Monk, QC, had informed them that Ledell was a fair man, with a record that veered towards leniency, and that was very definitely what they wanted for a manslaughter charge by reason of diminished responsibility.

Keeping her eyes lowered as she was escorted into the dock, Nikki tried to draw strength from the fact that her closest friends were all here today, not only David, Danny and Mrs A, but the whole crowd from the Factory and some of her neighbours too. Along with Spence, her greatest rock of all, and her parents, of course, she knew everyone was rooting for her, and even DS McAllister, whom she'd seen briefly before coming in here, had given her a friendly smile. No one wanted her to be found guilty, she understood that, but the law was the law, so due process had to be seen to be done, even if she knew in her heart that the entire truth had not been told during this week.

'All rise.'

As the court stood and the judge, in his red robes and horsehair wig, entered, Nikki felt her insides turning weak with fear. She almost wished she hadn't insisted on doing this now, but it was too late to turn back, and even if she could, she knew in her heart that she wouldn't. She would never have been able to carry on a normal life with her father in prison, suffering in ways she didn't even want to imagine. It wasn't that she condoned what he'd done to Zac, but she blamed herself too, because if she'd taken Zac upstairs with her, or stayed with him and slept on the sofa, he might still be with them now. And no matter how forcefully and angrily Spence and her mother had tried to talk her out of her decision, she hadn't faltered. The strongest argument of all had come from her father, who'd ordered, begged and even threatened her if she didn't see sense and let him pay for what he'd done.

'You say you won't be able to go on with your life thinking of me behind bars,' he'd cried, 'but can't you see it's the same for me? How I am supposed to go on, knowing you're paying for a crime that I committed?'

'It won't happen like that,' was her stock answer, while praying she turned out to be right. 'As Zac's mother there will be much more sympathy for me, and even if I do get sent down it probably won't be for long.'

'But you don't know that,' he'd said desperately. 'No, Nicola, I'm sorry, I can't let you do this.'

'It's out of the question,' Spence had shouted. 'You can't cheat the law, Nikki, not the way you're proposing . . .'

'The way I see it, it's not cheating the law,' she said savagely, 'it's cheating fate. Why should it be allowed to inflict a horrible disease on a child, and then expect the rest of us to stand back and do nothing? We're not helpless. We can take decisions for ourselves, and I, for one, am glad that Zac isn't going to be forced to stay here going through God only knows what kind of pain and suffering, because we're too squeamish or cowardly or stupidly moral to help him.'

'We all understand how you feel,' Spence growled, 'and I'm not arguing with any of that, I'm just saying that you can't put yourself up in front of a judge and jury for something you didn't do.'

'Yes I can, and I will.'

'No,' her father said firmly. 'I won't let you.'

'You're damned right you won't,' her mother shouted. 'I'm not letting her . . .'

'Stop, stop!' Nikki cried. 'My mind is made up about this,

and Dad, even if you go to the police and make a full confession I'll tell them that you're trying to take the blame for me. They're much more likely to believe that than they are the other way round, so please don't do it. It'll just complicate things even further, and they're already complicated enough.'

'It's absolutely straightforward, as far as I'm concerned,' Spence told her furiously, 'you have obviously completely lost your mind, and I will not stand by you over this. I'll go to the police myself, and make sure they know that your father's telling the truth.'

'And they'd think you're doing the same as him, trying to protect me,' she pointed out. 'No, I'm sorry, I've told you what I'm going to do, and if none of you wants to support me, I will try to respect your decision, but it will hurt me a lot not to have you there with me.'

In the end, it was her father's first suspected heart attack that had cooled some of the arguments, and even convinced her mother, at least, to start seeing things her way.

'You have to think about how you're going to survive if Dad gets really sick or goes to jail,' Nikki told her. 'I don't mean to be rude, but you're a bit old now to be starting a new career – which isn't to say I don't think you can, but it's not going to provide anything like the kind of income you're used to.'

'I'm living on a lot less these days,' her mother reminded her.

'Yes, and you're hating it and it's still more than you'd be able to make on your own. Please try to understand, I have to know that everything's sorted out for you two before I can get on with my life.'

'We're not your responsibility,' her mother cried. 'We're adults, and *you* haven't committed a crime.'

'Don't let's keep going back over that,' Nikki protested. 'You're my parents, so of course you're my responsibility, and I wouldn't have it any other way.'

Her mother shook her head in despair. 'How did you get to be like this?' she demanded. 'So headstrong and . . . *moral*. You certainly didn't learn it from me.'

'Maybe I did,' Nikki replied, 'especially the headstrong

bit, but that's a discussion for another time. What matters now is that we don't add any more to Dad's stress load. His heart's weak, his blood pressure's high, so think about what it might do to him if we suddenly turn around now and say, OK Jeremy, you can take the rap, good luck with the prison sentence, hope the other inmates don't get to find out what you're in for, but if they do there's a good healthcare unit inside.'

Remembering now how her mother's face had sagged when she'd said that, Nikki felt her own starting to drain as she listened to Adam Monk winding up his closing statement. The whole courtroom was in his thrall. No one moved, or even coughed, apparently not wanting to miss a word he said. He was certainly persuasive, she was thinking, at least to her ears, and she tried to tell herself that if she was on the jury, after listening to him she'd definitely return a verdict of not guilty. She even saw a couple of jurors dabbing their eyes as her own streamed with tears when Monk talked about Zac and his disease. She still longed for him so badly that it broke her heart each night when she went to bed, and again when she rose in the morning. She wished the jury could have known him, not because she thought it would have influenced them about the verdict, only because she wanted the world to know him for the beautiful, lively little baby he'd been, instead of the innocent victim of a rare and incurable disease.

Suddenly everything seemed to be tilting out of kilter, making the lawyer's words and her instincts come and go through her mind like strangers, finding nowhere to settle so moving on to a place she couldn't reach them. Then the walls of the court, high and white, started to remind her of those in the prison, and the way they'd closed in on her. She could feel herself becoming swamped by those inter-minable, terrifying few days she'd spent at Eastwood Park and what had happened at the end.

Her throat was too dry; she couldn't swallow. Her head was still spinning. Had Serena and her friends really intended to kill her? Would they have gone that far if a warder and other inmates hadn't dragged them off her? She'd lost consciousness and for all they knew she might have drawn her last breath, so maybe they would have carried it through.

A terrible heat was spreading through her body. She could be spending the next five or more years with women like that. What would she be like by the time she came out? Where would Spence be? Why hadn't she considered him more during all this? He'd said he wouldn't stand by her, but he had, because he'd been here every step of the way.

Would they be saying goodbye at the end of today?

As he sat through the summing-up with his wife's hand gripping tightly to his, Jeremy Grant was racked with more shame than he could bear. Since the words in themselves were like a punishment, and his soul needed to feel it, he wouldn't allow himself to shy away from them. He took each of them into his heart, adding them to the insupportable burden of sorrow and guilt that was already there. Though he was saying nothing now, barely even moving, he knew, without a single shred of doubt, that no matter how loudly and forcefully his daughter might protest, if the outcome of this trial didn't go the way they hoped, nothing in the world would persuade him to let her pay for a crime he'd committed. He'd done it once before with her mother, and to say he regretted it would be an understatement without equal. It had tormented him ever since, and he knew it would continue to do so for the rest of his days. His only excuse for allowing Adele to take the blame for Matthew's death was that in the heat of the moment he'd panicked, and by the time he'd come to his senses she wouldn't allow him to turn back. He'd have forced the issue if she hadn't made him realise how much she and Nicola needed him: she was still deeply traumatised by what had happened and barely able to cope with her own life, much less a baby. So he'd let things be, and over time they'd done their best to put it behind them, but it was always there, in the shadows, seeping through the cracks in their marriage, affecting almost everything they did.

Maybe losing everything had been a just punishment for his lies.

What he'd done to Zac, though, was far, far worse.

Though the baby had still been breathing when he'd left, he was absolutely certain he had, Jeremy knew in his heart, as they all did, that he'd played a part in Zac's untimely passing. The fact that his existence would have been blighted by all kinds of handicaps and pain didn't in any way excuse what Jeremy had done, in some ways it seemed to make it worse. God knew, he'd give anything, his freedom, his own life, to be able to bring the baby back to his mother, but he could no more do that than he could change the gene that had afflicted him.

What he could do, though, was make sure his daughter never spent a single minute suffering the punishment for a crime he'd committed.

The judge had finished his summing-up now, and the jury were being sent to begin their deliberations. As Nikki watched them leave her heart was pounding so hard that she almost couldn't hear the scrape of chairs and murmurings around her. Though she'd stolen looks at their faces throughout the week, and especially this morning, trying to gauge how they were reacting to the prosecuting counsel, and then Adam Monk, she still had no idea what they might be thinking. Her own thoughts were like quicksilver, escaping the instant she tried to pin them down. She couldn't be sure which way her mood was swinging, she was only aware of the weight of dread that was making it almost impossible for her to walk out of the dock.

However, when she joined Spence and the others in the private room Jolyon Crane had found for them she was determined not to let her fears show. Instead, she put on a bright smile, and agreed with them all as they remarked on what a brilliant closing statement Adam Monk had delivered.

'I was watching the jury,' Danny told her, 'they're definitely on your side.'

'Absolutely,' David agreed. 'You could see it, and the press are all saying the same. You should have heard them on their way out.'

Needing to stay in a parallel world to the press for as long as she could, Nikki turned to Mrs A. 'Thanks for being here again today,' she said, embracing her hard, 'it means a lot to me.'

Mrs A patted her back comfortingly, then held out her hands to greet Nikki's parents, who were coming in through the door. It gave Nikki a great deal of pleasure to see the warmth that was developing between Mrs A and her mother, because God knew Adele had needed a friend during this time, someone she could talk to and confide in who wasn't a part of the family. In her usual unflappable way Mrs A had been there, every step of the way, and though Nikki knew they'd all leaned on her far too much already, it offered her some comfort to think that Mrs A would be there for her mother if the jury returned a verdict of guilty. What that might do to her father she couldn't allow herself to consider, she just had to hope it didn't happen.

Mrs A had brought her usual basketful of sandwiches and dips, but no one managed to eat much, and as the time wore on it became clear that everyone's nerves were working their way closer and closer to the surface. Nikki sat with her father, holding tightly to his hand, while Spence and the others did their best to test her mother on an encyclopaedic knowledge of old films that Nikki hadn't even known she possessed.

'If they find you guilty,' her father murmured, 'then I shall . . .'

'Ssh,' Nikki whispered. 'Don't let's talk about it now.'

'But I want you to know . . .'

'No, Dad. Please. I know what you're going to say and this isn't the time to discuss it,' and letting go of his hand she walked to the door, reaching it just as someone knocked and pushed it open.

'Jury's back,' Jolyon told her.

For one awful minute Nikki thought she was going to run. Then quickly reminding herself that everyone she loved was behind her, and that she could do this, she put her shoulders back and walked out of the room.

Minutes later she was in the dock, watching the jury filing back into their seats. She tried again to read their faces, then realising that none of them was looking at her, she felt an icy fear creep through her soul. The fact that they weren't meeting her eyes could only mean one thing.

More time ticked by. She kept losing the sense of what was happening, as though it was a film shifting in and out of focus. She was told to stand and the officer beside her touched her arm. She rose to her feet and looked across the well of the court to the judge. Someone had already handed him the verdict, written on the piece of paper he was holding. He knew, but there was nothing in his expression to tell her what it was.

'Members of the jury, have you reached a verdict?' The question echoed portentously around the room.

The foreman was a short, balding man with round glasses and a double chin. 'We have,' he replied.

'Then please tell the court how say you on the count of manslaughter by reason of diminished responsibility?'

The small man seemed to stretch up his neck as he said, 'We find the defendant guilty, your honour.'

As Nikki started to sway the officer next to her caught her, holding her steady.

'It's all right, I've got you,' he murmured.

She was aware of someone shouting and the judge calling for order, but it felt as though it was happening somewhere else.

Eventually the court fell silent. Nikki listened to the judge thanking the jury and dismissing them. She watched his face, but all she was seeing was the inside of a prison van, taking her back to Eastwood Park. The clatter and grind of keys. The cold, dank showers. The stench of women who didn't wash. The walls closing in on her. She hadn't allowed herself to believe this would happen, but it had, and now, at last, she was realising how delusional she'd been even to contemplate trying to trick the law.

The judge was still speaking, saying he would hear mitigation now if the defence was ready. Adam Monk rose to his feet, but as he began stating the reasons why there should not be a custodial sentence, all Nikki could think about was her father. He'd be feeling even worse than she was now, so she must do her best to make him think she was strong enough to cope with this. She knew he was probably already on his way out of the courtroom to tell someone, anyone, that she was innocent and he must pay for the crime he'd committed. If anyone listened they'd probably put it down to a father's natural grief; his need to take on his child's suffering.

'. . . when taking into consideration the psychiatric reports submitted to the court,' the judge was saying, his voice breaking through the maelstrom in her mind, 'together with the reports from the health visitor and paediatrician, I have no difficulty in concluding that the defendant was under a considerable amount of stress at the time of the baby's death. All the expert evidence suggests that this condition was temporary, and that she has now regained full control of her faculties. This leads me, therefore, to the view that even though this case passes the custody threshold, a suspended sentence of one year's imprisonment for a period of two years would be appropriate. However . . .'

His next words were drowned by whoops of triumph from the public gallery.

The judge called for order.

Spence, David, and Danny obediently sat down again, but Nikki could feel their excitement and relief threading through the air, as though to bind her to them.

'However,' the judge repeated, 'I would recommend that the defendant undergo a continued period of psychiatric treatment in order to satisfy herself, and her family, that the trauma she has suffered has been appropriately recognised and dealt with.' To Nikki he said, 'Thank you, you are free to go.'

Nikki's heart stood still. *Free to go! Free to go!* She suddenly felt as light as air, as though she could float like a bubble from the court into a sky full of blue. The others were jumping up and down and cheering. Tears were streaming down her cheeks. She was afraid she might be dreaming as she was led out of the dock, and the next thing she knew she was in Spence's arms, clinging to him as though she might never let go. Then her parents were there, crying and laughing, and Mrs A and David and Danny. The Factory crowd quickly surrounded them, along with the neighbours. They were like a rugby scrum with Nikki at its heart.

In the end, Jolyon Crane managed to break his way through. 'The press will want a statement,' he told her. 'I prepared one just in case, but if you'd rather deliver one of your own . . .'

Nikki turned to Spence.

'I think,' he said to Jolyon, 'if you don't mind reading out yours that would be the way to go. It's not that we don't have anything to say, but as great a result as this is, I'd like everyone to remember that Nikki and I have still lost our son, so we'd really appreciate some space to get over all this and to try and get back to normal.'

Understanding perfectly, Jolyon shook them both by the hand, and after a curious glance in Jeremy's direction he went off to deal with the press.

'Mr Monk,' Nikki said, as the barrister came to join them, 'I wish I knew how to say something bigger than thank you. I can still hardly believe it . . .'

'You did the most amazing job,' Spence told him. 'You were right on the nail about the judge, he was definitely lenient . . .' He laughed, as though still taking it in.

Appearing every bit as satisfied as his clients, Monk congratulated them, and after wishing them well he followed Jolyon out to the street.

'You know what I think we should all do now?' Danny cried. 'We should go back to the Factory and get smashed.'

As everyone agreed Nikki spotted her parents hovering awkwardly on the edge of the crowd, and going to them she drew them both into an enveloping hug. 'Come with us,' she whispered. 'I know it's not your kind of thing, but . . .' She stopped as her mother broke into a smile.

'We'd love to,' Adele told her, and as their eyes met Nikki's heart soared to realise that something good was going to come out of this after all.

'I want you to know,' her father said, in the taxi on the way to the Factory, 'that I would never have let you go to prison.'

Realising how important it was to him that she believed that, Nikki hugged his arm as she said, 'Thankfully, it's not an issue any more, but yes, I do know that.'

He seemed cheered by her reply, but by the time they

arrived at the Factory she could tell he was withdrawing into himself again.

'Take your mother in,' he whispered, as Nikki got out of the car behind him, 'and make sure she has a good time. I'll go back to the house and have a lie-down. I think it's all been a bit much for me today.'

He suddenly looked so old and beaten that Nikki felt a twist of alarm go through her. 'Do you need anything?' she asked. 'Are you feeling tired, is that it?'

His eyes went down. 'Ashamed,' he corrected gruffly. 'I wish I'd put my foot down and stopped you doing this . . .'

'I'm a grown-up now,' she reminded him gently. 'I get to make decisions too.'

He touched a hand to her face, and gazed deeply into her eyes. 'I've made a lot of mistakes in my life,' he told her, 'but thank God they haven't changed you from the person you are. I'm so proud of you, Nicola, I . . .' His voice faltered and as a tear splashed on to his cheek Nikki's eyes filled up too. 'You shouldn't have done that for me,' he said brokenly.

'Yes I should,' she argued. 'You saved me and Mum all those years ago. Then you wanted to save Zac from that awful disease. So the way I see it, it was my turn to save you.'

Still seeming to consider himself unworthy of being cared for so much, he said, 'I'm going to make this up to you. I don't know how yet, but I promise you, I will.'

Her eyes turned mischievous. 'You could begin by coming inside,' she said softly, and as her mother came round the car to join them she linked both their arms to follow Spence, and to her relief her father didn't voice any more objections.

Chapter Twenty-Eight

Ten days later Nikki and Spence were at one of her parents' favourite restaurants in Bath, enjoying a quiet celebration of Spence's twenty-second birthday with them. Ordinarily, they'd have spent it with their friends, either whooping it up at the Factory, or throwing a big party at the house. However, now that all the tension and drama of the trial was behind them, the process of grieving for Zac had finally begun, leaving them much less keen to make a splash. Not that they were allowing themselves to become maudlin, or self-pitying, it was simply that their usual style of raucous celebration really hadn't felt appropriate this year, particularly when they'd only laid Zac to rest the day before.

The image of her father and Spence carrying the little coffin into the crematorium was one Nikki knew would always stay with her, and probably always make her cry. It had moved everyone present, as had Spence's words when he'd stood up to speak in a voice that was strong and proud, and occasionally broke with grief.

'He was only with us for a short time,' he'd said, 'but Nikki and I are so much richer for having known him. He brought us great joy and a lot of laughter, he also tested us in many ways, but we loved him from the instant we knew we were going to have him, and we always will.'

There had been a reception afterwards, at the Factory, which was when Adele and Jeremy had asked Spence if they would consider spending his birthday with them.

So here they were, just finishing their starters as a waiter topped up their wine.

When he'd gone, Jeremy raised his glass. 'I'd like to make a toast,' he said.

Nikki's heart turned over to hear the tremor in his voice, and when her eyes caught her mother's she could see that Adele was feeling emotional too.

'First of all,' Jeremy said to Spence, 'Adele and I want to wish you a very happy birthday, and to say thank you for agreeing to celebrate with us.'

'Happy birthday, Spence,' Nikki and Adele echoed, clinking their glasses to his.

Spence's eyes were shining and slightly curious as he accepted the toast. This was going somewhere, he could feel it in his bones, but as yet he couldn't work out where.

'I owe you so many thank yous,' Jeremy continued, 'that I hardly know where to begin, but the biggest, and perhaps the most important of all, is the one for finding it in your heart to stand by us all this time, in spite of what I've put you through. I know you wouldn't have done if it weren't for Nikki, so a very close second in my line-up of thank yous is for loving her as much as you do. I have no doubt at all that she's an even better person than I already knew her to be for knowing you.'

Spence glanced at Nikki with a self-conscious smile and gave her a wink.

'I don't imagine you've thought too much yet about whether you'll have any more children in the future,' Jeremy went on, 'but I hope it might help if I tell you that I've sought some professional advice over this last week, and I'm assured that the chances of the same thing happening again are extremely unlikely. You can be screened during pregnancy and if all is well, you will have nothing to worry about.'

Though Nikki and Spence already knew this, and had even decided that when they were ready they might consider adopting, rather than have a child of their own when there were so many already in the world who needed to be loved, neither of them wanted to spoil Jeremy's moment. Besides, it was all a long way off, because they'd agreed that, for the foreseeable future at least, they were going to grieve for Zac while doing what they could to get their lives back on track.

'There are also many apologies I need to make,' Jeremy

continued, 'not the least of which is for delving into your background the way I did. I've come to learn over these last few months that in spite of all the privileges and so-called good upbringing I've had, I'm not even half the man you are, and probably never will be. I've learned a great deal from you, Spence: forgiveness, humility, loyalty, integrity, open-mindedness, the list goes on, but I can see I'm embarrassing you, so perhaps I should stop.'

As Spence caught her eye again, Nikki pressed her fingers to her lips to try to stop herself from laughing and crying.

'You asked me a couple of weeks ago,' Jeremy went on, 'if I would contact the person who'd looked into your background to see if he could find out whether the man whose name is on your birth certificate really is your father.'

Spence had become very still, so had Nikki. This was going to be a momentous discovery for Spence, and she was praying to God that it would be what he wanted to hear.

'It turns out,' Jeremy said, seeming to glow a little, 'that your aunt was right. Keith James was incarcerated in Wandsworth prison ten months before you were born, and wasn't released again until you would have been almost a year old. So I'm happy to tell you that you can't possibly be related.'

As Spence seemed to collapse with relief, Nikki wrapped her arms around him, squeezing with all her might. 'I knew it,' she exulted, 'you're so not like that and anyway, even if he had turned out to be your dad, it doesn't mean you'd have to take after him, because it doesn't always work like that.'

'Indeed it doesn't,' her father confirmed, 'and it was unforgivable of me ever to have suggested that it might. So another apology, Spence, that I . . .'

Spence's hands went up as he laughed. 'Hey, I'm cool,' he told him. 'You're off the hook.'

Jeremy gave a chuckle of delight, seeming to enjoy the vernacular in a way Nikki couldn't remember having witnessed before. Then, looking suddenly worried, she said, 'I wonder if we'll ever find out who your real dad is.'

'Ssh,' Spence warned in a whisper, 'keep it down, or they'll be queuing round the block for the privilege.'

As everyone laughed, Jeremy and Adele exchanged glances.

'I have something to say now,' Adele told them.

'Oh, this is such fun,' Nikki teased. 'Me next.'

Her mother smiled, then turned her eyes to Spence. 'Of course, I want to echo everything my husband's just said,' she began, 'but what I want to add is this: Jeremy and I are ready to do everything we can to try to make up for the way we've thought about, and treated you. It's plain that our daughter is far more intelligent and insightful than we've ever been when it comes to seeing good in people. Thanks to her, and you, we've done a lot of growing up over these last couple of months, and not before time, I hear you say.'

As Nikki and Spence laughed, Jeremy put a hand over his wife's and gave it a squeeze.

'Spence,' Adele continued, 'I will quite understand if this isn't welcome, but Nikki has told me how much it means to you to be part of a family, so I would like to tell you that it would be a great honour for us to consider you a part of ours. I know we haven't got off to a good start, but, as I said, Jeremy and I intend to do everything we can to make up for that.'

As a rush of emotion stole Spence's reply, Nikki said, 'Thanks Mum, and Dad. That means so much to us both.'

'Yeah, it really does,' Spence assured them hoarsely. 'Thank you.'

'You know we're moving to London at the weekend,' Nikki said, 'but it's not far, and we'll . . .' She broke off with a splutter of laughter as she spotted the waiter hovering with a very worried look on his face. 'I think the next course is about to arrive,' she told them, and after their plates were set down she had the wonderfully happy experience of watching Spence hugging both her parents, while all of them laughed at the need to dab their eyes.

Two days later Nikki, Danny and David were all at the house in Bedminster, clearing the place completely of their belongings ready for the next tenants to move in at the end of the month.

'Have you got everything?' Danny called out from the hall.

'I think so,' Nikki shouted back from the bedroom.

'Then I'm taking this lot out to the car,' he told her. 'Your parents have just turned up. Looks like Spence is with them.'

'He'd better be,' Nikki said, coming to lean over the banister, but Danny had already gone.

'I didn't realise I still had so much stuff here,' David grunted, struggling to shift a heavy box out of his room. 'Do you need a hand with anything?'

'When you've got a spare one,' she answered, and disappeared back into the bedroom to check that all the drawers and cupboards were empty before they set out on the journey to London. Even Mrs A was coming with them today, partly to help transport everything to the house in Shepherd's Bush, and partly to be close to the airport ready for when Mr A flew in the next day.

'Killing two birds with one stone,' she'd chirped happily, when she'd told them her plans.

Now, as Nikki took a last look round the bedroom she and Spence had shared for what felt like a lifetime, but had, in fact, been little more than eight months, she felt her heart contracting with emotion. She looked at the bed where they'd lain so many times with Zac; the little dents in the carpet where Zac's cot had been; the chest of drawers that used to be laden with fluffy toys, and the corner where they'd kept his car seat. Everything was gone now, mostly given away to friends, or charity shops, off to start a new life, much like her. All that remained here in this house was the little wristband he'd worn when she'd first had him. *Baby James.* She'd kept it to put with the letters she'd written and all the photographs Spence and the others had taken. These were the mementos they'd keep, tucked away somewhere in a place only she and Spence knew about, reminders of their first baby who hadn't stayed long, but had changed them in ways that were still making themselves felt.

'Hey,' Spence said softly, coming into the room behind her.

She smiled and leaned back against him.

'Are you OK?' he asked.

'Mm,' she murmured. 'I missed you last night.'

'I missed you too,' he said, kissing her neck. Then, tightening his arms around her waist, he said, 'So what are you standing here thinking about?'

She gave a gentle sigh. 'Zac, of course. I was afraid it was going to feel as though we were leaving him behind, but strangely it doesn't.'

'That's because he's still here, in our hearts, which means he's coming with us.'

Turning to put her arms around him, she said, 'That's a lovely way to think of it, and you're right, because he will always be with us.'

After kissing her, he stroked back her hair and gazed down into her eyes.

'Did Mum tell you that there's four thousand pounds left in the kitty?' she asked. 'She and Dad want us to have it to help get us started again.'

Spence's eyebrows rose. 'But how are they going to manage?' he asked.

'Dad told me not to worry about that, because he's got ideas.'

Spence didn't look convinced. 'He's still not well,' he reminded her.

'I know, but I think it might make him feel better if we accept the money. Or at least half of it, anyway. So now, tell me how it went with Drake. Has he washed his hands of us? I won't blame him if he has, but I was hoping . . .'

Putting a finger over her lips, he said, 'He wants you to know that there's a desk and chair waiting for you as soon as you feel ready to take it up.'

Nikki's eyes shone with amazement as they filled with tears. 'You're kidding me,' she said.

'Straight up,' he promised.

'Oh Spence,' she gulped, throwing her arms around him. 'We're so lucky, aren't we, to have someone like him? I don't know what we'd be doing otherwise.'

'We'd find something,' he assured her, 'but I admit, he's making it a lot easier.'

'So who else did you see while you were there?' she asked. 'Val?'

'Yeah, and she sends her love. The shoot went really well, apparently. Everyone seemed happy, and she was like, "This directing thing really rocks, Spence. Got to do it more often."'

Laughing, Nikki said, 'I'm glad for her that she got her first break, but I could wish it had happened another way.'

'You and me both,' he said soberly. 'I saw Kristin too,' he told her.

Nikki regarded him carefully. 'To speak to?'

He nodded. 'She wants to know if she can ring you.'

Surprise gave a jolt to Nikki's heart.

'She pointed out that she did her best in court to play down the chat you had with her that day about Zac. And she's really sorry she told the police about it in the first place.'

Nikki sighed, and shook her head. 'I suppose she didn't have a choice, really,' she said, finding herself able to weigh it more objectively now.

'Pff,' Spence said disgustedly.

'Well, I did say those things,' she reminded him. 'Anyway, what did you tell her?'

'I said I thought she had a bloody nerve,' he retorted, 'but the decision has to be yours.'

It didn't take Nikki long to say, 'You know, I don't think it'll do either of us any good to start bearing grudges, and we know how hard she finds it to keep friends, so I'll give her a call myself sometime next week.'

Spence laughed, and rolled his eyes. Her response was pretty much as he'd expected it to be, because he knew she wasn't capable of staying mad at anyone for long. And if forgiveness was measured in fortunes, then she was already rich beyond their wildest dreams.

Hearing someone coming up the stairs, he wrapped her in his arms again and said, 'Come on, we best get this lot on the road.'

'Ah, there you are,' Danny said. 'Thought you might like to know that there's quite a crowd gathering down there.'

Nikki looked puzzled. 'Why?' she asked. 'What's happened?'

Danny laughed. 'You're leaving,' he reminded her. 'They

all want to wave you off. Even . . . Wait for this . . . The detective woman. What was her name again?'

Nikki looked astounded. 'DS McAllister's here?' she said. Then, thinking of her father, her insides turned over. *Please God don't let him have done something stupid. Not now.*

Leaving Spence to carry out the rest of their belongings, she ran down the stairs and out into the street, where the crowd was milling around the two cars that were being packed up ready for the journey to London.

Laughing as a cheer went up, she looked round for her father, praying she wasn't going to find him in earnest conversation with DS McAllister. She finally spotted him studying a map with Mrs A, with no sign of McAllister in close proximity. Allowing herself to breathe, she began hugging everyone and thanking them for coming, and in spite of being ready to move on now, she couldn't help feeling sad to be leaving them. They'd stay in touch, obviously, at least for a while, but she guessed, over time, they would all go their separate ways and this time in Bristol would start to fade into the past, as everything did in the end. Even the terrible ache of longing for Zac, though that was much harder to imagine right now.

'It's wonderful to see how many friends you have,' her mother commented as Nikki came to join her. She was standing to one side, watching the goodbye scene unfolding, her eyes shining with pride.

'Are you OK?' Nikki asked her, taking her arm.

'Of course.' Adele smiled. 'I'm glad Dad and I are coming to London with you today. I'm looking forward to seeing where you'll be living.'

'You'll love it,' Nikki assured her, trying not to think of Zac and how ideal it would have been for him, too. Now wasn't the time to let her feelings get caught up in grief again, it would happen often enough in the weeks and months to come, and today was about new beginnings. 'I hope you'll be coming to visit us – lots,' Nikki told her.

'Oh, I will,' Adele promised.

Nikki smiled, then tilted her head to one side, feeling a bit awkward as she prepared to ask her mother a question that had been on her mind for a while now. 'I was wondering,' she began, 'well, do you reckon my grandparents might still be around?'

Adele lifted a hand to Nikki's face as she gazed into her eyes. 'I thought you might ask,' she told her, 'so I made a couple of calls and yes, they are. Both of them. I haven't been in touch personally, I thought it best to wait till you were ready.'

Nikki's heart suddenly felt very full. 'I think I would like to meet them,' she said shakily. 'Maybe not right away, but soon.'

Adele smiled and continued to gaze into her daughter's eyes. 'I think they'll be very proud of you,' she told her. 'I know I am.'

Nikki gave a shrug of embarrassment.

'You remind me a lot of Matthew,' her mother went on, with a misty look in her eyes. 'He had your spirit, your way with people, before things started to go wrong for him.'

Feeling strangely pleased by the words, Nikki said, 'Do you think that bothers Dad?'

'Sometimes,' her mother admitted. 'Or let's say, it used to. Things have changed a lot lately.' Her eyes showed an irony that made Nikki want to laugh and hug her.

'Did you hear back from the psychotherapist Mrs A put you in touch with?' Adele asked.

'The one in London? Yes, and he's willing to take me on, so hopefully the judge will be happy.'

'Never mind him, what matters is that you are. This experience will have taken a greater toll on you than you're probably aware of right now, so it's a good thing to have some professional help.' Then, in a lower voice, 'We have a lot of time ahead of us for talking, and right now there's someone here who seems to be waiting to speak to you.'

Nikki turned round to find DS McAllister hovering close by.

'Hello, Nikki,' Helen McAllister said, holding out a hand to shake.

Taking it, Nikki said, 'Hello. I'm surprised to see you here.'

'I heard you were leaving today and I wanted to wish you luck.'

Nikki looked into the detective's eyes and saw only friendliness. 'Thank you,' she said. 'That's really kind of you.'

McAllister nodded, and continued to hold Nikki's gaze. 'It's funny that we never found out who the blue Mercedes belonged to,' she commented.

Nikki's throat turned dry.

McAllister's grip tightened on Nikki's hand as she leaned towards her and said, 'That was an incredibly noble but bloody stupid thing you did. I'm just glad it didn't backfire.'

As she walked away Nikki stared after her, too dumbfounded to move.

'And I want you to promise me right now,' Spence said, when she repeated the conversation to him, 'that you will never, *ever* do anything like it again.'

Nikki was about to reply when her eyes suddenly turned playful.

'Oh no,' Spence warned. 'The promise, Nikki, or I swear, I'm off.'

'But what if *you* get into trouble?' she said.

'Tell you what,' he said, 'I'll give you my word here and now that I won't.'

Laughing, she threw her arms around him and swore with all her heart that she really wouldn't do anything like that again.

Or she probably wouldn't, anyway.